GHOSTS
IN THE
GRAVEYARD

Also by E.F. Winters:

MEMELOOSE: The Island of the Dead
First in category winner
Somerset Awards
Chanticleer Writing Competition

SHARKS AND MINNOWS
The Jolie Chronicles
Book One

THE PEOPLE'S GIFT

Watch for:

EBULON
Book One of
The Keepers of the Truths

GHOSTS IN THE GRAVEYARD

The Jolie Chronicles

Book Two

E.F. Winters

Edited by: Victoria Winters

Kenspeckle Productions

2016 Kenspeckle Production

Published in the United States by Kenspeckle Productions
Distribution by Lightning Source via Ingram Books

Library of Congress Cataloging-in-Publications Data
E.F.Winters & Kenspeckle Productions
ISBN 978-1-940531-03-8

Printed in the United States of America

Book design by E.F.Winters & J.L.Winters

Acknowledgements:

To my friends and family and all of the young women in the "Girls Group", your strength inspires me, your trust honors me, your support moves me forward.

Thank you, Tus, V, Laura, and Jay. You make me a better writer and a better person.

E.F. Winters

CHAPTER ONE

Bumped hard from behind, Jolie Figg fell forward.

"Hey! Watch it," she barked as she caught herself, her books flying from her arms.

Proving her theory of the fickle nature of reality, the books went slow-mo, hanging suspended mid-air like birds struggling to fly into the face of a storm. The school hallway disappeared as vision replaced reality.

Car brakes screeched. Metal slammed against metal and a battered yellow skateboard corkscrewed into the blue sky in a futile bid for freedom. Gravity pulled it down into the mess of a car accident below.

Jolie's vision broke as the board shattered against the pavement, her books thudding onto the floor and sliding away in three directions.

"Sorry," a dark haired boy shouted over his shoulder. "I'm late for class."

"Jerk," Jolie muttered as she tried to retrieve her books, dodging between semi-truck football players and smaller sportier student models.

Her Biology book became a hockey puck.

"Score," the muscle-bound jock leered. "Oh, was that yours, Witch Girl?" His entourage laughed, celebrating with high fives.

"Surfs up!" English One got a new life as a surfboard, while Geometry raced toward the stairwell, saved from a dead drop by striking the corner post.

The vision of a crash swirled through Jolie's mind, fogging out the scene in the hallway. The hard, cold surfaces of a hospital room replaced it.

No. Jolie gritted her teeth, pushing the vision away.

She hated this. She was always careful not to touch anybody, walking with her head down to avoid eye contact, keeping to herself. The last thing she wanted, was to be burdened by her peer's stupid secrets. But it wasn't enough anymore. Things were changing. Her ability to hear other people's thoughts was becoming harder to avoid. It wasn't fair. How could someone who didn't want to be psychic become more psychic? She didn't want to know these things about other people and their rotten lives. She didn't want to get involved in their problems. With a mom who treated everything in her own life like it was disposable, including her daughter, Jolie had enough problems of her own. Her friend and mentor, Faith was helping Jolie learn to work with her gifts, but the visions and headaches that had begun to accompany her psychic disability were getting more intense.

Once again the vision won, and the fog of someone else's life enveloped the gifted teenager.

The image of a young man covered with abrasions bloomed in Jolie's mind. An oxygen mask covered most of his face; the tubes sprouted from his body making him look like a medical Chia pet.

"Get out of my head," Jolie demanded, grabbing at reality. *"This has nothing to do with me."*

A pale blond "Brady Bunch" mom stood by the boy's bed with one arm around a younger version of herself.

The mom and the sister, Jolie thought, though something seemed not quite right about that. If the boy was part of this family, someone had colored him with the wrong crayons.

A golf-tanned doctor, with an expensive haircut and perfect manicure, entered alongside a haggard businessman, his frazzled appearance contrasting sharply with the physician's cool.

"I'll give you a few moments. Just let me know when you're ready." Doctor Cool checked his watch, hinting he had somewhere else to be.

The man's eyes were red-rimmed and puffy. He'd been crying. He would no doubt cry again, but not where his family could see him. He and the blond woman looked at each other across the room, and Jolie understood that more separated them than the space of a few feet. The father's grief was deep, troubled, and honest. This boy was the child of his heart, the legacy of his first love. His loss opened old wounds that the blond woman's affection could not touch, and she resented it.

He looked away, knowing that his second wife saw his memories of his first family as a betrayal of their life together. But it was too late. Guilt, regret, and pain worked like worms in the minds of the two adults, exposing the secrets that whispered to them in the heart of the dark night.

He turned sadly to his daughter. "Are you ready, sweetheart?" he asked, including her in this most final of family decisions.

"There's no use waiting," the mother said, through tight lips. "Nothing's going to change."

"I think we should wait for Hoke," the girl said in a soft but firm voice. "He'd want to be here."

Disgust hardened the features of the mother's beauty queen face.

"That could take days, weeks if he's off on one of his trips. We can't wait that long." The words sounded harsh and mean-spirited, but she did not try to sweeten them.

"We need to give him a chance," the daughter said, pressing an auto dial number on her cell phone as she stepped out of the room.

The mother rolled her eyes. "She has him on speed dial?"

"He's family." The father shrugged. "It doesn't matter to Hoke that she's not his blood."

"This shouldn't be happening," Jolie heard the father think. "I'm so sorry, Mara. I thought I could keep him safe in my world, but I was wrong. I should have let Hoke take him. I failed you. I failed you both."

The girl came back into the hospital room and slipped her hand into her father's.

"All I could do was to leave a message." She stared at her brother, tears welling in her eyes. "This is all wrong. He is the best of us," her voice caught. "What will we do without him, Dad?"

Her father pulled her into his arms, holding her close. "We'll carry on, and we'll help each other, just like he'd want us to." In spite of his resolve, the father's chin trembled and a tear appeared.

After a few minutes, the blond woman caught his eye and a silent agreement passed between them.

"But your mom is right, honey. We have to think of us now. Who knows where Hoke is or when he'll get your message. He could be back on the res or up on a mountain somewhere. Dragging this out will only make it harder.

"He'll come. He will."

"When?"

Her dad put his arm around her thin shoulders. "Hoke will understand."

The girl shrugged her father's arm off. Her lower lip quivered, but she did not argue.

The boy's father went to opened the door. "Nurse, will you tell the doctor that we're ready."

The girl watched determinedly, her eyes shining with tears as the doctor removed the IV's, the tubes, and

Chapter One

finally the oxygen mask, exposing her brother's ruined face. She did not turn away.

Jolie reconsidered her earlier assessment of the sister. She was not a copy of her mother; she was better, stronger.

One by one, the monitors went dark until only the heart monitor beat out the final moments of the young man's life.

And then it too stopped, and he was gone.

But he wasn't.

Jolie emerged from the vision, like a drowning person rising from underwater, gasping for breath. Reality had returned, and she was standing in the middle of the hallway of Chaparral High School. Somewhere close by, the young man she had just watched die was alive and breathing, and maybe, just maybe, she could keep him that way.

The warning bell blared from a corner of the hallway. She was going to be late for class, again.

CHAPTER TWO

It rarely rained in the brightest spot on the planet, but when clouds did appear, they were the stuff of artist's fantasies: white puff balls like the fake ones airbrushed onto the fake sky ceiling of the Forum Shops at Caesar Palace.

Close to the boundary for Mountain Time Zone, the sun rose early in Southern Nevada. Las Vegas had been a hard sell for Jolie during her first lonely summer there, and her opinion hadn't changed with the onset of winter. She had to admit, though, that spring was pretty great: except, of course, when the wind kicked up knocking over everything that wasn't bolted down, and sandblasting your eyeballs. You didn't need to use exfoliants to lose a layer of skin in Sin City; all you had to do was stand outside on a windy spring day.

But on a good day, like today, when the morning air kissed your skin like lips cooled on a frosty glass, it was heaven.

As the day aged from early promise to a glorious maturity and the temperature warmed, people began to shed their clothes like pagans at a festival. Bare shoulders, arms, legs, and toes appeared perfectly trimmed, buffed, and painted, as if their owners were born that way.

Las Vegans, both natives, and transplants donned their shorts and sleeveless shirts with glee, hiking, biking, and bragging about the weather to their East Coast relatives, who were still shoveling snow. None of them talked about the price they would pay for this early

Chapter Two

season preview when the heat of July, August, and September melted tires and sucked the moisture from everything it touched. That came later. Today, they were living in the moment.

Jolie walked home oblivious to the spring day, or the cars and kids that passed her, lost in her own concerns. Her mind jumped from problem to problem: the upcoming Geometry test, the Chem reading she needed to finish, her mom's bad boyfriend addiction, passing Driver's Ed, and saving up for a car now that she was sixteen. And then, of course, there was the dilemma of what to do about Skateboard Boy. None of her peers interrupted her or tried to drag her into their little dramas. Their interest in Jolie had peaked last winter when fate declared that it was her turn to be the center of their derision. Now that her notoriety quotient was back in the single digits, she intended to keep it that way until she graduated.

Jolie had goals. She had priorities. High school was an obstacle course she was forced to run. She did not have to like it.

And so, ignoring the abundant sunshine that would have melted a Midwestern winter, Jolie Figg walked home, wrestling with the ethical question of whether it was possible to alter the course of someone else's future, and if so, did knowing that future mean you were required to do something about it?

Jolie watched a lot of television, including a lot of old movies. In the movies, when someone tried to change the future, things got messy. People who were meant to die died no matter what you did, and the universe punished those who had interfered. But that was Hollywood, and simple repetition of a fantasy like the Tooth Fairy did not make it true.

Jolie had learned a lot about life from movies, but she also recognized that there were things that were real and things that weren't, and it was important to know the difference.

No one would even know that Jolie had seen someone else's future unless she told them and Jolie had no intention of doing that. So, if she didn't tell anyone, then no one would judge or blame her, whatever happened. Still, she would know, she reasoned. She might not know much about how her gifts worked, but she knew that her visions were real. The question remained: could an action taken by one person permanently change another person's future? Would just making that person aware of the possibility of a problem be enough to change the outcome, or did you have to physically be there to pull them back onto the curb?

"A person's path is always changing, Jo." Faith had reminded Jolie more than once. "We have free choice."

Jolie hoped that her mentor was right, but if she wasn't, and there was going to be some mysterious karmic repercussion for interfering and stopping Skateboard Boy's death, Jolie figured she would just have to pay it because she couldn't do nothing.

Jolie remembered a day when she and her grandmother, Mem, had been outside working in the vegetable garden at Mem's big house in the Garden District of New Orleans. *Her grandmother's arthritic hands pulled up a clump of multicolored carrots and rinsed them under the hose.*

"What do you think, Cherie? Shall we try to figure out why some of these carrots are orange, some are red, and others are white, or do you just want to eat them?"

"Eat them," four-year-old Jolie announced without hesitation.

Chapter Two

Mem handed her granddaughter a blood red carrot. "It seems like a waste of time to fret over why a carrot is what it is. Some things you just have to experience. Just bite it." Mem crunched down on her own chosen prize. "You're bound to learn something, even if it's only that you don't like carrots. There are some things you just have to accept, Cherie. Over-thinking life will make you crazy." Mem winked. "It's like family; you have to love them, so it's best not to hold them up to too much scrutiny."

During the ten years since Jolie's mother, Jessie Lynn had snatched Jolie away from her dad's family in New Orleans, Jolie had thought of a thousand things she wished she had asked her grandmother back then, but she had only been a little girl. The Boulette clan had underestimated Jessie Lynn Figg's penchant for self-destruction, and Mem had passed away not long after Jessie and Jolie disappeared.

Mem had been gone now for twice as many years as she and Jolie had shared together, but Jolie still missed her kind generosity every day. Only since Solstice, when Faith had taken Jolie into her close circle of friends, had Jolie begun to feel like she could trust someone enough to ask the heavy questions that weighed on her.

"Do you think that what you see are hallucinations, Jo?" Faith's paper thin skin wrinkled more deeply when she smiled, her white cotton candy hair wisping around her head. "Like it's some trick of your brain--a psychotic episode or something? Is that what you think?"

Jolie bit her lip. "People who have psychotic episodes are as convinced, as the rest of us, that what they're seeing is real. How do I know that what I see is any different, Faith? If I'm going, to be honest with myself, I have to ask that. Maybe I'm not psychic. Maybe I'm just crazy."

Faith chuckled. "You're not crazy, or even mentally ill, Jolie. Your brain just works different. An artist's brain doesn't work like a mathematician's; a savants doesn't work like an accountant's. We're all different. Being gifted doesn't make you mentally ill."

"It might in time," Jolie quipped sardonically. "I just don't want to be one of those people who makes decisions about their life based on a flattering lie, and then desperately holds on to their specialness, like some three year old in the deep end, clinging to water wings shouting look at me swim. I don't have a mysterious destiny. I'm just a kid who sees and hears things she shouldn't--and I don't want to. If I could give my gifts back, I'd do it in a heartbeat. But genetics will prove out, right?"

Faith leaned back, relaxing onto her pillows and closed her eyes.

"Genetics are a fascinating field of study. Have you ever considered that field?"

Jolie made a face. "Are you kidding? That stuff's for the smart kids."

Faith raised an eyebrow. "You seem pretty smart to me."

"There are kids at school who ace tests without even trying. I just work hard."

"And it pays off. I've seen your grades, Jolie. You do well--better than just getting by. I understand that there's a comfort in believing that our choices aren't important because we aren't important, but I hope you will see more worth in yourself than that. I do."

"No universal variant in the cosmos is hinging on whether I take calculus next year or not, Faith," Jolie said with her usual sarcasm.

Chapter Two

"And yet every decision you make affects the next one, connecting you to all sorts of possible outcomes, sending you along a uniquely personal path."

"You should teach philosophy or something." Jolie shook her head.

"I'm just saying that you are smart, you've proven that you can succeed when you work hard. Embrace that. A whole new world could open up for you," Faith argued, sweetly.

"I am going to graduate high school. After that, I'll find a job and try to live without hurting anybody. That's good enough for me."

"What about college?" Faith asked, not letting up.

"People like me don't go to college, Faith," Jolie answered, her face becoming tight.

"Your mom didn't, but what about your dad? Did he go to college?"

Jolie looked away. "Yeah, he was like a biologist or something."

"And your grandmother, Mem, she seems like a smart woman. I'll bet she had an education."

"I don't know," Jolie admitted. "The subject didn't come up when I was five."

"Education is the path to a better life," Faith stated.

"You sound like a friggin' billboard."

"I believe in you, Jolie. So I'm not going to give up on this. What are you worried about, that you can't handle the work, or that you can't afford it?"

"Look, Faith, I know you're trying to help, but I can't wait to get out of school. It's a hell hole for someone like me." Jolie threw her hands up in the air. "Why would I sign up for another four years of voluntary torture?"

"College isn't like high school, Jo."

"Bigger campus, bigger classes; same kids. It sounds the same to me." Jolie paused. "Anyway, I don't have any idea what I'd study. I don't know what I want to do."

"Genetics?" Faith teased.

Jolie made a face.

"Well, you know what you don't want," her friend pointed out. "That's a good starting point."

"You mean being a cocktail waitress?" Jolie joked.

"You are taking Driver's Ed like we planned, right?"

"It's on my schedule," Jolie assured her friend. Once Jolie got her license, she'd be able to run some of the errands that their friend, Iris ran now for Faith, freeing Iris up to have more time for her own affairs.

At eighty-seven, Faith was mentally sharp and focused, but she had never fully come back after her heart attack last winter. Once everyone's part in the Solstice debacle was known, and Faith's daughter-in-law, Mae's betrayal was revealed, there had been no question of them continuing to live together.

"You know, it doesn't seem to matter anymore what I did for a living, or how much I got paid," Faith reminisced. "The clothes, the cars, the houses.... All the things we spent so much energy on. What is still important to me, is that I'm comfortable with who I am, I'm near the people I love, and I know that they'll be okay after I'm gone."

"I don't think they teach that in college, Faith." Jolie leaned forward and kissed her friend's forehead. "But if they did, I'd sign up."

Faith took Jolie's hand. "It's hard to be an old soul in a young body."

"No harder than being a young soul in an old body," Jolie teased back.

Chapter Two

"Isn't that the truth?" Faith seemed to drift off, not saying anything more.

Jolie got up, thinking she should get started on her chores.

"If you are nothing special, Jolie, how do you explain saving those people on Solstice?" Faith asked, surprising her.

"I can't. Not even to myself," Jolie replied. "What happened that night doesn't sound real in any world that people accept."

Faith opened her clear blue eyes and studied her young friend.

"A little too Alice-down-the-rabbit-hole?"

"More like Night of the Living Dead." Jolie bugged her eyes.

"My question stands, though, sweetie. What do you think would have happened if a certain plucky teenager hadn't been there?"

"I think that a certain plucky old woman would have figured something out."

"I did. I figured out that a young person with untapped strength appeared in our lives just when we needed her, and I got her to help when no one else could have done the job. And for that help, I am eternally grateful." Faith reached out and squeezed Jolie's hand. "This old woman owes you a great karmic debt, Jolie Boulette."

"You don't owe me anything," Jolie said embarrassed.

A clever fox-look glimmered in Faith's eyes. "You do know that you can't say no to a heartfelt gift, don't you?"

"Is that like some old Wiccan rule or did you just make it up, so you won't lose this argument?"

"I saw Pay It Forward," Faith announced.

"And The Sixth Sense?"

"It was like seeing my life story up there on the big screen." Faith chuckled.

"Only I was a girl, not a boy," they both said, at the same time.

Like Mem, Faith believed in Jolie, and she did it in such a big way that it was hard for Jolie not to believe in herself at least a little bit...at least for a little while.

*****

Jolie was approaching the entrance to the apartment complex where she and her mom lived. *There has to be a way to change Skateboard Boy's future*, she told herself, coming back to her present problem. If there wasn't, what was the point of being given visions? If visions were just some accident of the brain, like Radio Woman's faulty fillings picking up radio stations, then they were a sick trick of nature.

Jolie noticed a sun-faded El Camino cruising slowly past her. A greasy feeling slipped over her. She clenched her teeth at the familiar sense of wrongness that accompanied her mom's skanky ex-boyfriend.

"Shit," she swore under her breath.

As a sideshow to the close of the ill-fated Solstice celebration, Jolie had banished Rick from their lives. She hadn't planned it or studied up on how to make a spell. She'd just spontaneously let her righteous anger go and commanded Rick to stay away from them. To Jolie's surprise, it had worked. She and her mom had quietly moved from the trailer park to the new apartment, and they hadn't seen Rick until now.

Was Rick's ability to get this close a sign that the effects of her spontaneous warding were wearing off, or had the sleaze-ball finally worked up the courage to look for them?

The self-proclaimed reincarnation of Simon Magus, historical wizard, was not the kind of guy who took "no" well. He and his devil-worshipping friends were dangerous, and if he was snooping around looking for Jolie and Jessie, they needed to be careful.

Jolie went past the complex's entrance without looking at the sign and continued walking down the block.

"Hey, Jo! Wait up!" a voice called out from behind her. Rebecca Grolund was a brainy girl with a love of all things computer and a loathing of activities that made her sweat. It was turning her teenage baby fat into an adult weight problem.

"I thought you were going home?" Becca let her backpack slip off her shoulder, sweat beading on her forehead.

"I was, but..." Jolie checked the street for the El Camino. He had turned around and was at the light on the corner. Rick had slowed down so that he would stop at the red light. "I changed my mind," she finished simply, trying to work out some plan that did not include telling Rebecca that she thought Rick was stalking her.

"Did you see the table set up in the Quad where you can nominate people to run for Student Council?"

"I guess I missed that. Why? Do you think I'm a shoo-in?" Jolie stepped back and kicked Rebecca on the butt. They both laughed and for a moment it was like the old days before the snarky shark girls had recruited Rebecca to help demolish Jolie's reputation at school, before Solstice, when Rebecca had been in the wrong place at the wrong time and gotten in over her head. In the beginning, they had just been two lonely girls hanging out together, making each other's lives a little easier.

"Megan Washburn's running for class president," Rebecca announced. "Doesn't that just fry you?"

Jolie shrugged. "No. I really don't care."

"But she's cheating. You have to have a three-point grade average to run for office and the only reason she has that is she's got that kid, Hugo, doing her homework."

"I doubt that. Hugo's not an idiot."

"Well, it started out as tutoring, but Megan's been bragging about how she's got him wrapped around her little finger."

Jolie didn't like the sound of that. Quiet kind Hugo did not deserve to be the subject of malicious gossip. "Hugo would never cheat like that."

"Are you kidding? He's so into her; he'd do anything. He's like in love with her. Everybody knows about it."

Everybody but me apparently, Jolie thought.

"So, are you going to Faith's today?" Becca changed the subject.

"No. That's Tuesdays and Thursdays." Jolie was considering walking over to Faith's now instead of going home because of Rick. It felt safer to be where there was someone else, and if she had still been naïve enough to believe that the adult world followed a set of rules designed to keep kids safe, she might have given in to the impulse. But Rick had been close to Rory, the jerk responsible for the dark events surrounding Solstice, and he carried a grudge. He would have no problem convincing himself that his grudge included Faith and Jolie, and she was not going to be responsible for leading him to her friend's new house. She checked the street.

Chapter Two

"Walk with me," she told Rebecca. Her friend hoisted her backpack up and fell in alongside Jolie.

Jolie had tried to warn Rebecca that it was not safe for her to go to the Solstice ceremony, but they had still been working through Rebecca's lapse of loyalty at the time, and Rebecca had stubbornly not paid attention to Jolie's warning. Becca had arrived all excited to see live witches and be involved in something really magical like she had stepped into a scene from her favorite fiction book.

The reality that unfolded, however, had been beyond Rebecca's sheltered understanding. After Solstice, she had become troubled, distracted, and unable to sleep. Her parents had sent her to a shrink who gave her a hefty bill, a bottle of pills, and encouraged her to return to her family's traditional values; in adult speak: "Go back to church, be a good little girl, and all will be well with the world again." That was bullshit, of course, none of what had occurred on Solstice would have been solved by going to Sunday school, but as long as Rebecca didn't examine the hypothesis closely, it seemed to be working for her; at least at the moment.

Jolie took Rebecca's arms and steered her onto the sidewalk of the corner mini-mall. The cluster of neighborhood stores bordered the east end of the apartment complex where Jessie Lynn and Jolie had moved. Jolie waited, and as soon as the El Camino turned the corner, she pulled her friend into the first shop door.

The cloying smell of cheap incense hit her like a mud ball.

"Can I help you?" a dark-eyed Latino woman parted a bead curtain at the back of the room. The short round-cheeked woman with a mass of colored bead necklaces hanging over her shelf-like bosom examined the teenagers with heavy-lidded eyes. In the curtained room behind the heavy woman, Jolie could see Tarot cards laid out on a table.

"No. We're just--" Jolie searched for an acceptable lie. "How much does it cost to get your fortune told?" As soon as she'd said it, Jolie realized the problem with her impromptu ad lib. "Do you have any money, Becca?"

Rebecca's eyes bugged. "Are you nuts, Jolie? No, I do not!" Rebecca now espoused the school of zero interest in the occult. She had found religion.

"I just thought maybe since you were having bad dreams--" Jolie explained, lamely.

"And you thought having my fortune read by some scam artist would help?" Becca's lip curled in disgust. "After what happened at Christmas, I would have thought you'd know better. You are just so lost, Jolie."

The bells on the back of the shop's door jingled angrily as Rebecca and her righteous indignation swept out of the shop.

Jolie bit her lip as her friend strutted across the parking lot. She liked the Rebecca who saw the hand of divinity in an elegant computer program. That Rebecca had been as close to a friend as Jolie had at school. This one was different. Friendships were expensive. They cost time and energy, and Jolie wasn't sure that either of them could afford the price of this one anymore.

"Is she right, your friend?" The shopkeeper's words were thickly accented. "Are you lost?"

Jolie spun around. The woman had moved closer, stepping from the scented darkness into the shop's moody half-light.

Her mid-length cotton skirt and brightly colored blouse were vaguely coordinated in an outrageous boho way, her dark eyes lined with a hard black pencil.

Chapter Two

"I am Yanna Maria," she introduced herself. The Latino woman reverently stroked her many colored necklaces. They were not just costume jewelry, Jolie realized. They had significance, and she wore them proudly. "You don't need to hide from me. Yanna Maria feels your spirit." The woman licked her lips like Jolie was a particularly delicious looking cupcake. "Your friend says you are lost. You think she is wrong, but she isn't. I feel the confusion inside you. We have met for a reason, you and me, because I can help you." A cold smile widened the woman's full, brown lips. Her pudgy ring-laden hands opened and closed as if she were folding the space between them, trying to draw Jolie to her.

"I didn't mean to come in here," Jolie backed away. "It was an accident. I was--."

"Trying to hide?" The woman arched a brow, knowingly.

Yes, Jolie thought, silently. The sense that this woman was about to open her up like a can of tuna fish was terrifying. She turned and ran.

Safely outside, Jolie stopped to catch her breath, feeling foolish. It was stupid being so frightened by the fortune teller. The woman was probably just a charlatan with no gifts at all, just a bunch of tricks and mind games.

Jolie checked the street traffic. Would Rick's car come around again, or had he given up when she disappeared? She closed her eyes and sensed the greasy feeling once again drawing near. With her eyes open she rescanned the mini-mall shops, looking for another door to use as an escape.

Marching past the fortuneteller's big front window, Jolie passed a Thai restaurant and an insurance office before choosing the discount mattress store.

Compared to the tightly packed knick-knackery of the fortune teller's dungeon, the mattress store looked empty. The stark white walls, pale gray linoleum floor, and strict straight aisles between rows of white beds reminded her of a hospital ward, sterile and uninviting.

An East Indian man with a bad toupee stood behind the counter and sized up her customer potential.

"May I help you?"

Jolie saw a restroom sign at the back of the store.

"I, uh, just need to use your bathroom," she lied quickly.

The man's eyes went squinty, and he pointed to a sign.

"For customers only. There is a sign."

"That's okay." She pointed at the parking lot, her heart stopping as Rick's truck drove in and parked a few spaces away. "My parents are right behind me." Rick's door was opening. "They'll only be a minute," she promised the shopkeeper. "I've just got to pee." She hurried through the store and out the back door into the alleyway behind the shops. The apartment complex was on the other side of the block wall. Jolie ran for it and scrambled over.

CHAPTER THREE

True to form, Jessie had surprised Jolie after school one day, announcing that they were moving. The apartments weren't far from the trailer park, probably not far enough anyway, but Jolie had begged her mom to be able to finish the year at Chaparral, and Vegas was not a small town.

Jessie Lynn Figg was an expert at disappearing. If Rick came by their old place, he wouldn't have realized they were gone until it had been re-rented and someone else had moved in, parking their cars in the driveway, and putting up their stuff.

The same hour that Jessie was approved for the new apartment, she had quit her job at the bar where she'd met Rick. She and Jolie had tossed one quick load into their old pickup truck and were gone. They didn't have much worth packing. They moved too often to acquire stuff, and the less it looked like they had left, the less likely the most recently dumped boyfriend was to start looking for them. The colder the trail when they started, the safer Jessie and Jolie were.

A few days after they had moved, Jessie had a new job, working the night shift at a new bar.

As much as Jolie hated the trailer park that she and her mom had lived in when they first moved to Vegas, the apartment complex they traded it for was a questionable improvement. They had an actual bathtub now, one you could sit in with your legs straight out, and the doors to the bathroom weren't made of accordion-folded mystery fiber, but it was far from the tropical resort the advertisements claimed.

It wasn't that the new apartments were bad exactly; the worst neighborhoods in Las Vegas looked good compared to the low rent areas in big East Coast cities, but the skinny overgrown palm trees that lined the driveway had skirts of brown fronds below their new growth, and the misshapen boxwood bushes along the walkways protected patches of grass that were only green in little circles around where the sprinklers managed to spit a little calichi infused water.

Ground floor apartments each had an eight by ten concrete patio. Upper floors had similarly sized worthless balconies; most of them piled high with boxes of junk, the standard satellite dish, and a dead Christmas tree.

The complex advertised having a swimming pool, which residents were informed opened on Memorial Day, in spite of the fact that by April it would be as warm in Vegas as it would be on the fourth of July in most of the rest of the United States. The water in the pool currently was too green for swimming but showed real promise as a science project involving tadpoles and algae, so Jolie's emotions about it were mixed.

The apartment's other facilities were basic: a communal laundry room where the savvy never let their clothes touch the ground for fear of diseases, and a seventies era clubhouse fitted with cheap retro metal frame furniture. On Thursday nights, the wifely half of the management team ran bingo games there, justifying the little gold nametag she wore with "activities director" engraved above her name.

In the trailer park, people understood that there was no privacy and therefore no anonymity for bad behavior. If you did something wrong, people would know, and

Chapter Three

word got around, so you could expect to be treated accordingly. A person might choose to pretend they didn't care what their neighbors thought, and some chose that path, but the creed of helping out required the community's goodwill. If you were living on the edge, at some point you were going to need a hand. It was a given. People paid into the system in advance, helping others so that when they needed it, help was there for them. People who interacted every day, felt comfortable borrowing a cup of sugar, or jumping a dead battery, or loaning a spare propane tank when someone ran out before pay day. A trailer park was a village.

Apartment people were a different breed. If someone was being mugged in the apartment complex, Jolie figured the neighbors would draw their curtains and turn up the music.

Apartment people were very important and busy, always on their way somewhere, their hard heeled shoes clicking self-righteously against the cement walkways, clothed in the determination of their ambitions. No one admitted to planning to stay. No one believed that they belonged there. The apartments were a temporary stopover in the upward mobility of their lives, and they furtively snuck in and out like they were hiding gold bullion or dead bodies behind their doors.

It didn't take long for Jolie to realize that the apartment's walls were only slightly more solid than a trailer's, but apartment people clutched the pretense of privacy as if it was written in their lease. No one would ever acknowledge hearing or seeing anything that happened behind closed doors.

Jolie unlocked the apartment door and went inside. A damp towel had been tossed over the back of a chair with another thrown carelessly on the kitchen floor. The scent of Herbal Essence shampoo, Aquanet hairspray, and leftover Chinese food made her want to gag. The empty boxes from Chinese take-out made a paper model town on the chipped dining room table. The sink was a junkyard of dirty dishes. To Jessie Lynn Figg, having a girl-child meant having a live-in maid.

"I work to keep this family going," she justified her actions when Jolie complained about her mom's messy habits.

"And I go to school," Jolie countered. "It takes about the same amount of time, minus your extra-curricular activities."

"You can't possibly compare the two," her mother objected. "I'm on my feet all night, bringing drinks to jerks who think giving me a couple of bucks means they can grab a handful of whatever part of me is closest. I think that trumps your little high school social scene."

"There was plenty of uninvited groping in school hallways, and I haven't gotten a tip yet."

The old Betty Boop clock on the kitchen wall had one leg up over her head in a Rockette kick while the other leg was stretched out to the side.

"Three o'clock." Jolie sighed. She had pulled the spunky clock-girl off the wall and stuck her in a box herself, to make sure that Betty didn't get left behind. There was something determinedly sassy about the cartoon character's painted on smile, no matter what position time forced her legs into. Jolie felt oddly inspired by Betty's ability to return to normal twice a day between five twenty and five forty, no matter what gyrations her legs visited the rest of the day.

Jolie threw her backpack onto the tweedy couch they'd snagged at a moving sale a few doors down, and went to check the fridge.

When people left the apartments, they left the past behind, especially their make-do furniture. Whether they were leaving because they were accepting their failure in the big city, or because they had made it and now they were moving up in the world, the crappy furnishings they had collected had no value other than providing a little cash.

Jolie gave up on the contents of the fridge, downed a glass of water, and checked the chalkboard she'd bought for a dollar at the same moving sale. The note she'd written to Jessie three days ago saying she had gone to the library after school, was still the only thing on it. Jessie never used it. Next time they moved, it would be left behind.

Jolie headed to her room and dropped onto the bed. Staring at the ceiling, her mind rewound to the problem of what she could do about Skateboard Boy and his impending death without coming off like a psycho.

There's something about the sister, she thought, sure that she'd seen the girl somewhere before. Closing her eyes, Jolie imagined the girl's face, accessing the memory, then noted the surroundings. *Chemistry.* They had Chem class together, fourth period.

Jolie considered how she might approach the girl; "Hi. I know we've never spoken before, and you'd probably rather be dead than be seen talking to me, but I just wanted to let you know that I think your brother is going to die in a fatal accident pretty soon." Yeah, that would work well. "Yes, I'm serious." She played through the scenario a little further. "No, it's not a bad joke. How do I know? I'd rather not say because I saw it in a vision." And at that moment all the anonymity Jolie had regained in the last few months would vanish. Every detail of her life would be chewed on, digested, and regurgitated for the consumption of the general student body. It would be complete social suicide.

Just stay quiet and keep your head down, a small voice in her head advised.

It would be so easy. It would be so wrong.

Still trying to work out her plan, Jolie fell asleep to the sound of the drunk upstairs starting his evening tirade.

The gangly creatures crushed the low rocky hills like a mass of soldier ants, climbing over each other, biting, and pushing to get on top. The desert floor writhed with black shadows, a noxious miasma of evil intent that completely covered the ground. Behind Jolie was the circle of celebrants, ignorant of what approached. Jolie stood on the hill petrified by the realization that she was all that stood between this mass of demons and the innocents who had come to celebrate the return of the sun.

Jolie turned to the circle of Solstice celebrants and shouted a warning, but the scream went deep inside her, not out. She lifted the cell phone in her hand, but when she spoke, all that came out was nonsensical garble. She put a hand to her mouth. Her lips had been sewn shut.

The black creatures swarmed past her, over the hill, and down into the bowl where the celebrants were circling. Clamping their tentacles onto the people, the creatures began to feed.

"What is it, Jolie?" Faith's voice asked worriedly from the phone. "What's happening?" Jolie screamed into the phone, unable to form words with her stitched up lips.

She woke up. Her cell phone read two o'clock AM.

Jolie got up and stumbled to her mom's room. Jessie Lynn was still not home.

She went back to her room and texted. "r u ok?" Then took out her Chemistry homework, looking over her notes while she waited for Jessie's answer.

At three, she gave up and called the bar.

"Hi, I'm sorry to bother you, but it's Jolie Figg, Jessie Lynn's daughter? Is my mom, there?"

"She left at the end of her shift," the bartender told her.

"Alone?"

"No. She was with some guy."

"Thanks." Jolie hung up, turned on the TV, and opened her Social Studies book. She never slept well when Jessie wasn't home; she might finally fall asleep, but she didn't sleep well.

At six o'clock in the morning, Jolie had finally nodded off when she heard keys turning in the front door. Her stomach knotted as her mind flashed back to last winter when Rick had come in uninvited, and forced her to get in his truck to go to the Solstice ceremony. Jolie relaxed when Jessie Lynn came through the door. She was still dressed for work in a short tight black skirt, a low-cut tank top, and black heels.

"Hey, Baby." Jessie threw her leather jacket on the couch. "Are you up already? Have you got a test today or something?"

Jolie ignored her mother's attempt at cheerful deflection.

"I thought we agreed you'd text me if you were going to stay over somewhere?"

Jessie sighed as she stepped out of her high heels. "I didn't stay over. I'm here aren't I? I came home." Jolie gave her mom a disgusted look. "I met a really nice man." Jessie Lynn wiggled her drawn-on eyebrows. In Jessie's world, men came in many flavors, and she was making it her life's work to try them all. "His name is Brett."

Jolie frowned. "He sounds like a high school quarterback. What is he, twenty-five?"

"No. He's a grown man with responsibilities and everything."

"Responsibilities like a wife and kids responsibilities?"

"No." Jessie pouted. "Give me some credit, Jo."

"Well, you know what they say about old dogs and new tricks. So this guy is not young, he's responsible which I'm guessing means old?"

"No. He's cute, in a western gentleman kind of way."

"If he's so responsible and gentlemanly, what's he doing at a dive like the Golden Horseshoe?" Jolie gathered up her homework and stuffed it into her backpack.

"Meeting some guy on a business deal." Jessie shrugged. "Just my luck, huh? But he's not a bum. He's got property and his own company and everything."

"Everything but a good woman, like you." Jolie could just hear the lines this guy had been feeding her mother. "So did this businessman with his own company ask you to play secretary?"

Jessie Lynn picked up a shoe and threw it at her daughter, laughing. "Be nice. You should be happy that I finally met a nice man."

"That remains to be seen, " Jolie muttered.

"What did you say?" Jessie looked up, unbuttoning her blouse.

"I am happy for you, Jess. Can't you tell? I can hardly contain my excitement." Jolie yawned. "So are you two kids going steady now?"

Jessie stuck her tongue out at her daughter. "You watch too many old movies."

"I outgrew Sesame Street," Jolie quipped. "But seriously, Mom, you could at least have texted, so I didn't worry."

"God, how did I raise such a straight-laced pain-in-the-ass kid?" Jessie Lynn dropped onto the couch and pulled off her skirt so that all she was wearing were her skivvies. "I'm not going to stop and tell a hot guy that I have to text my kid because I think this is going to take awhile. Get real."

"You'd expect me to do it."

Jessie Lynn raised an eyebrow. "Is there something you're not telling me, Jo? Do I need to get you a doctor's appointment? Because I am not ready to become a grandmother."

"No. I'm not stupid," Jolie assured her mom.

"And I'm not a high school kid breaking curfew," Jessie countered. "You're the kid. I'm the parent."

"It'd be hard to prove it by me," Jolie mumbled. If Jessie heard, she ignored it. "I saw Rick today."

"Where?" Jessie was suddenly sober.

"He was driving past the apartments. Don't worry; I didn't let on we lived here."

"You talked to him?"

"Are you kidding? I just ducked into a shop at the mall on the corner. I don't even know for sure that he saw me."

"Maybe he was just driving by, you know, and it had nothing to do with us," Jessie said, hopefully.

"Maybe." Jolie didn't believe it.

"Do you think he followed you from school?"

Jolie shrugged. "I don't know. I didn't see him until I was almost here."

"Well, we always knew he could find us if he tried. We should have moved across town--changed schools."

"I've got seven weeks left before the end of the school year, Mom. That's not too long to dodge a sleaze ball like Rick. I think we can manage it."

Jessie Lynn nodded, yawning.

"It's been a long day, Jolie. I'm going to bed. I'll see you tomorrow night after work."

"Unless Brett wants to go out again," Jolie added.

Jessie stopped. "He's not a bad guy, Jo, really. This one is really decent."

"They always are, in the beginning."

"Screw you." Jessie Lynn flounced into her bedroom and slammed the door.

Jolie went back to her own room and sat on the edge of the bed. There was no point in trying to sleep now. It was almost time to get ready for school. She headed for the shower.

CHAPTER FOUR

Jolie kept her head down for her first few classes and focused on her school work, waiting for Chem class.

Weaving her way through the crowded hallway toward fourth period, someone tried to grab her boob. She slapped their hand and bulldozed her shoulder into the obstacle on that side.

"Don't touch me," she hissed. She didn't know if she'd hit the right person. She didn't care.

"Oh my God, what's that smell?" Megan Washburn came up from behind Jolie, pinching her nose closed.

"It smells like a dead body," her friend chimed in. Both girls looked at Jolie.

"Oh, it is a dead body," Megan added, a malicious smile thinning her sticky glossed pink lips. "It must just be impossible to get the smell of death out of your clothes, huh, Jolie?"

Megan's groupies snickered behind their hands as they sashayed down the hall, their perky buns wriggling above their bottle tanned legs.

Jolie knew there was no point in saying anything. None of Megan's crowd had been at the Solstice ceremony. Anything they'd heard was second-hand at best, and while it was true that Rick's mentor, Rory, had died that night, Jolie had nothing to do with it.

"Hey, Becca," Jolie greeted her friend as she entered the Chem room. She pulled her books out of her bag and opened her notebook, laying it on the lab table.

"I really am sorry about yesterday, Becca. It was just a spur-of-the-moment thing. I wasn't thinking."

"It's okay; I probably overreacted," Becca admitted.

"Did you read the chapters?"

"I had youth group last night, but I skimmed them this morning at breakfast."

"You can't go all the way through high school and never do any homework, Rebecca. That just wouldn't be fair."

"I do homework," Becca protested.

"Because you're a goody two shoes, not because you need to study," Jolie pointed out.

"Well, I do it," Becca repeated. At sixteen, Rebecca would have traded being smart for being pretty in a millisecond. Jolie was betting that by the time her friend was twenty, she'd realize that as a computer geek from a supportive family, who had been able to set aside a college fund for their daughter, the world was her oyster, and she had all the tools she needed to crack it. When Rebecca went away to college, everything would change.

Jolie usually made a point of not noticing the other kids in class unless she was forced to, but today's mission required a new strategy. She spotted Skateboard Boy's sister sitting at a lab station with a girl from the student government crowd.

Great, Jolie thought to herself. *Just what I needed; a credible witness. Why couldn't it have been someone that no one would have believed?*

She listened carefully while Mr. Wexler called student's up to collect their lab reports. Pretending to look at her notes, she waited to catch the girl's name: Madison, Madison Bishop.

Once the teacher finished his drawn out explanation about how to do the lab, Jolie gave Becca an excuse and wandered over to the blond girl's station, trying to mold her face into an expression exhibiting the proper amount of awe and submissiveness expected by girls in Madison Bishop's social set.

"You're Madison Bishop, aren't you? I'm Jolie Figg." Jolie wanted to barf.

"I know who you are," Madison replied, bluntly.

"I heard you were running for student council?"

"Yeah. I hope you'll vote for me." The words were polite, but Madison's tone was cool and cautious like Jolie was a panhandler about to ask for money.

"Against Megan Washburn? I'd vote for a scorpion," Jolie stated. "No offense."

"None taken." Madison almost smiled. "I hope you'll encourage your friends to vote against Megan, too."

There was an awkward pause; both girls realizing that Jolie didn't really have any friends.

"What a pain, right?" Jolie tossed her head toward Mister Wexler's thick middle-aged figure. His plain button down shirt was half un-tucked, and his pants were frayed at the bottom where they drug along the floor. "We could be almost done with this lab by now if he hadn't droned on for so long explaining it."

"Speak for yourself," Jolie heard Madison think. *"I'm completely lost with this stuff."*

There was another awkward moment. Jolie was about to ask if they wanted her help when the Student Council chick spoke up.

"Is there a point to this conversation, because we need to get to work here?"

Yeah, Jolie thought. *But like this Chemistry lesson, you're just not going to get it.*

Ignoring the partner, Jolie turned again to Madison.

"I bumped into your brother this morning. I guess it's more like he bumped into me. He's kind of shy, isn't he?" *Stupid, stupid, stupid,* Jolie scolded herself. By tomorrow it would be all over school that she had a crush on Madison Bishop's brother.

"Remy?" Madison looked surprised. *What would Jolie Figg want with Remy?*

Jolie didn't have any intention of explaining. She had what she needed; Skateboard Boy's name was Remy Bishop. Now all she had to do was make an acceptable exit.

"Yeah. He was blushing like anything."

"He was probably freaked out that he bumped into you." Madison looked alarmed at what she'd said and how it could be taken. "Not that there's anything wrong with you. It's just he's a nice guy, and he'd be really embarrassed about something like that." She glanced at her lab partner, clearly uncomfortable.

"Right." Jolie nodded. "He probably doesn't bump into too many girls at the skate park." Madison looked at her as if she'd lost her mind, but Jolie was used to that. "It must be kind of nice having a brother who's so close to your own age, huh?" she added, still looking for that graceful exit and hoping it was coming soon.

"You must be an only child," Madison rolled her eyes.

If she couldn't change Remy's future, Madison Bishop would probably regret saying that for the rest of her life, Jolie thought. She truly hoped that wouldn't happen, for all their sakes. In spite of Madison's questionable choice of friends, Jolie liked her--or at least she liked the person she thought Madison could become. Hell, by the time she and Jolie were in their twenties and high school was behind them, they might even become friends. But not here. Not today.

"Well, I'd better get back to my station. See you around."

Chapter Four

Madison's lab partner snorted. "I'd rather smell dead fish." Madison glared at her but didn't call the girl out. Jolie didn't hold it against her. Not every teenager was built to handle being socially ostracized by their peers.

Jolie walked back to where Becca was measuring out the chemicals required for the day's assignment.

"How's it going?"

"A piece of cake."

"Hey, Becca, I really need to go to the office real quick. Can I owe you this one?" She indicated the lab work. Rebecca didn't even look up from her task.

"Sure. No problem. Go."

"I'll make it up by doing next week's write up, okay?" Jolie approached the teacher's desk.

"Mr. Wexler, I have to go to the nurse's office." He opened his mouth to give her some excuse why she couldn't leave his class, but Jolie cut him off. "Now." She gave him the look every female past the age of puberty knows how to use on any male who questions her need to go to the bathroom. Wexler scribbled out a hall pass and Jolie hurried to the Administration office. Fourth period she had an ace; Hugo Aiza was the office aide.

Last December she'd stood up for Hugo against some bullies, and he'd been in her corner ever since. Jolie wondered if that was why Megan Washburn had targeted him to be the butt of her abuse, but there was nothing she could do about it now.

"Hey, Jo." Hugo smiled shyly as Jolie came into the office. A large bruise covered his eye and three-quarters of his right cheek.

"Whoa. What happened to you, dude?" Jolie asked, examining the damage.

"I had a disagreement with some fellow students."

"What about?"

"They thought my face was a punching bag and I didn't."

"Shit," Jolie swore under her breath. "That looks like it hurts, Hugo. Did you report them? You should report them."

Hugo gave her a withering look. "What would I say that would change anything?"

"Yeah, I guess." Jolie eyed his shiner.

"At least now, I know how it feels to get punched, and I can stop worrying about it." Hugo touched his eye gingerly. "It appears there are worse things than getting punched, like the anticipation of getting punched."

Jolie shook her head. "That's messed up, dude. Nobody should have to go to school worrying they'll get beat up."

"Who's worried?" The chubby geek smiled, transforming his face into something angelic. Jolie had never noticed before how lush and dark the eyelashes that fringed his brown eyes were. They would have made many a girl jealous. "Promise me that you're not going to try and do something about this on your own?" Hugo asked.

"It's wrong, Hugo," Jolie insisted.

"Yeah, but it's my wrong. I need you to let me deal with it in my way, Jo."

"Okay. But I need you to do something for me, too."

"Sure, if I can."

"I need to know what class Remy Bishop has this period." Jolie plopped her elbows down on the counter, giving him a front-row seat to the cleavage plumping out of her bra beneath her tee shirt.

Hugo glanced at the crease between her breasts then brought his eyes back up to her face.

Chapter Four

He's either a really nice guy, or he's gay, Jolie thought. She was betting on nice. Still, sometimes it was hard to tell at this age.

"I don't have access to that kind of stuff, Jo. I just answer phones, file stuff, and play courier."

"But you could get it, couldn't you? Come on, Hugo; this is kindergarten stuff for you. You're probably the smartest kid in the school." Jolie remembered what Rebecca had said about Hugo doing Megan's homework for her. Was this how that had come about? Suddenly, she felt like she was abusing a friendship.

"You don't have to try to flatter me to get my help, Jo." Hugo's disappointment added to her embarrassment.

Jolie stood up straight. He had never been anything but nice to her and manipulating him cheapened their friendship.

"I'm sorry, Hugo, but I wouldn't ask if it weren't important."

"If I tell you, is it going to get us in trouble?"

"Absolutely not." Jolie shook her head. "Because no one will ever know, and even if they did, it's not a big deal. I just need to deliver a note to his class."

"You're not stalking him or something weird, are you?"

"No. Cross my heart. No stalking. Just tell me what room he's in. I'll write the note, and that'll be it."

"Okay." Hugo went to a school computer.

"Great." Jolie smiled. "I'll be back in five minutes." She went into the nurse's office. By the time she returned Hugo had a room number and "Senior English" scrawled on a piece of scratch paper. He pushed it across the counter toward her.

"Thanks. You're a life saver. She raised on tiptoes and leaned across the counter, giving him a quick kiss on the un-bruised side of his face. "I owe you one."

As soon as she was out in the hall, Jolie stopped to write on the hall pass she'd snagged from the counter.

Danger. Don't go to the skate park, she wrote. Leaving it unsigned, she folded it twice, then headed for Remy Bishop's classroom. She could give the hall pass to his teacher, who would give it to Remy, and that would be the end of it. Whatever happened after that, her conscience would be clear.

CHAPTER FIVE

Jolie was sitting at a table outside in the commons at lunch, when the pass she had written her warning on, was suddenly dangling in front of her face.

"Do you want to explain this?"

She looked up. Remy Bishop was much better looking in person than he was lying on his deathbed. A rakishly mussed thick head of jet black hair framed the kind of features required of old Hollywood leading men; a strong jaw, sculpted cheekbones, and unnervingly bright eyes that looked as if they were eternally amused.

Not here, Jolie pleaded, silently. *Please, not here.* "You can read can't you?" she said out loud.

"Yeah, but what does it mean?" He sat down beside her.

Jolie shrugged, trying to slow her heartbeat. "How would I know? It's not mine." She turned away because all she wanted to do was look at him.

"But you brought it," Remy pointed out in a completely reasonable tone. "I saw you." His amused eyes seemed to twinkle "I caught you," in Morse code. Jolie bristled.

"I was in the office, and they needed someone to deliver a note. I was going that way."

"That's it? That's all you know?" He wasn't buying it.

"Look, we don't know each other," Jolie worded her reply carefully. "Whatever that note says, it's for you. It's got nothing to do with me." She stared him down.

"I'm sorry," he caved. "It seems like I'm making a habit of apologizing to you."

"Maybe you should stop doing stuff that you need to apologize for." Jolie picked up her stuff and stood to leave.

Remy stopped her. "Look, I'm sorry that I bumped into you yesterday. It was rude, and it wasn't right that I didn't stop to help you, but this note thing.... Well, it's just kind of weird, you know?"

"So naturally you thought of me. Nice." Jolie started to walk off.

"I didn't mean it like that." Remy caught up with her, shortening the stride of his long legs to walk beside her. He smelled like fir trees, campfires, and summer nights under the stars. It was completely distracting.

"Good. Well, I'm glad you got that off your chest." She kept walking.

"Okay, I give up. Stupid kids." Remy muttered wadding up the note. He tossed it in a garbage can and split, presumably toward his next class. His yellow skateboard was sticking up out of his backpack.

Shit. He thinks this was just a prank, Jolie realized. *Leave it be. You've done what you can,* the little voice inside her advised. But, she hadn't. She had not actually said; I get visions. Usually, they come true, and Remy Bishop is going to be in a terrible accident. It has something to do with his skateboard. Whatever release from responsibility Jolie had fantasized, she would get by writing that note, had not played out per plan. This thing with Remy Bishop was not over.

No matter what went on during school, everything that happened to a high-schooler had to fit into either the three minutes between classes, the twenty minutes of lunch, or before or after school. The unnatural suspension of unresolved issues resulted in drama and emotional explosions.

Jolie's frustration was tangible as she entered the Driver's Ed room.

After school, Jolie lingered in the parking lot skimming the next chapter for English, while she waited for one of the Bishops to come out and start for home.

This is not stalking, she told herself, aware that it was suspiciously like it.

A string of shiny SUV's, with soccer moms at the helm, made their way along the street in front of the school, stopping to pick up kids whose Moms didn't work at a bar--at least not anymore. Vegas society was full of good looking mothers who had been showgirls or dancers, either exotic or "legit" before they married.

Jolie felt her neck hairs stand up and twirled into the cover of a pickup truck as Rick's El Camino came down the street. Cruising by with his window rolled down, Jessie's ex-leaned one arm on the car door, searching the schoolyard.

"Get away from me," Jolie muttered, clenching her fists. "Or by God, I swear I'll kill you."

The El Camino rumbled down the street. If Rick was hunting them, he wasn't trying very hard. Staying alert, Jolie resumed her "I'm waiting for someone" posture.

Madison Bishop and some friends came out of the school and turned left. Jolie mentally patted herself on the back. If Madison used these doors to go home, chances were her brother would do the same, although that was assuming that they were both headed home.

A few minutes later, her guess paid off, and Skateboard Boy-Remy ambled out, his backpack with the yellow skateboard slung over one shoulder. His thick black hair stood up stubbornly in some places and lay down in others like it had its own ideas about what it should do, but it came off as charming, not messy. *There was something about this boy*, Jolie thought, watching him. There were a hundred other kids milling around outside the school, but it was like her new awareness of him put a spotlight on Remy Bishop. It didn't matter what clique he passed, the other kids turned and smiled at him.

He's like some damn Greek God or something; Jolie mused, grudgingly.

Remy looked over, and their eyes met. She had meant to try to talk to him again, to try to nudge him toward thinking the note was not a prank, but the instant their eyes met her resolve became a puddle of goo.

He'll think I'm completely nuts. She spun around and headed down Annie Oakley Drive.

It was Tuesday, and she was expected at Faith's.

She hadn't gotten off the school's long block when Remy jogged up alongside her.

"Hey."

"Hey," Jolie replied, surprised.

"What was that about?"

"What was what about?" Jolie played innocent, feeling her cheeks getting hot.

"Why'd you give me the cold shoulder just now?"

"I don't know what you're talking about," she lied.

"Just now, in the parking lot, when you saw me. It looked like you had something to say to me, but then you just left."

"I-I didn't see you," Jolie stammered. Where was the legendary Jolie Figg hard shell? One smile from this doomed boy and she had melted.

"You're the strangest girl," Remy declared, his open smile making it sound like a compliment. "You send notes that you don't send. You wait to talk to me, then pretend not to see me and run away. I can't figure you out, Jolie Figg. Are you a player or just confused?"

"Those are my choices?" She stopped and looked up at him. His smile was genuine, his eyes bright with good-natured humor.

"You're not like most girls I know."

"Do you know many girls?" Jolie retorted, trying and failing to resist his teasing.

"A few. I've got a sister, and she has friends. But none of them are like you."

"I'm not surprised. I've seen some of your sister's friends." Jolie tried to frown, but she couldn't get her mouth to go that direction. Remy Bishop just made her want to smile. "You're not making this easy for me, you know," she scolded him, letting the smile lurk at the corners of her lips.

"If you mean I'm not making it easy for you to brush me off, like you do everyone else, then no, I'm not. You put yourself on my radar. That wasn't my doing. You can't blame me if I find you fascinating."

Was he flirting with her? Jolie bit her smile in two, trying to hide it.

"Look, I'm not trying to be fascinating or weird or anything. I just didn't see you."

Remy looked at her and laughed, shaking his head.

"Right. You didn't see me like you didn't write that note. You're a terrible liar, Jolie Figg."

"I'm a good liar."

The boy leaned in and whispered, "That act might work with other people, but I see through it."

Jolie didn't know what to say. She didn't consider herself a dishonest person. Her lies were matters of expediency--part of her survival kit.

If I tell him the truth, he'll never talk to me again. What should I do? She liked talking to this boy, and he seemed to like talking to her, but if she didn't tell him what she knew, he was going to die and then he wouldn't be talking to anyone.

"Is it really so hard to tell me the truth?" Remy prodded.

"I could explain, but it would be awkward." Jolie sighed. "And you wouldn't believe me anyway, so what would be the point? Maybe you could just take the note as a friendly warning and let it go?"

"Did you just admit to writing that note?" Remy grinned. Jolie's color rose again.

"I'm just trying to say that it's important you take it seriously and don't write it off as a prank."

Remy studied her face as if reading more there than her expressions.

"Okay. I'll accept that if you agree to meet me someplace later and explain--everything, the truth. It can be anywhere you name, any place that you feel comfortable, but if you want me to accept the warning, I need to understand what it is." He looked at his watch. "I've got track practice now, but I could come by your place about six thirty? Then we'll go wherever you say."

Jolie's eyes narrowed. "This isn't like a date or anything, though, right?"

"If it makes you feel better, we'll go Dutch." Remy reached for Jolie's phone, punched in his number, and pressed call. "Tell me where you live." Jolie hesitated. "I can't pick you up if I don't know where to pick you up at," he explained.

"This isn't some bizarre "Carrie" thing, is it?" Jolie asked, completely out of her comfort zone. "Or one of those; let's mess with the weird girl bets?"

"God, I hope not." Remy made a face. "But since it's not prom, I think we're probably safe."

Chapter Five

Jolie spoke into the phone. "Okay. The Tropical Paradise Apartments on Mountain Vista just off Flamingo. See you at six thirty."

"Great." Remy flashed her a dazzling smile.

"He smiles all the time. What's wrong with that boy? "Jolie muttered to herself. "People are going to think he's simple or something." *You're a damned idiot, Jolie Figg,* the voice in her head chided as the lanky boy jogged down the block.

"He's the best of us," Madison had told her father in the vision. Jolie was beginning to believe it was true. Remy Bishop felt clean and good and honest. If anyone deserved to live, he did. Not getting involved had always been one of Jolie's cardinal rules and she was breaking it big time.

She was walking east when she noticed an old red pickup drive out of a side street. She stepped off the curb to cross the street and it drove slowly by her. A Native man with skin textured like tree bark, nodded to her. Jolie couldn't place him, but she felt sure she had seen him before. As the truck passed, she caught a glimpse inside the cab. There was a woman in the passenger seat who looked like the fortune teller, Yanna Maria. Jolie frowned as the truck headed east towards Boulder Highway.

CHAPTER SIX

On Tuesdays, Thursdays, and most weekends, Iris and Jolie met at Faith's house. Sometimes their friend Mickey and her little girls joined them, but mostly it was just the three of them. Jolie would have been happy to help Faith out for free, but Iris always found a way to slip a little something into the front pocket of Jolie's backpack, which gave Jolie a little independence and stability, and meant that she didn't have to worry so much about her mom forgetting to save some of her tips for Jolie's lunch.

Iris was in charge of all Faith's financial affairs since Faith had left Mae's, from buying the new house, managing investments, groceries, appointments, and dealing with insurance companies. But the relationship went beyond practicalities. They had history. They had become a family.

Jolie or Iris often spent an afternoon reading to Faith from one of her favorite books; something by Jane Austen, Louisa May Alcott, or Maya Angelou. Some days they played cards. They talked, read, listened to music, cooked, and ate together. But most of all they laughed: the brilliant, sharp-tongued Iris, sweet, wise fragile Faith, and the hard-shelled teenager, whose shell was falling away. They were not commonplace friends. Separated by decades, their love of interesting conversation and good music bonded them, giving each the support to grow.

Fashion conscious Iris bought an iPod and now had playlists that included Iron and Wine, Norah Jones, and

Bon Iver, while Jolie had gained an appreciation for the warmth of vinyl records and the classic crooners. Iris brought Jolie quirky and cool fashions from her endless closet of designer clothes, collected during years spent in the New York fashion world. Jolie felt safe in their company, physically and emotionally. If she had a question, the older women seriously tried to help her find an answer.

Jolie walked up to Faith's. A 1960's Harley motorcycle was parked in the driveway next to Iris' classic black Cadillac.

Sean, Jolie thought, her heart thumping like a rock band's bass drum. *Sean's back.*

Faith's errant grandson had taken off right after New Years without a word to any of them. When he finally called, Faith and Iris had been so relieved they hadn't challenged his lame excuses. But trust came hard to Jolie Figg, and Sean tossing that trust aside and running off made her feel uncomfortably vulnerable.

"Why would he do this? Why would he just abandon us?" she had demanded. "He knows how much we need him."

"Sean's not a thinker, Jolie. He doesn't plan," Faith explained. "He just gets something in his head and does it. It isn't meant to be hurtful. He just forgets to think about the rest of us."

Jolie didn't buy it. "It's wrong to make people you care about worry like this."

"You're right, Jo, but it won't do any good to scold him. He'll just get defensive and run off again. Tell her Iris," Faith sought her friend's support.

"Don't look at me." Iris pursed her lipsticked mouth together until it looked like a tiny red cabbage. "I'm with Jo on this. I think Sean acted like a spoiled jerk."

Faith turned up her hands in a helpless gesture. "I'm not blind to it, but it's not my place to judge him. When he gets it right, he's a delight, and when he doesn't--. Well, he knows that I'll be there waiting for him when he comes back around. I always have. He counts on that."

Well then he's in for a big surprise, Jolie thought to herself. *Because one day, he's going to come running home, and you won't be here.*

She hated to think about it, but she knew it was true. Faith was more frail every day. Of course, Jolie would never have said that out loud.

Too late, she realized. She didn't have to. Faith had probably heard her thoughts. The old woman looked up at Jolie with sad eyes, confirming Jolie's suspicion.

But even if I am not here for him, you will be, won't you, dear? They seemed to say.

Jolie broke the link between them, ashamed.

Sean and Jolie had no official relationship, beyond friendship. Everything else between them had been casual flirting and teasing, except on Solstice when they fought side by side to thwart the darkness. There had been a connection that went beyond this life, and both had seen it. For Jolie, the existence of connection elevated Sean's self-absorbed character flaw to the level of willful abandonment. Faith was kinder.

"He's just young," she explained as if that excused all of her grandson's self-centered misbehavior.

"He's older than I am," Jolie protested.

"Only chronologically," Iris argued. "You're an old soul, Jolie. You've probably forgotten more in this life than Sean will remember in his next three."

"I don't know, Faith. You know how you said that souls travel together through many lifetimes?" Jolie countered. "Well, I "saw" Sean. I saw who he really is and he is so much more than this irresponsible overgrown kid."

Faith sighed. "Maybe not this time."

Remembering Sean's trespasses, Jolie's initial excitement about his return faded.

"I don't care how happy I am to see him. I'm going to throttle him," she growled as she stomped up the driveway. "It's just me," she announced, entering. She dropped her backpack by the door.

"Jolie," Faith called back. "Come see who's here."

Jo entered Faith's sitting room, an area between the kitchen and the family room. It was the sunniest place in the house, with a big plate glass window looking out at a desert oasis backyard that had been lovingly planted by the previous owner.

Faith was holding court from her chaise lounge, her white hair framing a face with tissue-paper skin stretched over delicate bones. She wore the silk dressing gown that Iris had bought her when it became too difficult to get dressed every day.

"A woman deserves to look good whatever she feels like." Iris had insisted, lifting the robe from its tissue papered box.

"You shouldn't have spent the money, Iris." Faith said, smiling at the lovely material. "The last thing I need is more things."

"Just because Las Vegans think that dressing up means wearing socks, doesn't mean we all have to lower our standards," the aged fashion icon stated. "This, my dears, is real silk." Iris gently pressed the material against her friend's cheek. "Not that cheap polyester stuff they try to pawn off on people these days. It's as soft as a butterfly's wings but will wear like iron. You could wear this robe every day for the rest of your life--" she stopped abruptly, her eyes wide with horror at what she had said.

"It's all right, Iris. None of us gets out of this alive. I have no illusions about my future," Faith assured her with a smile. "Oh, it is a pretty thing, isn't it? Jolie, will you put my old bathrobe in the Goodwill bag? Iris, help me into this lovely little bit of gossamer. I'll feel like a fairy queen when I wear it. What a wonderful gift, my friend." She had worn it almost every day since.

Faith and Iris sat opposite Sean, looking up at Jolie with a sense of great expectancy, foolish grins pulling their faces sideways.

Jolie's eyes met Sean's, and she knew that something was wrong.

"You shaved," she said bluntly. His signature blue jeans and leather jacket remained, but his usual tee shirt had been replaced by a ludicrous "business casual" cream-colored button down. Sean's eyes flickered to his left and Jolie realized there was a fifth person in the room. A willowy blond sat next to Sean.

"Hey, Jo." He crossed to Jolie and crushed her to his chest. The scent of his skin flooded Jolie with memories: the uncertainty of her home life, the danger they had faced together, the safe zone he had become for her. Now, here he was, back again, but he was not alone. What did it mean? Jolie pushed him away, glaring at the slim intruder.

"Who's this?"

"This is Adrianna." Sean scratched the back of his neck, looking awkward and uncertain. "Adrianna, this is Jolie. She's a friend of the family." The young woman stood and offered Jolie, her hand. Jolie didn't take it.

"I'm very glad to meet you, Jolie. I've heard so much about you." There was a charming foreign lilt to her voice. Jolie hated it.

Chapter Six

I've never heard anything about you; she wanted to say. Instead, she said, "You're French?"

"I'm American, but my father is in the diplomatic corps, so I lived in France until I was thirteen."

"How nice for you." It sounded rude even to Jolie.

Faith smoothed the blanket spread across her legs.

"Jo, could you be a dear and make us a little tea?" "Coffee for you, Sean, and some cookies or cake?" she asked.

"Don't go to any trouble for us, Mrs. McBride," Adrianna said, politely.

Jolie glared. *Us? Us? When did she and Sean become an "us"?*

"It's no trouble," Faith demurred. "Jolie knows where everything is. The three of us have a little tea together most days." She smiled at her grandson, but the message was clear. Jolie was there. Sean was not. "Jolie has become my right hand since I left Mae's. She helps me out in so many ways. I wouldn't be able to live here on my own if it weren't for her and Iris." Sean looked down at his hands, guiltily. "Jolie, please, see what we've got in the kitchen for our guests." Faith's clear blue eyes directed Jolie to the kitchen. *I know Sean bringing this girl is a shock. Give yourself a moment,"* she said, silently directing her thoughts at Jolie.

"Of course, Faith. Excuse me," Jolie headed for the kitchen, a model of civil behavior.

"I'll help." Sean bolted through the doors before anyone could stop him.

Jolie and Sean stood at opposite ends of the kitchen; the linoleum floor stretched between them like a battlefield.

"What are you doing here, Sean?" Jolie demanded.

"What do you mean? I came to see Faith, and you, of course."

"Four months. Four months you've been gone." Jolie turned away, got out the tea tray, and began throwing open cupboards, pulling out packages of cookies and muffins, and tearing them open like they were Sean's head.

"I told you, I went north to look for work."

"No, you said you were thinking about going north to look for work. There's a big gap between thinking about it, and leaving without telling anybody." She retrieved a silver tea set and china cups out of another cupboard. They rattled and clinked as she set them down a little too forcefully. "What if Rick had put some bad juju on you, so you crashed your motorcycle, or strung you up and cut your heart out, or some crazy shit?"

"He didn't."

"How were we supposed to know that?"

"Maybe you could use your amazing psychic powers," Sean bit back.

Jolie hurled a muffin at him. "Do you have any idea how worried your grandmother was--how worried we all were?"

"I needed to get out of town, Jo--away from Rick and his crowd. Grandma understood that."

"You had to get away, but it was okay to leave us here with Rick prowling around, trying to sort out who was responsible for Rory's death, and the rest of that mess on Solstice?" Jolie filled half a plate with cookies, stacking muffins on the other half. "Yeah, you're a real stand-up guy, Sean. Let the old ladies and the girl take care of it. I'm out of here." She set the water on to boil.

"I couldn't sleep. I was going crazy. I kept having these dreams...." Sean left the sentence dangling. Jolie understood about the dreams.

"Yeah. I have them, too," she admitted, her voice softening.

"There are pictures in my head from that night that don't make any sense," Sean confessed.

"We saved them," Jolie said firmly. "That's the part we need to remember."

"We didn't save Rory."

Jolie's jaw set. "Rory didn't deserve saving."

"No one deserves that kind of death," Sean protested.

Jolie wondered what Sean had seen when Rory died. How much did he really understand?

"What happened to Rory was on him, not us," she insisted, firmly. "He should never have been doing any of that shit. He was in way over his head."

Sean walked to the kitchen window and looked out. "I should have known that something was wrong about him--I mean before all of that stuff came down there at the end. How come I didn't know the guy was such bad news? It was my fault--all of it. I'm the one who introduced Rory to Aunt Mae. If I hadn't done that, none of it would have happened, but I didn't see him for who he really was until it was too late."

"Nobody did, except Faith," Jolie pointed out. "He fooled all of them."

"Not you. You had him pegged from the moment he walked into Mae's that first afternoon, didn't you?"

Jolie shrugged. It was true. None of the others had recognized Rory's egocentric evil. She had always thought that spells were a historic hangover from the dark days of medieval witch hunts. They made no sense in a science-based worldview, but the events of last winter had led her to question her assumptions. Something had blinded Mae's and Faith's friends to Rory's true nature. Something had kept them from voicing any concerns about him when they did come up; right up until the spell was broken.

Sean was studying the toes of his boots.

"Sometimes, I think it was all a hallucination. Like somebody put something in the Kool-Aid, you know?" He looked up, desperate for an explanation that made sense in the everyday Western world.

"It may be hard to accept what happened, Sean, but it did happen. Pretending it didn't isn't going to make you sleep better."

"It might," Sean mumbled.

Jolie resisted calling him out as a coward. "So, did you follow me in here to tell me that you found your dream girl; Adrianna 'is the one'?"

A crooked grin screwed up half of Sean's face. "I don't know, maybe."

Jolie spun around ready to spit out a stream of jealous girlfriend put downs. Instead, she took a breath, walked over, and tugged playfully on the collar of the cream-colored shirt.

"It won't last you know. She's not your type."

"Adrianna picked it out." Sean looked embarrassed.

"I can see that."

"Look, I know that you and Grandma and Iris are disappointed in me, and I guess I deserve that. I've been selfish, but I can change." Sean straightened up, losing his habitual slouch. "I've changed already."

"Yeah, you let some girl pick out preppie clothes for you at Banana Republic."

Sean winced but let it go.

"The point is, Jo, you don't need me. You do fine on your own. You proved that on Solstice."

So that was it. Jolie could read it on his face. It was there in the air around him. Sean had come back to say goodbye.

"Solstice didn't prove anything except that bad things can happen to good people without them having

Chapter Six

any idea about what's going on." Jolie tried to keep the emotion from her voice.

"And there are good people who will stop those things from happening," Sean countered.

"If they're there," Jolie protested. "I didn't fight that battle by myself, Sean. I had help: you and Tru, Marty and Mickey, Faith and Iris--you were all a part of it."

"I remember." His tone made it clear that it was not a good memory. "And if it weren't for you, we would all have been in deep shit."

Jolie wiped her hands over her face and sighed. She was just a kid that Sean knew; a friend of the family he had said. That was all. What did she expect?

"So that's it? You've decided. You're going?"

Sean crossed the room and pulled her into a reluctant hug. "You'll be fine. You're the bravest hard-ass I know, outside of my grandmother," Sean tried to soothe and quiet her, but it wasn't his voice Jolie heard. It was not even his touch she felt caressing her hair. The vision took over, and it was Mem's.

"You're going to be just fine," Mem crooned in her refined contralto. It was sunny, the air smelling of wet earth, savory herbs, and lush flowers. The bees were buzzing in the fruit trees overhead.

Jolie had fallen and skinned her knee. Mem had answered her cries, and already it didn't hurt so much. Her grandmother had always been there to fix things for her and then suddenly; she wasn't.

Jessie had woken Jolie in the middle of the night and spirited her away. With Mem gone, there had been no one to fill the void in Jolie's life until Faith had pulled the confused teenager into her own family circle.

"Mem's here," Jolie's grandmother had stroked her granddaughter's brown hair. "Mem will always be here."

That was a lie; grown-up Jolie thought as she was transported from Mem's garden, re-emerging in Faith's kitchen.

She pushed away from Sean.

"You're such a douche."

"I don't mean to be," he apologized. "Uncle Robert used to say that Trouble liked the way my name tickled its tongue. I'm trying to be better now, Jolie, really. Adrianna is helping me."

Jolie snorted. "To be what, her toy poodle?

Sean frowned. "Don't do that. It's unbecoming, and it's not fair. Don't blame Adrianna for what's wrong between us."

"There is nothing wrong between us, Sean," Jolie spit back. "Because there is no "us", there's just you and what you need--what "you" want. Trouble doesn't have your name--that's just more of your charming bullshit. It wasn't just Faith you dragged into this mess with Rick and Rory. You got me into it, too, remember? I'm going to impress my friends by getting Jolie to be the Solstice virgin," Jolie mimicked Sean's voice. "I'll introduce her to Faith. Everyone loves her. There's no way Jolie will say no to Faith."

"Oh come on, Jo, you have to admit that part worked out pretty well, even if you and I didn't." Sean took a cookie and popped it into his mouth.

The water began to boil reminding Jolie of her task. She took the pot off the stove and poured the hot water into the tea pot.

"Don't flatter yourself, Sean. This isn't about some disappointed schoolgirl crush," Jolie cautioned him as she worked. "I'm not falling apart because you needed some comfort between the sheets and I was too young to do the job. I never expected you to wait for me to grow up, but I did expect you to be a friend. For Faith's sake,

Chapter Six

and for your own, you should stick around. Faith can't take any more of your little backsliding episodes. She's not well."

"God, I wish everyone would stop talking about my grandmother like she was half dead already," Sean complained. "Faith's the strongest woman I know. She'll probably outlive us both."

Jolie just looked at him. "You're a friggin' idiot. She won't be able to get out of bed tomorrow, and maybe not the day after that."

"Why? Because of me?"

"There's only so much energy left in her--only so many heartbeats."

Sean glanced back at the closed door. "She looks fine."

"She's thrilled that you're here. I think she was worried that she wouldn't see you again."

"First, you're pissed at me because I'm not here, and now you're going to guilt trip me because by coming I'm making her tired? I just can't win with you, can I?"

"You could. You could stay and take care of her until she crosses over; be the grandson she deserves."

Sean hung his head. "I'm no good at taking care of other people."

"You're not so good at taking care of yourself either, but you are her grandson. You have history--that means something, and no matter how much affection she has for me, or Iris, we can't take your place. We shouldn't have to."

"What about Aunt Mae? She's family."

"That woman will never come close to Faith again. Iris will see to that. Now, it's time for tea, so put your Mister Roger's smiley face on and let's go give your grandmother a nice memory." Jolie donned her own poker face, picked up the tea tray, and pushed through the swinging door into the sitting room. "Tea, ladies," she announced.

None of the women said anything about whatever they might have overheard from the kitchen, but a sadness shadowed their polite smiles. Like a favored princeling, Sean had returned, but he would not be staying. Jolie sat straight-backed on a dining room chair watching as the others chatted about whatever was safe and unimportant, carefully avoiding any hard truths that might take the conversation somewhere real or honest. She felt trapped; like someone had sawed off her legs.

Faith said that the four of them had been born and re-born into different roles throughout many lives. Jolie knew it to be true as surely as she knew she had five fingers on each hand because she had "seen" it. Maybe, that was why Sean was attracted to someone like Adrianna; a woman who didn't come with expectations built up over lifetimes, who wasn't waiting for him to become something greater than just a pretty decent guy with minimal baggage. Maybe sometimes a soul got tired of fighting the good fight and just wanted to phone it in for a life or two. Jolie didn't know much about the spiritual world, but she was pretty sure there was a karmic price to pay for that kind of spiritual wimping out.

"So, Grandma, I've decided to go back to school," Sean announced as he took the last muffin. "I'm going to study engineering."

"Here at UNLV?" Faith asked, hopeful.

"No." Sean hesitated. "I've been looking around. I think I like the University of Washington." He glanced at Adrianna. "I'm planning to start there next term if you're okay with that?" he added, quickly.

"That's what your grandfather always hoped, that you would get a solid degree once you figured out what you wanted to do with your life," Faith replied, trying not to show her disappointment.

Sean looked at Adrianna. "And now I know."

Jolie's heart twisted. She had been so sure that she and Sean's destinies were entwined--so sure that they were perfect as lovers and helpmates, but Sean just wanted to escape.

In what life did you become such a coward, Sean Flahretty? She asked, silently.

Faith leaned forward and took Sean's hand. "He'd be so proud of you, Sean. Are you staying the night? I have a guestroom."

"No thanks, Grandma." Sean glanced at Jolie. "We don't want you to go to any extra trouble."

"We have reservations at the Bellagio," Adrianna explained.

"But I'll come back in the morning and straighten out the trust fund stuff and all that if that's okay?"

"Iris takes care of that," Faith informed her grandson.

"I'll notify the bank that you are coming, so they know to expect you," Iris replied in her curt, businesslike manner.

Sean and Adrianna rose, and Sean kissed Faith's cheek.

"Don't come too early tomorrow," Iris cautioned Sean in a low murmur. "It takes her awhile to get going in the morning, especially after a day like today."

"When have you ever known me to be early, Aunt Iris?" Sean smiled, nervously glancing at his grandmother.

"I'd better get going, too." Jolie stood and began to clear the dishes. "I've got homework and a friend's coming by later."

Sean and Adrianna were out the door before Jolie had finished washing up. He looked back at the house and waved at the kitchen window, and then he was gone.

"Goodbye, Sean," Jolie whispered. Maybe next time there would be a different ending for them.

Iris came into the kitchen, giving Jolie a sympathetic smiled. "Come on. I'll give you a ride home."

The long spring twilight was still lingering when Iris dropped Jolie off at the apartments.

Jolie had showered and was drying her hair when the trouble started upstairs.

CHAPTER SEVEN

"Shut up, you stupid bitch." Something heavy thudded against the floor of the apartment overhead. The walls of Jolie's room trembled like a junkie with the shakes.

Jolie froze with the blow dryer pointed at her tousled hair. The old woman upstairs was a mouse of a thing, as shrunken as a Halloween jack-o-lantern three weeks into November. Jolie had only seen the old woman outside of her apartment once since she and Jessie had moved in. The poor thing was furtively fetching the newspaper from outside her own door, and when she'd seen Jolie, she'd become so frightened that she'd dropped it in her rush to get back inside.

The floorboards overhead transmitted the woman's whimpers, oozing her misery through the ceiling. Jolie switched off the blow dryer and steadied herself against the counter, overwhelmed by the intensity of the woman's fear.

Breathe, Jolie. Just breathe. It's not happening to you, she tried to tell herself.

"Get up, you dried up old bag," the abusive husband shouted. "Get up and face me like a human being." His words slurred, bleeding one into another without consonants.

He's drunk again, Jolie thought.

It wasn't the first time Jolie had been forced to take a front row seat in the theater of their failed marriage. The woman's bleating noises sounded like a wounded animal.

"Did you hear me, Helen? Get up or I'll hit you again." The woman mumbled something unintelligible into the floor. "Stand up and face me, or I swear I'll kill you where you lay," the man threatened.

If the points of his consonants were being blurred by alcohol, something else had trampled the old woman's completely flat. She begged the old man for mercy in a voice Jolie's ears could not understand.

She's ill, Jolie realized. *She can't speak.*

There was a scuffle, then the sound of something being dragged across the floor. Shrieks rang out over the percussion of heels scrabbling against the floor.

"Is this what you want?" Slap. "Why do you make me do this?" Slap. "Stop crying, Helen. You know how upset I get when you cry." Slap. "Stop it now." Slap.

Helen's protests weren't in any dictionary, but Jolie understood them. Helen was begging for her life.

Jolie picked up a shoe and threw it at the ceiling.

"Shut up, up there. You know I can hear you down here, don't you?"

"Who the fuck cares? Who is that, that little whore from downstairs? Mind your own business you little bitch." There was another slap, and Helen cried out in pain.

"Stop it!" Jolie shouted. "Stop hitting her or I'll call the police."

"Get the fuck up off the floor, Helen," the man's attention returned to his victim.

"Leave her alone!" Jolie shouted again. "I'm calling nine-one-one." She pulled her phone from her pocket and dialed. "Do you hear me? They'll be here in a few minutes."

"Stand up or I'll kick you again," the man shouted at his wife, ignoring Jolie. "You know I will."

Chapter Seven

Helen screamed in a half-human voice that sounded like the death shrieks of rabbits attacked by wolves on a National Geographic program she'd watched.

"Nine-one-one, what's your emergency?" the voice on the phone sounded like the start of a comedy routine, but right now nothing was funny.

"There's a man upstairs beating his wife. We're at the Tropical Paradise apartments on Mountain View; Quad F."

Helen screamed.

"Hurry!" Jolie dropped her phone onto the couch and ran out of the apartment, taking the stairs two at a time.

"Leave her alone, old man. Do you hear me? Don't touch her." Jolie reached the landing and threw herself against the door, banging her fists against it. "Helen, are you all right? Helen, open the door. Let me in."

The door flew open. A wiry old man stood framed in the doorway, looking like a piece of dead fruit tossed out to rot in the sun. His stained t-shirt hung over his shriveled body like half peeled skin. The whites of his eyes were jaundiced, and he stank.

"Helen, are you okay?" Jolie tried to see past him. "I called the police. They'll be here any minute." She could hear Helen sobbing, inside. "Helen?" There was no answer. "I'm coming in," she warned the man, standing in a dazed stupor near the door. Jolie slipped by and into a chaos that folded around two realities: the world everybody saw and the other world that sometimes bled through.

The rancid smells of filth overpowered even the old man's sour scent. Helen's sobs came from behind a barricade of furniture in the living room. The man moved past Jolie and stepped in front of it, his eyes blazing.

Helen crawled out from behind the torn and toppled furniture, her face bruised, her lip bleeding down her chin.

"Are you okay, Helen?" Jolie asked.

"G'oaaaaw," the old woman gurgled motioning for Jolie to leave.

"Get out of here, bitch!" the old man growled. "What I do in my house is none of your business." His voice and his body language looked like they had been copied from the creature that Rory had summoned on Solstice. Jolie's hands began to shake.

"What you're doing is wrong. You're going to kill her." She stood her ground. "That can't be what you want." The man looked down at Helen, and for a moment the demonic disfiguration on his face softened, changing it to the face of an unhappy, aging man. He looked around at the room as if he wasn't sure where he was or why Helen was bleeding on the floor. "You were angry just now," Jolie explained carefully, hoping he could hold on to his humanity. "But you didn't mean to hurt her. I know you didn't. You care about her. Please let me come over and clean her up." The man frowned as he backed up into the kitchen.

Jolie moved cautiously forward, careful not to make any sudden moves, and knelt beside the old woman.

"It's going to be okay. Help is on the way, Helen."

"Noooo," the old woman moaned, shaking her head.

There was a growl from the kitchen and a body slammed into Jolie. Claw-like hands pressed deep into the tendons of her neck, stopping her breath, compressing her vision into a shrinking black dot with a pin prick glow of a demon's red eye at the center. Her hands frantically scratched at the flesh and bone vise around her throat, but it did not budge.

Thtop! Thtop! Helen's hands stroked Jolie's arms, unable to reach high enough to get to the point of crucial contact.

"Please stop, Axel." Jolie heard the voice locked inside Helen, the voice that had been hers before a stroke had imprisoned her inside her aging body. *"They'll take you away and lock you up. Then what will I do? What will happen to me? What will happen to me?"* she wailed.

The red glow in the black dot faded. A small, bright iris took its place.

"Joliette?" Jolie heard Mem's, voice. *"What are you doing?"*

"Dying," Jolie replied very matter-of-factly. *"Life wasn't like you said at all. You weren't there. I was alone and it sucked. So, I'm done,"* she announced smugly.

"Sweetheart." Jolie could hear the patient smile in Mem's voice. *"Things are not the way either of us wanted, but you can't just give up. You've barely lived. You have so much left to see and do, Cherie. You're a Boulette, and we Boulette's don't give up. You need to fight back, Jolie. Fight back, now!"*

Something deep within Jolie pulled itself together into a tight spinning ball of energy then let go.

The room exploded like a hand grenade, the old man's hands raking gouges in Jolie's neck as he was thrown across the room.

Air rushed into Jolie's lungs and she collapsed onto the floor, coughing.

"Jolie? Jolie, are you up here?" Remy's voice penetrated the muddle of Jolie's mind. She looked around, disturbed by the condition of the strange place. It looked like a hurricane had hit it.

"Shit." Remy stood in the doorway staring at the aftermath of Jolie's battle for her life. "What happened?"

Helen groaned from the floor.

"Axel." Jolie heard the old woman's thoughts, though her physical speech was still a tortured exercise in language gone awry. Jolie's eyes tracked Helen's grief-stricken gaze.

The old man lay bent back over a chair that had slid up against the counter, in a most unnatural position.

Helen turned to Jolie, mumbling words she could not push past her paralyzed lips.

"You need to go," Jolie heard the woman's thoughts. *"It's no use you staying and getting caught up in this. The police have been here before. The thing they won't understand is you and your part. Leave now, before they come."*

Jolie tried to get to her feet, gasping in pain as she failed, and then Remy was there, lifting her into his arms.

"Hold on to me," he commanded. Jolie wrapped her arms around his neck and leaned her head against his chest, unable to do anything more. "I think we need to talk about all the things you didn't do, Jolie Figg," Remy said as he carried her down the stairs.

"Not now." She struggled to get air past her crushed vocal chords.

"No, not now," Remy agreed as he settled her behind him on his scooter. "Right now, all I want you to think about is holding on to me. Don't let go."

Jolie remembered anchoring her awareness to Remy's heartbeat, her arms wrapped around his waist. The cool evening wind washed the tears off her cheeks, a field of stars stretching across the sky above them.

She had no understanding of distance or how long they drove. The traffic and the city fell behind, the scents of sage, creosote, and pine pulling them into the desert's embrace, wiping away the ugliness of the scene in the apartment.

The dramatic stone escarpments of Red Rock National Conservation Area loomed tall and powerful beneath the rising full moon, glossing the stone peaks in silver light while their bases remained as dark and solid as the bones of the ancient dinosaurs hidden beneath them.

Remy turned his scooter onto a dirt road, slowing as he wove around the pot holes. Somewhere nearby, a burro brayed, the haunting hee-haw echoing off the red stone faces that protected Calico Basin like a pair of protective arms. The shaggy animals came into view, standing in a group not far from the road. An old black jack stood guard over them, standing between them and the road. He watched Remy and Jolie go by on the scooter as if taking their measure, his solemn face resigned to his herd's plight. The city was encroaching on his world and the greed of expansion had never been kind to those who had come before, be they two or four-legged.

Jolie turned her head, looking back over her shoulder until she could see him no more.

"Where are we going, Sean?" she tried to whisper through her crushed vocal chords.

"Sh. Don't talk, Jo. Just hold on," the boy in front of her whispered back." It was not Sean's voice, but it was a gentle voice. "I'm taking you someplace safe."

Skateboard boy. Jolie remembered. *Remy.* Remy had scooped her up and taken her away. The sharp, brittle edge that Jolie hid behind wanted to laugh and mock this doomed boy for the notion that he could keep anyone safe, especially her. He was about to be killed and she--she knew things, saw things that he did not. But what had happened at the apartment, had drained and separated Jolie from all of her sharp-tongued sarcasm.

She had seen death up close before. But with Rory, she had merely nudged the scales of justice. What had happened at the apartments was something different. She had pushed Axel away from her with what? Her energy? Magic? Her intention? How was that possible? She had acted purely on instinct, not knowing what she was doing. *I was just trying to get his hands off my throat,* she thought, frightened. What else was she supposed to do? He had been trying to squeeze the life from her.

"Remy? What's happened?" a woman's voice broke into Jolie's confusion.

The scooter had stopped and the looming shadows of the red rock mountains curved around them.

"Dear Creator. Bring her inside, nephew. Put her in the little room in the back." Jolie felt her bits gathered up like a package that had been ripped apart. Remy laid her down on a bed and pulled up a cotton blanket with a multi-colored star quilted onto its face. The bare beams of a log cabin supported the roof above. Mismatched furniture: a vintage dressing table, old chests of drawers, and trunks were pushed up against the walls as if they needed the support to stand.

"Just try and rest, dear." The woman's voice was as kind as her face. "We'll talk in the morning." She tucked the quilt around Jolie, there was the soft swish of fabric and the door closed to allow a sliver of light to come in from the next room.

"What happened to her?" a thickly accented woman's voice demanded.

"Remy hasn't had a chance to explain. Is everyone ready to go in, Yanna?"

"I'll just put the wasna in a bowl," the second woman replied.

Chapter Seven

"Okay. I'll get them lined up."

Jolie had just closed her eyes when the wooden door swung open again, spilling light over her in the bed.

The fortuneteller's face hovered over her like a disembodied head.

"So you were lost. Rest easy. I have found you."

"Yanna Maria, we're waiting for you," the kind voiced woman called from the outer door. The fortune teller's face vanished and the light from the door waned back to a crescent sliver.

Jolie looked out the little wood-framed window that faced west. Twin peaks in the escarpment, like a pair of rounded breasts, shone in the moonlight. She could not have said how long she lay there, just looking at the red rock cliff face, but once again light spilled across the bed. Remy pulled a chair up beside her.

"Sleep, if you can, Jo. I'll be right here." He gently moved the hair back off her face, touching her forehead with cool, gentle fingers. She longed to take his hand and curl herself around it. Wavering between waking hallucination and haunted sleep, Jolie's mind drifted away on the sound of drums beating out the heartbeat beneath the stone breasts shimmering outside her window.

CHAPTER EIGHT

The morning sun struck the red rock mountains on the west side of Calico Basin, waking Jolie like a thunderclap. Clutching the faded star quilt, fear coiled in her belly. Where was she? She took in the small low-ceilinged bedroom. How did she get here? The smell of the desert and the images of ghost-like burros and towering rock cliffs tickled the edges of her memory. Then, she remembered and wished she hadn't.

The old man's body had been flung back over the chair like a deflated blow up toy, discarded and forgotten.

A flood of questions pulled at Jolie's mind. Had her interference in the argument between Axel and Helen made matters better or worse for the old woman? Would there be repercussions for her impulsive actions? What if Axel pressed charges? Helen would never stand up to her husband to support Jolie's version of what had happened. The old woman was too cowed. Helen's life might not seem like a good one to those on the outside, but Axel was all she had.

"They'll take you away," the old woman had cried, locked inside her post-stroke world. *"What will happen to me?"*

"I did the right thing," Jolie insisted, with more conviction than she felt. Doing the right thing had never been a guarantee that things would go well for her. Sean had joked that Trouble knew his name but Trouble thought it had a place set at the table in the Figg house.

Chapter Eight

Jolie rolled over and looked out the bedside window. Sunlight was moving down the red stone mountains that formed the west wall of the basin, dripping like golden frosting running down a red velvet cake. As she watched, the sun reached the foot of the mountains and began to spread across the valley floor.

A burro's bray split the quiet, bouncing off the stone cliffs surrounding the oasis valley. Jolie smiled, remembering the old black jack on the road, shaggy-coated, his ear torn, he too had seemed like an old soul.

Jolie took a deep breath of the clean desert air; breathing in pure wonder. Something ancient and powerful lived here. She felt it kiss her skin, burrowing into her bones, and smiled. Feeling strangely safe in this odd little house, she snuggled more deeply under the blankets, letting her eyes wander over the details of the room. The sloped roof and rough wood walls gave it an unfinished lean-to feel. The white enamel frame of the cast iron twin bed she lay in was chipped and rusted at the welds. A vintage vanity opposite the bed looked like it had been stolen from the set of one of the Thin Man movies from the thirties, with its frameless, circular mirror and rounded corners. Two dressers and an old trunk had sprouted a collection of collectible Avon bottles, their round bellies and long necks poking up like the minarets of a miniature Turkish village. None of it was dusty. These were the mementos of a personal museum, the small treasures in which resided some family history.

Voices drifted in from outside, followed by the staccato thwacking of someone splitting wood. The smell of a campfire was what finally lured Jolie out of bed. Still dressed in blue jeans, a sleeveless shell, and a button down shirt with Remy's oversized hoody thrown over it, she found her tennis shoes neatly tucked under the bed and slipped her sockless feet into them. Fighting the impulse to wrap the star quilt around her and take it along, Jolie smoothed the cotton blanket over the bed and tiptoed into the connecting room.

It was a welcoming space, open and airy. Morning light streamed in through a bank of windows facing East. Another bank of windows brought in an inspirational view of a huge pink mountain that bounded the basin's edge to the north.

A hand-woven wool rug covered the center of the wood plank floor between two overstuffed couches, and colorful Indian blankets transformed the room from tatty to secondhand chic. Two more pieces of fine woven art hung on the opposing wall. Between the couches, balanced on a wooden pedestal, was a coffee table made from a single slice of a giant tree. The feel was homey, interesting, and eclectic, if not strictly matching.

Jolie peeked into the kitchen, then found the bathroom, adjusting the hood of Remy's hoody to hide the bruises that Axel's hands had left on her neck. Stepping outside the house, she filled her nose and lungs with the earthy smells of the desert. An undertone of horse accompanied the more powerful scent of burning wood.

Following the smoke, Jolie made her way around the north side of the house, past the big windows, to the east end. A cleared space was separated off from the rest of the yard by a row of juniper trees and a rickety mesquite branch fence. Jolie could see a fire pit and a small mound of dirt. A stick, with a feather tied to it, stood in its center. Behind this, a bowl-shaped hut had been covered by a dusty olive green tarp. Remy came out from behind the round hut and walked to the fire, gently moving sticks of wood into place with a pitchfork, maintaining unbroken walls of wood around a hot center. When he was done, he looked up at Jolie.

"You're awake." He smiled. It was like pulling back the drapes of a dingy room and flooding it with sunshine like he opened his soul and invited her in.

Jolie blinked, unnerved by this sudden intimacy. Only yesterday, she and this boy had been strangers. Were they now something else? How was that possible?

"Hold on to me," Remy had said, as he scooped her up like a stray kitten. Why had he brought her here? How had he known not to just take her downstairs to her own apartment?

Remy picked up a blanket from a stump beside the fire, stepped out through the little gate and wrapped the blanket around Jolie's shoulders.

"Come sit. You've had a rough night." He guided Jolie to a makeshift bench made up of stumps and a board that sat at the edge of the fire's warmth.

"How long did you stay with me last night?" Jolie asked self-consciously.

Remy shrugged. "Awhile. I had to start the fire before dawn." Jolie glanced sideways at him. What kind of a boy sat beside a girl all night, just watching her sleep when he barely knew her? "How do you feel?" he asked.

Jolie tapped her throat. "Hurts," she whispered, not recognizing her own voice.

"You probably shouldn't try to talk too much. It'll take time to heal."

"So you're a doctor now?" she rasped.

"No. Just someone who cares."

Jolie wanted to ask if he meant he cared about everyone in general, or if he was saying that he cared about her in particular, but such a discussion felt too exposed.

Another burro call pierced the basin's peace. Jolie grinned.

"It sounds like we're on Tatooine, and the Sand people are about. They are easily startled, but they will be back, and in greater numbers," she tried to mimic Obi Wan Kenobi's voice, doing a poor job of it with her damaged vocal chords.

"It's not a galaxy far, far away but it is like another world here," Remy agreed. "This is my Aunt Rose's ranch. It's a good place, a safe place."

Safe. Short snapshot images began playing through Jolie's mind. She closed her eyes, waiting for them to pass. When she opened them, Remy was patiently leaning on a pitchfork, gazing into the fire.

"What happened last night?" she asked in her froggy voice.

"You'd know better than I would. I think I came in after the finale."

"And took me away. I remember that part. Thank you."

"Fireman," a woman called from the round hut, startling Jolie, who had assumed they were alone. Remy squatted down by a ground level opening that apparently served as the hut's door and listened to instructions from the woman inside. He nodded, then pulled down the heavy blankets that were looped over a thick mesquite branch, covering the opening. A drum began to beat inside and a woman's voice joined it.

The small hairs on the back of Jolie's neck stood up, vibrating with the rhythm of the drum.

Jolie looked into the sky. A swarm of spirits was coming toward them.

"What's going on, Remy?" she asked, anxiously.

"Aunt Rose is singing a calling song, calling in the Spirits."

Chapter Eight

And they're coming, Jolie realized. She felt the spirits approaching the round hut, some tentative, others eager, swooshing by Jolie, focused on the voice of the woman inside the hut. Remy was right, she had walked into another world.

Remy crouched beside the fire and closed his eyes. Jolie could see that his energy was linked to whatever was nestled in the heart of the fire. The energy went through the objects to the woman inside the hut, as she raised her voice in song inviting the invisible beings to join her.

The calling song ended and a new song began. This time the singer was a younger woman, joined by the tentative voices of others with voices nearer the timbre of her own.

The women sang four songs, accompanied by the heartbeat rhythm of the drum, then called out an unfamiliar phrase in a language Jolie did not recognize, and Remy opened the door flap. The woman inside handed out a bucket of water to him. Once again sitting on his haunches by the door, he waited for instructions, then began going back and forth to the fire, bringing hot stones from the fire back to the hut. Jolie could hear him whispering to the stones as if they were newborns, as he gently carried and deposited them inside the hut, sliding them inside on his pitchfork.

"Thank you for coming, Grandfathers. Thank you for helping us," Jolie caught a few words of what Remy said.

After a few trips, he handed the water bucket back in and again closed the door flap. When he had repaired the fire's burning log wall, he sat down beside her again.

"What are they doing in there?" Jolie asked.

"They're praying, in a very old way. It's a Stone People's lodge. Most people call it a sweat lodge."

It was not like any praying Jolie had ever heard of before, but she couldn't argue; she had heard the spirits being called, and she had seen them answer that call.

Remy continued to tend the fire and wait on the women in the lodge, carrying stones to them, refilling the water bucket, fetching objects off the little mound outside the doorway. Each time he closed the lodge door there was singing, heartfelt, and sometimes agonizing in its raw need. During the third round, the song became raucous and triumphant as if the young women were getting ready to take on the world. In between the songs they spoke in hushed voices so that all Jolie heard was murmuring.

Where have you brought me, Remy Bishop? Jolie asked silently, trying to take it all in.

The sound of car tires on the gravel driveway announced a visitor. A car door clicked shut and Officer Wrangler in a cowboy hat and boots sauntered up to the little stick fence.

"What's he doing here?" Jolie pulled her blanket up around her face.

"Don't worry," Remy assured her. "He's not here to arrest anyone."

"Well, Miss Figg." Wrangler doffed his broad-brimmed hat. "I didn't expect to see you here."

"She came with me, Cowboy," Remy explained.

"Hey, Rem, thanks for doing the fire for the girls today." Wrangler looked from Remy to Jolie and back again, chewing over the bit of bruising he noted on her neck. Jolie pulled Remy's hoody up higher.

"No problem."

Wrangler turned to Jolie. "You didn't go in?"

"She's just visiting," Remy explained. "They'll be out in a few minutes. They're almost done."

Wrangler nodded, sitting on the opposite end of the bench from Jolie. She glanced at him, cautiously.

"Cowboy?" Her voice sounded like she'd been on a three-day binge, smoking, and drinking, but if Wrangler noticed, he didn't say anything.

"It's a nickname my friends use."

"So you're friends with Remy's aunt?" Jolie asked.

"Yeah, and I usually bring the girls." He tossed his head toward the lodge. "Some of them have gotten to like doing a women's lodge with Rose. It's good for them. It gives them a sense of belonging and connection, and it's the full moon, so it's a good time for them."

Wrangler seemed to think Jolie understood the reference, which she didn't, but she didn't ask him to explain. The women chimed out in unison again, and Remy opened the door for the fourth time. Steam poured from the hut, filtering the morning sunshine. The kind-faced woman Jolie remembered from last night crawled out on her hands and knees, mud caking her dress, her long salt, and pepper hair fluffed out from the heat and steam. Remy gave her a hand and helped her stand.

"Welcome back, Aunt Rose."

"Thank you, nephew." Rose hugged him, her face flushed. She stepped to the side of the door as one by one teenage girls, muddy from head to foot, crawled out into the world, their faces ruddy and glistening with sweat, their eyes bright. They all wore long skirts and tee shirts, or loose fitting dresses similar to Rose's, some tattered and faded, all mud-stained and sagging wet. Wrapped in a world of their own, their faces radiant, they hugged Rose, then hugged each other, heart to heart, whispering secret encouragements that brought smiles and tears.

Wrangler and Jolie did not seem to exist.

Jolie felt a pang of jealousy at their closeness. It wasn't hard to be a loner in a plastic, superficial world, where you could easily tell yourself that no one was worth knowing, but faced with the honest friendship between these fresh-faced girls, it was harder.

"Get dressed, ladies, then we'll feast." Rose turned. "Ah, Cowboy. You're here. You'll join us for the feast, won't you?"

"The girls cooked? I wouldn't miss it."

"And you too, Jolie?" Rose offered. "You must be hungry. I'm sorry I wasn't around to greet you and be a proper hostess this morning. It gets a little busy here around the full moon."

Jolie looked to Remy for guidance, uncertain about leaving his side.

"Go on," he encouraged her. "I have a few things to finish up here and then I'll be in."

Jolie followed Rose and the girls into the house. The girl's muddy footprints lead to a curtained off area and Jolie could hear them talking quietly as they changed back into their street clothes.

Rose came out of a side door dressed in a caftan, her long hair framing cheeks still red, her skin so clean it was glowing. She rubbed her hands together.

"Okay, what needs to be done first?"

The oldest girl came out from behind the curtain.

"You aren't allowed to do anything else today, Auntie Rose. You've done enough. Sit down and put your feet up. We'll take care of the feast and the clean up."

Rose sighed. "Thank you, girls." She smiled proudly as they came out from changing, now looking like the modern teenage girls they were, and began to take food out of the oven and the refrigerator and place it on the counter, removing lids and foil covers, and putting serving spoons or forks into each dish.

"Is there something I can do to help?" Jolie offered, tugging the hoody up around her neck.

"Nope. We've got it." The older girl grabbed a mop and began swabbing away the footprints from the floor.

"Come sit by me, Jolie." Rose patted the couch beside her. "We can talk."

There was no polite way to refuse. Jolie sat gingerly on the arm of the couch, giving herself as much personal space as she could. Rose gave her guest a warm smile.

"I'm glad Remy brought you." Rose combed her fingers through her tangled hair. "We don't usually get to meet his friends from school. I think he likes to keep his two worlds separate." She eyed Jolie. "You seem to be feeling better."

"I am, thank you."

"Rose, the spirit plate is ready," one of the girl's interrupted.

"Jolie can take it." Jolie started to panic. "Just give it to Remy. He knows what to do," Rose assured her as the other girl handed Jolie the paper plate.

Jolie carried the plate with little bits of food on it back outside to the lodge area, grateful to have escaped questions about what had happened last night.

Remy had spread out the coals from the fire so they would cool and was standing by, watching the red coals wink at him. Jolie hesitated, loath to interrupt. This was a deep boy with many layers that she suspected he had only just begun to share with her.

"Remy? Rose said to bring this to you."

"Thanks." Remy took the plate, placed himself in front of the fire and turned slowly clockwise, stopping four times before placing the plate onto the fire so it would burn.

"So, you even feed ghosts at these things?" Jolie asked.

"Spirits," Remy corrected her. "It seems right to honor them for their help."

"Do you do this a lot?"

"Tend the fire?" He shrugged. "Rose usually has one of the women do it for the girls, but I fill in when she needs me, and sometimes I do it for mixed lodges or men's lodges if none of the older guys can make it. My uncle says that tending fire is a good place to learn."

"I didn't know that you were Native."

"Lakota--half, on my mother's side. The family left the reservation when Mom was little so she never spent much time there. The men in the family became horse trainers and loggers, so they moved around a lot."

"So, Madison...?"

"Is my half sister. My mom crossed over when I was a baby," Remy explained.

As Jolie had suspected, the blond woman was not Remy's blood relative, she was his stepmother, and pale, perfect Madison was her daughter. Jolie wasn't the only one leading a double life, but maybe Remy's experience with a culture where spirits were seen as real, meant that explaining her vision to him wasn't going to be so impossible after all. Of course, Christians recognized spirits too, selectively anyway--the Father, the Son, and the Holy Ghost--and she wouldn't expect them to understand. Still, it gave her hope.

"Remy, you know that note?" Jolie began cautiously.

"You mean the one you didn't send?" He grinned.

"Yeah, that one. Well, sometimes I see things, like spirits," she indicated the air around the sweat lodge. "And other things, too, like things about people: stuff that's going on with them, or that might happen to them."

Chapter Eight

"Visions?"

"Yeah; visions. That first day when you bumped into me, I saw something about you. You were in an accident. It was really bad and... you didn't make it." She was afraid to look at him. "That's why I wrote the note. I wanted to warn you, but I didn't know how to explain and make you believe me." Remy didn't say anything. He just began to rake out the hot spots in the coals. "Crazy, huh?" Jolie added, prodding him to say something that would let her know what he was thinking.

"Well, it's certainly the most unusual introduction I've ever had to a girl," he teased.

"This isn't a joke, Rem. You're in danger," Jolie bridled.

He stopped raking and looked at her. "From who, Jo?"

"I don't know: the world--some random stranger. I don't know, but I think it has something to do with your skateboard."

"I don't own a skateboard," Remy announced.

"You do." Jolie blinked, perplexed. "I've seen it in your backpack. It's yellow, just like the one in my vision."

"That's not mine. It's my friend, Bodhi's. So..." Remy shrugged as if this one fact should effectively erase her concerns. Jolie clenched her jaw.

"I know what I saw."

"Okay. I'm not saying you didn't, Jo, but what do you want me to do about it, hide in my room for the rest of my life?"

"Don't be dumb. I just want you to take this seriously."

"What makes you think I'm not? I don't disbelieve you, but I don't know how to change the future, and apparently you don't either. You don't even know where the threat is coming from."

"It's the skateboard. It's something to do with the skateboard," Jolie insisted.

"That's not much to go on," Remy argued.

Jolie's frustration was beginning to show in her voice. "I'm only trying to keep you safe."

"Now you sound like my Uncle Hoke. Look, Jo, I promise not to run with scissors and I'll look both ways before I cross the street, but there's no one out there trying to get me. I don't have enemies. I'm not a controversial kind of guy."

"And you think that's going to protect you? The most dangerous things in my life happened because I was doing the right thing. And yes, it is a hell of a lot easier to pretend you don't see what you see, and you're not who you are, so you can get by at school." Remy blanched. She had hit a nerve, but it was too late to stop, the words were already taking a dive off her tongue. "But it won't protect you from shit. Does anyone really know you, Remy? Do you even know yourself?"

"I thought you were different. I never thought you were mean." He walked away and crawled inside the lodge.

"I'm not mean. I'm just honest," Jolie shouted after him as he disappeared through the dark opening.

Cliff Wrangler effectively ended any more discussion by coming around the corner and approaching the lodge area.

"Food's ready," he announced.

"Tell Rose I'll be there in a minute," Remy called from inside the lodge.

Jolie was about to pass Wrangler when he stopped her.

Chapter Eight

"Can I have a word with you, Miss Figg?" The arm barring her way didn't really give her a choice. "Quite a night last night, huh?" His eyes went to the bruises on her neck. "Anything you want to tell me?"

"Nope." The trick to talking to prying adults was to say as little as possible. Eventually, they'd write their own story, filling in the blanks to their liking. In the end, they were happy, you were happy, and they had a version of events that made sense to them. Jolie looked up and saw the old black burro standing across the road, looking at her.

Wrangler turned to see what had taken her attention.

"Old Black Jack," he commented. "That burro must be older than Satan, but he just won't give up. One or two of the younger jacks tests him every year, but he's a tough old codger. He just runs them off." The old burro continued to stare at Jolie. Wrangler looked back and forth from Jolie to the burro. "He's sure interested in you."

"Probably thinks I've got a carrot in my pocket," Jolie tried to diffuse Wrangler's interest.

"Not that one. He's too crafty to be taken in by an easy handout. Handouts are dangerous for wild critters. It teaches them that people and the road they travel on are sources of food. It gets them killed. I've seen that guy chase his herd away from the roads even when tourists are tossing fries out of their car windows." Wrangler turned his focus back to Jolie. "Most people around here figure Remy Bishop for a decent kid." He looked meaningfully at her injuries.

Jolie realized that he was asking her if the marks on her neck had anything to do with Remy.

"And they'd be right," she agreed. "He's a good guy--a good friend. The kind of friend who helps you out when you need it."

Wrangler nodded. "You were at home last night?"

"Until Remy picked me up and brought me here."

"Nine-one-one got a call from a girl reporting a domestic situation at the apartment above yours. You want to tell me anything about that?"

"Nope."

"Do you mind if I look at your cell phone?"

Jolie felt her pants pocket. "I must have left it at the apartment. I was in a hurry when we left."

"Anything to do with the argument going on upstairs?"

Jolie stiffened. "It's hard to listen to that stuff."

"Yes, it is. You know, whoever made that call did the right thing, Jolie. If you ever find out who it was, maybe you could let them know that the woman, Helen, is okay. She's in the hospital for now, but her family back in Illinois have been notified, and they're on their way to fetch her and take her back home with them. They haven't known where she was the last twenty-five years. Anyway, she won't have to suffer anymore."

"What about Axel?" Jolie asked. "What will happen to him?"

"He didn't have any assets. Probably drank them up years ago. The county will bury him."

Jolie's jaw went slack. She couldn't breathe. Axel was dead. Was that her fault? Had she done that? She realized that Wrangler was watching her closely--too closely.

"This is probably a lot to take in," he said. "Maybe I should take you home."

"Now?" Jolie was trying to find her poker face, but it seemed to be missing. "But Remy..."

"It'd probably be better if someone official brought you back and talked to your mom," Wrangler explained. "She, uh..."

Chapter Eight

"Turned me in as a runaway," Jolie finished the sentence. "I'm surprised she noticed I was gone. It must be some kind of a record. I'd like to thank Rose and the girls before I go, if that's okay, Officer Wrangler?"

"There's no hurry. Go back inside and eat. We're all riding together."

As Jolie went back into the house, she noted the black burro had moved on.

Everything was cleaned up and the girls were saying their goodbyes, but a plate had been set aside for her.

"Can we come again next month at the full moon, Rose?" a skinny girl with a boy-short haircut asked.

"I'd be disappointed if you didn't, Carly."

"And will Remy do the fire for us?" the older girl cocked her head to one side flirtatiously, as Remy came in to take the kitchen garbage out. "You're the best fireman, Remy."

"Thanks, Carmen." Remy smiled as he tied up the bag, oblivious to her interest in him. Rose was not nearly as dense.

"We usually use a female fire tender for a women's lodge, but we'll see. Will you make your wonderful lasagna again, Carly?"

The skinny girl brightened. "If I can. My foster mom made kind of a fuss about buying all the cheeses and stuff."

"If you give Officer Wrangler a list, I can have the ingredients here for you, and you can put them together before we go in. Tell him I said it was all right."

"Okay, thanks," Carly lifted her head up proudly.

"And what about you, Jolie? Rose turned. "Will you be joining us next time?"

"I don't know. I'm glad I came, though. It was nice. Thank you for taking me in last night."

"I hope we'll see you again soon."

Jolie met Remy coming back from garbage duty. "Officer Wrangler's going to take me back to town," she said.

"If that's what you want."

"It's not what I want, it's just that my mom reported me as a runaway so, you know, he probably needs to clear things up with her. Look, Remy, if anybody asks, you didn't see anything upstairs at the apartments, okay? You were never there. When you picked me up I was already downstairs."

"Whatever," Remy replied, still feeling hurt.

"I'm really sorry about saying what I said," Jolie apologized. "You've been so great, and I want to thank you for taking care of me and everything. I was just spouting off, you know? It's just my dumb mouth."

"I understand." An awkward silence hung between them.

"Jolie, we're ready," Wrangler called from the van.

"I'm coming," she called back. "I meant what I said, though, Remy, about keeping you safe. I'm not going away. I'll be there. Whatever it is that's coming, you're not alone." Jolie took off his hoody and handed it and the blanket back to him, then headed to the front of the house.

As the van was about to leave, an old red pickup pulled up.

"Hey, Hoke," Wrangler greeted the man in the driver's seat.

"Hey, Cowboy." It was the same man that Jolie had seen outside Chaparral High, the one she had recognized but not been able to place. The next breath immersed her in vision.

Jolie was in the desert on Solstice, fighting for her life and the lives of a hundred strangers. Faith had tried to help, Tru and Marty had done their part, and Sean

Chapter Eight

was there beside her, but the weight of responsibility had still made her feel isolated and alone. How could one girl stand against so many dark creatures?

"You are not alone," she had been told and white flames had begun popping up around the landscape, dotting it with the heart-fires of allies who also fought, each in their own way. Focusing on the spirit nearest her, Jolie had been transported to the campfire of a Native man; this man, who Cowboy called Hoke.

Hoke: the name of the person that Madison had wanted to call from the hospital when Remy was dying, the man Mr. Bishop had called family.

Yanna Maria got out of the passenger side of Hoke's truck.

CHAPTER NINE

*J*essie Lynn's childbed screams rang out like an alarm clock as she labored to push the tiny infant from her body.

"Go on now. It's time to be born," Mem encouraged Jolie's reluctant spirit.

"I'm not ready," Jolie held back.

Jolie relived the dream regularly.

"It's time, Jolie," Topi's spirit whispered.

Topi, the man she had thought would marry her mother and save them both. But Jessie Lynn had refused to be saved, and Topi had fallen in love with cousin Tessa-of-the-beautiful-hair. Now, Topi and Tessa had a family of their own in New Orleans, and Jessie and Jolie only had each other.

Jolie felt herself being sucked through a tunnel toward the tiny lump of flesh that her spirit would inhabit for the rest of this life.

"It's all right. We'll be right there with you," her spirit family lied. Maybe they hadn't meant to lie, but that didn't change the fact that they had.

Hands grabbed baby Jolie, pulling her from the slippery red tunnel into the cold, empty space of the birthing room. Jolie opened her eyes. Yanna Maria was holding her.

"And so we meet again," the fortune teller announced.

The dream was changing.

The doctor entered, and Yanna Maria handed Jolie to him.

Chapter Nine

Peering at the new world from inside the infant body, Jolie felt herself flipped upside down. Liver spotted hands held her by the ankles and Axel's face, bigger than life, zoomed into hers. His breath reeked of alcohol and a rotting liver.

"I have you now, you little bitch!" he wheezed. "Kill me, will you?" He slapped her baby buttocks. "Kill me?" He slapped them again.

Baby Jolie opened her mouth and howled, her tiny fists clenched in impotent rage.

The spirits of her family who had gathered for the birth, gasped in horror as a cyclonic wind caught them up in its twisting body, flinging them to the far reaches of the universe.

"No! Don't go!" Jolie's soul shrieked. "Don't leave me." The baby wailed, the tiny body flailing in the empty air.

"Scream away. There's no one to help you." Axel cackled gleefully.

Something moved behind the old drunk's eyes, something that skulked in the darkness of his twisted mind, lusting for revenge. The shadow shifted into a low banked, demonic glow. Something was hiding there, deep within Axel. He leaned into Jolie and opened his mouth. It grew larger and larger until it was the size of a cave, the roof, and floor ringed by low walls of tooth fencing. The noxious gasses of decay and death was unbreathable.

The cave-mouth began to close over Jolie.

"No!"

Jolie woke up thrashing in her sheets, trying to claw her way out of Axel's cave mouth.

"I am not an infant. I am not helpless, and Axel is dead," she told herself firmly, working to slow her breathing. "There is nothing he can do to me in this world. It's just a stupid dream."

The birth dream always left Jolie feeling uneasy, but she had been dreaming it for years, why was it suddenly changing? It had never changed before.

You never killed someone before, her subconscious answered.

If Jolie accepted that hypothesis, then had her subconscious added the old drunk to the dream because she was struggling with the guilt of his death? Probably. She was no psychologist, but it made a certain mind-game kind of sense. You couldn't kill someone and not have it affect you unless you were a psychopath. Jolie tried to remember what the dream had been like before, and consider if there had been any other changes.

Had the nurse always been Yanna Maria? Maybe Jolie had just never noticed because she hadn't met the fortune teller yet. She wished she could remember the face of the nurse before, but she couldn't. Dreams were like that, mercurial; changing the moment you tried to define them in words. If Yanna Maria was indeed a new presence in the dream, what was her subconscious trying to tell her?

The fortune teller had said something to Baby Jolie. Jolie didn't remember the nurse in the other dreams ever saying anything, except maybe, "It's a girl, Miss Figg." Was it possible that the fortune teller had the ability to appear in other people's dreams, or was she a symbolic stand-in for something else?

Jolie unwound the sheets from her legs and walked to her bedroom window, sliding it open.

A warm breeze brushed her skin. The full moon was beginning to wane, but its light played over the city's red tile roofs in shadowy violets and purples.

Chapter Nine

When she and her mom had first come to Southern Nevada, Jolie had hated everything about Las Vegas.

"It's brown and ugly," she'd complained. "And whatever isn't all dried up, is plastic and fake. It's a big con, Mom. How can you buy into this shit?"

It had been Faith who showed Jolie that there was more to Vegas than tourist attractions on the strip.

"Maybe you could just start with noticing the world around you," the older woman had suggested. "Not the man-made world--the natural world, the sky, the plants, birds. If you pay attention to them, they can tell you things."

"You sound like Mom's witch friends." Jolie grimaced. Faith looked out the window, a blissful look came over her face, more than just an upturning of lips, it transformed every feature, giving the old woman a soft radiance.

"Feeling connected gives you a foundation that you can count on, Jo. Even when people fail you."

"I don't think I can connect to a whole anything," Jolie groused. "I have trouble just being around a few people."

"I like sunrises and sunsets here," Iris chimed in, setting lunch down on the coffee table. "The reds and oranges are so vivid and the sky is so big. It doesn't look like that back east. But the best is the stars. There's nothing like them anywhere else." Iris' face, too, was lit up.

Jolie frowned. "The only stars I've seen in Las Vegas are the Elvis and Marilyn impersonators down on Fremont Street. There's too much light pollution here to see real stars."

"You have to get away from the city," Iris advised. "I stayed overnight in Death Valley once, and when I went outside that night, there were so many stars. I'd never seen so many stars, layers, and layers of them, going on and on forever. You could actually see that space is three-dimensional--not flat like it usually looks. It was humbling and amazing."

"The desert has subtle beauty," Faith agreed. "Not everyone has the stamina to walk out and look at it up close, but if you do, you'll discover something very special." She winked at Jolie.

Sometimes Jolie wondered if Faith and Iris lived in the same world that she did. Neither of them had ever killed anyone. They were good people. She wasn't so sure about herself. Would her own life change if she somehow managed to believe more in Faith's and Iris' world and less in her own? If she did, would she still be herself, or would she become someone unrecognizable, even to herself? Part of Jolie longed for the new start that would come with such a change. Another part was terrified even thinking about it. But if she and her friends lived in different worlds, those worlds magically intersected in Faith's sitting room, and for that, she was grateful.

Jolie pulled her bedroom curtains shut, turning her mind to more practical matters. The big questions of the universe would have to wait; it was a school day and that meant teachers, kids, and a math test.

*****

"Hey, Jo," Hugo greeted Jolie at lunch.

Jolie started to scoot over to make room for him, but he walked on by, following two boys wearing black and white martial arts school tee-shirts. Hugo threw her an apologetic smile.

"God, I hope she understands," she heard him think.

Chapter Nine

She did, of course, and this time she didn't feel guilty for hearing his thoughts. Hugo had decided not to live in fear of the bullies who stalked him and had found someplace to belong, someplace where he could gain some confidence, someplace he wouldn't be an outsider and people noticed he was there.

Good for him. Jolie sighed. *Alone again,* she added just before Remy Bishop plopped his tray and then his butt down beside her.

"Hey guys, over here," he motioned Hugo and the other boys to come back. "You didn't want to sit here all by yourself, did you?" He grinned at Jolie. "Don't worry. They might look tough, but they won't bite."

"Remy!" The stockier boy took the sandwich from his lunch tray and scarfed it down in one mouthful. "See?" he tried to talk around it. "I told you I could do it."

"How ya doin', Brutus?" Remy laughed as the boys did a one armed, hug man style.

"Hey, Rem," a sullen elfin-faced Asian boy sat down across the table from Jolie and Remy, scrutinizing them. "We missed you at practice this weekend. Where were you?"

"Sorry, Bodhi. I had family stuff," Remy sidestepped explaining the sweat lodge, or Jolie, or any of the rest of it. "This is Jolie," he added.

"Hi." Jolie glanced briefly at the newcomers. Brutus smiled past the glob of sandwich. Bodhi glared. Hugo just grinned, looking from his new friends to Jolie, surprised and pleased.

"Do you know Hugo, Rem?" Brutus asked. "He just started down at the school."

"Cool. What are you taking?" Remy asked the chunky teenager.

"Everything I can," Hugo announced with shy pride.

Remy nodded. "Is that where you got that shiner?"

"No." Hugo touched the yellowing bruise. "That's from before I started at the Lohan school." The boys exchanged knowing looks.

"Well, just keep going to class, Hugo. Pretty soon you'll be begging people to punch you."

Brutus jumped to his feet. "Punch me, Rem. Right in the gut, as hard as you can." Remy did. Brutus didn't even flinch. "I've been doing Iron Body." He wiggled his eyebrows pulling up his shirt to show off a strongly muscled midsection. Remy shook out his hand. Brutus was short and stocky, but the person who mistook his bulk for soft fat would have a rude surprise

"It's working for you," Remy gave him an approving thumbs up.

"Being a Lohan is the greatest," Brutus bragged. "You get to learn cool Fu, and you get to hang out with us. Awesome!" Brutus and Hugo jumped up in the air and slapped their hands together in a vigorous high five.

"You guys are such nerds." Bodhi's mouth twisted in disgust.

"Don't hate us because we're beautiful," Brutus shot back, hitting a magazine model pose that looked absolutely ridiculous on his build. Everyone laughed, and suddenly they were friends. "What about you, Jolie? Do you study?" Brutus asked, settling back down and attacking the bowl of pudding on his tray.

Bodhi made a face "You're kidding, right? Look at her. She's got no muscle at all, not even her hair has body. She's a total girl." He sneered.

Jolie glared, thinking how much she'd enjoy tossing him across the commons with her mysterious energy. She hadn't needed muscle to stop Alex from killing her. She had other talents. She glanced at Remy, hoping he hadn't heard about what happened. Death, during a domestic violence incident, was not so unusual in Vegas that it made the news, and she couldn't see Remy coming out and saying, "*Hey, remember that guy you killed?*"

"Bodhi doesn't think girls belong in the martial arts," Remy explained.

"They don't," the smaller boy insisted. "Forms aren't about pretty dances--they're about fighting."

"Sifu says the original Taoists were women," Brutus pointed out before gulping down a bottle of water.

"Shut up, Brutus." Bodhi scowled. "There weren't any women in the Shaolin temple."

"Personally, I like having girls in class." Brutus belched. "I think girls who can fight are hot." He wiggled his eyebrows at Jolie.

Bodhi rolled his eyes. "Which proves my point. A girl studying Kung Fu is a distraction."

"You're such a misogynist, Bodhi," Remy chided.

"Sorry guys, I forgot my burka today," Jolie quipped. "But don't worry, I'm not interested in invading your boy's club. I will sit here quietly and finish my lunch, though if that's okay with you?"

"Sure. Go ahead." Brutus nodded, missing her sarcasm. The conversation moved on to what classes the other boys thought Hugo should take and how he could best organize a solid Kung Fu practice. Bodhi did not participate, sinking instead into a moody silence while he pushed his food around his plate.

Jolie watched him surreptitiously. He was sweating a lot--more than made sense for the spring weather--and an odd metallic odor came from his pores. When his fork slipped from his shaking hands and he looked around to see if anyone had noticed, he caught Jolie watching him. She had been on the receiving end of more seriously malevolent glares in her life, but not many.

"I'm out of here." Bodhi grabbed his tray, dumped the contents into a nearby garbage, and disappeared into the lunchtime swarm.

"We're taking off, too. My next class is way across campus." Hugo and Brutus picked up trays and backpacks and headed off.

"What's that Bodhi kid so mad about, Remy?" Jolie asked.

"He just gets in moods. He's got a lot of stuff going on at home right now."

"Yeah? So take a ticket. Getting himself a drug habit is only going to add to his problems."

"What are you talking about, Jo? Bodhi doesn't do drugs." Remy defended his friend. "He's a serious martial artist. He'd never abuse his body like that. You just don't know him."

"Oh, I know him alright," Jolie disagreed. "I could write his life story. The names and dates would be different, but the format is usually pretty standard: there are problems at home, he doesn't know what to do, it's messing him up, and he can't deal with life. So now, he's not just a jerk, he's a jerk with a drug problem."

"Not Bodhi," Remy's insisted.

"He may be your friend, Rem, but this is my area of expertise. I've lived the homework, and I know what I'm seeing. That boy's using."

Remy shook his head. "Well, this time you're wrong. We're buds, Bodhi and I. We train together, we hang out, we play video games. I would know about something like that."

"Then you should know that your best bud is in trouble. My guess is meth or heroine, something chemical with a bite."

Remy's jaw tightened. "Are you always like this?"

"Like what?"

Chapter Nine

"So sure that you're right about everything?"

Jolie got up from the table. "When I don't know, Remy, I'll tell you. When I do, I'll tell you. It's your choice what you do about it." She walked away. She wasn't the kind of girl who would dumb down to please a boy, and for Jolie dumbing down wasn't just about pretending you weren't smart. She knew things that she shouldn't: private things, and right now, she knew that Remy's friend, Bodhi, needed help.

CHAPTER TEN

Mister Wexler read the note Hugo had given him, then looked up, scanning the room.

"Jolie Figg? You're wanted in the counselor's office." Jolie rolled her eyes at Becca, who was writing up their latest lab work, retrieved the hall pass from Wexler, and followed Hugo out.

"Ms. Warren wants to see you," Hugo said. "I don't know why, so don't ask me."

Jolie fell in beside him. The halls were plastered with big sheets of poster paper bearing the slogans that students running for next year's Student Council Officers had made up to campaign for themselves. Written in primary colors, the lame slogans were as laughable as they were untrue.

"A vote for Megan is a vote for you," one proclaimed.

"Don't fool yourselves; a vote for Megan is a vote for Megan," Jolie muttered. Hugo grunted his agreement.

They came upon the next poster. "Vote Megan: she'll put things right."

"In her mouth," Jolie added, sardonically.

Hugo chuckled. "How about that one," he pointed. "Megan Washburn wants your vote," he read.

"Cross out 'vote' and add 'body.'"

"Megan Washburn wants your body." Hugo nodded. "I like it. You should be her campaign manager."

"In what universe?" Jolie scoffed.

"Too bad no one will ever see your improved versions, they'd be a big hit."

Chapter Ten

"So, do you like this Lohan Kung Fu place?" Jolie changed the subject.

"Yeah. I think it's a good school. It's a temple school so they don't just teach kicking and punching, they teach the spiritual stuff, too. Sifu talks about Qi: you know, the energy that is part of Kung Fu, and he teaches about using it to heal, and tells us to meditate; stuff like that."

"Cool."

They entered the high school's main office and parted silently as Jolie went to the door marked "COUNSELOR". Ms. Warren's office was open.

"Ms. Warren?" she knocked on the door frame tentatively. "What's up?"

"Come in, Miss Figg." Ms. Warren's hair style had undergone a change since Jolie had last been in her office. It was smaller, and straighter, while her earrings were larger, and she was actually wearing makeup.

She's seeing someone, Jolie realized, hoping she would not pick up anything more personal than that. All she needed was to get a kinky vision of her school counselor getting sweaty with some shirtless Mensa geek to make the week really special.

"I realized today that we haven't talked in some time." Ms. Warren's smile looked forced. "So I thought I should check in to see how you were doing."

"I don't expect to be elected prom queen, but I think I'll finish the year with a 3.5 or above. So, I think I'm doing pretty good," Jolie answered.

"Your grades are not the problem, Jolie."

So what is? Jolie wondered.

"You're a good student," Ms. Warren went on. "You work hard. You turn in your assignments." She paused. "I was talking to Office Wrangler yesterday, and he mentioned that there'd been a death in the apartment above yours?"

Here it comes, Jolie thought. Had Wrangler looked into things after all and begun to wonder about how Axel had died? Did they suspect her? Jolie waited for the other shoe to drop.

Ms. Warren waited for Jolie to say something.

And there they sat, looking at each other across the desk, each waiting for the other to speak up, both refusing to be the first to give in.

"That must have been traumatic," Ms. Warren caved. "Do you want to talk about it?"

Obviously not, Jolie thought. Did Ms. Warren really think that all Jolie needed was a verbal nudge and she'd open the floodgates of her life, pouring out all of her deep dark secrets? What bullshit. She did not want to talk about Axel, or how he'd died, or how it made her feel, or the nightmares she was having since it happened. Ms. Warren clearly didn't get it; Jolie's silence was her answer. Ms. Warren continued to look expectantly at Jolie.

"No," Jolie finally defined her position, stating the obvious.

"You look..." Ms. Warren hesitated.

Jolie's mind filled in the blank, *Tired? Worn out? Distraught? Hell yes, I'm distraught. I have nightmares from the moment my head hits the pillow until I wake up in a grateful panic. What do you expect?*

"...thin," the counselor finished her observation.

"I have a high metabolism," Jolie said, relieved that the counselor had missed the mark so thoroughly.

"So, you're okay?" Ms. Warren prodded.

"Yes. Thank you for your concern." The counselor was testing Jolie's patience, but Jolie knew the value of not letting that get the best of her judgment.

The conversation was not going the way Ms. Warren imagined it would. *Why do I always feel like I'm in a chess match with this girl and she understands the game better than I do?* The counselor considered her next move.

"Okay then, good." Ms. Warren mentally checked off the dead guy upstairs as a dead end and abandoned that line of questioning. "So have you had any more problems with the other students?"

Is this what she really called me here for? Jolie realized that the thing with Axel's death could have been just fishing, prodded by Wrangler's concerns, but that incident had been days ago: ancient history in the high school world. Whatever Ms. Warren was really after, had to be more recent.

"Nothing out of the ordinary," Jolie replied, thinking about the half dozen tricks her fellow students had played on her since winter break: none of them significant. "People aren't really my thing, Ms. Warren. I'm kind of a loner, as I'm sure someone with your education and intelligence has realized."

"It's just that I heard about an incident in the hall the other day, and I thought maybe I should give you a chance to tell me your version?"

My version? That sounded sinister.

"I didn't see the event myself," Ms. Warren explained, "but other students have reported that someone was dancing down the hall screaming: 'I want to be naked, take me dark powers'." It wasn't a quote but it was close. "Do you want to tell me what that was about?"

"I'm the wrong person to ask," Jolie shrugged.

"I can't help you if you won't talk to me, Jolie," Ms. Warren prodded.

"What is it you want me to say, Ms. Warren? A girl danced down the hall shouting crazy stuff. It's high school. Kids do dumb things all the time. You know that."

"I do." Ms. Warren nodded. "And sometimes it's a cry for help."

"And sometimes it's just noise."

Ms. Warren leaned over her desk and lowered her voice, "Was that girl you, Jolie?"

"Me?" Jolie gaped, blindsided. Why would Ms. Warren think that it had been "her"? The incident had been aimed at mimicking some twisted version of her, yes, but Jolie had been a witness, not a participant. "It wasn't me. It was just some girl," Jolie stammered.

"Some girl?" Ms. Warren leaned in."Who?"

"I don't know, some dumb chick that Megan got to do it on a dare or something. Ask her."

Ms. Warren's tone was studied. "You misunderstand Megan, Jolie. Miss Washburn has great compassion for you and how you carry on in spite of your difficult home life. She's a thinking and caring person."

"Yeah, she thinks about herself and carries a lot of shopping bags," Jolie shot back. "It wasn't me, Ms. Warren. There must have been fifty kids in that hall--and they all know it wasn't me. And if you stopped interviewing the students who Megan conveniently remembers being there and talked to anyone that, I don't know, maybe has a class nearby at that time, and therefore would logically have been present, you'll find I'm telling the truth." Jolie stood up. "Of course, if you do that, it will tarnish that gold star you've got pasted to Miss Washburn's forehead. So, if you're not ready for that, you should just accept my word and let this go. It wasn't me." Jolie didn't ask if she could leave and go back to class. She would have choked on the words.

*****

Chapter Ten

Jolie had finished dinner and done her homework before Remy called.

"I've been thinking about what you said today about Bodhi," he started off. "I'm sorry. I understand that, because of your gifts, you see things that other people miss. If Bodhi really is struggling, and I'm any kind of a friend, I'd want to know so that I could help." He sighed. "I guess it's up to us to let him know that he has our support and he's not alone, right?"

This was the point when Jolie would usually have run the other way, reminding herself not to get involved, because unless Bodhi's friends were druggies as well, Bodhi "was" alone. But this was Remy talking--Remy saying "us", like an inferred we, and she couldn't walk away from him.

"You know, you're turning out to be a lot of trouble, Remy Bishop." she laid down, dangling her feet off the edge of the bed and staring up at the ceiling.

"Sorry. I promise I'll try to be worthy of all the trouble I cause you and all of your efforts on my behalf. Who knows, maybe you'll get a twofer and end up saving me and Bodhi both."

"Great, more pressure, but right now all I can deal with is Wexler's Chem final. See you tomorrow."

"Sweet dreams," Remy signed off.

Sweet dreams, Jolie thought, ruefully. *Like that's going to happen.*

*****

Jolie hung by her ankles like a spider's dinner, not a baby Jolie, like before in the birth dream, but Jolie as she was today.

"Kill me?" Axel lashed her over and over again with arms grown long and boneless, ending in tentacles. "Kill me?"

Jolie's body swayed and struggled while demon Axel opened gashes across her back. Usually, in the birth dream, Jolie was worried about Jessie Lynn's lifeblood gushing away. Now, it was her own she felt slipping like warm honey across the gory red channels in her flesh. Her skin flinched with every breath of air, waiting for the sear of the next cut. The blood dripped off her body and into the mouths of black creatures crowded eagerly below: the creatures that Rory had called up. They had become fixtures of her nightmares since Solstice.

Jolie twisted around on her spider-web thread, scanning the pit below her. Where was their leader? The demon she had spoken to that night?

"Show yourself, you coward," she shouted. "Stop hiding and show yourself!"

Axel's face materialized in front of hers, his eyes burning with an unnatural glow.

"Oh, my God," Jolie muttered, recognizing the demon's essence inside the tortured man's spirit. "Axel, what have you done?".

She woke up with a gasp. Her tee shirt and unders wet through. Even the sheet beneath her was damp with sweat.

There was an evolution to her dreams. New characters with sinister motivations were beginning to emerge. The guilt of being born in her original dream had not been easy to live with, but being tortured and eaten alive was even more disturbing.

Jolie climbed out of bed and stumbled to the living room. The lights were on, but Jessie Lynn was fast asleep on the couch, still dressed in her work clothes.

Chapter Ten

"What's wrong honey?" Jolie imagined her mom waking up and saying. *"Come sit by me and tell me all about it."*

It would be nice to have someone care if you had a bad dream--nice to have someone listen to you while you told them about it--then, even though they couldn't do anything, it would be nice to have someone say *"Everything will be all right."* Jolie could really use a good pep talk and a reassuring hug right now, but this wasn't a TV sitcom. Jolie turned off the TV, got a blanket and covered Jessie, being careful not to wake her.

"Good night, Mom," Jolie whispered as she turned off the lights and went back to her room alone.

CHAPTER ELEVEN

Having Remy in her life changed things for Jolie. There was someone to talk to about the crazy things that happened in the halls of greater learning. There were other kids who assumed she would sit with them at lunch--kids she could stand around with before or after school, instead of pretending she was waiting for someone. The Fus didn't share anything important in their lives. Talk centered around tests and teachers and who had a trip to what competition. Jolie knew that she wasn't a real member of the Kung Fu boys club, but because of Remy, she was allowed to hang with them.

Except for Remy and Hugo, her connection to the Fus was one of convenience. When the boys were together, she didn't exist. Their world centered around their practice; who nailed what form, or knocked someone out, and what level they'd reached in some video game, but no one else knew how far out on the fringe of the group she was.

Jolie might have been able to take some wicked revenge on the bullies who persecuted her if her life had been scripted in Hollywood and she had any control over her abilities, but it wasn't, and she didn't. But her new alliance to the Fus had come with an unforeseen perk.

Now, when she walked by a potential tormentor, a flash of doubt crossed their face as they were forced to question whether the Kung Fu boys would stand up for this weird girl and kick their asses if they bothered her, or if it was still safe to pick on her?

Chapter Eleven

By the time they finished questioning the wisdom of their actions, Jolie, and the opportunity had passed.

"Hey, Jo." Madison Bishop approached Jolie in the courtyard before school. "I thought maybe since you're dating my brother, you and Remy and Skie and I could go out together, like a foursome? Maybe catch a movie and grab a pizza or something? How about tomorrow night?"

Jolie frowned. "Remy and I aren't dating."

"You eat lunch together every day. He texts you all of the time."

That was true, but outside of school Jolie barely saw Remy. He had track practice, then Kung Fu practice. An hour or two for homework left him just enough time to call Jolie before he fell into bed. They hadn't gone anywhere together since their first trip to Rose's.

"We're friends," Jolie replied cautiously.

"Okay. Friends can go out," Madison persisted.

Megan Washburn stopped beside them, a triumphant smirk plumping out her glossed lips.

"How's your campaign for President going, Madison?" she asked, twirling a corded necklace.

"Fine, thanks." Madison gave the cheerleader a tight-lipped smile. Megan held the necklace up so the symbol on the end swung back and forth. Madison fell for the ploy. "What's that?"

"It's a talisman against witches and evil spells," Megan replied, with obvious glee. "Cool, huh?"

"And very useful in suburban Las Vegas," Jolie added, her voice dripping sarcasm.

"Apparently, they're the new thing here at Chaparral," Megan went on. "All the really cool kids are wearing them. At least all the kids who vote for me. I'm giving them out free with a promise for your vote. Oh, but that would be weird, wouldn't it, because you're running, too, so if you wore a necklace it would be like saying you wouldn't vote for yourself. Oops. Later." She flounced off, swinging her short pleated cheerleader skirt.

"Two more years. Just two more years and we're free." Madison sighed.

"You're singing my song," Jolie agreed. They shared a smile. "I'll ask Remy about Friday." Jolie nearly gagged on the words. Like she couldn't have just said, "no this is the worst idea ever," without pretending she needed to talk to Remy first. But their mutual dislike of Megan had created a moment between them, and now, she was stuck. Still, it got Jolie wondering; what exactly was her and Remy's relationship? Did she even know?

The Fus beat her to the lunch table and were already involved in an animated discussion about their most recent leveling on some video game. Jolie sat beside Remy and waited, hoping the other boys would leave before the break ended. They didn't get the hint.

"I know this is kind of weird, Remy," Jolie finally said, trying to keep her voice low so that the others wouldn't hear. "But do you want to go to a movie or something tomorrow night? Madison asked us."

In unison the Fus stopped eating, the food halfway to their mouths.

"Did you just ask him out on a date?" Bodhi's words were as sharp as a porcupine's quills.

"It wasn't my idea. It was Madison's," Jolie said, defensively. "But for some strange reason, Bodhi, she asked me, not you." Jolie picked up her books. She'd had just about enough of Bodhi's snarky comments and depressed bullshit. "We can talk about this later, Rem, when we don't have an audience." She stomped off across the commons.

Chapter Eleven

"Wait up, Jo!" Remy ran to catch up with her. "Are you mad at me?"

"No. Why would I be mad at you?"

"You act mad."

"But not at you."

"So, this is about Bodhi?"

Jolie stopped and squared off, facing him. "I don't get you and Bodhi. You're so not alike. Why are you even friends?"

Remy shrugged. "We've known each other since second grade."

"You "know" each other? Really? So does he go to sweat lodges with you and talk to you about spirits and stuff?"

Remy's expression darkened. "You know that I don't share that part of my life with other people, Jo."

"You shared it with me."

"You're different."

"You mean I'm not one of the boys." Jolie put a hand under a breast and pushed it up. "Thanks for noticing." Remy got that hurt look again. "Look, Rem," she softened her tone. "I appreciate you letting me hang out with your friends, but I just don't fit into the boys club. I'm tolerated, but I'm not welcome. Bodhi's made that perfectly clear."

Remy shook his head. "I don't understand. You two seemed to have gotten off on the wrong foot."

"So he's been a perfect gentlemen to all the other girls you've brought around?"

"I've never brought any other girls around."

"Remy, Bodhi's a petty tyrant and an addict. The only reason he's still functioning is because you and the Fus babysit him, spoon feeding him Kung Fu all the time. What's going to happen him when the rest of you grow up and get lives? He's going to be completely lost. No one else is going to put up with his bullshit."

"Bodhi's my friend, I will always put up with his bullshit," Remy stated with finality. "Just like I will always put up with yours, for the same reason."

"Right." Jolie took a deep breath. "I think maybe we need to back off a little. People are getting the wrong impression about us."

"'And what impression is that?"

"That we're a couple--that we're dating. Your sister asking us to go out with her and Skie, pronounced Sky but with an I E. God, isn't it bad enough that people saddle their kids with bizarre names? Why do they have to make it worse by spelling them weird? Other people don't think they're creative, they just think they can't spell."

Remy's eyes crinkled at the edges as if he wanted to laugh but wasn't letting it out.

"So Madison thought we were dating, huh?" he changed the subject. "What did you say?"

"I didn't know what to say. I told her we were just friends."

"That sounds safe." He paused, "So, do you want to go out Friday?"

Jolie's eye narrowed. "Are you making fun of me, Remy Bishop?"

"Never. I've just been waiting for you to feel like the whirlwind had passed, and you might be able to trust someone. I was hoping that someone could be me."

His smile was like a tooth whitening commercial. Jolie reached up and closed his lips.

"Close your mouth, dude. You're blinding me." His lips were soft and warm under her fingertips. Her mind started listing all the reasons she should not let this go on a minute more. *Shut up,* she told it, stretching up, and kissing him.

There were no fireworks, no crazy chemistry, stained by the angst of a doomed young love. It was a kiss of affection between two people who had known less of love than they should have and desperately needing someone to accept them as they were.

"Woo-hoo!" A kid passing them called out. "Get a room, you two."

Jolie and Remy stepped apart.

"You have track practice," she reminded him. "And I have to get to Faith's." Jolie cleared her throat. "Call me tonight?"

"I always do." Remy kissed her lightly. He tasted like salted sunshine.

I have to find a way to save him, she thought watching him jog away, but she had no idea how to do that.

*****

"Faith," Jolie called out as she let herself in the front door of the house. "It's me." Iris' Cadillac was not in the driveway. Jolie went to the sitting room. Faith was propped up on her chaise lounge looking alert, a little color in her cheeks.

"Where's Iris?"

"Out on errands. We knew you'd be here soon, so I told her to go ahead and get started."

"Is the color in your cheeks you or has she been at you with her makeup again?" Faith was the kind of woman who had worn lipstick twice in her life, to her wedding and her husband's funeral, and never again. Iris wouldn't go to the mailbox without putting on her "face".

"It's just me." Faith tilted her head, presenting her cheek to be kissed. "How was school?"

"No one went postal, so good, I guess. I had a weird conversation with Remy's sister, though. She thought he and I were dating and asked us to go out with her and her boyfriend on a double date. I mean how weird is that?"

"I think that it sounds nice."

"Are you kidding? It would be a disaster. What do I have to talk about with Madison Bishop?"

"She is Remy's sister, maybe you'd be surprised. Anyway, that's why you go to a movie and then out to eat with people you don't know yet. It gives you things to talk about; the movie, the food. You don't have to talk about big issues or important things."

"And the point of that is?"

"It's the way people start to get to know each other, Jolie, the way we feel other folks out to see if they're worthy of trust and friendship."

"I think you missed that step with Rick and Rory," Jolie countered.

"I never broke bread with either of those two men." Faith sniffed. "Even in my dotage, I'm more discerning than that."

Jolie liked that Faith used words like dotage: words that were all but extinct in the average vocabulary. She liked that Faith never asked if she understood what they meant. Her friend didn't talk down to her. Faith operated under the assumption that Jolie was as intelligent as any of her other friends, in spite of her age.

"So, does this mean you and Remy are officially dating?" Faith inquired.

"Well, we are going to go out on a date," Jolie hedged.

"Good." Faith patted Jolie's hand. "You should have friends."

Chapter Eleven

"I have friends, you and Iris."

"And we love you, but I meant you should have friends your own age, Jolie."

Jolie pouted. "Why? You can't talk to kids my age about anything important."

"You judge your peers too harshly. You may not find many who will become friends, but if you keep looking, you'll find a few. You need to give them a chance, though. Now, how about some chocolate?"

"Yes, Ma'am."

Jolie fetched the tea tray, dressed with packets of gourmet hot chocolate and some of the little pastries that Iris always bought, and sat down beside her friend to share the moment.

"Faith, why can I see stuff about other people's lives, but not my own?" Jolie asked after awhile.

Faith blew on her cocoa to cool it down.

"People say you can't use your gifts for personal gain without repercussions. I've never known anyone personally who had it happen to them, so I can't say if it's true or not, but there are stories about gifted people who used their abilities to gamble themselves to a fortune and then lost their gifts. Other misuses would be manipulating a romance or a career move."

"Really? Like poof, no powers; gone? Where do I sign up?"

"Don't be so eager to give up your gifts, my dear. You don't even realize how much you rely on them, or how much a part of you they are because you've never been without them. People breathe without thinking about it. Can you learn to breathe more efficiently if you practice? Of course, but whether you practice or not, you'll keep on breathing at some level, until you die. It's just a part of your life experience."

"So, you're saying I could just ignore my gifts and leave them undeveloped, or I could learn how to use them better, but either way I'm stuck with them?"

"Essentially, yes." Faith smiled.

"When Remy took me to his friend Rose's, in Red Rock, they were having a sweat lodge," Jolie told her friend.

Faith raised an eyebrow. "Did you go in?"

Jolie shook her head. "No, but I saw things...spirits. When Rose sang the songs to call the spirits, they actually did it; they came. It was pretty amazing."

"There are aboriginal people all over the world, who keep the old ways," Faith acknowledged. "You were fortunate to have had a chance to see that."

"It was strange. The people at the lodge just accepted that there were spirits in the world like it was normal. The spirits were real to them."

"Different cultures view the world and reality quite differently. So your friend, Remy, he accepts this view of the world as well?"

Jolie hid her smile behind her cup of chocolate. "Yeah. He does."

"And will you go to a lodge again, then?"

Jolie shrugged. "Maybe. They invited me to."

"There are many paths that could teach you about your gifts and how to use them, Jolie."

"I'm not interested in using my gifts," Jolie assured her friend.

"There are practices a person can do that will develop their minds so that they can see other worlds and do extraordinary things--things that seem quite impossible to most people. Things that come naturally to you."

Chapter Eleven

"I'm not interested in doing impossible things, Faith. Only geeky teenage boys and egomaniacal dictators are stupid enough to chase after that stuff."

"This is not something you should accept Hollywood's version of, Jolie. It takes a person of strength and wisdom to live with abilities like yours. That's why the skills to gain them require commitment and perseverance and are not taught lightly, or commonly. If a person is not ready, opening the mind like this can be dangerous. That is why in most disciplines there is a gatekeeper that decides who, when, and if someone gets taught."

"A teacher."

"Exactly," Faith acknowledged.

"I don't know why anyone would even try to do that," Jolie sulked.

"Because the ultimate goal is not the abilities, my dear," Faith explained. "The gifts are just side effects. The goal is enlightenment."

Jolie made a face. "I can do and see stuff, and I am definitely not enlightened."

"But you were born with your gifts. You are what the Buddhist teacher, Padmasambhava, would call, naturally anointed." Jolie looked skeptical. "Spiritual seekers study and practice their whole lives just to get a glimpse of what you have, Jolie Figg."

"Because they don't know what it's like to live with it, or understand what it costs." Jolie thought about how helpless she had felt on Solstice when the black horde of creatures had come rolling over the desert toward her. "You're right about one thing, though, Faith. Living with gifts isn't like it is in the movies, or on TV. It's not Bewitched or I Dream of Jeannie; it's not a sitcom. If anything, it's a horror film."

Faith held one frail hand to Jolie's cheek. "The mind is an amazing thing if you explore its possibilities. Unfortunately, most people find it just too frightening."

"So, they burned us," Jolie joked.

Faith remained serious. "Yes, and that is why there are so few of us left today to pass on the wisdom of how to live with gifts."

Jolie gathered up the remnants of their snack and took the tray back to the kitchen. What would Faith think if Jolie told her that she had already misused her gifts? Was there ever a justification for killing someone with your powers? And then there was the whole quandary of Yanna Maria appearing in her dreams. Jolie wanted to ask Faith about that but didn't think she could without revealing the whole story of what was troubling her. It was a slippery slope.

The sun was going down, throwing dramatic shadows over Frenchman's Peak, the mountain that served as the valley's eastern boundary. It wasn't tall enough to have a snow cap, but it turned a pretty pink, the sky behind it a pastel palette of muted lavenders and blues. Sunrise Mountains they called the small range. They didn't rival Red Rock but they were pretty.

Jolie felt the same sense of wonder that had warmed her to the core in Red Rock, creeping over her. Faith had been right, bearing silent witness to the larger changes in the world around her made her feel connected. No matter what happened to her today, tomorrow the sun would start its dance across the sky and for a brief moment, if she stopped to watch, she could be a part of it.

The light faded from the eastern peak, leaving it a faded peach. Jolie finished the dishes and went back into the sitting room.

Chapter Eleven

"I think the vegetable starts we got last week have hardened off. Do you want me to plant them?" she asked as she entered the room.

Faith didn't answer. She had fallen asleep. Jolie walked quietly to the chaise lounge and removed the book from her friend's hands.

Faith's white hair made soft curls around her face. A feeling of deep affection flooded through Jolie for this dear woman who had befriended her, giving her a second home, then she realized Faith was not breathing.

CHAPTER TWELVE

"**F**aith! Faith!" Jolie shouted, afraid to shake her friend, but desperate to do something. She pulled her cell from her jeans pocket.

"Nine-one-one, what's your emergency?" a voice answered.

"My friend--she isn't breathing."

"Okay, calm down. Where are you?"

"At her house; 3218 East Meadow Crest Drive." "Are you safe? Can you stay there?"

"Yes. Please tell them to hurry. I think she's dying." "I'm sending the paramedics now. Stay with me--"

Jolie ended the call. "Hold on, Faith, please. Don't die now. You can't. You just can't."

Faith's eyes fluttered open and she took a breath. *"Of course I can. It's the most natural thing in the world,"* she answered Jolie, silently.

"No." Jolie shook her head, tears blurring her vision. She wiped them from her eyes with the back of her hand, wanting to keep Faith in her sight, as if she could will the older woman to live.

"It's okay, Jolie." Faith put her hand over Jolie's. *"Let me go."*

"But it's not okay. It's not even remotely okay."

"You made these last few months something special, but I'm ready to move on now."

"Please, please stay, even for just a little longer, a year, a month, a week." She stroked Faith's arms...her head... her cheek, feeling the deep chill seeping into her friend's body.

"It doesn't work like that, honey. Look after Sean for me, will you? And don't be afraid to lean on Iris and Mickey. They care about you, too. Don't push them away." Faith sighed. *"I love you and I'm so proud of you."* Her

eyes closed.

"Faith? Faith, stay with me." Jolie could hear the wail of the ambulance siren in the distance. "Do you hear that? They're almost here." The front door opened and Iris came in.

"All hail, the great hunter returns bearing dinner," she sang out, cheerily.

"Iris," Jolie wailed. "She isn't breathing! Faith isn't breathing!"

Iris dropped the boxes of Thai take-out and ran to her friend's bedside. The paramedics were right behind her, grinding the spilled noodles into the carpet.

"Step aside, please," one of them commanded.

Iris pulled Jolie out of their way. Holding the girl tight in her arms, the two women watched the paramedics trying to revive their friend, but Faith was gone.

The paramedics put Faith's body on a stretcher. The sirens stopped. The EMT's left, their busy energy following them.

Jolie and Iris were alone.

The house felt like an empty shell as if Faith's spirit had been its beating heart, and now it too was dead.

Jolie stood at the edge of the sitting room staring at the empty bed. The happiness that had anchored her here was already becoming a collection of memories. What would her life be like now, without Faith in it? All she could imagine--all she had known--was the life she'd had before: adrift, isolated, confused.

What will become of me? the old woman, Helen, had pleaded. Jolie understood her despair. There was something inherently selfish in grieving for a loved one.

"Should I take you home?" Iris asked, uncertainly. "Or do you want to stay awhile longer?" She glanced at the Thai food on the floor. "I should at least get you some dinner. You need to eat."

"I'm not hungry," Jolie muttered, vacantly.

"Me neither." Iris stood in the middle of the floor as if she wasn't sure which direction to go. "You don't have to go home, you know, Jo. You don't have to be alone. You could come back with me to my place. I'd be happy to have the company."

Jolie felt like a stray puppy. Iris probably had a hundred things she needed to do right now, all of them more important than babysitting Jolie.

"Thanks, but I have school tomorrow. I'll be fine."

Iris' perfectly lined eyes filled with tears. "I'm not sure I will. I don't seem to know quite what to do."

"Cry?" Jolie suggested.

"Crying has always seemed to me like such an indulgence. It doesn't change things and it doesn't help anyone. What's it good for?" She wiped away the tears logic could not stop.

"You and Faith were friends a long time," Jolie pointed out.

"Yes, we were," Iris whispered as if closing a prayer.

They stood together breathing in the silence with their memories.

Outside, the afternoon had slipped away, leaving them to the growing uncertainty of a dark house. The small book light on the table beside Faith's chaise clattered to the floor, blinking on when it hit the rag rug.

Iris picked it up and turned it off, returning them to darkness.

"I suppose someone should call Sean," Jolie said. Iris turned the tiny book light back on, using it like a flashlight.

"Yeah. Just give me a minute." She sniffled. "I just want to tidy things up in here a bit." Iris was proud, Yankee stock. Not the kind of woman who was comfortable showing emotion in front of witnesses.

"You go ahead." Iris turned on a side lamp, then went to the closet for a broom and dustpan. Jolie left her to her sorrow, going to the kitchen to find the notepad Faith had

CHAPTER TWELVE

written all her important numbers on. Sean's was three-quarters of the way down the page. Once he'd gotten his trust fund, he'd gone back up North and disappeared into his new life. Jolie wished he had been a better grandson. She wished that whatever cathartic change Faith had been waiting for, had happened while she was still alive. She punched in Sean's number.

Voice mail picked up.

"Sean, it's Jolie." Her voice failed. Saying the words out loud was so final. "You need to come home," Jolie stumbled around how to say it. There was no sense being subtle. Subtle would be lost on Sean. "She's gone. Faith is gone." Jolie broke down crying and hung up so Sean would not hear.

CHAPTER THIRTEEN

The creature that hunted her snarled from low in the darkness.

Jolie couldn't see it through the thick, ebony midnight of her dreamscape, but the moment she became aware in her dreams, she felt it stalking her.

How did it track her, this thing that wore Axel's face and howled about retribution for his death? Did it hear her heartbeat, or follow her scent like a bloodhound? Did a person even have a heartbeat or a scent in the dream world? Jolie didn't understand the rules, but somehow the creature always found her.

At first, she tried to explain to Axel that what she had done to him had been an accident, but there was no reasoning with this raving remnant of a man. He had tumbled over the edge of lunacy just before he died and was stuck there, his warped spirit focused on one thing: revenge.

Each night he chased her, his image a little less solid as if the further he got from the physical life that had been his, the more of himself he lost.

"You owe me," he growled the same three words over and over again.

With fear balled up in her belly, Jolie turned and shouted at him, "Leave me alone!" The tomb-like darkness split open, becoming a pair of red tooth-lined jaws.

Terrified, Jolie spun and ran.

In front of her, all she saw was darkness folded on darkness. Behind her was this thing that looked and felt

Chapter Thirteen

like Axel, only bigger and more powerful, smelling of malevolence and death. Jolie looked back over her shoulder and saw the demon creature riding Axel's spirit like he was a bristle-hide boar it had haltered and saddled.

The shadow creature laughed maniacally as it stood in the stirrups and melted down into Axel's ghost.

The boar's visage became more cruel. Part Axel, part demon, it raised up on its hind legs. Growing robes made of carnage, grisly human fetishes hung like prizes from its stiff-haired shoulders; a shank of human hair, a finger still wearing its wedding band, a child's shoe. Spaghetti shreds of bloody meat and viscera dripped off the boar creature's shoulders, and hung from its arms, swaying and slapping like bloody fringe as it ran.

"You can't escape," it gloated in its sepulchral voice. "You are in my world, and here, I have the power." Its body swelled forward, growing larger until it overcame Jolie from behind like a flood unleashed, tumbling her through space.

Bile rose in Jolie's throat as the demon engulfed her, digging at her skin to get inside her.

"No!" Jolie screamed, swatting at its unsubstantial form like she was plagued by wasps. "Get away from me. Get away!"

Yanna Maria's voice violated Jolie's awareness.

"The old man is nothing," her voice claimed. feeling like a stab in Jolie's brain. "The further he gets from life, the weaker he becomes. The demon is all that gives him the power to pursue you."

"Welcome to my new bargain," the demon crowed in deranged satisfaction.

Jolie could feel its intent, like carving-knife fingers, working to get inside her head.

E.F. Winters

"Control it, Jolie," Yanna Maria shouted, her excited commands as uncomfortable as the demon's attempts at brain excavation. "Tether it with your power!" the fortuneteller shrieked.

"I can't. I don't know how." Jolie felt the demon's animus burst through the shell of her being and begin to crawl through her brain like a slow carrion slug.

"Get out of my head!" she screamed, beating her skull with her hands. "Get out! Get out! Get out!"

"Foolish girl." Yanna Maria's contempt tasted like poison. "You have no discipline--no learning. You are as helpless as a baby." Jolie felt herself becoming an infant again. "You think Rose can help you? Do you think Hoke can? I am the only one who can save you," the fortune teller's incorporeal voice offered. "But you must ask. Ask for my help," she commanded.

"Help me!" Jolie screamed. "Help me!"

*****

Rolling out of bed, Jolie's body arched and contracted with dry heaves, trying to vomit the dream from her body. When she was done, she leaned back exhausted on the bed, wiping her mouth on yesterday's tee shirt. Going to sleep at night was like being under attack, and the nightmares were escalating.

"Welcome to my new bargain." The creature's triumphant words vibrated through her bones like warning tremors before an earthquake. *"Welcome to my new bargain."* What did that mean? Who had made this bargain? Not her. And what exactly had the first bargain been? Jolie thought she might know if she could only remember, but she couldn't make the fragmented thoughts in her head fit together into anything resembling logic.

She remembered Yanna Maria talking to her in the dream. What was it the fortune teller had said about the demon? And when had Axel gotten himself a demon? *"Welcome to my new bargain."*

Jolie remembered the black shadow creatures that had come to feed at Solstice. Their leader had said something to Rory about a bargain.

"Axel, you stupid old fart, what have you done?"

Jolie crawled up onto her bed and closed her eyes, imagining she was in the little bedroom in the back of Rose's, Red Rock's healing energy pulsating through her like the earth's heartbeat. Maybe if she could sit quietly, she could calm the calamity scrambling her brain. Today of all days she needed to be able to function.

It was Saturday, the day of Faith's memorial.

Jolie had never been to a memorial before. She had been five years old and three states away when Mem died. Neither she nor Jessie Lynn had known that the Boulette Matriarch had passed and been laid to rest in the family crypt in St. Louis Cemetery Number Three until three years later.

Jessie had conveniently forgotten Faith's memorial and picked up a day shift, and Remy had a track meet, so Jolie was on her own. She'd figured out the bus route and how long it would take to get to the church when Mickey called.

"Hey, Jo. Iris gave me your number. I hope that's okay? The girls and I were wondering if you wanted to ride with us to the memorial service tomorrow? I've got a sitter for the baby. She'd just cry the whole time anyway. She's a terror right now; teething again, you know. I'm hoping to leave my house at twelve thirty. We could be at your place at about one. How would that be?"

Jolie gulped back a surge of emotion, feeling weak and stupid for coming so close to tears just because someone had offered her a ride.

"Great. If it's not too much trouble."

"It's no trouble. We're family," Mickey replied. "That's what family does; we look after each other."

Not where I come from, Jolie thought sullenly, but she thanked Mickey and said goodbye before any more inconvenient emotions embarrassed her.

Mickey's call was the first she'd heard from any of Faith's friends since Iris had called three days ago to tell her where and when the memorial would be. Jolie told herself it wasn't a problem, that she didn't need help, that she was used to being alone and doing things for herself. After all, she'd done it for most of her life. Faith had only been in her life for a few short months. But with the nightmares and lack of sleep, she was feeling beaten down.

Trying to figure out what to wear, Jolie tried on and discarded most of the clothes in her closet. It was all secondhand, and none of it right for a funeral. In the end, she chose a short black denim skirt, black leggings with blue flats, a blue shirt, and a denim jacket. She tied her pink streaked hair back in a low ponytail so that most of the color didn't show, and loosely wound the scarf that Iris had given her for Christmas, around her neck, hoping she looked respectful.

Mickey arrived fifteen minutes late, dressed like Wednesday Addams, the Goth daughter from the Addams Family, in a short black dress with its schoolgirl cuffs and collar.

"Sorry, I'm late," she gave Jolie a quick glance as they headed for the minivan. "How are you holding up?" She gave Jolie a second, more thorough look-over.

Chapter Thirteen

Jolie hung her head, wishing she hadn't tied her hair back. With her face in full view, there was no place to hide from prying eyes, and Mickey's eyes could be more prying than most.

Mickey was a member of Faith's original group of friends, intuitive, and experienced in reading people. If Jolie was uncomfortable knowing private things about other people, she was doubly uncomfortable with them knowing things about her.

"I haven't been sleeping too well," she mumbled. Of course, at this point, she was trying to avoid sleeping, using her old habit of watching movies and old programs on late night TV until Jessie Lynn got home, then staying up and reading until it was time for school.

It wasn't working. Eventually, her body gave in, and when it did, Axel's demon appeared and the chase resumed. Now, she was so exhausted that she was having trouble staying awake, drifting off whenever she sat still.

"I'm sorry. This must be hard on you." Mickey apologized. "You and Faith had gotten pretty close." Mickey changed the subject, talking about her girls' activities and achievements at school, saving Jolie from having to figure out what kind of small talk was appropriate. She began to nod off while the girls played a game in the back seat.

"It's my turn to be the ghost in the graveyard, Gita. You're the dead person," the older girl announced. "Oooo. Gotcha."

"Stop that, Rhea," the younger sister insisted. "There's no touching in Ghosts in the Graveyard. Ghosts can do anything except touch you."

"I wasn't touching you."

"You were too. That's touching." She repeated her sister's transgression, giving her hair a yank.

"Girls, stop, please," Mickey intervened, patiently. "Do we need to go over the rules of the game?"

"No, Mother," they answered together.

Mickey made a face and grinned at Jolie.

"People say boys are easier, but how would I know? All of my little indigo angels are girls."

Indigo children. Jolie blinked away her drowsiness and looked into the back seat. The girls looked back at her, their large brown old-soul eyes examining her matter-of-factly. What did they see, these kids whose parents claimed they were a new, more spiritually evolved generation? Was Jolie one of the first of their generation, or was the whole Indigo Child thing a new agers' retort to helicopter parents and their overachieving progeny?

When Jolie turned back around, she noticed that Mickey was studying her.

"Are you sure you're okay, Jo? I'm worried about you."

"I'm fine," Jolie lied. The young mother did not press, but Jolie sensed Mickey listening with senses other than her ears and vowed to keep her internal dialogue silent. It wasn't that hard. She drifted off again.

The memorial was being held at the church around the corner from Mae's house, at Father Owens' parish, where Jolie had gone last winter for help on the night Faith was attacked. The help she'd been given had been questionable: Father Owen had locked her up, then turned her over to her mother with a mini-sermon on good parenting.

Mickey parked the minivan.

"Okay, here we go." The girls, dressed in their princess best, spilled out of the van, bumping, giggling, and whispering to each other behind their little girl hands.

Chapter Thirteen

Jolie's stomach clenched as they headed toward the steps that led up to the church's big double doors. Sean would be here, Mae too, and god knew who else.

"Behave now, girls," Mickey cautioned her indigo angels. "We're here to say goodbye to Nana Faith, so think about all the nice memories you have of her, wish her well, and if you see her spirit hanging around, just keep it to yourselves."

"Yes, Mother," the girls answered in unison, their eyes round with excitement at being included in the grown-up event.

As they approached the church's stone steps, a black limo pulled up to the curb. Faith's daughter-in-law, Mae McBride, stepped out dressed smartly in a black tailored suit, pointy stilettos, a Prada bag, and equally snobby name brand jewelry.

"The queen has arrived," Mickey muttered. Like any mama bear, the young mother was fiercely protective of her cubs, and Rhea and Gita had been at the Solstice ceremony that had taken such a terrible turn. Mickey had not forgiven Mae for putting her children in harm's way. "She probably spent more on that outfit than I spend on groceries in a year," Mickey complained, looking down self-consciously at her own clothes. Everything about her black dress screamed that it had been pulled from the back of a spare closet, where women who can't afford to throw things away stash them just in case they come back in style. Mickey shot Jolie an embarrassed half smile and shrugged. "It was the right color."

Mae patted her freshly styled hair with a manicured hand, then looked around to see who had witnessed her arrival. Her eyes met Mickey's and hardened. Mickey gave as good as she got, glaring back.

"She's never even had the character to apologize," she muttered.

The door on the other side of the limo opened, and Sean got out.

Jolie saw him as she had on Solstice: a prince, powerful and strong, aware of all he was and had ever been, her friend, lover, and partner of lifetimes past.

Sean. Her lower lip quivered. Sean would understand how much losing Faith had hurt her. Sean would make it better. The pull of their many lives together drew Jolie to him. She stumbled forward, tears blurring her eyes.

"Sean," she called out to him.

Sean turned back to the limo and helped Adrianna out as if he had not heard her. It was Mae who turned to face Jolie, her thin, stingy mouth set in a tight-lipped grimace.

"So, the little juvenile delinquent had the gall to show up," Jolie heard Mae think. *"I can't believe Faith didn't see the minx for the gold digger she is,"* Mae whispered something in Sean's ear.

A petulant scowl transformed Sean's handsome features. When he looked in Jolie's direction, it was as if she wasn't there. Jolie froze like she'd been sprayed with liquid nitrogen. Pointedly ignoring her, Sean folded Adrianna's arm possessively over his, and they ascended the church steps.

Jolie stood at the foot of the steps, feeling as if she'd been slapped.

"Forget about it, Jo." Mickey urged her. "He's just upset, and who knows what lies Mae's been telling him. When Sean gets over his grief and thinks about it, he'll come around. He probably won't remember how he acted today."

"What's wrong with him?" Jolie asked, bewildered. "Why would he act like that?"

Chapter Thirteen

Mickey shook her head. "Grief and guilt play games with our minds and Mae is going to capitalize on that if she can."

"By shutting me out? I lost Faith, too."

Mickey sighed. "And everybody that matters knows how much she loved you. Look, I know you and Iris haven't had a chance to talk yet, but after Solstice, Faith rewrote her will, removing Mae as the executor of her estate. Iris is in charge of everything now. Mae found out about it a few days ago, and I'm guessing she didn't take it too well."

Jolie frowned. "That has nothing to do with Sean and me."

"Maybe not, but Sean and Mae are blood family and you aren't--we aren't. You were close to Faith, Jo. You were there, spending time with her during her last days. That can be awkward for blood relatives who were not, and like I said, guilt makes people act all kinds of weird. Let it go, and let's go find seats." Mickey and the girls flanked Jolie as they climbed the stone steps to the church doors.

They passed through a set of center doors and the foyer. A dozen oversized pictures of Faith were displayed at the front of the nave: Faith as a young woman, trim figure, trim suit. Faith with Mae's husband Robert still a little boy, the baby sister who would become Sean's mother in her arms. Dark haired Robert bore a strong resemblance to Sean, the same mischievous grin, and casual cool.

All the pictures from Faith's later years featured a smiling Mae by Faith's side, telling a slanted tale of closeness that fulfilled a not so hidden agenda. The picture frames that held them, were gaudy gilt things that stood on ornate gold easels and draped with creamy white chiffon. Faith would have hated them.

Since the attack, and her sickness last winter, Faith's social circle had shrunk to only a few special friends, but she was fondly remembered in the local spiritual community, so the church was packed.

Mickey led Jolie and the girls into a pew near the back and they settled in to wait for the memorial service to begin.

Vases and wreaths of flowers covered the steps leading to the altar, making it into a summer garden. One huge wreath encircled a picture of Faith as Jolie had known her, her face, soft with compassion and sweet with age. Beside the urn with Faith's ashes was a huge wreath of hot pink roses, with "Mom" emblazoned in large gold letters on its white satin banner. Faith hated pink. It was all wrong. Jolie looked around. *Where was Faith in any of this?* She couldn't think why she had even come. *This wasn't about Faith, it was about Mae.* Jolie glowered at the woman.

Faith's daughter-in-law might have found it easy to snub Jolie, but Iris could not be so easily dismissed. She and Faith had known each other since college. They had been friends and confidants for most of their adult lives, and now, Iris was Faith's executor. Pressed and polished in vintage Channel, Iris sat in a place of honor up front, next to Sean and Mae.

From where she sat, Jolie had a narrow view of Sean. He kept shifting his shoulders and scratching at the collar of his shiny new suit. A chunk of heavily gelled hair fell into his eyes. Adrianna reached up possessively and tucked it back into place.

He's not mine, Jolie reminded herself. *Not in this life.* It was okay. Adrianna could have him. Whatever time he and this stranger spent together would never wipe out the many lives he and Jolie had shared. Adrianna might love Sean, but there were things that she would never understand about him, and someday, though he and Jolie might never be lovers, it would be Jolie he would seek out to talk to about the things his grandmother had said to him that he still needed to understand.

"Got room for any more misfits in this row?" A young woman with bright maroon hair and a little steampunk hat with an iridescent green veil squeezed in beside Jolie.

"Tru!" Jolie's eyes lit up. Tru and her boyfriend, Marty, were a surprise package from the universe: friends who had popped up when she needed them and stuck without making any demands. Tru crushed her young friend into an exuberant embrace.

"Come here, you brat. I would have called as soon as I heard, but someone changed her number and didn't tell anybody."

"Sorry. We were trying to hide from Rick," Jolie whispered.

"That doesn't mean you have to leave your friends behind," Tru gave her a mock scolding, softened by a genuine smile.

"Hey, kid." Marty leaned in to give Jolie's arm a squeeze. "It's good to see you."

Emotion swept over Jolie like a tidal wave.

"Damn. Do you guys have some kind of conspiracy going on to make me cry in front of everyone?" Jolie pulled away from Tru, wiping her eyes.

"How are you holding up, honey?" Tru asked.

"She's a mess," Mickey answered before Jolie could lie. "Just look at her."

Tru did. "What's going on, Jo?"

"She's not sleeping," Mickey butted in again.

"What do you expect?" Marty defended Jolie in his masculine baritone. "It's like she's losing her grandma all over again. Cut her some slack."

"Sh." Tru hushed him.

"Do you really think that's all it is, Tru?" Mickey whispered from the other side of Jolie. Tru examined Jolie.

"Do you want a microscope?" Jolie quipped, feeling like a bug under glass. "You do know that I'm right here, don't you?"

"Something's wrong," Tru agreed, ignoring Jolie's sarcasm.

"Something's wrong," Mickey echoed.

"Nothing's wrong," Jolie insisted.

"See? Nothing's wrong." Marty supported Jolie. "Stop trying to make something out of nothing."

"Shush, Marty. They're starting," Tru faced forward.

Marty rolled his eyes as Father Owen stepped up to the altar.

"A Catholic priest for Faith McBride? I don't understand." Jolie frowned. "Faith wasn't Catholic."

"But Mae is," Mickey explained. "And Father Owen has been their neighbor for a long time."

"Mae McBride's the witch with the coven isn't she?" Marty looked more confused than usual.

"She's Wiccan, Marty. Nobody calls them witches anymore," Tru corrected him.

"She was Wiccan," Mickey explained. "But before it was fashionable to dabble in magic, Mae McBride was a devout Catholic, and last winter's little mishap scared her right back into the fold."

"I can't imagine what all of this cost."Jolie shook her head. "Faith wouldn't have wanted any of this."

"Memorials and funerals aren't for the dead, Jo," Tru pointed out. "They're for the living."

Chapter Thirteen

"And this one is about Mae McBride trying to regain status in the church," Mickey groused. "She's buying her way back into the ladies auxiliary."

"But you said that Iris was in charge now. Why would Iris give in to her like this?" Jolie demanded.

"A good general picks her battles," Mickey answered. "And Iris is no fool." Mickey leaned over and whispered to Tru as Iris walked to the pulpit to begin Faith's eulogy. "Mae's throwing a fit about the will." She glanced pointedly at Jolie.

Everyone turned their attention to Iris. The flowers and pictures might not have been to Faith's liking, but what her friend said in summing up her life, made up for all that. Iris knew Faith inside and out and when she talked about Faith's talent for seeing the potential in others and drawing it out, Jolie could not stop the tears that rolled down her cheeks.

Sean turned and looked back at her and their eyes met. He, too, was one of his grandmother's projects, and in that moment, Jolie knew that Sean might need to sit this life out, but he would be back.

CHAPTER FOURTEEN

*J*olie ran up and up the stairs, leaping two steps at a stretch, the demon's splayed claw-like fingers grabbing at her feet. The spiral stairway curled like the unbroken coil of an apple peel, climbing into an empty abyss above. Jolie had been here before, climbing one step ahead of the demon. The stairs never ended.

She remembered one of her mom's friends talking about some addiction recovery wisdom that said doing the same thing over and over again with the expectation of change didn't work. They called it magical thinking. As Jolie leaped from stair to stair, climbing the never ending spiral to nowhere, she thought about this: if she ever got to an end, what would happen? Did she really think that she would get away from the creature, or would this hide and seek play out as it always had, with the demon fighting its way into the little burrow it had been carving out for itself inside her mind?

"Where do you think you're going?" the demon's rough bass demanded, echoing her own thoughts. "You can't get away from me. We are one now."

"No, we are not," Jolie shouted, adamantly.

Faith had taught Jolie that learning to control your actions in the dream world was an important skill.

Jolie stopped climbing and spun around to face the demon.

"Stop following me," she commanded. The demon stopped an arm's length away and they stared at each other.

Chapter Fourteen

"That was it?" The creature smirked. "That was your big strategy?" It threw back its head and laughed, breathing out a slaughterhouse stench. Jolie gagged.

"You're disgusting!" She turned back around and began climbing again.

But as long as the demon hunted and chased her, it did not have a hold on her. It could not dig in. Surely, if she could avoid it catching her for long enough, a way to get free of it for good would present itself. Jolie leaped up another step and stopped, balancing precariously. The stairs had ended.

There was no door, no landing, nothing beyond them but infinite emptiness. They had just been stairs, without a purpose, leading nowhere.

So why had she climbed them?

"Give me a break," Jolie shouted.

The demon was three steps below and coming forward.

There was nowhere left for her to go except into the emptiness. She could face the unknown, or face the demon; those were her choices.

Jolie turned and gathered her courage, ready to fight to the last. Whatever happened to her, this thing could not be let loose to wreak havoc on the world by inhabiting her. She had felt remorse for Axel's death. This demon would not.

"I have you," the creature purred with satisfaction.

"No. You don't," Jolie replied. "And you never will, because I will not give in to you, never." She forced herself to wake up as the demon dove into her.

Jolie's eyes popped open, her chest heaving like she'd been running a marathon. Gradually, she slowed and deepened her breath. She was in her body, in the physical world, and she was still herself. She rolled over on the bed, trying to breathe out the fear humming through her. That was all she ever seemed to bring back from these dreams: fear. Everything else faded to confused images.

"Damn effing demon." She threw off the bedcovers and headed for the shower. No one was going to cut her any slack at school because a demon was trying to possess her, and she had a big day ahead. She was going to drive a real car for the first time in Driver's Ed.

*****

Hugo made the sign of a cross with his fingers like he was warding off a vampire. "Whatever it was, I didn't do it, honest."

Jolie felt like her body was a cement log she had to drag around.

Nothing felt right. The world was not her friend.

"What's wrong with you?" Hugo asked, munching his burger.

"Why does everybody keep asking me that?" Jolie grumped.

"Because you look like you're auditioning for the undead. I think you've got a shot."

"Just for that, I'm not going to go to the dance with you, not ever. So don't ask."

Hugo looked perplexed. "I don't dance. Anyway, aren't you Remy's girl?"

Bodhi plopped down on the bench glowering like the dark elf he impersonated most days. The look he shot Jolie had daggers in it.

"Remy doesn't have a girl, Hugo," the moody boy sneered.

"What is that, Bodhi?" Jolie demanded, not bothering to hide her annoyance with him.

"What's what?" Bodhi feigned innocence.

Chapter Fourteen

"That grim reaper look you get whenever anyone mentions me and Remy in the same sentence."

"I don't know what you're talking about."

"You know exactly what I'm talking about. You've got a problem with Remy and me." Jolie was ready to pick a fight and didn't care who knew it.

"You're hallucinating," Bodhi accused.

"I don't use drugs." Jolie countered, smugly. "Now you say it." Bodhi didn't speak. "I didn't think so. Only a coward lies to his friends. Take away all that Kung Fu crap, and you're just another scared punk, aren't you, Bodhi?"

Bodhi was shaking with anger. "If you weren't Remy's friend..." His fists clenched.

"You'd do what? Punch me? A girl? That'd show everyone what a great warrior you are. Remy would be so proud."

Bodhi's right hand shot out and grabbed Jolie's wrist, his left hand held her elbow. He pressed her arm down hard against the table.

"Say that again, bitch," he hissed, venom oozing from every syllable. His left elbow pushed into the hollow spot of her left shoulder and he leaned in, bringing Jolie's other arm all the way down to the table. It hurt, but with a little more pressure, it could hurt a lot more. With a little more effort, Bodhi could either break her arm or pull it out of its socket.

Hugo's eyes went wide. "Bodhi, stop," he warned his friend, alarmed.

Bodhi didn't move.

"You can't control it, can you?" Jolie egged him on. "The drugs have you at the edge all the time, and you can't get free."

He pressed his elbow deeper into her shoulder. Jolie winced, but she didn't back down. "Admit it, Bodhi, you're a junky, and you need help."

"Both of you stop it!" Hugo stood up ready to intervene as Remy came out of the crowd and walked up to the table.

"What's going on?" He dropped his backpack onto the bench seat.

Bodhi released Jolie's arm.

"Nothing. I was just giving your friend a demonstration." A dark undercurrent of anger smoldered beneath his fake smile.

"A demonstration of what?" Remy looked from one to the other.

"Just how easy it is to pull someone's arm out of their socket if you know how." Bodhi took the apple off Jolie's lunch tray. "See ya." He looked at Jolie and mouthed "bee-otch", bit into the apple, and melted into the crowd.

"Are you alright, Jo?" Hugo asked.

"Yeah." Jolie rubbed her shoulder.

Remy frowned. "What was that all about?"

"Like he said, he was showing me how easy it is for him to hurt someone," Jolie explained, dodging the bigger issue and Bodhi's ill intent toward her.

Remy looked to Hugo, expecting he would fill in what Jolie seemed unwilling to share.

"Don't look at me, Rem. I had nothing to do with it. I was trying to stop him."

"Stop him from what?"

"Nothing. Let it go," Jolie tried to end the discussion.

"It wasn't nothing, Jo," Hugo interjected. "He could have really hurt you."

"Sifu would have thrown him out of the school if he had." Remy examined Jolie. She refused to look at him. "Are you okay, Jo?"

"I'm fine," Jolie snapped.

"I'd better go to talk to him," Remy hoisted his backpack.

Jolie picked up her own backpack and stood. "You do that, Remy. He needs a lot of help. Has he taught you how to tie him off yet? Frigging idiots." She started to leave. Remy stopped her.

"What's the matter with you? Why are you so damn prickly?"

"I'm fed up with Bodhi's bullshit, and I'm tired, Rem." Jolie wiped a hand across her face. "I'm so tired." She held back the tears by sheer willpower. "I can't sleep. I mean I could, but I don't dare. It's the nightmares." She looked up at Remy, her eyes begging him to help her. "I've been having them ever since that first night when you took me to Red Rock, but they're getting worse and worse, and it's getting so hard."

"Is this about what happened in the apartment?" Remy asked.

"What happened in the apartment?" Hugo asked, confused.

"It's making me crazy, Rem," Jolie admitted, feeling exhaustion fissuring her resolve.

"I'm so sorry, Jo." Remy pulled her into his arms and held her.

Kids streamed around them like Remy was a rock: her rock. "What if I come over for a few hours tonight and just sit with you while you sleep?"

Jolie smiled, weakly. "That's sweet, but I don't see what difference that would make."

"I'll bring some sage and sweet grass and we'll smudge out your apartment to get rid of the bad juju. I hear that there have been some weird things going on upstairs." He smiled his sweet smile.

"'You're going to banish my bogeyman?" Jolie laughed.

"Absolutely. I'll be over after practice. Okay?"

"Okay," Jolie agreed.

Remy gave her a quick kiss and headed off to class.

"What happened at the apartment?" Hugo asked again.

"It's a long story, Hugo." When Jolie turned to leave, Bodhi was staring at her from across the commons, rage fixed on his face. He had been watching her and Remy from the crowd. "Great." Jolie sighed as her cell vibrated.

"Hey, Jo, it's Tru. Got a second?"

"I've got three, maybe four tops. Class is about to start." Jolie kept walking.

Tru hesitated then blurted out, "Marty asked me to marry him."

"Wow, congratulations. What took him so long?"

"I don't think we saw ourselves as the marrying kind, but I've got to say that now that we're actually engaged, things feel different between us: sweeter, and more romantic. It's really sudden, I know, but we've set a date for next month, and I want you to be a bridesmaid."

"Gee, Tru, I don't know what to say," Jolie stammered, hurrying along the breezeway. "I've never been to a real wedding before. I was the flower girl at a biker wedding once. Will it be anything like that?"

"God, I hope not." Tru laughed. "Not with my mom involved. But you'll do it, won't you? It would mean a lot to Marty and me to have you be a part of it."

"'Sure. I guess I could do that," Jolie sprinted the last few strides to get into the classroom.

Chapter Fourteen

"Good. I'll text you the date, and the fitting times, and all that."

"Fitting times? Wait--what?" Jolie skidded her butt into her chair just ahead of the bell.

*****

Drivers Ed went better than Jolie feared. She didn't fall asleep or crash into anything, and she kept a tight rein on her smartass mouth. Mister Anderson was a nice, fatherly Mormon who believed driving was a serious thing that left no room for joking.

Oddly enough, there were a lot of Latter Day Saints living in Sin City and working in the casino industry. Las Vegas was a popular place to raise a nice Mormon family, just one more of the city's strange incongruities.

It was Tuesday after school, and without Faith, Jolie had nowhere to go. She lingered at the top of the steps outside the school, watching the other kids go off to their afterschool activities. There was nowhere she wanted to go, and no one--except Remy--that she wanted to go there with. But Remy had a full life without her. She had come into his life to try and save him, but it seemed more like he was saving her lately. She sat down on the school steps.

Some days, she almost forgot about Remy and the accident. She'd had the vision those few times early on, and then nothing. All she'd done for Remy so far was cause him trouble.

Rebecca strolled across the lawn toward her. The black lined lips and heavy eyeliner of her Goth phase were gone along with her jet black dyed and ironed hair. Without makeup hiding them, you could see Rebecca's freckles. Her naturally curly brown hair was two toned, the ends still clinging to the black dye, while the roots grew out a warmer brown. She had even taken to wearing her glasses. Jolie sensed her friend's new comfort with herself. Not all change was bad.

"How was the memorial thing?" Becca sat down beside Jolie.

"Weird."

"Weird because it was about someone dying, or weird because Sean was there with another woman?"

"It was very...Catholic."

"I thought your friend was a New Age witch or something?"

"Well, she was definitely not Catholic," Jolie said, wryly.

Becca fingered the gold cross that hung around her neck.

"Sometimes people come to God in the last moments of their lives, and he accepts them even then."

"And sometimes people imagine things because they want so badly for them to be true," Jolie countered.

"Have you ever been to church, Jo?"

"Yep. More than one. Some of the buildings were really nice." Jolie stood up. "But it didn't make me want to go to Sunday school."

Rebecca chuckled. "Yeah. I can't quite see you wailing out 'Jesus Loves Me.'"

Jolie chuckled. "I learned the words."

"Really?" Becca looked surprised. "I would have paid good money to see that."

"Yeah, I was there a whole two days. They had graham crackers at snack," Jolie confided. "And there was this really cute boy who's mom taught the class..."

Rebecca laughed. "Ah, and now the truth comes out."

Chapter Fourteen

"She didn't like me much. After the second day, she handed me a Parks and Rec. flier, and suggested I might be better suited to their Backyard Scientist camp."

"You know, we're not all like that, Jo."

"I know." Jolie smiled. "And she did me a favor. I was much happier at science camp. It would never have worked out between me and her son anyway."

"I know that we're very different people," Becca said. "But we can still be friends, can't we, Jo?"

"Sure." Jolie shrugged. " As long as it's okay that I'm a heathen."

"That's cool, as long as you don't try to convert me to your pagan ways," Becca teased.

"Ditto."

"Then we're good?"

"Well, you are anyway." Jolie gave her friend a devilish grin.

"So, do you want to go to the library?" Rebecca asked.

Jolie considered her chances of staying awake sitting still in a quiet library.

"Only if we can stop for coffee on the way," she decided.

"Done. I just have to get my books." Becca headed back into the building.

Jolie closed her eyes, trying to steal a moment of calm. Focusing within, she sensed the demon, relaxing as she relaxed, settling into the little space inside her that it was trying to claim as its own. For a moment Jolie felt as if she could actually "see" it and it could "see" her. They studied each other, not forming thoughts or judgments; just observing.

Weird, Jolie thought, unable to put any other description on the interlude.

She felt a sort of ripple in the air. Opening her eyes, she brought her awareness back to the physical world.

The pickup of the Native man she had seen at Rose's was parked by the curb in front of the school.

Jolie got up and sauntered over.

"Hi. I know you, don't I? You're a relative of Remy's, right?"

"Yes. His uncle, Hoke." The man's voice was a soft low shushing, like the heads of ripe wheat rubbing together. "And you are the girl in Cowboy's van." Remy's smile had come from this side of the family, but his uncle used it much more sparingly, smiling mostly with just his eyes.

"One of them, yes."

"We met before that, though. You came to visit me out in the desert last winter."

"You saw me?" Jolie asked. "You remember that?"

"Of course." He nodded. "It is a night that would be hard to forget."

Every hair on Jolie's body was standing up as if Hoke's presence was electrifying the air around them. How much did he know about the events of Solstice?

In spite of his weathered face and salt and pepper hair, the energy radiating from the man was vibrant and powerful, but it was more than physical power. Jolie sensed a strength that bridged multiple dimensions.

"So, you go to school with Remy?" Hoke said in his soft-spoken voice.

Jolie nodded. "I've seen you parked by the school before. You just drive over and sit and watch the school? Why? What are you doing?"

"Nothing really. I just come to make sure my nephew is okay."

"Remy's not really the kind of kid who gets in trouble," she pointed out.

Chapter Fourteen

Hoke shrugged. "It's something his mother asked of me."

Jolie frowned. "His dead mother?"

"And so you see why I must come." There was something Remy's uncle was not saying, but he expected her to understand--something he was leaving out. "You care about Remy. I can see that" Hoke went on. "Like me, you care what happens to him."

"Yes." Jolie shifted, uneasy. "You hang out here just in case something happens to him? That's kind of weird. What do you think is going to happen?"

"I don't know. What do you think is going to happen?"

Jolie fidgeted. What was taking Becca so long? Her mind tried to back out of the lariat hold of Hoke's presence.

"I think you understand my concerns because you have similar ones," Hoke said.

"I don't," Jolie said, quickly. It wasn't a big lie but it was a lie, and when she looked at him, she could see that he knew it. She felt the blood rush to her cheeks, uncomfortable with what else he might know about her.

"Relax, I am no danger to you," Hoke said in his wheat-field voice. "We are on the same side, you and I. I am glad to know that when I am not here, you are here looking after him. Pilamaya." The old Indian tipped his hat and started his pickup. He was driving away when Rebecca came up beside her.

"Who was that?" Becca asked as they fell in step together, headed for the library.

"No one."

It was a much bigger lie. Remy's uncle, Hoke, was many things, but he was not no one. He knew things; important things, but for some reason, he chose to pretend he was just a cowboy in an old pickup truck.

Like I pretend to be just a teenage girl, Jolie reminded herself.

"They don't know anything," Yanna Maria had sneered at Hoke and Rose.

Jolie did not believe that was true. Which raised the question: why would the fortuneteller say it?

"Because she did not want you to seek your answers from them," a voice from inside her answered. *"She wants you dependent on her."* Jolie considered what that might mean, but even before questioning the truth of the statement, she had to question its source. Was this voice the demon answering her internal question, or some part of herself? How could she know the difference?

The fortune teller had been a guest in Rose's house, a member of the sweat lodge community. Jolie had seen Yanna Maria riding with Hoke in his truck. Those things indicated a friendship, didn't they? At the least, they were spiritual colleagues. Jolie knew from her experience with Faith, and Rory, and the coven women, that just because a grownup claimed possessing spiritual wisdom didn't mean it was true, and it didn't mean they were trustworthy. Some were, and some weren't.

Why can't people just be who they say they are? Jolie thought in frustration.

"Don't be naive," an inner voice chuckled, sardonically. *"Where would be the fun in that?"* Jolie was sure that voice was the demon.

Shut up. No one asked you, she told him. She had no interest in such a chaotic universe.

*****

On and on, Jolie ran along the twisted stairway following it as it curled sideways, then upside down, mocking any sense of gravity.

Chapter Fourteen

Ahead of her, a door appeared, so far away that she wondered if she could ever reach it, or so small that she would have to shrink to the size of a mouse to fit through.

"Leave your body behind," something inside her suggested.

"That's dumb," Jolie realized. "I have nobody. This is a dream." But if she didn't have a body, then how was she running away from the demon? "If I can only reach the door and get through it, maybe I will be safe. Maybe he cannot follow me through it."

She needed someplace where she could close the demon out, leave him behind, and shut him out forever.

"The rules of the human world do not apply here," the inner voice reminded her.

The steps became taller, forcing Jolie to climb from tread to tread like a crustacean. As soon as the thought came into her head, Jolie's body changed into a crab's.

Ten jointed legs scrabbled from stair to stair stretching, pulling, and grasping over each lip.

She missed a step, and with nothing to grab, went bumping down the stairs, banging her shell with each bounce.

Crab-Jolie lay on her shell back on a landing at the bottom of the stairway she had just climbed, her broken crab legs twitching helplessly in the air above her.

A figure of dark smoke appeared from out of the darkness.

"Together again," the demon wheezed.

Jolie inhaled and the creature rode the breath inside her.

CHAPTER FIFTEEN

It wasn't hard to ditch Rebecca the next day and go to Yanna Maria's. Jolie left directly from her last class without going to her locker and hurried off campus.

"Yanna Maria, I need to ask you--"

"I will teach you nothing, foolish girl," the fortune teller said petulantly as Jolie entered the shop. "You think you can do this all on your own. You know nothing." She waved her hand in dismissal and flounced off into the back room.

Jolie stood in the shop uncertain what to do. Who else could she ask? No one. Swallowing her pride, she took the broom from the corner and began to sweep the floor.

"Wax on, wax off," she muttered the classic line from Karate Kid.

A leggy business woman in a fitted gray suit jacket and skirt, her dark hair pulled into a professional chignon, came in. She did not wait to be invited or greeted, instead, she walked directly to the back room as if she knew the way and was expected.

There was an excited conversation between the two women, most of it in Spanish. Ten minutes later the woman emerged, sweeping past Jolie as if she did not exist. Jolie craned her neck to see out the shop's big front window. The business woman got into a silver Spyder and drove away.

Yanna Maria came to the doorway of her reading room. Holding aside one drape, she watched Jolie sweep a pile of dirt into a dust pan and empty it into the garbage. No one told her to do it, but Jolie took a spray bottle out from under the counter, found a roll of paper towels, and began cleaning the fingerprints off the shop's glass door.

"Humph." The fortune teller dropped the drape behind her and retreated into the back room. As Jolie moved on to washing the big front window, she could hear Yanna Maria talking on the phone in Spanish accompanied by the soft click of cards being laid out on the table. She was giving readings to clients over the phone.

Who was this woman, really? Jolie recognized how little she knew.

The front door bells jingled and a young Latino man, in work clothes and heavy boots, entered the shop. His jeans were spattered with mud, and he smelled like freshly mown grass. Jolie looked out the window. The truck, now parked where the Spyder had been, was a recent model, clean and waxed with Guillermo's Lawn and Garden Service on the doors in vinyl lettering. The trailer behind it held a lawn mower, wheel barrow, shovels, and rakes.

He, too, went into the back room, and Jolie could hear him and Yanna Maria talking, though she could not hear what they said. When the landscaper came back out, Jolie caught a glimpse of Yanna slipping a roll of paper money into her cleavage.

"So you are the new girl?" the landscaper, presumably Guillermo, studied Jolie. "Helping our Madrina out, eh?"

"It's no big deal," Jolie replied.

"Washing windows? No, it isn't. Anyone can do that, but what the santara does; now that is special."

"I guess." Jolie shrugged, noncommittally.

"You guess? What are you doing here, little girl?"

"Nothing. Yanna Maria just asked me to help out a little is all."

"And what favor did you ask of her?"

Red flags went up in Jolie's head. "Nothing," she lied.

He examined her again, more closely. "What are you, Gringa, Latino, Black?"

Jolie stopped wiping the glass. "What I am is none of your business."

The lines of Guillermo's face set like concrete. "We don't like outsiders coming around our ways and making trouble for us," he said, threateningly.

"I'm not here to take anything from you or Yanna Maria. I'm just helping clean up around the shop because she asked me to. There's a toilet brush in the bathroom if you want to pitch in." Jolie went back to polishing the window.

Yanna Maria opened the back room drape.

"Leave Jolie alone, Guillermo. She has work to do."

"I'm not stopping her, Madrina. I'm just supervising, making sure she does a good job for you." He leaned back against the display case and crossed his arms over his chest. Rick's El Camino pulled up in front of the shop.

Jolie froze.

"This girl, she is full of fear, Madrina," Guillermo informed the fortune teller. "Look at her. She is like a scared rabbit."

Heat began to rise from the depths within Jolie where the demon lurked. The anger she felt was part her own, part something foreign and unnatural, but it made her feel powerful and much bigger than her own small self.

Chapter Fifteen

"Oh, she didn't like that, did she?" Guillermo taunted. "Are you sure you want to teach this one, Madrina?"

"Who said I was teaching her?" Yanna Maria snapped, her eyes searching the room as if looking for something. "You know better than to make assumptions about me and my business, nephew."

"I do." Guillermo grinned.

Rick was sitting in his truck, talking on his cell phone, but any minute he could look up and see Jolie.

She could not be here.

"I have to go." She set down the spray bottle and tossed the paper towel in the waste basket.

"What? Right now?" Yanna Maria's eyes narrowed. "But we haven't finished yet."

"I think maybe we have," Jolie looked from Yanna Maria to the truck outside. She didn't know what the fortuneteller's game was, but no matter how talented or knowledgeable she was, if she was connected to Rick, Jolie wanted no part of it.

"You haven't even finished washing the window," the heavy woman argued.

Jolie didn't care. "Get your gardener to do it," she said, flippantly.

Guillermo laughed. "I think you forgot to give this one the speech about obedience, Madrina."

"Shut up, Guillermo!" She told him, impatiently, continuing to seek the source of the strange energy rising in the room.

Closer to the surface than Jolie had ever felt when awake, the pressure of the demon's desire pulsated through her as it prowled just behind her eyes. It's attention zeroed in on the mocking gardener.

A demonic growl escaped Jolie's lips, issuing from deep in her belly. The demon was waking, ready to test its boundaries to find a place from which it could act.

"I have to go." Jolie headed for the back door that opened onto the alley behind the mini-mall.

Yanna Maria blocked her way.

"There is no path for you this way."

The El Camino's door clicked open, then thudded closed. Fear, stress, and the demon all three pressed at Jolie's mind, making it impossible for Jolie to think.

"No," was all she could say.

Yanna Maria's face became red. "What did you say?"

"I said, no," Jolie repeated. It was a denial of everything and everyone trying to force her into action according to their wishes: demon and human alike.

The sound of Rick's cowboy boots approaching on the sidewalk was like nails hammering into her skull. A moment more and she would lose it, screaming the world down around her. Her last thread of control was unraveling. The demon surged forward, pouring itself into the spaces inside her mind that it had long coveted.

Jolie's eyes glowed with the reflection of an aberrant spirit.

Yanna Maria backed away as understanding finally came, frustration and greed turning her round childish face, ugly.

"What have you done, you foolish girl?"

"I think, with this one you may have bitten off more than you can chew, Madrina Yanna," Guillermo warned the santara.

"Get out of my way," Jolie warned with a voice not entirely her own. "Nobody is taking any bites out of me." The demon's focus shifted to the person about to enter the shop: Rick.

Chapter Fifteen

"This one is mine. He was promised to me," it announced, gleefully. *"A bargain was made."* It expanded, trying to force its will on Jolie's mind.

"I had no part in that." The stoic teenager shoved past Yanna Maria. The fortune teller caught Jolie's arm, holding her with a surprisingly strong grip.

"You have no idea what you are doing," the santara warned. "You cannot control this thing. You do not know how. It will devour you. I am the only one who understands it. I am the only one who can help you."

"You've done a real good job of it so far," Jolie countered.

The fortune teller released her with a flourish.

"When you come to your senses, you will be back."

Jolie hurled herself at the back wall, tearing at the drapes covering the reading room's wall, searching for the door she knew must be hidden there.

The shop bell jingled. Jolie's hand found the round doorknob and she was out.

When Jolie got home, Remy was sitting on the steps waiting for her.

"I left practice early," he explained.

Placing himself on the couch, he insisted Jolie lay down with her head on his lap. Within minutes she had drifted off to sleep.

Coiled up in a corner of Jolie's parietal lobe, the demon glowered like a sullen kitten, jealous of the stranger's unwanted intrusion.

"What is he doing here?" it demanded.

"Keeping me safe," Jolie answered, curtly.

"From who?"

"From you."

"I wouldn't hurt you," the demon scoffed. "We are one."

"Your math sucks. We are not one. I am one, and you are another, and that equals two."

"We don't need him." The demon continued to argue for Remy's removal. "You only need us."

Wriggling its way deeper into Jolie's mind, the creature seemed to have tireless energy to focus on its goal of merging its will with hers, running a propaganda monologue to convince her that their purposes were aligned against the rest of the world, and if she just gave it more control, all her problems would be solved.

"With us, you will never have to be alone again," the demon promised.

"I'm not the one who is afraid to be alone," Jolie argued.

"Because you stay awake for hours and hours and leave us with nothing to do." The demon pouted. "We get bored. We hate being bored."

The longer the thing spent connected to Jolie, the more it sounded like a petulant teenager. "Let us help you in your world, then we won't be bored anymore," the demon whined. "We can help you solve your problems."

"You mean problems like Rick? Oh no. I saw what happened to Rory after he bargained with you."

"We could make the one you hate go away," the demon tried to persuade her.

Jolie connected to the calm she recognized as Remy, found the kernel of her own will, and imagining it as a bright light, made it grow larger and larger.

"Stop!" the demon squealed. "You can't just push me out."

"I'll test that theory for myself, thank you." Jolie kept expanding the light, filling all the dark corners she could find until there was no place left for the demon to hide. With a victorious yelp, she pushed it out.

She was free again.

Chapter Fifteen

Jolie woke up on the couch in the apartment with her head in Remy's lap. Her mom was just coming in.

"Well, hello there." Jessie Lynn stopped just inside the door, surprised to see Remy. "You're cute. Who are you?"

"Remy Bishop, ma'am." he slipped Jolie's head off of his lap and stood up.

"Mom, what are doing home?" Jolie rubbed the sleep from her eyes, squinting at the athletic middle-aged hunk who had followed her in.

"They let me go early," Jessie dodged the question. "Oh, this is Brett. Brett, this is my daughter Jolie and her friend, uh, I'm sorry. I'm terrible with names."

"Remy."

"Right."

Everyone looked at each other awkwardly.

"It's nice to finally meet you in person, Jolie," Brett offered her his hand.

Jolie looked at it like it was a snake that was going to bite her, and turned away. All she needed was to know her mother's new boyfriend's dark little secrets before he'd gotten the chance to lie to her and tell her what a great guy he was.

Brett's button down shirt was crisp if slightly worn. His blue jeans were broken in, but not thrashed. His hair was beginning to gray at the temples and he wasn't trying to hide it, so he wasn't vain, but his haircut was a good one, so he wasn't entirely unaware of his genetic jackpot in the looks department. His split lip and the way he kept massaging his right hand told Jolie that he had recently been in a fight. Aside from that, he was not Jessie Lynn's usual type.

Jessie came from the kitchen with a drink in her hand. As she walked into the dining room light, Jolie saw her mother's black and purple cheek.

"My God, what happened to your face, Mom?"

Jessie touched the spot gingerly and glanced at Brett.

"Is this your work?" Jolie turned on Brett, her accusation fierce. "Did you hit her?"

"No. Oh God no, Jo." Jessie jumped between them. "This wasn't Brett's doing."

Jolie scowled, looking from one adult to the other.

"Well, I'd better be going." Remy picked up his hoodie. "It was nice to meet you, Mrs. Figg."

"Please, Jessie Lynn is fine."

"Okay, Jessie Lynn. I was hoping to take Jolie out to my Aunt Rose's in Red Rock on Saturday if that's all right? I'd pick her up in the afternoon and I'd bring her back on Sunday after breakfast," Remy promised. "I know that sounds a little strange, but my Aunt Rose invited Jo to a Morning Star ceremony. We go into the lodge in the middle of the night and come out at dawn. We'll be totally chaperoned the whole time, I promise."

"It's fine." Jessie shrugged dropping onto the couch. "Jolie knows better than to come home pregnant."

"It's a women's lodge, ma'am," Remy explained, politely. "Traditionally my people don't mix genders in a sweat lodge, and never in a women's lodge."

"Hence the name," Jolie added.

"Getting all hot and sweaty with a bunch of women? Where's the fun in that?" Jessie Lynn gave Brett a suggestive smile.

"Right. Well, good night, ma'am, sir." Remy nodded at the adults.

"Coward," Jolie teased as he made his exit. "Thanks for standing guard while I napped. I think it did help." Jolie turned on her mother as soon as Remy closed the door behind him. "So what really happened?" She indicated the bruise on her mom's cheek.

"Don't make a big deal out of it, Jo," Jessie tried to sidestep the issue again.

"I think she should know, Jess." Brett moved up behind Jessie and began to rub her shoulders. "What if he shows up here? She could be in danger."

"He, who, Rick?" All Jolie's alarms were clanging. "Did Rick do this?"

"He showed up at the bar," Jessie admitted. "Brett threw him out." She giggled. "You should have been there, Jo. Brett beat the shit out of Rick's skinny ass. You would have loved it."

Rick. Twice in the same day he had tried to get to them. *Either there had never been a true warding spell or the magic was wearing off.*

"So, he knows where you work, and he knows where I go to school, and now he's decided to cause trouble. Perfect." Jolie sighed.

"Tomorrow, I'll get my lawyer to draw up a restraining order," Brett offered. "It's against the law for him to harass you like this."

Jessie Lynn grinned. "Isn't he great? I told you, didn't I, Jo?"

Brett looked embarrassed. "The man is on retainer. He needs to do something to earn his money." Jessie rolled over onto one hip, propping her forearms on the back of the couch, all coquettish and flirty.

"Are you sure that you won't reconsider that nightcap I offered, Brett? I feel like I owe you."

Brett shook his head. "I'm going to follow Jolie's friend's lead and say goodnight to you, ladies." He put on his cowboy hat. "Get some rest."

"You don't have to go, you know. You could stay." Jessie Lynn stretched her legs out on the couch like a cat settling in for some serious petting.

Jolie thought she might barf.

Brett glanced toward Jolie, clearly embarrassed by Jessie's open expression of sexuality in front of her daughter.

"Thank you, but I'd better get going.

"'See you tomorrow?" Jessie Lynn persisted.

"I'll check in." He tipped his hat.

"You really are a gentleman cowboy, aren't you?" Jolie said as she walked him to the door. "I thought they were only in the movies."

"There are still a few of us around if you know where to look."

"And I guess that would be Wyoming?"

"Montana." Brett corrected her with a smile.

"Well, thanks for looking after my mom. In case you didn't notice, she's a bit of a trouble magnet."

"I noticed."

"But it didn't scare you off?"

"She's not a bad person. She's just..."

"Damaged. Yeah, I know. But hey, ya gotta love her, right?" Jolie said, sarcastically.

Brett frowned. "Look, Jolie, just to set the record straight, I'm not looking for another ex-wife. I've got a set already."

"Good, because I'm not looking for a dad. I'm glad we got that straightened out, but you might want to let Mom in on the plan."

"I don't think your mom has any illusions about our relationship."

Jolie winced. "Then you don't know her very well. My mom lives on illusions. She can get them about almost anything, and usually does, but she's especially susceptible when it comes to men. Just so you know."

Brett nodded. "I'll try to keep her expectations low."

Too late, she thought. "Thanks. Well, good night." Jolie closed the door.

Chapter Fifteen

"You're not trying to scare off my beau are you, Jo?" Jessie Lynn asked. She finished off her beer and leaned back on the couch, closing her eyes.

"No. You're right. This one seems like a nice guy." *Maybe too nice,* Jolie wanted to add. What would a guy like Brett want with a messed up piece of work like Jessie Lynn, aside from the cheap sex while he was out of town on business in Vegas?

"Get me some ice, will you, Jo? My face is killing me."

"Sure." Jolie went to the fridge and took an ice tray out of the freezer. Turning it upside down, she ran hot water over the back. Scooping up the fallen cubes, she dumped them into a plastic bag.

"Do you really think a restraining order will keep Rick away?" Jolie wrapped the bag of ice in a dishcloth and brought it to her mom, seating herself on the back of the couch.

"I don't know, babe. I hope so." Jessie Lynn took the ice bag. "Bring me another beer."

Jolie got the beer. This was not the time to talk to her mom about her drinking.

"I've got five weeks of school left, Mom. I can't leave now." She set the beer on the coffee table. "You know what happened last time we changed districts in the middle of the term. I could lose credit for the whole semester. It could cost me a half a year to make it up."

Jessie sighed as she put the bag to her cheek. "I can't keep jumping from job to job, Jo. People won't hire me if they think I'm not stable."

"Vegas is a big town," she argued. "There's a ton of bars here."

"It's a lot smaller than you think, and people talk."

"Like if you get a reputation for bringing in trouble?" Jolie suggested, cautiously. "Is that why they let you go early tonight? They blamed you for the fight?"

"He came in looking for me, and he wasn't shy about announcing it," Jessie Lynn admitted.

"Of course he wasn't. Why should he be? He's got nothing to lose," Jolie complained. "What did they say?"

"They gave me a warning and said don't let it happen again." Jessie changed the subject. "You really liked Brett, didn't you? I mean you really liked him?"

"I said he was nice."

"Maybe when he goes back to Montana, he'll take us with him. We could live in a house like a real family and not have any more problems." Jessie's voice drifted off.

We'd just have a whole new set of problems, Jolie thought, privately. But then, she knew that Gentleman Brett was not going to scoop them up and take them off to his oversized cabin under the big Montana sky to live happily ever after. Jessie Lynn Figg's life story was not a Victorian romance, it was contemporary smut, dirty, and gritty, and uncomfortably real. In Jessie Lynn's world, women got their hearts broken and their faces beat up, and when they fell into the gutter, no one cared. It was unfair, but that was the way it worked.

Jolie wished that for once in her life things would go smoothly and stay that way long enough that she could catch her breath, but that was the wishful thinking of a kid, not the understanding of a sixteen-year-old who knew better than to trust the magical thinking of an alcoholic.

"I'm going to bed." Jolie went to her room and closed the door.

Jolie lay down and curled up in a fetal ball. When her cell buzzed, she almost didn't answer it, but the ringtone was Sean's.

Chapter Fifteen

"What do you want, Sean?" she asked, trying to make it clear that it was no big deal that he'd called.

"You weren't at the reading of Faith's will. Iris invited you, didn't she?"

"I had school, and you know, that's family stuff. It's got nothing to do with me."

"You know that grandma thought of you as family?"

Tears jumped to Jolie's eyes. "Don't be nice to me right now, Sean. It's too confusing."

"Look, Jo, I'm sorry I couldn't talk to you at the memorial. There were a lot of people there, and a lot of expectations, and you know I'm not good at that stuff."

"Maybe Adrianna can teach you, along with sit and stay," Jolie quipped, sarcastically.

Sean chuckled. "You're such a pain in the ass. Actually, Adrianna and I sort of broke up a few nights ago."

Hence the call to me, Jolie realized.

"What's the matter, did she tell you that you had to sell your bike?"

"Something like that. Anyway," Sean continued. "I got this wedding invitation from Tru and Marty. What a thing, huh? I thought maybe since neither of us is attached that we could go together?"

Jolie thought about that. Sean might be free now, but was she? What would Remy think if she went to the wedding with Sean? But then, Sean wasn't just a guy, he was an old family friend--not even an old boyfriend, really. It was perfectly natural that they should go to the wedding together.

"I guess that'd be okay," Jolie decided "I'm a bridesmaid, though, so I can't sit with you at the ceremony or anything."

"That's okay. We can hang out at the reception. I'll tell Tru to put us at the same table."

"Okay. Whatever."

"And you should ask Iris about Faith's will. It's important."

"On a scale of one to ten, you've got no clue what's important in my life right now, Sean." It was an effort to keep the tears out of her voice.

"I'm sorry, Jo." He sounded genuinely contrite. "We'll talk at the wedding."

"That'd be good." Jolie hung up and rolled back onto the bed in a ball. Waking or sleeping, she was still in deep shit.

CHAPTER SIXTEEN

Jolie woke up in the dream world on the landing at the bottom of the stairs. She was still rolled over on her crab shell back, her broken crab legs peddling fruitlessly in the air.

This shell sucks, she thought.

Instantly, the shell became a dark soft body with thousands of microscopic hairs covering it. Ten legs became eight, and Jolie looked at the dreamscape anew, seeing it with a spider's eyes.

There were patterns and designs everywhere; in every detail, large or small. The many layers of a subtle world lay themselves out before her: realities unrecognized, potential futures, worlds that overlapped her own with a myriad of connections weaving them all together.

The threads from Jolie's own spider body spun out into it in every direction, touching other webs, other lives. Some Jolie recognized by their vibration, others, she had yet to know.

Ignoring the stairway, spider-Jolie walked out onto the tightrope threads of her own webbed life.

Some of the glistening threads were strong and shone with an inner light, drawing her focus to their patch of the greater pattern.

"What are you doing now, foolish girl?" Yanna Maria's voice shouted at her as if she had caught Jolie with her finger in the frosting of someone else's birthday cake. "The door; remember? You are seeking the door," the woman urged.

Jolie became a girl again, precariously balanced on threads stretched over a tomblike nothing extending into forever. The door was far above.

She began to climb toward it, hampered by the stickiness of the spider threads and the clumsy inappropriateness of a girl's body on a spider's web.

"That's it," Yanna Maria encouraged her. "Keep going. Focus on the door," the commanding voice faded.

When Jolie finally climbed off the web and onto the landing, she felt weak and drained, the despair of trying to elude the demon once again overriding her focus. She reached for the doorknob and the door flew open, torn from its hinges by the howling wind on the other side. She turned back to look behind her.

The demon crouched a few steps below.

Jump, her inner voice urged. Just jump and be done with it.

"Go ahead, try it," the demon goaded as if it could hear her inner voice.

Jolie turned back to the chaos of the storm. Beyond it was a woven net of glowing threads, moving in the wind, anchored firmly at the ends. Laughing, she leaped off the landing, sailing into the nothing: free. And then the demon was there beside her.

"Foolish girl. You need me. We are one." It wrapped itself around her, weaving its energy through hers, binding them back together as they fell.

*****

Something has to change, Jolie told herself again and again when she woke from dreaming, but she did not know how to make that happen.

Yanna Maria. The name came into her head, clear and persistent.

Chapter Sixteen

Ask Yanna Maria.

For the next few days, she avoided the fortuneteller's shop. She dragged herself to school, sleepwalking through class, just trying to get through the day, worn out and beaten down. Avoiding her friends as well, it felt like she was watching everything from a distance. Feeling as if her insides were shriveling, finally, she could take it no more. Something had to change.

As soon as school was out, Jolie went straight to the fortuneteller's shop.

Hesitating at the corner of the mini-mall, she scanned the parking lot for Rick's El Camino, then once she was sure he was not around, straightened her shoulders, took a long breath, and went in.

The tuneless bells on the back of the shop door announced her. She stood just inside the door, waiting for the fortune teller to appear.

Yanna Maria stood up from behind the counter.

"So, you're back." The plump woman pursed her lips. "You're a mess. I can feel it from here."

"You said you knew what was going on with me and that you could help."

Yanna Maria's pudgy hands slipped through her rope of necklaces.

"You have not earned my trust."

"And you haven't earned mine," Jolie retorted. "What should we do about that?" There was only silence. "Look, Yanna Maria, if you're not going to help me, what are you doing in my dreams?"

"Ask yourself." The woman shrugged. "They are your dreams, not mine."

"If you don't know how to get rid of this thing, just tell me. I'll find someone else." Jolie was walking the blade of a knife.

Yanna Maria snorted. "It is not as easy as you think." She studied Jolie for a long minute. "You do not want it?"

"The demon? God, no."

"Very well, but you must do exactly what I say and not ask questions," the fortune teller warned.

"That's never been my strong point," Jolie admitted.

"Those are my terms." The fortune teller crossed her arms making the upper end of her cleavage rise to meet her double chins.

"What do you want me to do?" Jolie agreed, reluctantly.

"Come with me." The fortuneteller led Jolie into the back room.

*****

Jolie sat in the coffee shop with Hugo and Brutus. The afterschool crowd was thinning and the second jobbers were trickling in for their evening shot of career juice, but mostly the teenagers had the place to themselves. Rebecca had been there when they arrived, so she came over and sat down with Jolie and the boys and began her usual nervous chatter.

Jolie had no idea what her friend was going on about, and she didn't care. She'd come for the caffeine and because Brutus had hunted her down, asking for her help with Algebra. She felt bad that she'd been avoiding them lately, and Brutus had never asked her for anything before, so she'd given in.

The equations danced before her eyes. Outside of a vague recollection that the groupings were supposed to have meaning, she had no idea what she was expected to do with them. The numbers and letters kept turning into

Chapter Sixteen

little dark figures that scampered and jumped around the page.

As she watched, the figures rearranged themselves into a digital image and a scene began to play out before her fogged eyes.

"Put the gun away, Rick." Jessie Lynn backed away. Rick grabbed her arm and jerked her around, using her body as his shield. "Whoa! What are you doing, baby? You're hurting me," she wheedled, sweetening her tone as if they were still a couple and he was playing too rough. "Come on, lighten up, honey."

"You stupid bitch!" Rick spun her around to face him. There was a loud slap and Jessie Lynn fell to the floor.

This equation Jolie understood.

"I have to go." She jumped to her feet and scooped her books into her backpack.

"But we haven't finished my homework," Brutus protested.

"Sorry."

"Are you coming back?"

"I don't know."

"Is something wrong, Jo?" Hugo asked, interrupting his conversation with Rebecca.

"I think my mom needs me."

"What's going on?" Rebecca added her concern.

"She's in trouble."

"How do you know that? Extrasensory perception?" Brutus joked.

Hugo and Rebecca exchanged glances.

"I'll go with you." Rebecca stood.

"No." Jolie stopped her. "There's nothing you could do, Becca. Go home."

"Do you want me to call the police or something, at least?"

"No." Jolie hesitated, her mind split between the scene in the bar and the questions she was being asked in the coffee shop. "I have to go--now!" Jolie stumbled from the table, struggling to navigate with the vision of her mother being beaten filling her head.

"I'll text you later," Becca called out after her.

Hugo finished texting, tucked his phone away, and rose to follow. "Let's go, Brut."

"I don't think you should. She said there was nothing we could do," Becca protested.

"That's not what she said. She said there was nothing "you" could do, Becca," Hugo corrected pushing Brutus through the swinging doors.

By the time Jolie got to the bar, sweat had soaked through her shirt and was running down her face. She ran like an athlete on super drugs, rocket-fueled by adrenaline, but now, her supply was running low. For weeks she had worked to suppress Axel's violent anger and the demon's desire to meld its strength with her physical being; now, bereft of any natural reserves, what they offered was a temptation.

"We are here. Just use us. We can give you the strength you need," the demon promised.

"I'm going to kill him," Jolie growled.

"We'll help you." The demon's energy coiled tight within her belly.

She noticed Rick's car in the parking lot near the door. Jolie burst through the bar door, blinded by the abrupt plunge into darkness. She blinked to help her eyes adjust and looked around. There was no one behind the bar and only a few stunned patrons, pretending to focus on their own business, real or imagined, were in attendance.

Chapter Sixteen

"Stop this baby, you're hurting me." Rick held Jessie in a choke hold, tight against his body. "Come on, let go of me. I'll get you a drink and we can talk about this."

"Let go of my mother," Jolie snarled from the doorway. A middle-aged couple skittered past her like rats.

Rick spun around, dragging Jessie Lynn with one arm. There was a gun in his other hand.

"There she is, miss high and mighty, 'don't ever come near me or my mother again'. Who do you think you are, you little bitch?"

"I know who I am." Jolie planted her feet, standing as tall as her small frame allowed. "It's you who's confused about it."

Rick moved the gun from Jessie Lynn's head and pointed it at Jolie. "I don't feel confused."

"Jolie, turn around and walk out those doors," Jessie Lynn ordered her daughter. "Do you hear me? Go home. This is between Rick and me. It's got nothing to do with you. It's just a lover's quarrel. Nothing we can't get past, right, Rick?" Jessie looked up at Rick, her face begging. "You always did like making up after a fight. I haven't forgotten what you like."

Jolie felt sick. "Why do you do that?" she confronted her mother. "Why do you demean yourself to this piece of shit?"

Jessie Lynn bugged her eyes in exasperation. She had a game plan and Jolie wasn't playing along.

"If it had been just us, Jess, it would never have been a problem," Rick claimed. "But this little slut of your loins here was always judging me." He indicated Jolie with the gun. "Swishing her tempting little tail around, trying to come between us. Nothing's been right since Solstice. Everything's been 'off', you and me, work. Everything's gone wrong. I don't know what you did to us on Solstice," he accused Jolie. "But I'm going to undo it; starting with your mom and me."

"Whatever happened on Solstice was you and Rory's doing," Jolie argued. "You were in so deep, that you hit the iceberg and still thought you were having a party."

"Shut up," Rick shouted.

"Rory made a deal, then wouldn't ante up," Jolie refused to stop. "Bargains made with the underworld have to be kept, Rick," Jolie's voice was acquiring a sibilant hiss. "Rory paid his debt. Now it's your turn. I think he needs company."

Rick licked his lips, his finger beginning to curl against the trigger. "I agree, but it won't be me."

"No!" Jessie threw her weight against him, toppling them both to the floor. The gun went off just as a woman came out of the bathroom. She screamed and ran back through the swinging doors.

Jolie was on Rick like a lion, her hands locked around his throat, pressing her thumbs hard into his larynx.

"Keep pressing. Don't let up until you see his eyes glaze and hear the last heartbeat." Axel had done this before. *"Keep pressing. Harder,"* he teetered on the edge of pleasure, anticipating Rick's death.

"Stop, Jolie! Stop!" Jessie Lynn was pulling her daughter's hands from Rick's neck.

Chaos churned inside Jolie.

Gathering a ball of energy in her belly, she compressed it, then forcefully exploded it at Rick.

The gun went off a second time. Jessie flew across the room, hitting the wall. With a moan, she slid down like a dropped rag doll.

The breath rushed back into Rick's body and the gun was back in Jolie's face; much, much closer. The rage inside her was building again. Whether the thoughts in her head were hers, Axel's, or the demon's, she neither knew nor cared. Rick had to die and if that meant she died too, well, it didn't seem any harder than living had been lately.

"Screw you." Jolie opened her mouth and closed her lips around the gun's cold hard metal barrel, daring him to pull the trigger.

"Crazy bitch," Rick muttered, throwing her off of him onto the floor. He was getting to his feet when a tennis shoe clad foot came flying through the air and caught him in the side. Rick crumpled back down like a bag of wet laundry.

Hugo stepped out of the shadows and grabbed Rick's arm. Rick was still trying to figure out what had happened when Hugo wound Jolie's attacker's arm up behind his own back.

"I've got him, Jolie," the fledgling Fu declared, nervous and triumphant.

"Get away from him. He's mine," Jolie threatened as if Hugo was a rival predator trying to move in on her kill. Hugo looked perplexed.

"I'm just helping out, Jo."

"I don't need your help." Jolie rose to her hands and knees and began to creep toward Rick like a cat stalking its prey.

"What are you doing?" Hugo blinked, fascinated and horrified.

"Hunting." Jolie's lips rolled back from her teeth. "Him, at the moment." Her eyes tracked back to Rick, leaving Hugo staring, dry-mouthed at the bizarre scene before him.

"Oh shit," he muttered.

From somewhere in the dark bar Bodhi appeared, placing himself between Jolie and Rick.

"Stop. This is over, Jo," he said, firmly.

"Get out of my way, Bodhi." Jolie moved forward.

"No." Bodhi shook his head. "The police will be here any minute." Sirens could be heard in the parking lot. "We're going to step back now, and let them take it from here."

"The police?" The unctuous derision of her words hid that her voice was not her own. "When did the police ever know what to do, or how to do it right?"

Bodhi shrugged. "That's not ours to debate tonight. Tonight, they take him away and lock him up so that you can focus on helping your mom over there." He nodded to where Jessie Lynn lay against the wall. "She needs you, Jo." Brutus stepped into the light holding the drama within its circle. Bodhi walked toward Jolie and held out his hand, offering to help her up. "I called Remy. He'll meet us at the hospital."

CHAPTER SEVENTEEN

Jessie Lynn was unconscious when the EMT's carried her out of the bar on a stretcher. Bodhi made sure the team knew the stunned girl sitting beside the injured woman was her daughter and that the girl should ride with her mother. Bundling her into the back of the ambulance, Bodhi buckled Jolie in like she was six and going to grandma's alone for the first time.

"We'll see you there," he told her in a tone of gentle confidence. Jolie looked at him and nodded, tears welling in her eyes. Bodhi was a pain in the butt, but he was good under pressure. Hugo surged forward and grabbed Jolie's hand, squeezing it as if he could give her some of his own new found strength.

"It'll be okay, Jo," he promised.

"Stop hovering, Hugo." Bodhi pulled Hugo back to stand with Brutus and himself. "She's fine, she's strong, aren't you, Jo?" he prompted.

Jolie just stared at the three of them, not knowing what to say. She had always considered herself strong, but the veil of subterfuge had torn, revealing a profoundly troubled girl, who was not nearly as tough as she pretended to be.

"We'll meet you at the hospital," Hugo repeated as the EMTs moved the Fus out of the way and closed the ambulance doors.

The red flashing lights, the siren, the trucks engines whirring: it was all background noise to the war inside Jolie.

The demon was triumphant, excited by getting to act in the physical world. Axel was psychotic. The parasitic spirit's emotions fought Jolie's own relief over Rick going into custody and her concerns for Jessie Lynn. The flashing lights spinning outside the ambulance windows and blaring siren jangled her already raw nerves.

Focus. Get it together, Jolie scolded herself. Cautiously, she reached over and lifted the edge of the sheet that covered all but her mother's face. A dark red stain was soaking through the gauze bandage taped to Jessie Lynn's thigh.

"Don't do that, kid." The EMT beside her said.

"How bad is it?" Jolie asked. The man hesitated, not wanting to answer. "She's my mom. Just tell me."

"There's a bullet in her thigh," the man acquiesced. *It's too close to the artery,* Jolie heard him think, but he didn't say it. "She's got bruises, maybe an internal hematoma, and her arm is broken.

"But she'll be okay, right?" Jolie prompted him.

"She's going into surgery as soon as we get to the hospital," the EMT replied. "Is there someone you should call, your dad? A grandparent?"

Jolie shook her head. "No. It's just Mom and me."

"I'm sorry." He seemed to mean it. "Don't worry, it's a good ER. They do this kind of stuff all the time."

Of course, they did. It was Las Vegas; playground to the rich and the desperate; home of the con, a garden of expectations where dreams were manufactured in plastic that evaporated when exposed to too much sun. And there was always plenty of that.

Jolie could feel the Axel-demon entity peeking out through her eyes, voracious for more of what it had tasted.

Chapter Seventeen

"What about him?" it asked, focusing on the EMT as a possible new victim. Jolie felt the creature's malicious intent like a lump in her belly.

"That's not the way this is going to work," she warned, speaking out loud. The EMT glanced at her uncertainly and she turned her head to look out the window, hoping to change the demon's focus.

Looking out the backdoor windows, Jolie could see an elderly woman at a bus stop, carrying an oversized shopping bag.

"What about her?" the demon suggested. *"No one knows or cares where she is. No one will even notice that she's gone."*

"Stop," Jolie snapped back.

The EMT checked to see if Jolie was talking on a blue tooth. She ignored him, focusing on controlling the creatures inside her.

They passed a skinny teenager on a bicycle.

"We could take him out with just a swerve of the car," the demon played its perverse game.

"I can't drive," Jolie reminded it. "I don't even have a license."

"You will have soon."

"I don't have a car," Jolie refused to give in.

"We'll steal one."

"The world is lucky you're dead, Axel," Jolie derided him.

"We could--" it started to make another suggestion.

"Shut up," Jolie shouted. The EMT was getting seriously worried now. Jolie's stomach rolled and jerked. "I think I'm going to be sick."

"There's a sick bag by your right arm," the guy told her. "Don't worry. It happens all the time." He tried for a reassuring smile, but Jolie could see that he was nervous, ticking off her symptoms and questioning what action he should be taking. Axel and the demon were toying with the hypothetical killing of others, but the EMT was within reach. She could not let them get control again.

It had been so easy to give in to them when things got tough at the bar. It was not so easy to get the damn things back into their box.

The ambulance slowed, then stopped. The siren went silent. The doors were thrown open and stranger's hands pulled Jolie's mother out and took her away.

Jolie climbed out onto the dock and watched Jessie Lynn being swallowed up by the hospital's double doors. The ambulance lights went off. The driver came around the back and closed the doors, then got back in and pulled away. Jolie stood outside the hospital, alone.

A brilliant sunset of reds and oranges brushed the lavender sky as the sun sank behind the Spring Mountains to the west.

The weather isn't right. If this was a movie, it would be rainy and bleak, Jolie thought. That was how she felt inside.

"Jolie!" Remy called from across the parking lot, she turned from the bright sunset to Remy, and then she was his arms. "It's okay, I'm here. I'm here, Jo." Jolie stood as stiff as a stick, numb and unresponsive. Remy held her out at arms' length to look at her. "Are you alright?"

Slowly, as if the air was Jell-O, Jolie reached a hand up to Remy's face and tried to press the worry lines out of his skin with her fingers.

"You shouldn't worry, Remy," she whispered. Her voice was eerie and unconnected. "You're face is too pretty to be all scrunched up."

Remy gently cupped her hand in his, holding it against his heart. "Boys aren't pretty, Jo. They're handsome... or not." He gave her a crooked smile.

Chapter Seventeen

"You definitely are. You could be on a magazine cover."

"How pretty would he be, lying dead in a box," the demon inside her muttered.

"Shut up," Jolie ordered it, feeling her awareness split, rejoin, then split again. When she looked back at Remy, the worry wrinkles were deeper.

"What's going on, Jo? Why are we talking about my career options?" he asked, troubled.

Jolie looked around the parking lot. Hugo and Bodhi were there.

"What?" she frowned. Unable to remember what they had been talking about.

"Brutus couldn't come. How's your mom?"

Jolie stared at him, not comprehending.

"Your mom just went into the ER, remember?"

Jolie squirmed under her friend's knowing eyes.

"He wouldn't be hard to kill," Axel suggested. *"He's soft, trusting, and unaware. He wouldn't even see it coming."*

"Don't touch him! Get out of my head!" Jolie began to hit her head with her fists. Remy grabbed her hands.

"Whoa. Who are you talking to?"

Jolie stopped and blinked. She saw the hospital's double doors and reality stampeded her.

"Mom..." She ran. Pushing through the doors, Jolie threw herself at the receptionist's desk. "Where is my mother, Jessie Figg?" she demanded.

"I'm sorry, honey, but you aren't allowed in this area," the nurse sitting at the desk told her. She looked like a doctor's wife in the making, tight uniform stretched across her breasts, too much makeup, perfectly straightened hair. "The waiting room is over there." She pointed.

"Where is my mother?" Jolie repeated as if the woman hadn't spoken.

"Is she a patient here?" The words were polite, the attitude was not.

"They just brought her in an ambulance."

"Ah." The nurse glanced at one of the trauma rooms. "Her condition is being evaluated. If you'll just wait in the waiting room, over there." She pointed again, impatiently, "We'll send someone out as soon as we know something.

"What about her?" the demon suggested. *"You'd like to kill her, wouldn't you? Perky assed and so full of herself."*

What were you before you died, Axel, a mafia hit man? Jolie demanded.

"Oh come on, Jo, we could do her and be out the back before anyone knew anything had happened."

"There's cameras all over this place," Jolie disagreed, out loud. "I'm not going to prison just so you can get your jollies." The nurse looked up from her computer.

"Hey kid, you can't stay here. It's hospital policy. Go to the waiting area. Just down the hall and through those doors." She stood up and came out from behind her desk and reaching for Jolie's arm.

"Don't touch me!" Jolie warned her. The woman was too close, too tempting. Jolie pulled away. The demon's energy was rising like molten lava inside her: dangerous and invigorating.

"It's okay. Calm down. No one's going to hurt you," the nurse assured Jolie, looking around for help.

"Why would you say that?" Jolie demanded. "You know it's a lie. Everyone is going to hurt you." She began to pace back and forth like a caged animal, her

Chapter Seventeen

breath shallow and fast. "That's all they do is hurt you, over and over again, and there's no way out of it."

"Do it now," the demon urged her. *"I know you want to. We'll wipe that smug look right off her face."*

"Stop talking to me," Jolie shouted. "I'm not listening to you."

"Yes, you are, and in another minute you're going to let go. You'll feel so much better, I promise. You'll feel alive and free--"

"And perverted. Shut up!" Jolie grabbed her head with her hands and pressed hard against her temples.

Remy came running in, followed by Bodhi and Hugo.

"I'm sorry, gentlemen, but you can't be in here," the nurse started to repeat her spiel.

"I'm with her," Remy explained, approaching Jolie.

"Oh." The nurse stopped, obviously okay with someone else taking charge of the reckless teen.

"Jo? Jolie?" Remy tried to get Jolie to look him in the face. "Where are you, Jo? What's going on?"

Jolie shook her head back and forth like a pendulum.

"What's wrong with her?" Hugo pushed the others aside to get to his friend.

"I don't know," Remy muttered.

"You need to leave," the nurse repeated. "You can't-
-"

"We know: we can't be in here," Remy interrupted her. "We're trying to figure out what's wrong with our friend. As soon as we do that, we'll go. Okay?" The woman seemed willing to back down for the moment and Remy turned his attention back to Jolie. "Jolie?" He tried to take her arm and pull her along the hallway. She twisted away from him, her face red with fury.

"Let go of me."

Hugo joined Remy. "Jolie?"

Jolie dropped her head and looked up at him through the tops of her eyes.

Alarmed, Hugo backed away. "What the crap, Jo?"

"Jolie." Remy grabbed both Jolie's arms and tried to force her to look at him.

"No. I won't do it!" She flailed against his grasp. "I won't do it!"

"Settle down, Jo. Settle down. It's just me, Remy." That seemed to mean something to her because she stopped trying to get away.

"Remy? You're alive?" Jolie's face changed from violent anger to confusion and sadness.

"Yes, that's it, Jo. Just take nice deep breaths," Remy coached her.

"She seems pretty upset," the nurse hedged. "I'd better call someone."

"No, she's fine," Remy assured her. "I think we have her under control now."

"You won't call anyone," Jolie growled in Axel's baritone, his anger blazing. Twisting from Remy's grasp she closed her fingers around the woman's neck.

"Jolie, no!" All three boys jumped forward to pull the women apart. "What are you doing?" Remy tried to stop her. "This isn't you. This isn't you!"

"Maybe it is," Bodhi piped up. "She was kind of like this at the bar, too."

Hugo stared at the scene, completely undone. "I don't understand any of this: people getting beaten up, shot--trying to kill each other. I'm an extra in a horror flick."

"Get him out of my way, or I'll tear his heart out of his chest while he's still breathing," the demon roared.

"Jo! Jo!" Remy got hold of Jolie's shoulders and shook her. She growled and spat at him like an animal

Chapter Seventeen

caught in a trap. He did not let go. "Listen to me, Jolie. It's Remy. It's Remy. Stop this."

The world stopped moving like etch-a-sketch granules, and recognition flickered in Jolie's eyes.

"Get away from me, Remy. I'll hurt you," she gasped.

"You'd never hurt me. You're going to save me, remember?" he reminded her.

"Save you? Save you from what, Remy?" Bodhi demanded, staying close enough to intervene.

"It wouldn't be me," Jolie admitted. "But "he" will hurt you."

"'He', who, Jo? Who are you talking about?" Remy grilled her.

"I can't control him. I can't hold him back anymore. All the pieces keep flying apart." Jolie's eyes lit on Bodhi. "You have to look out for Remy, Bodhi. You have to watch over him when Hoke can't be there. Keep him safe. I thought I could do it, but I'm just putting him in danger. Protect him, Bodhi. Promise me. You get clean and protect Remy. Promise me!"

Bodhi positioned himself in front of Jolie, stiffened his hand and in a move almost too fast to see, gave her a chop to the neck. She collapsed at his feet.

"What did you do that for?" Remy began to gather Jolie up into his arms like a bundle of rags. "That was a little extreme, wasn't it?"

"I don't think so. I think it was necessary. You heard her rambling on." Bodhi turned to the nurse. "We're really sorry about this." He oozed charm. "Our friend's had a really rough night. Her mom just got shot and she was right there." He touched the woman's arm. "She saw everything and she was trying to stop it but...."

The nurse nodded. "Everyone handles trauma differently. Look, I really should call someone."

"No," Remy stopped her again. "We've got this."

"We do?" Hugo looked around, dismayed. Bodhi silenced him with a look.

"Yeah, we do. She can call here and check on her mom later, right?" Remy asked the nurse.

"We should know something in a few hours," the nurse agreed. "Are you sure you've got her under control?"

"Absolutely," Bodhi jumped in to dissuade any doubt.

"There's a lady she sees--a counselor," Remy explained. "I know the place. I've taken her there before." He hiked Jolie up higher in his arms and carried her from the hospital. Hugo swept up Jolie's fallen backpack and followed, trailing behind Bodhi who remained close to Remy.

"What was that?" Hugo demanded as they walked across the parking lot.

Remy chuckled. "Which part? Jolie going all Exorcist or Bodhi using his special powers to bewitch that nurse into not calling security?"

"Either... both. I don't know. I've never seen shit like that before, except in the movies." Hugo's eyes were as round as a Japanese anime character.

"Welcome to the world of a Spiritual Warrior, Grasshopper," Bodhi mocked a Chinese accent. "The Force can have a strong effect on the weak minded," he added, dropping it.

"And you call "them" geeks," Remy laughed.

"It worked, didn't it?" Bodhi defended himself. "Sifu says that lots of the stuff in Star Wars was based on Taoist practices."

"Sifu understands that this generation doesn't read philosophy books, they watch movies," Remy countered, stopping at the edge of the parking lot. He looked both ways along the street.

"Did anyone bring a car?"

CHAPTER EIGHTEEN

"I came on my scooter," Remy informed his friends.

"We came on the bus." Hugo and Bodhi exchanged apologetic looks.

"Great." Remy stood holding Jolie's unconscious body, trying to figure out their next step.

"Let me take her for awhile," Hugo moved in for the transfer.

They made it to the bus stop on the corner, propping Jolie up against Hugo on the bench

"Do you really have a plan for where we're going?" Hugo asked.

"Red Rock," Remy checked the bus schedule.

"Do buses go there?"

"They go close. I should be able to get us a ride if we can get to Summerlin." He tried Rose's number. There was no answer.

It would only take one transfer to get to Summerlin, the closest neighborhood to Calico Basin.

The city bus slowed, came to a stop, and the Fus climbed on, trying to look nonchalant about the unconscious girl among them.

"What's going on with her?" the bus driver eyed them, suspiciously.

"She passed out," Bodhi started his charm act.

"'Can't hold her liquor," Hugo added, improvising. Remy punched his arm and gave him a look.

The driver frowned. "You kids been drinking?"

Chapter Eighteen

"Not us, sir. Just her. We're on a mercy mission, you know, save the girl. You understand." Bodhi was laying on the charm thing.

The driver finished scrutinizing them then jerked his head toward the back of the bus. "Go on."

They clambered into four of the empty seats, hoping their luck would hold.

It didn't.

Jolie's eyes popped open. "Get your hands off me before I kill you," she growled.

"Calm down, Jo. It's us," Remy smiled nervously at the driver who was watching them in his big rearview mirror.

"I said, don't touch me, boy!" The demon pushed fully into Jolie's semi-conscious brain. With uncommon strength, she began to fight the Fus to keep them from restraining her. The few passengers on the bus tried to be small, huddling within themselves, and scrunching down behind the seats as the bus turned into a Jackie Chan style fight scene.

"Don't hurt her," Remy kept shouting as the Fus dodged the demon-driven girl's manic offensive.

"Don't hurt her?" Bodhi's reply was imprinted with his usual sarcasm.

"You kids, sit down back there," the bus driver shouted.

"Driver! Stop the bus. Stop the bus!" one of the riders started to scream.

"Sit down and stop playing around," the driver ordered.

"Get away from me!" a patron howled.

"Driver, stop!" another yelled.

The whole bus was a chaotic mess of arms and legs, angry faces, and shouting.

The bus stopped. The driver stood up, his face apoplectic.

Bodhi slipped in behind Jolie and gave her a quick chop. She collapsed back onto the bus' bench seat.

"Get off my bus," the driver ordered.

The Fus gathered up Jolie and obeyed. Standing on the corner, they watched the bus drive away.

"We need a car," Remy announced.

"And a driver," Bodhi added.

"Someone open minded who won't get too freaked out and ask too many questions," Hugo made his contribution to the wish list. "Got a Jedi mind trick for that, Bodhi?"

"Can you think of someone who would want to help this chick out enough to come pick us up, before the cops do?"

Hugo sloughed Jolie's backpack off his shoulder, pulled her phone out of the front pocket, and began scrolling through names.

"How do you know who to call?" Bodhi asked.

"I listen. I paid attention when she talked about her friends." Hugo shook his head. "You guys are hopeless. You're never going to have girlfriends."

Iris didn't pick up but Tru did. She and Marty were there in fifteen minutes.

Jolie was beginning to stir, indicating she was regaining consciousness as Tru opened the truck's door and got a good look at her friend.

"She looks awful. What happened?" she glanced, suspiciously at the boys.

"It's a long story. We need to get her to Red Rock, to my aunt's. I can't explain everything because I don't understand it all myself yet, but I'll tell you what I know on the way."

Chapter Eighteen

Jolie's eyes fluttered open. "Tru," she said groggily. "You met Remy?"

"Yeah, just now, sweetie. Are you okay?"

"He's a nice boy," Jolie said. "Nicer than I deserve." Her eyes flooded with tears. "I don't want him to die, Tru, but it's gotten so hard to fight him."

Tru looked up at Remy. "To fight who, Jo? Who are you fighting? Remy?"

"No, no, not Remy. 'Him'." She dropped her voice to a whisper. "The demon. I'm not a bad person, Tru. I'm not."

"No, you're not, Jo," Tru agreed. "You're probably the best, most courageous person I know, except maybe for Marty here." She smiled at her fiancé. "Not everyone would have done what you did on Solstice. Not everyone could have. Is that what this is about, what happened that night?"

Jolie seemed confused by the question. In a way it was, she had encountered the demon for the first time that night, but Axel's death had come months later.

"What happened on Solstice?" Remy asked, looking from Jolie to Tru, alerted that there might be a clue in this for him.

Tru hesitated. "You'll have to ask Jolie. It's her story to share, or not."

A police squad car drove slowly by, the officer on the passenger side taking a long interested look at the little group.

"They seem awfully interested in us," Marty noted.

"There was an incident at the hospital," Remy admitted.

"The hospital? Why was Jolie at the hospital?" Tru demanded.

"It sounds like we'd better get going," Marty muttered. "You can explain, like you said, on the way.

There's room for Jolie and one of you up front." The rest of you will have to ride in the back if you're coming with."

"I need to stay with Jolie." Remy climbed in beside Jolie, propping her up against him.

"I don't care where I ride, but I'm going," Hugo jumped over the side of the pickup and settled into the bed. Bodhi did the same.

"Try and relax," Remy told Jolie. He pulled up Rose's number on his phone and called. She picked up.

"Thank god," he breathed a sigh of relief. "Aunt Rose, it's Remy. Listen, I need you to find Hoke for me. It's important. We need to do an emergency wipe down for Jolie tonight. No. This is more serious than that. Have you got someone who can tend fire? Sifu's there? That's great. We'll be there in half an hour." He hung up and began to sing softly to Jolie in Lakota.

Tru looked over at him and smiled. "We really love this girl. Tell me she's going to be okay."

"I can't yet, but if anyone can help her, it's my uncle Hoke."

"Okay. Then we'll get her to him."

Rose met them at the gate.

"Sifu has started the fire. Go explain the prayer to him." Remy started to protest. "We've got the girl," Rose stopped him. "Go do your part."

Rose and Tru bundled Jolie out of the truck and into the house. They got her out of her jeans and tee shirt and into a long loose fitting cotton dress that covered her arms. Helping her into the little back room, they sat her down on the edge of the star quilt bed.

"There are still a few things I need to do," Rose announced. "Can you watch her?"

Tru nodded, smiling. "We're friends. She won't give me any trouble." Rose raised an eyebrow but let it go.

Chapter Eighteen

"Do you want to tell me what happened?" Tru asked Jolie when the other woman had gone. Jolie drew her knees up to her chest, hugging them, rocking herself gently as she looked around the room. "Remy said that Rick showed up and attacked your mom," Tru tried to get Jolie to talk. "You must have been terrified. It's a good hospital, though. Your mom will be all right."

"Everyone keeps saying that. They're just trying to make me feel better."

"Is it working?" Tru tried to lighten the moment.

Tears gathered at the lower lids of Jolie's eyes and trickled over, spilling down her cheeks.

"It wasn't all right before. Why would it be all right now?"

"Oh God, sweetie. The questions you ask," Tru pulled her friend into a hug. "You're alive, your mom is alive, and that scumbag, Rick, is going to be locked up for a long time. It may not be great, but it's a start."

Jolie wriggled out of Tru's arms, staring at her with hard, cold eyes. "Are you always this naive?"

"It's not easy but I do try."

Remy came in. Crawling onto the bed behind Jolie so that she could lean against his chest.

"Thank you for saving us," he drew the edges of the star quilt up around them both.

"I think saving you is overstating the case a bit, but you're welcome," Tru replied.

"Please let Marty know how grateful I am for his help--how grateful we both are."

"Sure." Tru studied the two young people, seeing how Jolie's body relaxed now that Remy was near. "Do you want me to stay?" she asked.

"It'll be a few hours before the fire is ready and we can take her in," Remy replied. "I'm going to try to get her to sleep a little if I can."

"Should I wait and go in--"

"No," Remy said, firmly. "I'm not trying to be mean or exclusive or anything, but this is not going to be a first timer's lodge. A wipe down is a special healing and this one could get pretty intense."

"Okay. I understand," Tru said, reluctantly. "You've got my number. You'll call me when she's out?"

"I will. And thanks again."

"I meant what I said before, about her being special. It wasn't just words. Jolie is...well, you don't meet people like her very often."

"No. You don't." Remy nodded. "She told me about her visions and how she sometimes knows things."

"And what did you think about that?" Tru asked, taking stock of this new boy in her friend's life.

"I think she is very brave."

"This thing, you're going to do, this wipe-down? Will it fix whatever has her twisted up inside?"

"I hope so. Hoke is a good man and he knows a lot about the old ways."

"I'll be waiting for your call." Tru left Jolie and Remy sitting together in the dark, wrapped up in the star quilt.

Jolie drifted through a foggy dreamscape, unable to see or find her way. Somewhere off in the fog, a young man was singing.

"Wakanta ha-ya wa-oo-way-loy yo."

She did not understand the words, but she felt their meaning vibrating her heart.

"Great Mystery, Hear me. Help me. Heal me. I want to live in a good way, but I am struggling, and I need your help."

Once during the night, Jolie opened her eyes to find Bodhi sitting in a chair beside the bed, watching Remy and her sleeping. His elfin face was a study in anguish.

Chapter Eighteen

Jolie felt Remy's heartbeat against her back and drifted back off.

She woke again. The rhythm of Remy's breathing had changed. His chest against her back stuttered and trembled; he was sobbing quietly. Bodhi's head hung low between his shoulders so that she could not see his face, but everything about him said that he, too, was crying.

"Remy?" Jolie murmured, sleepily. "What's wrong? Why is Bodhi crying?"

"Go back to sleep, Jo. Nothing is wrong," he lied, sweetly.

The next time she opened her eyes, she was alone under the star quilt. Remy was beside Bodhi's chair his arms wrapped around the slim boy. Sensing her attention focused on them, Bodhi looked up and held her gaze.

"I will take care of him. I will keep him safe. No matter what it takes," he promised her silently.

CHAPTER NINETEEN

Remy carried Jolie to the fenced boundary of the lodge grounds. Hugo and Bodhi followed like shadows, silent and cowed at finding themselves thrust into this unfamiliar world where their honored teacher took the role of a humble fireman. They knew that whatever happened, things had changed for them. Very few of the school's students had ever been to a lodge with Sifu. Being there had moved them into a coveted circle of his most trusted students, and they were determined not to fail their teacher's expectations.

Jolie's eyes opened and she took in her new surroundings, feeling disconnected from her body.

A large oval ball of energy lingered by the fire, its colors swirling, mixing, and changing. When they came together with enough density, a hand appeared, part of a body...a face; it was Rose's face. She stood by the fire, wrapped in a blanket.

Jolie's eyes wandered over the lodge grounds. There was life everywhere; all of it connected. The spirit of the fire was connected to the stones, those spirits were connected to the fireman, and he was connected to the universe as well as to some of the people in the lodge area; each of them connected to the others. Even the stick stuck in the middle of the humped hill outside the lodge door, with its feathers spinning in the breeze, and the buffalo skull below it was connected. All of it glowed with life--not human life, but life, nevertheless, palpable and real.

Chapter Nineteen

Jolie looked over her shoulder at the Fus. Bodhi's essence was dark with demons of his own, while Hugo's carried the clarity of his genius and innocence.

"Hang on, Jolie." Hugo smiled, reassuringly, though he did not know that she could hear him. *"You can get through this."*

Jolie tried to smile back, but she wasn't sure she'd been successful. She didn't seem to have full control of her body.

When Jolie had been to the lodge before, she hadn't noticed the tall sticks guarding the edge of the ceremonial area, marking the four cardinal directions. She saw them now; bright balls of energy clothed in colored pieces of cotton.

Wards, she recognized them for what they were. *They've put wards around the lodge area.* In these, too, there was spirit. The energy of intent had given them life.

A complex spirit, vibrantly visual, with large sweeps of colorful energy surging and whirling around it, approached the gate in front of her.

"You boys are free to go back in the house," Hoke spoke from it. "Or sit here outside the lodge by the fire and wait. But if you stay, you must be quiet. You cannot interfere in any way. No matter what you see or hear. Do you understand?"

"Yes, sir." The boys nodded.

Another light being appeared as if it had come out of the fire. This one was a complicated combination of light and dark, brightness and shadow.

"This isn't a game, boys," Sifu's voice came from it. "This is the real thing, maybe more real than you're ready for right now, and that's okay." The man's physical self became more solid. He was medium height with a solid build, the posture of a stone fortress and shoulders like battlements. Backlit by the fire, Jolie couldn't see his face, only the long dark hair that spilled over his shoulders. "There's no dishonor in waiting in the house." He turned his body so that the firelight caught his strong, Native features. Dark intense eyes pinned the boys to a silent promise.

"I'll stay, Sifu." Bodhi's voice was steady.

"Me, too," Hugo agreed.

Sifu nodded. "Okay. I'll make sure they don't get in the way, Hoke."

"Wait here," Hoke told the boys. "We'll bring you inside the gate once we've smudged Jolie down and gotten her inside the circle." He turned to Remy. "You know what to do, nephew."

Remy carefully stood Jolie up, steadying her while his uncle retrieved a coffee can from his teacher. The can belched fragrant smoke. Jolie felt the demon stir as if he were waking. As the smoke began to envelope her he leapt to full attention.

"What are you doing?" it shrieked, inside Jolie.

Muttering under his breath in Lakota, Hoke used a large bird wing fan, sweeping Jolie off from head to toe, as if removing something invisible that clung to her.

"Turn her." Hoke continued brushing her off with the feather fan, moving the smoke over her as Remy slowly turned Jolie clockwise.

The demon quieted, its presence fading, weakening.

"The smudge is burning really strong," Remy's voice was so low that only the three of them could hear.

"You should expect that in a case like this," his uncle replied, finishing. "Okay, now let's see what happens when we bring her in."

Remy took Jolie's arm and began to lead her through the gate into the protected ceremonial grounds.

"Hell no," the demon growled using Jolie's vocal chords. "I'm not going in there."

Rose came quickly to Jolie's side and took her arm.

"It's okay, Jolie. You've been here before. There's nothing to hurt you here."

When Jolie looked at Rose, she saw the amazing Technicolor of her spirit. When the demon looked, he saw a strength and power that he wanted no part of.

"I said, I'm not going in there." He eyed the glowing wards protecting the sacred circle. His kind was not welcome.

"Then stay out here," Hoke replied, calmly. "Remy." He nodded to Remy to bring Jolie in.

"No." Jolie's eyes, darted back and forth, her body writhing and twisting to free itself from Remy's grasp. Remy did not let go.

"You said I didn't have to go in. You said I could stay out here," the demon protested.

"And 'you' can," Hoke said. "But Jolie is going in."

Jolie felt the demon's fear, but she was not afraid and because she was not, she could separate his feelings from hers.

"Bring me in," she said, struggling to find her own voice.

Hoke grinned. "There's that plucky girl, I met out in the desert."

Remy looked surprised. "You know each other?"

"Not in this world, but we have seen each other before. You stood against a thousand dark creatures that night," Hoke reminded her. "All you need to do now is stand up to one."

"Noooo." Sweat glistened like diamonds on Jolie's brow. Her eyes bugged from their sockets, her body moving like a snake trying to shed its old skin.

"Gently now," Rose murmured. "Walk with me, Jolie." Jolie's spirit stepped forward and out of her body.

Remy scooped up her physical form as it collapsed.

"I have you," Rose's spirit assured Jolie, folding the girl's spirit into her embrace. *"You're safe here with me."*

"Bring her in, Remy," Hoke commanded.

"Can this thing get past the flags?" Remy asked, glancing at the wards.

Hoke shrugged. "We invited Jolie in. I think it will depend on how deeply their energies are woven together. How long did you say it had been?"

"I'm not sure. Three weeks maybe. But you definitely think there's something there, right, Uncle Hoke?" Hoke raised an eyebrow. "Sorry. Dumb question."

As Remy carried Jolie's body past the wards into the lodge area her body shook like he had just fished her out of the Arctic Ocean.

Hoke got down on his hands and knees and crawled inside the lodge.

"You'll have to go back inside your body now, Jo, so that you can crawl in," Rose told Jolie. "Do you think you can do that?"

"Yes," Jolie answered.

"I'll be right here. Put her down, Remy. She'll be okay," Rose instructed. "I'm going to crawl in, Jo, then you follow."

Remy leaned into Jolie. "I'll be right behind you," he whispered.

"Put her in the east gate," Hoke commanded. "Once the stones are in, Remy, I want one of you on either side of her."

Jolie crawled in on her hands and knees, feeling the bare ground scrape the skin over her kneecaps. Small

Chapter Nineteen

stones bit into her palms as she crawled around the edge of a shallow pit that was at the center of the space.

"Follow my voice," Rose beckoned her forward. Jolie crawled to a point halfway around the circle before Rose stopped her. "That's good. Now just sit there and try to relax."

Jolie expected it to be dark inside, but sitting in the east, she could see right past the mound of dirt outside the door, all the way to the fire. Sifu stood beside the fire like a strong tree, holding a pitchfork, waiting, as she had seen Remy wait when he was the fireman.

As her eyes adjusted to the darkness, Jolie examined the inside of the lodge. It was small and cozy with a low ceiling, brightened by different colored blankets, their patterns, and colors warmed by the glow of the firelight coming in through the door. The framework itself was a loosely woven basket made of long flexible branches, turned upside down, then covered. It reminded Jolie of forts she'd made from tables and chairs and sheets when she was little. Long strands of tiny red bundles had been looped into the branches above her head, where they came together in a star pattern. Each of the bundles glowed faintly like a firefly was held inside.

Remy crawled in. His spirit was made up of two lights, like flames. All of the others; Rose, Hoke, Sifu, Hugo, each had only one. Bodhi had two as well, Jolie realized, wondering at the significance.

"Remy has two spirit lights," she commented.

"Yes," Rose agreed, softly. "It is part of what makes him special."

Hoke leaned forward and began to draw a design in the dirt at the bottom of the pit.

Sifu crouched by the side of the doorway.

"Chanchega." Sifu handed in a drum that was passed to Rose. "Do your students know how to handle stones, Sifu?" Hoke asked him.

The man chuckled. "They know how to follow directions and how to be respectful."

"Then they can help you if you want. It's a lot of stones for an old man." The humor reflected the long friendship between them. "Okay, bring in the Grandfathers," Hoke said, quietly.

"How many?" Sifu asked.

"All of them."

The first seven stones were brought in one at a time and placed with care in the pit. Rose whispered to them as if greeting old friends or honored guests, placing fragrant herbs on each as they were placed in the pit. The herbs sizzled and burned, filling the lodge with strange smells that seemed to speak to something very ancient and basic within her. Jolie could see the faces of spirits in the stones, glowing at her from the darkness, as if putting them in the fire had revealed their true nature.

Her attention was drawn upward. Tiny flickering spirits, like fairy lights, flitted through the stick-woven star at the center of the ceiling.

"Are you doing okay, Jo?" Rose asked, softly.

"I'm good."

Rose followed her gaze. "You see the uwipi?"

"Is that what they are?"

"That's what we call them. Who knows what they 'are'? They are part of the mystery."

Hugo and Bodhi began helping Sifu, bringing pitchforks heavy with glowing hot stones to the doorway, then sliding them inside where Remy took charge of settling them in the pit. As the smoke in the lodge grew thicker, the demon's fear once again rose, the

Chapter Nineteen

tension building. The air became thick and stifling and Jolie felt as if she would either wilt or bolt outside.

"Sit up as long as you can," Rose advised. "But if you can't sit anymore lay down on the Grandmother." She patted the ground. "Lay right against her breast. Give her your burdens and ask her for strength."

Jolie nodded. Hugo's face appeared at the doorway, lit by the glowing hot stones he carried on the pitchfork. Caution, care, and worry made him look much older than his years. His eyes searched the smoke for his friends. Hugo disappeared and Bodhi replaced him at the door, subdued and uncertain.

"That's all of them," Sifu announced when the pile of stones had overfilled the pit. The heat was stifling.

"M'ni." Hoke addressed Sifu who then handed in a bucket of water. "Close the door."

Sifu drew a door flap over the opening, tucking down the edges until no light leaked in anywhere. Inside the lodge it was completely dark, except for the uwipi, flickering above their heads.

The world seemed to hold its breath, waiting for what would come next.

Jolie looked up at the ceiling again and there was no ceiling. The blankets that had covered the top of the lodge had melted away to reveal the sky with layer upon layer of stars winking down at her.

It's just like Iris said, Jolie felt her heart lift. *It's amazing.* Uwipi played and tumbled around her head.

The demon panicked.

"I think I'm going to be sick." Jolie gagged.

"That's okay," Rose handed her a small bucket.

"Just imagine you've swallowed something really nasty and let it all out," Hoke told her.

Rose began a slow heartbeat rhythm on her drum, raising her clear contralto, calling the spirits to come and help them.

A gentle rain of juniper-scented water began to sprinkle over Jolie's head and shoulders. She raised her face to the cleansing water and wept, adding her own silent voice to the prayer.

"Help us because we are only poor pitiful people but we want to live. Help us. We want to be better and walk this Red Road in a good way."

CHAPTER TWENTY

In the morning, Jolie found herself tucked in under the star quilt in Rose's back bedroom.

Hello? Is anybody there?

She turned her attention inward, tentatively scanning for the demon's presence within her. Not a growl responded.

They're gone. A sense of relief swept through her.

The events of the night before were like bits of smashed china. Looking at the different pieces you could suss out something of the original pattern, but the shards would never fit back together into a whole.

Jolie remembered the uwipi flitting around her head, weaving in and out of the woven star structure at the top of the lodge. She remembered the magical way the lodge's coverings had disappeared so that she could look out at the night sky and see all the layers of stars.

There were other less pleasant memories, too: confused images her brain was already overwriting. Some memories just didn't earn a "cherished" definition. Being possessed was definitely one of them. Jolie might never remember everything about the previous night, but she was okay with that. Having a demon banished from you in the presence of your boyfriend was akin to upchucking onstage in front of the whole student body.

Jolie took a long slow deep breath, feeling the energy moving freely through her. There was dirt between her toes and under her fingernails. She got out of bed. Her jeans and shirt had disappeared but she was dressed in a clean cotton shift like the ones Rose used for lodges. Her hair, caked with dust and frizzed from steam, was wild and stiff, threatening to curl into dreadlocks. Her cheeks were smeared with dirt.

She caught an image of herself in the round frameless dressing mirror, confirming she was a mess.

It didn't matter; she was finally free.

Jolie picked up her shoes and padded out to the main room of the house.

The morning sun flooded the big room, dust moats dancing on sunbeams as they tumbled along to the floor.

"Rose?" she called out.

"I'm out here, Jo," her hostess answered from out back.

Jolie hesitated, lingering in the doorway. She had never been in this part of the property before. The high curved wall of the courtyard swept in and out like the changing course of a river. Made of mud, red sand, and clay, its surface had been polished to a subtle sheen. The courtyard floor was covered with red stone pavers and fine red gravel. A large mesquite tree grew in the center of the yard, gently shading everything from the incessant Southwestern sun.

A wrought iron gate led out of the courtyard toward the south where Jolie could see a pair of horses munching hay.

A round earthen oven had been built into one of the alcoves in the courtyard's curved wall. A long handled wooden paddle lay on the flat surface next to the oven. A basket covered by a cotton towel could only be fresh bread from the smell of it. Jolie's mouth began to water. When was the last time she had eaten? She couldn't remember.

A larger silver kiln and a potter's wheel sat in the center of the area to her left, its legs splattered with red sand from rains past. At the end of the courtyard, three weathered garbage cans sat pressed against the mud wall. Beside them, blocks of clay, a box of red sand, and bits of broken pottery had been organized onto rough wooden shelves. Dried mesquite leaves and cobwebs told the story of their abandonment.

Rose was at the other end of the courtyard, sitting behind a large free-standing loom, weaving: her suntanned hands deftly winding and tying off wool threads.

Jolie drifted forward.

"That's really beautiful," she told Rose.

"It's a pictorial style piece," Rose explained.

"It looks like a sunset?" Jolie pointed. "And those designs look like mountains?"

"Yes. You have a good eye." Rose began to unbind a different set of threads, preparing to work with them.

"How do you figure out the geometric patterns you use on the edge?

Rose shrugged. "They just come to me."

"Do they have symbolic meaning, or are they just shapes?"

Rose laughed softly. "Well now, that's kind of a loaded question. Is anything an artist does just shapes?"

"I'm sorry. I didn't mean to be disrespectful," Jolie apologized.

"You weren't. It's an honest question. Some university did a study and found that some of the patterns that traditional weavers have been using for centuries look remarkably like DNA. Of course, weavers were using the patterns long before anyone knew anything about DNA, so the discovery increases the mystery for one school of thought and validates the Great Mystery for another. So, your question, do the shapes have meaning? Maybe more than we understand."

Jolie gazed wistfully at the weaver's work. "When did you start weaving, Rose?"

"One of my Auntie's was from the Dine' people, the Hopi. She taught me when I was a little girl, but I didn't come back to it until I was much older."

"Why? You're so good at it."

"I just lost my way for awhile during my early twenties. My birth family was not traditional. I grew up seeing the worst parts of the white world. I was a mature woman before I found the Red Road. This place and the man who brought me here gave me the patience to reconnect with what I had lost." She smiled at Jolie. "So, how are you feeling today?"

Jolie looked at the blue sky and the red mountains breathed in the desert scents of sage and chaparral and smiled.

"Like somebody gave my insides a good spring cleaning."

Rose nodded. "You're going to be very open right now--too vulnerable to be out in the world. You'll need to take special care of yourself, at least for the next four days. It's best to try to avoid difficult people and situations."

Jolie wondered how she was going to do that. "It's Friday. I should be at school."

"I think under the circumstances, they'll understand," Rose suggested.

"Yeah, I guess. I do need to go to the hospital though and see my mom."

"Remy will take you when he gets out of school. She won't be released for a few days, though. I thought maybe you'd like to stay here for the time being?"

Jolie bit her lip. "I don't want to be any trouble."

"It's no trouble. I'm glad to have the company." Rose glanced at the potter's wheel at the far end of the

Chapter Twenty

courtyard. "My husband and I always lived isolated lives together." Jolie looked at the abandoned potter's wheel and understood that Rose's husband had been the potter, but he had died, and now she lived alone. "You're not exactly a chatterbox, so I think we'll manage for a few days. It would be nice to have someone around but not underfoot. You might want to spend some time exploring the Basin."

"I'd like that," Jolie agreed.

"Good. The number for the hospital is by the phone." Rose went back to her work. "When Remy comes, he can take you back to your apartment to get whatever you need."

"Do you know where my jeans are?" Jolie plucked at the cotton shift.

"They're in a bundle by the fire pit." Rose lifted her chin in the direction of the lodge. "I thought you might want to burn them as a symbolic gesture of closure after what happened."

Jolie thought about that. "It's a nice idea, but I don't have that many clothes," she admitted, feeling a little awkward about admitting it.

"Then we'll just wash them." Rose smiled.

"Maybe I could hang them out in the sun to dry," Jolie suggested. "That ought to get rid of any bad juju that's left."

"There's no bad juju left for you to worry about, Jo. That's been taken care of," Rose assured her. "There's fresh bread in the basket there. Just tear some off, and there's lots of leftovers from the last feast. You can rummage around in the fridge until you find something that looks good.

Jolie helped herself to a hunk of bread.

"This is amazing, Rose," she muttered as the bread's warmth filled her mouth, spreading comfort through her distressed body.

"I thought that would hit the spot. I don't think you had anything left in your stomach after last night."

"You could probably see right through me."

"There were moments," Rose agreed.

Jolie popped the last bite of bread into her mouth and went back inside the house. The hospital's number was where Rose had said, right by the phone, but Jolie couldn't quite face thinking about Jessie Lynn and the future yet. She found some fruit salad in the fridge, poured herself a glass of orange juice, then went back to sit on the step in the doorway where she could watch Rose work.

The Native woman hummed as she wove the wool weft threads through the vertical warp strings, pushing them down firmly into place with a wooden stick.

"Why do the spirits come when you sing those songs, Rose?" Jolie asked. "I've seen them coming. I know it's not just music."

"A spirit calling song is a prayer. We don't sing sacred songs just anyplace or without the intention of them having an effect. We only sing them when we mean it. That way they keep their power."

Jolie considered the explanation while eating a second piece of bread.

"There are a lot of spirits in this place," she noted.

"Red earth: it's ancient sacred land," Rose agreed.

"Sacred to your people?"

"This is Paiute land." Rose continued to work as she talked, taking some threads and weaving them into the pattern, then tying them off and moving to others. "But some places are sacred to all people. You feel it when you are near them." She pushed down the newly woven

Chapter Twenty

threads, sliding them into place within the pattern. "There is just something special about them, like the earth's awareness, is very close in those spots. Sometimes, when I am working here and all the tourists have left the Basin, it gets very quiet, and I feel like I can hear spirits talking." Rose stopped, listening. "Like that just there." The weaver seemed to exude light, her face sweetly joyful. "Did you hear that?"

"No," Jolie admitted. She longed to feel the kind of peace that Rose lived with here. She had never been anywhere the energy was so strong, but there was also a real world outside of the basin, and that was where Jolie had to live.

"Whenever I look out at Red Rock, no matter where I am in the city, it just makes me smile," she confessed.

"A lot of people feel that," Rose said. "You've seen how the tourists stop just over the rise when they first see the red mountains? They feel it, too. They just don't know what it is. There are other sacred places that give you this feeling of awe or joy. There are also others that feel terribly sad, or incredibly powerful, even some that are downright frightening, especially after sundown."

"You're not Paiute are you, Rose? I thought you were Lakota, like Remy?"

"My husband was Lakota, but there are not so many of us who follow a traditional path here in Las Vegas that we can afford to be exclusive. Remy and I are not blood family, but we are lodge family. He calls me auntie out of respect."

"But Hoke is his blood uncle, right?"

"Yes. Hoke is Remy's mother's older brother, that is why he teaches Remy. It is the traditional role of the mother's brother." Her eyes wandered again to the abandoned potter's wheel. "We honor the gift of those who have come before us by passing their teaching on to a new generation."

Jolie let the deep silence of the desert basin settle around them, thinking about what Rose had said.

"Would you teach me, Rose?" she asked after a few minutes.

Rose smiled. "What is it you want to learn, Jolie? You already see the world as it is, not as most people see it, and I suspect that you have had that ability for a long time."

"My whole life," Jolie admitted.

"You are very lucky not to have unlearned what you saw, and understood naturally as a child." Rose continued weaving the tapestry before her as she talked. "You never pushed away your truth to accept other people's view of the world."

"It wasn't a conscious choice. I'm not brave or smart," Jolie insisted. "If I could have thrown this gift away, I would have done it in a minute. If I'd believed that my prayers would be answered, I would have prayed until my knees were raw just to be like other people."

Rose seemed to think about this for awhile before she spoke again. "Henry taught me that it's right and correct to see the world as connected and alive. Treating it like it's separate and inanimate is what causes us so many problems.

"There are good people and bad people among us, Jolie. It is when we accept our true nature and realize we are beings of infinite magic that our path begins to become more clear. Spiritual seekers throughout history have put themselves through terrible trials trying for a few moments of what you live with every day: true sight. What more is it that you are looking for, Jo?"

"Answers. Understanding," Jolie replied. "It's true that I see things. but I don't understand them, and I have no idea what I am supposed to do about them. You know how these things work, Rose. I need to know how to control things. You can teach me that."

Rose frowned. "Only a foolish, or a very egotistical person would try to do that. I am neither. Don't make me into something I'm not, Jolie. I'm a weaver who sometimes pours water. I am just a common woman."

Yeah, and Hoke is just a cowboy, Jolie thought.

"Come crawl into a lodge with the women," Rose encouraged Jolie. "You'll learn a lot about yourself. The women are very compassionate with newcomers."

"Could Hoke teach me? " Jolie persisted.

Rose frowned. "It would not be appropriate for Hoke to teach a young woman."

"He couldn't teach me because I'm a girl? Seriously?"

"The Lakota have a lot of rules, Jo. Sometimes a modern woman can find them hard to understand, but keeping the old ways is how we honor our teachers." Rose shrugged. "People who can't make their peace with that, move on and find something else. But once you start looking for your truth, it doesn't matter if you stop along the way to rest, or take a fork in the road. What matters is that you have begun. Everything that comes afterward is part of the journey."

Rose wove a new line while Jolie watched, giving silence another turn in their conversation.

"What is that blue line that you're adding, there, Rose?" Jolie pointed to the new strand. The rest of the threads were in purples and grays, progressing from deep, saturated colors to paler shades as the weaving advanced.

"That thread is you."

"Me? Why did you weave me in?"

"Because you needed a place to belong.

Jolie followed the sinuous blue line weaving its bulkier, less cultivated wool through the pattern. It disrupted the established pattern but gave the weaving a focal point, a character that pulled the whole design together. Jolie felt her chest swell.

"You're not going to tell anybody, are you?" she whispered.

"No. I won't tell anyone," Rose answered. "It is just for you and me and the thread to know. Now, if you've finished your breakfast, there's a package of tobacco on the coffee table. You might want to take it with you when you go exploring."

"I don't smoke."

Rose chuckled. "It's not to smoke, honey. I thought you might want to thank the spirits for their help last night. It's good manners to offer something in return and tobacco is traditional."

"I wouldn't know what to say."

"Just say: 'ho, mitakuye oyasin', or you can say the English version: all my relations. Then take some tobacco in your hand, and say the words that come into your heart. When you're done, let the tobacco go." Jolie turned back into the house. "Watch the sky," Rose added. "And stay out of the washes if it starts to rain. There are thunderheads building in the southeast. " She gave Jolie an encouraging smile.

Jolie found her tennis shoes by the door, picked up the tobacco pouch and a bottle of water from the twelve pack on the floor. With one more look at the number by the phone, she turned, and stepped out of the house.

CHAPTER TWENTY-ONE

Jolie's feet crunched in the dusty gravel. Ruts and potholes littered the rural dirt road. In some places, some past rainstorm had washed the road out, reducing it to a single lane. It didn't rain often in Southern Nevada, but when it did, the deluge could instantly change the terrain. Creek beds, dry for most of the year, altered their courses, trees were uprooted, and the asphalt layer on roads disappeared, simply washed away.

Taking the branch of the road that leads toward the mountain, Jolie followed it. It ended not far away at a weathered split-rail fence marking the beginning of the Bureau of Land Management's territory. The path narrowed to a single person footpath as it lead out into the wild.

Surrounded by the mountains that cradled Calico Basin, Jolie could neither see nor hear Las Vegas over the hills to the east. Instead, birds called in sweet sound bites. A lizard drew lazy "S"s in the red sand with its tail. A burrow brayed.

Jolie stopped and closed her eyes. She could have been a hundred miles from Las Vegas, or on a different world. Listening to the wind whisper secrets to the red hills, she felt the tickle of attention that was focused on her and understood that its source was not human. She opened her eyes and looked up at the huge pink mountain.

"Ho, mitakuye oyasin," she sent her own whisper out on the wind.

"Once you set your foot on the path...." Rose had said. Jolie looked down at her Converse high tops. Any part that had been white was now pink: laces, rubber toes, the sides that edged the sole. She took them off, removing her socks as well. Sticking the socks down inside the shoes, she tied the laces together and threw them over her shoulder, wriggling her toes down into the fine red sand. The smooth grains slipped between her toes like silk, changing from warm at the surface to a luxurious coolness several inches below.

Rose said that Jolie was fortunate in her gifts and the understanding they gave her. Faith had believed that too, but Jolie never felt fortunate. She struggled, wishing she could be someone else. It never changed anything, though. Time only made her feel more miserable, alienated, and disenfranchised. Maybe her friends were right. Maybe it was time to accept herself as she was and embrace the future that came of it.

Jessie Lynn had never seen any special worth in her daughter's abilities, and being young, Jolie naturally followed her mother's example, never seeing anything in them herself. It was a mystery to the troubled teen why others did. Jolie didn't recognize the person her friends saw in her, but then, you couldn't really appreciate someone if you spent all your time wishing they were someone else.

The cell phone in Jolie's pocket buzzed. Surprised there was service out here in the basin, Jolie looked to see who it was.

It was Iris. The older woman had left a few messages, encouraging Jolie to reach out when she was ready to talk, letting her young friend know that even though Faith was gone, she was still thinking about her. Jolie hadn't been able to face talking to Iris with everything else that was going on. They hadn't seen each other since the memorial, so it was expected that they would talk about Faith, or would try so hard not to that it would hurt as if they had. How would Jolie explain what was going on in her life? Iris had enough to deal with in settling Faith's estate. She didn't need to worry about Jolie's demonic possession. But things were better now, and it was cowardly to keep avoiding her friend.

Jolie pressed the screen on her cell phone and answered.

"Hi, Iris. I'm sorry I didn't call or text back. Things have been pretty weird around here lately." Jolie kept her emotions in tight check. She and Iris both prided themselves on being unemotional types, and Jolie didn't want to embarrass herself by blubbering to her friend the first time they talked after so long.

"I knew we'd get together eventually," Iris said in her crisp East Coast Yankee style. "So, school is okay? Home is...?

"Home is...." Jolie realized how much had gone on that Iris didn't know about. She took a deep breath. "Mom is in the hospital." If Iris hadn't realized that Jolie was trying to mask her pain before, she got it now.

"Oh my god, honey. Is she alright? What happened?"

Tears welled in Jolie's eyes. She wiped them away, glad that Iris couldn't see her.

"Rick shot her," Jolie's voice cracked. Talking about it brought it all back too vividly. "He found out where she worked, went there, and shot her."

"Jolie! When did this happen?"

"Uh, yesterday, I guess."

"Yesterday? Was this what that call was about? You didn't leave a message."

E.F. Winters

"I didn't call--at least I don't remember calling, but things are a little fuzzy. My friends might have called looking for a ride. It doesn't matter."

"The hell it doesn't," Iris disagreed.

"Everything's been just a crazy blur, you know?" Jolie went on. "And I haven't been in any condition to call anyone, but it's better now. Really, it is."

"Where are you?" Iris demanded. "At the apartment? I'm coming to get you."

"No, don't, Iris. I'm fine. A friend took me in." Jolie's voice quavered.

"Tell me what I can do, Jo, please," Iris insisted. "I feel so awful that you've gone through this alone, and so soon after Faith..." she didn't need to finish. "I should have been there."

Jolie shook her head in silent disagreement with her friend's assumption that what Jolie needed was an adult to fix everything.

"Everything's fine now, really," she repeated, feeling stronger. "The ambulance got there in time, and the police arrested Rick." She was going for the short version. "So the excitement is over."

"Honestly, Jo, let me come and get you."

"I appreciate the offer, Iris, but it's not necessary." Jolie looked around at the red mountains. "It's good here. Remy's aunt's ranch is in Red Rock and she's a really nice lady. I think it's better for me right now, to be out of the city."

Iris hesitated. "Okay. If you're sure?"

"I am. They've invited me to stay until mom is out of the hospital, so I'm going to do that. It's not that I don't want to see you, Iris. It's just that I'm kind of overwhelmed right now, and here, I have space to sort things out. I've got a lot of that to do."

Chapter Twenty One

"Okay. But if you need a shoulder, or an ear, or a shopping trip, or anything, you'll call, right? I mean it, Jo. Anything."

"Thanks. I'll talk to you again in a few days. I promise."

"Okay, honey. We need to talk about Faith's will. When you're ready."

"Yeah. I asked her to leave me my favorite teacup as a remembrance. Will you keep it for me, for now?"

"Of course," Iris said gently. "We'll talk about it later when things have settled down. There's no hurry."

"Okay. Thanks. Later." Jolie hung up and straightened her shoulders. With a breath of resolution, she took one step and then another along the red sand path.

Let this be the beginning of my journey as someone who can see, not just the problems, but the possibilities, she vowed, silently.

The narrow path branched off left and right. Standing at the intersection, as if guarding invisible gates, were two very large ravens. Behind them, the burro herd grazed, watched over by the old black jack. As Jolie drew closer, the jack raised his head and looked at her.

Voices drifted down from the path to the west. The jack's ears perked up, listening. Turning his head, he looked east, then looked back at Jolie.

"Okay, east it is." Jolie turned onto the path that curved around the east end of the mountain, jogging, then running, carried along by the buoyancy of the red earth, feeling it flood into the dark holes where the demon had burrowed, filling those empty places with a fresh and vibrant joy.

She felt triumphant and ridiculous, marvelous and amazing like she could do anything and become anyone.

Her old sarcastic self laughed at the hubris of this naive happiness.

"Shut up," she told it. "I'm alive and free and I deserve to celebrate it."

Boulders that had splintered off from the heights of the pink mountain and fallen to the desert floor during the last several thousand years, now hunkered at its foot, scattered among the chaparral, sage, and agaves. Jolie veered off the path and made her way to a large flat-topped rock. Scrambling up, she sat facing the mountain.

"I feel like a little girl sitting here," she said, speaking to the pink mountain. "Like I was sitting next to Mem again. Maybe if like they say, all energy is connected, then some part of her has become part of you and has been waiting here for me. Well, I've come now, Mem. I made it."

All of the problems that Jolie had been trying to hide from, suddenly crashed over her like a tsunami.

"Show me what to do. Show me who I'm supposed to be." Tears pooled over the dams of her eyes. "Because I don't know." Jolie lifted her tearful face to the mountain.

The events of the last few weeks had nearly broken her, but she had made it through. It was time to begin the process of rebuilding, but there was no pattern, no plan for her to follow. She pulled out the package of tobacco and opened it.

What should she say? Praying was something other people did; people like Father Owen, who kept a bible on their bookshelf, people who held to a set of rules that had no place for someone like her. But Rose had not sent her out to the desert to pray. She had sent her out to explore, and given her the tools to say thank you for the healing she had received.

Chapter Twenty One

"That I can do." Jolie dug out a handful of tobacco and held it up in the air. "Ho, mitakuye oyasin," she repeated the phrase that Rose had taught her.

The world hushed as if to listen. Jolie paused, formulating her thoughts around what weighed most heavily on her heart.

"Show me how to protect Remy." A lump rose, blocking her throat. *He should live,* she continued, forming her thoughts in the silence with the basin as witness. *The world needs him. His people need him. Help keep him safe.* Opening her hand, she let the shredded tobacco scatter over the desert on the quickening wind.

Clouds had been moving in as she sat on the rock, and now the sky rumbled. It was already raining somewhere to the west; Jolie could smell it on the wind. The bushes rattled like dried beans poured from a barrel. Jolie closed her eyes and let the storm climb over her.

Moisture crowded the air as the clouds released raindrops that evaporated before reaching the ground: virga, they called it. The subverted rain dripped from the sky like water color paints spreading over wet paper.

The wind wrapped her dress around her ankles and tugged at her dust coated hair. Thunder crackled across the sky, echoing off the red cliffs.

Big, juicy raindrops began to plop onto the dry, sun-scorched earth: one, then two, and three, until the clouds gave up their hoard and it became a stampede, millions of drops punching little hollows in the red sand.

Jolie held up a hand to catch the precious drops in her dusty palms. She leaned her head back, her face to the sky, and let the rain wash away her tears and the cares that had brought them. It was a new start and the rain's renewal of the thirsty earth, mirrored her own.

Waterfalls began to flow from crevices all around the red cliff, seeking the lowest point. The roar of a flash flood pounded the ravine to the north of the pink mountain.

Jolie jumped off the boulder and ran toward the sound. At the easternmost edge of the mountain, a large rock slab, fallen long ago, had wedged itself against a boulder, creating a small cave. Soaked to the skin, her hair and dress clinging to whatever part of her it touched, Jolie ran along the path toward the stone shelter, her bare feet crusted with wet red sand.

To her right, the plateau of land at the foot of the mountain dropped off into a box canyon of deep red stone. All of the rain from the north cliffs was now flowing to the upper ravine, gathering mass and racing toward the drop off that separated the upper and lower canyons.

Jolie walked cautiously to the edge and looked over. The deluge was coming so heavy now, that she could barely see through the sheet of gray.

A gush of riotous water plunged over the edge of the upper ravine, making a waterfall that only ran when it rained this hard in the basin. It was a phenomenon that few would ever see, Jolie realized.

The box canyon below had been a dry creek bed just minutes before, but the rainstorm had transformed it into a raging river. The sound was deafening.

Another clap of thunder split the roar and Jolie looked up. On the far side of the canyon, Yanna Maria stood, glaring down at her.

"Where is the demon?" the fortune teller demanded, imperiously.

"Gone," Jolie answered. *"Hoke sent it away."* Another thunderbolt struck the ground, this time very close to Jolie. She jumped in surprise but did not cower.

Chapter Twenty One

With the pink mountain at her back, she faced the fortune tellers' displeasure. *"You said you would help me get rid of it. You didn't. Hoke did."*

"What did he do with it?" Yanna Maria wanted to know.

"Ask him. I don't know and I don't care."

"Foolish girl," the woman growled. The fortune teller's image faded into the falling rain. Jolie turned back to the shelter of the cave, crouching and hugging her knees for warmth, as the storm raged, water rushing over the cliff.

Yanna Maria's ideas about what Hoke had done weren't important, she told herself. The demon was gone. That was what mattered. It was over.

As suddenly as it had come in, the storm passed. The clouds parted, the sun came out, and the sky went back to its accustomed bright blue.

The dust had been washed from the world, making it sparkle. The colors of the rocks became deeper and brighter. Every tiny desert flower released its subtle fragrance combining into a perfume that could not be bottled.

Jolie's were the first footprints pressed into the freshly washed sand. She headed back to Rose's.

As she approached the house, she saw an old Jeep Wagoneer parked out front, mud caked its wheels.

Yanna Maria was leaning against it, her arms wrapped in a shawl and crossed over her bosom, her brown lips pulled tight.

"Hoke did a wipe down? Rose should have called me." The woman scowled.

"Why would she?" Jolie asked. "As far as Rose is concerned, we haven't even met."

"So, you have kept our secret?"

"Yes," Jolie answered, wondering why Yanna Maria thought keeping their arrangement from the others was necessary.

"Good," Yanna Maria said, but she did not look as if she meant it. "Rose says you will be coming to lodges now. Then we will be seeing more of each other. We will become lodge sisters."

Jolie found the suggestion less than encouraging.

"Won't that make our "secret" harder to keep?"

Yanna Maria glowered. "The full nature of our relationship will remain hidden," she insisted.

"Why exactly is that, Yanna Maria?" Jolie demanded, her tone bordering on insolent.

"Because uppity apprentices can't resist making people think that they know more than they do, and they must be protected from themselves," the fortune teller replied, maintaining a tone of challenge. "You let me know if you have any questions about what you see or experience in the lodge. I will answer them for you."

"I'll keep that in mind if I decide I want to become someone's apprentice."

Yanna Maria snorted. "We are alike in many ways, you and I. The spiritual path is one of power, Jolie. If you are going to embrace your power, you will need a guide as fearless as you are. You will not find that in there." She tossed her head toward Rose's.

"Hoke seems brave enough."

"He will teach you nothing." Yanna Maria spat on the ground. "You are a woman."

"And it is not the Lakota way for a man to teach a woman," Jolie finished for her. "Yeah, I heard."

"A convenient excuse for hoarding knowledge. He won't teach us, but he will teach that boy, his nephew. When you are ready to take the next step, you know where to find me." Yanna Maria wrapped her shawl

Chapter Twenty One

around her, got into her Jeep and drove off through the puddles.

CHAPTER TWENTY-TWO

"It's just me, Mom." Jolie dropped her backpack by the door as she entered the apartment, sighing as she took in the mess. Jessie Lynn was laid up, or maybe laid down was a better description. All she'd done since she came home from the hospital was lay around on the couch or in bed, watching TV, and flipping through gossip magazines.

"She seems to get around just fine when I'm not home," Jolie grumbled, picking up a shirt and a bra that had been tossed over the back of the couch.

"Jolie, can you get me a Coke, baby? I'm dying of thirst," Jessie called from her room.

Jolie went to the kitchen and opened the fridge. There wasn't much in it, and there were no sodas. Jolie had bought a six pack yesterday. Two had gone the first night. Two were on the dining room table and two more were adding rings to the already stained coffee table. Jolie went to the sink and filled a glass with water.

The blinds in Jessie's room were down, the window half closed over a box fan that blew warm air into the stuffy room. In a few weeks, when the valley's temperatures hit triple digits, there would be no question of going without air conditioning, but in the upper eighties, the dry heat was livable, and the issue of how they were going to survive while Jessie Lynn was laid up, had not been resolved.

"Thanks." Jessie Lynn grabbed the glass and took a sip. "Blah. What's this? Water?"

"Yea," Jolie confirmed the obvious.

"And tap water at that. What are you trying to do, poison me? You know I don't drink that shit. It tastes like a swimming pool."

"There isn't anything else, Mom. You drank all the sodas and we can't afford bottled water anymore. You don't have a job, remember?"

"My disability money is going to kick in any day now," Jessie said as if her own determination was all it would take to make it happen.

"Well, when it does, we can buy more groceries, but a temporary disability check is not going to pay for a six pack a day soda habit to replace the beer you're not drinking."

"Don't be mean, Jo. I'm bored and I'm in pain. What else is there for me to do here all alone all day? Anyway, stop worrying, we'll be fine. Brett said he'd help out."

That stopped Jolie. "You can't ask Brett for money, Mom," she objected.

"Why not? He's got plenty, and he wants to help us out."

"There's plenty wrong with it, and you know why," Jolie argued. "Isn't it bad enough that you got him involved in all this in the first place, fighting with Rick?"

"Rick will no longer be a problem," Jessie declared.

"Until he posts bail or gets out on parole. Rick is a vengeful moron. Brett could find himself in the middle of all kinds of problems that he didn't ask for. And you know that owing someone for that kind of help opens doors that aren't easily shut. We talked about this. It puts us in Brett's debt and makes you feel like you have to say yes when you should say no." It was just the kind of poor judgment that had marked the beginning of more than one of Jessie Lynn's romantic entanglements, ending in her and Jolie making a late night getaway across the nearest state line. Some people learned from their mistakes. Jessie Lynn was a practice makes perfect girl with a penchant for self-delusion.

The door bell rang.

"Speak of the delicious devil," Jessie Lynn re-arranged her hippie girl skirt so that it covered her injured leg. "That will be Brett now."

"Hello? Jessie?" Brett opened the door a crack and stuck his head in.

"Come on in, darling. Jolie and I are back here," Jessie chimed, musically.

Jolie should have realized that Brett was expected. Jessie Lynn had dressed for the occasion, putting on a tight, low-cut tank top. The crinkly material of the long skirt was so light and thin, that when she bent her good leg, it showed off its shapeliness. Conveniently, it was also easy to get up, get down, or get off. Jessie had full war paint makeup on her face, and her nails on both the good arm and the broken one had been freshly pinked and shellacked. She was ready for the hunt, and she was the bait.

"I almost feel sorry for him," Jolie muttered.

"There's my sweet man," Jessie held out her arms and puckered her lipsticked lips for a kiss.

"You're looking better," Brett complimented Jessie as he came in, handing her a bouquet of flowers. Jolie added up what a dozen roses cost, wishing Brett had been more practical and brought them dinner.

"How sweet. You're such a gentleman." Jessie dutifully stuck her nose in the bouquet. Brett nodded to Jolie.

"How do you feel?" he asked Jessie, glancing at her injured leg.

"Better, now that you're here." Jessie flirted.

Chapter Twenty Two

Brett didn't seem to notice. He rolled the brim of his cowboy hat, turning the hat slowly in his hands. Something was on his mind.

"So, I've had a full day," he announced. "Do you want the good news or the bad news first?"

Jessie's eyes flashed. "I don't want any bad news, anymore, ever. You can keep that to yourself, but you can tell me the good news."

"I talked to my friend Chase today. He has a place out in Tecopa, and he's agreed to let you stay there until you can get on your feet, free of charge, of course." He looked at them, expectantly.

"Tecopa? Where is Tecopa?" Jolie asked, googling it on her phone.

"And why would we want to live there, Brett?" Jessie questioned him, taken aback. "We have an apartment."

"But you can't keep it. You know that, Jess. If you're not working, you can't afford this place. It's too expensive."

"I'll get disability," Jessie insisted, puckering up for a pout.

Brett shook his head. "I had my lawyer check. You're not going to be out of work long enough to save the apartment. Disability won't kick in until after eight weeks, and your doctor said he could release you in a month or so."

"That was just an estimate." Jessie crossed her arms over her chest, increasing her cleavage. Brett gave her a moment to calm down.

"Look, you need to think realistically, Jess. Next week is the end of the month, and your rent's going to be due."

"I know, but you said that you were going to help," Jessie whined.

"I am helping. Having this house in Tecopa means you'll be okay. You can stay as long as you need to get well, and you won't end up homeless. And because Chase is letting you stay for nothing, I can take care of the utility expenses, and get you set up with groceries." He looked at Jolie. "This will make whatever you have saved stretch further, and when you're well and can work again, you can get a new job, come back and start again."

"Tecopa, California?" Jolie asked Brett. "That's ninety miles away. Isn't that like out where Charles Manson and weirdos lived?" Jolie wanted to shout *How can you do this to me?* but she knew that adults made decisions all the time without considering what it would do to kids' lives. She understood that Brett was trying to help, but who was he to make these kind of decisions for them? He was just some casual do-gooder, trying to make himself feel better after banging her mom for free for a few months. Remy was still in danger. She had friends here. Tru's wedding was in a week. After all the months and months of hating Las Vegas, why did this have to happen, when things were finally turning around?

"I can't leave now, Mom. You know I can't," Jolie protested. "What about school?"

"There's a high school in Shoshone. It's small but..." Brett let the sentence fall off without finishing it. "And there's a library with internet access, so taking classes online would be another option."

"And what about you, Brett?" Jessie Lynn asked quietly. "When will I see you if I'm all the way out in Tecopa?"

"Well, that's the bad news, Jess. My business here is done, so I'm headed back up north at the first of the month."

Chapter Twenty Two

Jessie looked stunned. This was not how she'd thought today was going to play out.

"I'll stay to see you settled in," Brett went on. "But I've got a business and a ranch to run in Montana, and I need to get back to it. I reserved a truck to move your things this weekend."

"Well, it seems like you've just taken care of everything," Jessie said. There was an edge to her voice. "That was real friendly of you."

"I'm sorry, Jess. I know the timing is not great, but we always knew this was coming. I never made a secret of the fact that I was here for a short time, and that I would be going back."

Jessie Lynn's smile was forced. Saying anything would only make her look weak, and weak was not desirable. As long as she put a good face on Brett's departure, there was always a chance that he'd have second thoughts, that he'd miss her, or realize what a wonderful woman she was, and come back for her. She had watched Pretty Woman way too many times.

"Don't give it a second thought, honey. You've been more than generous," she said, smiling through the lie. "You're a good friend."

Brett turned to Jolie. "Jo, can you help me get some stuff out of the car?" Jolie followed him outside. There were several sacks of groceries in the back seat.

"I didn't want to give your mom money because I wasn't sure what she'd do with it. She's uh ..."

"An impulsive alcoholic?" Jolie finished for him, silently wanting to point out that if Jessie Lynn had not been impulsive, he would not have gotten laid so easily, or so often on such a short acquaintance. "It's okay, Brett, I know how my mom balances her checkbook."

"I'm sorry if I've offended you, or if that was disrespectful to your mother, Jo. I just want to make sure that there's food in the house, and she's not drinking it all away, that's all. So, do I give you the cash or...?

"I'm not taking money from you," Jolie informed him. "You've done enough. Whatever else you do or don't do, you'll have to work that out with my mom. If I had my way, she'd never take a dime from you."

"I respect that, but you need help, Jolie."

Jolie wasn't sure where this guy was going with this sudden desire to promote her into the adult club. Taking her into his confidence wasn't soothing her worries over him moving them to some mysterious hovel in the sticks where nobody could hear them scream. In Jolie's experience, there was only one reason for an older man to try and make a young girl feel more grown up, and it had nothing to do with respect.

"My mom's made some poor choices," Jolie admitted. "But she's still my mom, and it may not look like it to an outsider, but we have each other's back when it counts. She isn't the kind of mom who would stand by and let someone take advantage of her daughter."

Brett didn't miss a beat. "Yeah. I see that." He seemed to genuinely have no idea what she was inferring. "And she's real proud of you, Jolie," he added. "You should hear her brag about her girl."

"When I'm not around to hear it, right?"

"Lots of parents are like that. They don't want to give their kids unrealistic expectations."

Jolie smirked. "No fear of that here. What about your kids?"

"Never had any," Brett admitted. "I kept marrying the wrong kind of woman I guess, and now, it's too late."

Jolie started getting nervous again about the direction of the conversation.

Brett must have sensed her nerves. "I'm not looking for anything from your mom, Jolie, or from you. I'd just feel wrong if I left you in such a pinch without trying to help. There was a time or two in my life when I was down and people helped me. Let me return the favor. I'll walk away; no strings attached. I promise." He gave her a friendly smile as he picked up the other two bags of groceries.

They were headed back to the apartment when Jolie's phone chimed that she had a text.

It was Sean: "Change of plans. Can't go to the wedding with you. Sorry."

She should have known better than to count on Sean. She should probably have asked Remy in the first place.

Jolie slid her phone back into her pocket without replying to Sean's text.

CHAPTER TWENTY-THREE

"**P**lease come, Jo. Please." They were sitting at their usual lunch table before the boys arrived. If Becca's whining hadn't been so annoying, Jolie might have been tempted to agree to go to the Grolund family barbecue. After all, they were friends. But the event was a week away. Jolie didn't think she'd be living in the state by then. She didn't want to say that, though. Rebecca was lousy at keeping secrets. If Jolie told her anything, it would be all over school in a flash, and she hadn't decided if she would tell her friends or not. She hated the whole goodbye thing. Sometimes, it was just cleaner to move and send a text afterward saying goodbye. She could always blame the suddenness on Jessie. Usually, ducking out this way didn't bother her, but this time it felt cowardly. What was going to happen to Remy after she left? Who would look after him? Bodhi? Was Bodhi ready for that? Had he understood what Jolie was asking him to do when she charged him with the task that night out at Rose's or had he just dismissed the whole incident as more of her confused ravings?

I can't leave. I just can't. Jolie felt like a stone weight in her belly was ripping her insides apart.

"I just don't think I can make it, Becca," she tried to beg off.

"Why? Oh, come on, please. You're practically the only friend I have. What is it, your mom? I thought you said she was going to be okay?"

"She is. I mean she's getting better, but she still needs a lot of help."

Chapter Twenty Three

"So you're worried that she'll need you home that night?"

"Maybe. I don't know. Right now everything is up in the air. They let Mom go at work and we haven't figured out our next step," Jolie admitted.

"Oh my God," Rebecca figured it out. "You think she's going to make you move."

"No, I don't. Well, maybe." Jolie was conflicted. On the one hand, she didn't want anyone to know, and on the other, she longed to share the burden of her situation. Rebecca would not have been her first choice, but there was no going back. She had already said too much.

"But she can't make you leave now, Jo," Rebecca insisted. "It's practically the end of the year."

"Tell me about it. Please, don't say anything to anyone, Becca. Nothing's been decided for sure and there's no sense stirring things up."

"I don't know what I'd do if you left. I'd be completely lost," Becca insisted, ignoring anything Jolie said.

"Nothing would change that much," Jolie argued, wishing she'd kept her mouth shut.

"But we're like sisters. I know that we've had our differences, but no one understands me like you do, and no one else understands you like I do, Jo."

Jolie wasn't entirely sure those statements were true, but she appreciated that Rebecca believed them.

"We can text, and see each other, and stuff," she offered lamely, knowing that it would never equal face to face time: talking, laughing, and sharing. "If Mom loses the apartment, we have to move. What can I do, Becca?"

"I'm not accepting defeat," Rebecca announced, gamely. "There has to be something we can do." She began texting on her phone.

"Hey, guys," Remy and Bodhi joined the table. "So what time do you want me to pick you up for the wedding, Jo?"

"I told you, Rem. I have to be there early because I'm a bridesmaid. They want to dress me up, and do some stuff with my hair."

"You mean they don't trust you to do your own hair? Imagine that." Bodhi flicked the rag wrapped mess Jolie had scrunched on top of her head.

"It's some girly thing they do for weddings, I don't know. Just meet me there, okay, Remy?"

"Do you have a ride?" Jolie didn't answer because the answer was no. Remy raised an eyebrow. "Then let me take you, Jo. I won't be in the way. I have a phone, I can entertain myself."

"Fine," Jolie gave in. "Pick me up at nine."

"AM?"

"Yes, AM. They're not getting married at one o'clock in the morning, dork."

"The wedding is at one o'clock, but I'm picking you up at nine?"

"Forget it. I'll walk." Jolie got up to leave.

"Stop. I was just teasing. Why are you being so sensitive?"

"I'm not." She tried to keep her face neutral.

Remy studied her. "You're lying, but okay, if you don't want to tell me right now, I'll wait. Nine o'clock is fine.

"He'll be late," Bodhi added.

Remy punched his arm, playfully. "Bodhi, stop trying to cause me problems."

"Who, me?" Bodhi did his innocent look.

"'Who, me?' You have a face like a puppy, Bodhi." Jolie tried to imitate his "it wasn't me" face.

Chapter Twenty Three

"Sorry, Jo. It's just not the same," Remy shook his head.

Jolie's relationship with Bodhi had changed since the night Jessie Lynn was shot. They might never be close, but a truce had been called.

I should tell them. Jolie felt her conscience gnawing at her like a colony of starving rats. She wanted to tell them she was moving; she just didn't want to be there when they found out.

"Just make sure that you look really hot for the wedding, okay, Rem?" she kept her poker face on. "I want all the other girls to be jealous."

"Don't forget the boys," Bodhi joked. Remy glared at his friend.

"I'll get Madison to take me shopping," he promised.

Bodhi rolled his eyes. "Oh my God, he'll look like a Mormon girl's wet dream."

"Justin Bieber," Becca suggested, still carrying on her marathon texting session. "And by the way, good Mormon girls don't have those kind of dreams."

"Then how do they get such big families?" Bodhi teased.

"If you show up looking like Justin Bieber, I'll pretend that I don't know you," Jolie warned Remy. Maybe after the wedding, she would tell Remy that she was leaving, like when he dropped her off. Then they could have a nice private goodbye.

The bell announced the end of lunch, everyone hefted their backpacks and headed off to their afternoon classes.

"Boom!" Rebecca punched the air. "Problem solved," she announced, triumphantly. "And you 'can' come to my barbecue now, because you'll be living with me."

"What?"

"If your mom moves, my parent's just agreed that you could move in with me," Rebecca repeated.

"But your parents don't even like me," Jolie protested.

"Sure they do, and I like you. That's what's important. So, problem solved."

"Problem solved," Jolie echoed, wondering why she didn't feel more relieved.

By Saturday, everything would be settled. Brett would load the moving van and drive Jessie Lynn and their meager belongings up to Tecopa. Jolie would go to the wedding, then come back to the apartment, clean it, turn in the keys, and move in with the Grolund's so that she could finish out the year at Chaparral.

*****

Jolie caught a glimpse of herself in one of the huge gold framed mirrors that hung like wallpaper around the casino's wedding area. She would have liked to believe, when they placed full length mirrors every six feet along both walls, the intention was to show blushing brides how beautiful they were as they walked toward their blissful futures. But they were just as likely a cruel joke on the unfortunate bridesmaids forced to look at themselves over and over again, all the way down the hall, every time they went to take a leak.

To Tru's credit, she had made an effort to get around the demeaning tradition, refusing to wear a white gown set off by a complimentary bouquet of friends in pastel frocks. The flaming redhead had opted for a deep green gown for herself with her bridesmaids in classic little black cocktail dresses.

"Maybe, I could use it as a Halloween costume," Jolie muttered under her breath, examining the effects of her transformation under the spell of the black sheath dress, stilt-high heels, glamour photo makeup, and Texas beauty queen hair.

"It's like Rocky Horror meets Cinderella," Jolie complained. It had taken hours to put it all together. It would take twice as long to undo it and she would come home from the wedding dressed like Magenta from The Rocky Horror Picture Show, take off her stilettos, and go straight to cleaning the apartment. Jessie Lynn, Bret, and the little U-Haul with their meager possessions would already be gone, along with everything but the few clothes that Jolie would need between now and the end of school.

One more night of freedom, and then she'd be living with the Grolunds.

"Her dream: my nightmare," Marty entered the hallway from the groom's dressing room with a sigh. "I thought we'd just have some friends over, say how much we love each other, then the band could play, and we'd have a party. It was such a simple plan in the beginning."

"What happened?" Jolie asked.

"Tru's mother, that's what." Marty rolled his eyes. "Her folks insisted their little girl should have the wedding of her dreams." He looked at Jolie and did a double take. "Whoa, Jo!" He blinked. "That's a change."

"When I told Tru I'd do this, I had no idea what I was getting into," Jolie tugged at the hem of her dress, trying to wriggle it closer to her knees.

Marty let go a belly laugh, completely at odds with the rented tux.

"Welcome to the club. None of us did, but you clean up nice." He pulled at the stiff white collar circling his neck. "I feel like a trussed turkey. I can hardly breathe."

"You and me both," Jolie commiserated, trying to fill her lungs against the restriction of the dress's plastic stays.

Marty held up a patent leather clad foot.

"If you look down, you can see your reflection in my shoes."

"Don't let Tru know about that. If she figures out that you can see up some girl's dress just by standing next to her, you're going to end up one dead bride's groom."

"Jolie Figg, you have a truly perverted mind." Marty gave her a devilish grin. "I love it."

"Don't pretend you hadn't thought about that. It's my duty as a bride's maid to keep an eye on you."

"Hey, I'm an almost married man." Marty held his hands up in a gesture of surrender.

"Yep and the bachelor party is over."

Marty sat on one of the velvet covered love seats and took off one of the offending shoes. "I thought I rented a tux, not a torture chamber."

"Quit being a wimp. I've got it much worse than you." Jolie stuck out a high heel so tall, she was literally walking on the tips of her toes.

"I don't think so. I'm wearing a corset, and you, clearly are not," Marty one-upped her.

The door at the end of the hallway opened and Sean's on again off again girlfriend, Adrianna stepped in. She was wearing a conservative sun dress that could have been on the June cover of Good Housekeeping magazine, her hair braided into one tasteful French braid down the back.

"I think the bathrooms must be in here somewhere, Sean." She caught sight of Jolie. "It's okay, honey, I found it. You just wait for me there." She tried to keep Sean from coming any further, but it was too late.

Chapter Twenty Three

Sean saw Jolie and stopped halfway through the door, his mouth hanging open like a wide mouthed bass.

"Hi, Jo."

"Hi, Sean," Jolie replied coolly. "Adrianna."

"I was just looking for the ladies room." Adrianna gave Jolie the once over. As much as Jolie hated being put on display like a department store manikin, she could not deny a little surge of pleasure watching Sean's girlfriend's face. Jolie had never shown up on Adrianna's "watch out for this one" meter but she was reassessing that dismissal now.

Sean was too. The Jolie standing in front of him was no kid.

"I'll be right back, honey." Adrianna gave Sean a kiss, that doubled as a declaration of territory, before exiting into the lady's room.

"Wow, Jo, I almost didn't recognize you." Sean didn't seem to know what to do with his face, smile, frown, gape. "Did you do something new with your hair?"

"No. Someone else did. Tru said to do something retro and out came the highlight foils, the rat tail combs, and cans of hairspray. It's guaranteed if I disappear my hair will stand here all by itself."

Sean chuckled. "Well, you look good kid--damn good."

Jolie noted the inclusion of "kid" in that sentence. Sean was trying to remind himself that he was an adult and she was not. Adrianna reappeared.

"Well, we'd better get back, honey," she took Sean's arm possessively and pulled him back through the carved double doors at the end of the hall.

"Meow," Marty made cat claws with his hands. "I wouldn't trade places with that dude right now, even to get out of these size eleven nightmares."

"If he's not happy, he's got no one to blame but himself," Jolie pointed out. "He already broke up with her once."

Marty shrugged. "Some guys are slow learners. Look, Jolie, I know I'm not your dad or anything, but would you do me a favor tonight?"

"You know I will, Marty."

"Just be careful. Tru's parents have spared no expense on this shindig and the alcohol will flow freely. I wouldn't worry if it were just the band and our friends, but there are people here that Tru's parents invited that she hasn't seen in twenty years. We don't really know them."

"What are you trying to say, Marty?"

"People get a little crazy at wedding receptions, and right now, you don't look like anybody's idea of a sixteen-year-old, but you're every guy's idea of hot. So just keep your head about you, okay?"

Remy entered through the door that Sean and Adrianna just went out.

"Don't worry, Marty. You have your best man, and I have mine." Jolie tucked herself under Remy's arm. Marty offered a hand to Remy and they shook hands.

"'Nice to see you again, Remy."

"Nice to see you, too, Sir. Congratulations on your wedding, and thanks again for your help the other night." Remy's sincerity and charm teased Marty into a relaxed smile.

"No problem. It seems like everything worked out okay." He glanced at Jolie.

"I'm fine." Jolie raised her hand like she was giving an oath in court. "I promise not to foam at the mouth or let my head turn around backward. Come on, Remy, let's go get this chump married." She smiled as she linked Marty's arm in her other arm.

Chapter Twenty Three

The wedding ceremony was what Jolie expected from watching movies: full of sentimental mush and weeping relatives, but this time it was her friends saying the words. Maybe she was more vulnerable because of everything that had been going on. It felt strange that Jessie Lynn was moving away without her, kind of like she was being abandoned, and even though she thought she had wanted to stay, moving in with strangers seemed like the separation before a divorce.

The cliché of crying at a wedding was old and tired, but here she was, listening to her friends promise to love each other forever, and pretending there was something in her eye.

There was so much naked truth in Tru and Marty's promises to each other, that it made Jolie's chest ache. Would she ever find a Marty to love her? If she did, would she recognize his feelings as real and be able to hang onto him, or had all the years in her mother's shadow made her so jaded, that she would never be able to accept something so inexplicably naive and hopeful as love?

Jolie looked out over the congregation and locked eyes with Sean, remembering past lives when the two of them had been at the center of similar ceremonies.

Friends and neighbors shouted encouragement as bagpipes skirled in the background. Clasping hands, the Jolie and Sean of a different lifetime looked into each other's eyes and jumped over a broomstick.

The scene switched. A man draped in a white toga took a younger Jolie's slender hand into his.

"Go with him," the little girl's father commanded her, sternly. "Be a good girl and do what he tells you."

Jolie looked up at the tall, muscular man beside her wearing his shiny breastplate and feathered helmet. He looked down at Jolie and smiled kindly: it was Sean.

"Would you like to see your new house?" he asked, as gently as if he were trying to tame a woodland fawn. Jolie nodded and followed him like a bee to honey. They had eight children in that life, Jolie remembered as the image faded.

But this time Sean would not be hers. Instead, Remy had stepped forward when she was in trouble. Remy, who needed her, and who had shown her a world where she was not an outcast.

Jolie turned her eyes from Sean and sought Remy's face. When she glanced back at Sean, his expression was troubled. He might not want to admit that he remembered any life but this one, but he didn't like the idea that someone else might have her heart.

He's jealous. Jolie smiled, pleased by the prospect. She flashed Sean a provocative smile, feeling the kind of power that had nothing to do with making a deal with any demons other than her own natural desires.

Sean was moody the whole reception. Pushed outside Tru and Marty's inner circle by his new relationship, he sat pouting, refusing to dance, so that Adrianna was completely isolated and bored.

Not my problem, Jolie reminded herself, watching the young woman struggle with her escort's black mood.

Iris came by and hugged Jolie, reiterating her promise to help out. Jolie almost told her about Jessie Lynn's move, and how she had to go live with the Grolunds, but Iris lived miles away from the school, and Jessie Lynn already had the papers granting the Grolund's temporary guardianship. All Jolie had to do was make sure her mom signed them and deliver them to the school office.

Besides, it's only for a few weeks, she told herself.

Chapter Twenty Three

The new couple was about to drive off for their mini honeymoon when Marty turned and grabbed Jolie and bussed her right on the lips.

"I'm just so happy, Jo--so happy. I never thought she'd choose me." His eyes shone.

The food was good, and the band was solid, even with the new bass guitarist sitting in for Marty, and everyone seemed to have a great time.

"Thank you for coming with me," Jolie's arms encircled Remy's neck as they danced to the evening's closing song.

"Thanks for asking me."

Jolie glanced at the table where Sean and Adrianna were sitting. Sean was watching them. Jolie reached for Remy's hand and moved it down to her butt. His body was so close to hers, all of their most vital bits were just inches apart, with only a few layers of fragile clothing separating them. She leaned into him, pressing her hips against his, her chest against his, looking deep into his eyes. It was a silent offer that would be hard to misunderstand.

Remy moved his hand back to her waist, his color rising, the look on his face confused as if she'd just sliced his heart open.

He is a tortured soul as well as a gentleman, Jolie told herself. She might not be able to do much about the tortured soul part, but she thought she could do something about the gentleman. Almost as tall as he was in her stiletto heels, she leaned forward and kissed him long and deep, drinking him in. When she was done, she stayed close, so that the silhouettes of their faces were interlocking jigsaw puzzle pieces ready to be pressed together into perfect union.

"I'd like you to take me home now," Jolie whispered. It was her last night of freedom here in Las

Vegas. Who knew if they'd ever have another chance to truly be together. So many times, she had thought about throwing away her virginity in a fit of anger. This was the first time she had thought to give it in love. The apartment would be empty except for her clothes and a sleeping bag, but they wouldn't need more.

*****

"What do you mean you can't?" Jolie repeated Remy's words, trying to make sense of them. "You mean it won't work right now or something?" She looked down at his crotch, trying to see past the shadows cast by the street light. He had borrowed his folk's car for the event, and they had pulled up into the parking lot at the apartments. Jolie leaned over and kissed Remy. "I don't want to be alone." She took his hand and began to slip it down the tube of her dress. This night would be special for them for the rest of their lives, no matter where their lives took them.

"No." Remy said firmly, pulling away. "This isn't right--not for us, Jo. I'm flattered and I do love you but-"

"But what? You're not worthy? You're not ready, you're not interested? What? Go on finish the sentence."

"I'm gay," Remy blurted it out.

CHAPTER TWENTY-FOUR

Jolie got out of the car and staggered toward the apartment, tears blinding the way.

"Don't push me away, Jo." Remy came after her. "Don't write me off just because I can't give you what you expected." He grabbed her shoulders and spun her around to face him. "We're supposed to tell each other the truth. I don't want that to change, and I don't want to lose you." Jolie twisted away, continuing her march toward the apartment. Doggedly, Remy followed.

"You don't want to lose me? I'm a little confused." She got to the door, got out her key, and opened the door. "'You' kissed 'me', Remy Bishop." She stomped inside. He hesitated, not following her in. "We are not having this conversation in the middle of the apartment complex so all these jerks can have a free show," she announced. "If you want to talk to me, you'll have to come inside." Remy came in and closed the door. "If you're gay then what was this shit about how you were waiting for me to be ready for a deeper level of commitment?"

Remy sank to the floor hanging his head.

"I wanted that. I wanted to believe that we could have that. My feelings for you are so strong, Jo, that I thought maybe it meant that we had a chance, that maybe I was straight after all, or at least bisexual. I wish to God that I was because my life would be so much simpler, but that's not how it is." He looked up at her, his face twisted with despair. "You are my dearest friend in the world, and I don't want to lie to you."

Jolie put her hands on either side of her skull and pressed.

"No, it's so much better that you pull out my bleeding heart." She flopped down on the carpet beside him. "I'm such an idiot. I thought you wanted 'me'--that you loved 'me', in spite of how I am." She lay down on her back, tears streaking her glamour shot eye makeup into punk rock war paint.

"I love you, Jolie, just--."

"Don't friggin' say, 'but not that way'. If you do, I'll cut off your balls."

Remy lay back beside her. "I never wanted to hurt you."

"Well, that worked out well."

"You say it was important to you that I accepted you the way you are, and loved you anyway. Don't you see that's what I'm asking you to do for me now?"

"Yeah, well it sucks." She had never picked up a stray thought, never seen a glance that gave her a clue-- or had she?

She thought about that night at Rose's, when Remy and Bodhi had kept vigil beside her. It had been right there in front of her that night. She had just not wanted to recognize it for what it was.

"Okay, so we aren't going steady or some dumb stereotype like that. So what?" Remy propped himself up on his elbow, looking down at her. "We don't fit those stereotypes. We never did. We don't even like them. We laugh at them. The friendship we have goes beyond that," Remy stated, passionately. "We love each other as human beings. Really caring for someone goes beyond sex, doesn't it?"

"Maybe when I'm eighty, I'll be happy with just holding hands, but that's a long way off. I'm still young,

Chapter Twenty Four

Remy. I want someone to love me in every way possible."

"And I want that, too," he agreed. "And it will happen, for us. It's just not going to happen for us with each other."

With her hormones settled down, Jolie realized that it was probably a good thing that Remy had stopped her from adding one more problem to her already complicated life, but seeing the humor in their situation was still a few years off.

"I'll be there, Jo," Remy promised, reaching out and taking her hand. "I'll be right there beside you commiserating over all your relationships: the good, the bad, and the ugly, because what we have is beyond some fleeting teenage romance."

"Ouch." Jolie winced. "That's what you thought of us? That's flattering." She wondered how long Remy had known about himself. Had he been using her to look straight to kids at school, or was this revelation something he was just discovering, something he was not sure about yet? She turned her head and looked at Remy's face and knew that her friend would never have purposely toyed with her feelings. He had wished things could be different too, but they weren't. He was just being honest. They lay on the carpet, staring up at the ceiling.

"You've thought about this, haven't you, Rem?" Jolie asked, quietly. "I mean, I know it's better than it used to be for gay people, but it's still hard. There's so much prejudice."

"Yeah, a gay Native American dude: I'll be on the unwanted list of most of white America."

"But not your people?"

"It's different with them."

Jolie thought about that, remembering seeing Rose and Hoke's spirits in the lodge before the wipe down. They had only had one flame, while Remy and Bodhi had two.

"You have two spirits. That's why Hoke is teaching you, and why Rose and Sifu put so much store in your abilities, right?" Remy nodded. "I saw it that night in the wipe down. You were so beautiful. Rose even said something to me about it, but I didn't understand."

"In my world, those who are two spirited are not outcasts. Instead, we're recognized as people of unusual power and abilities."

"Because you have both a male and female spirit?"

"Yes. The belief is; we understand things differently. Hoke knew about me, of course, from when I was born, because he could 'see' my two spirit lights. That's why he fought dad so hard to raise me in the Native world, but Dad was sure that he could give me a better life."

Jolie didn't want to say how much Remy's father would regret that decision if she was unable to save his son.

"So Hoke just hung around all these years while you were growing up?" she asked, instead.

"He jumped in and out of my life, teaching me in bits and pieces, showing me things when he thought I was ready, always hoping that one day I would accept my heritage, and step up."

"And you're doing that." She squeezed his hand. "I'm sorry I was so selfish. I was thinking of me and what I wanted when I should have been thinking about how hard it was for you to come out to me. It's a big deal that you trusted me enough to tell me. I know that."

"Sometimes you just love someone, and you can't help it. I love you, Jolie Figg."

Chapter Twenty Four

"Right, but not 'that' way." Jolie's lips trembled. She knew it was silly, Remy had not rejected her, but she still felt the loss of the closeness that she had hoped would be hers. Remy seemed to sense this.

"It was wrong for us, Jo. Lying to you and pretending would only have made it hurt more, later."

Jolie's heart twisted. She took Remy in her arms and stroked his hair.

"You're too good, Remy. I usually really love that about you, but right now, it just kind of sucks." She pulled away, wiping her eyes. "At least now, I know why Bodhi is so jealous."

"You don't hate me?" Remy asked

"People like us don't find other people like us very often," Jolie said, putting a big emoticon smile on her face to mask her broken heart.

Remy nodded. "Lovers will come and go, but we'll always have each other." Remy took her face in his hands and kissed her on the forehead.

As long as I can keep you alive, Jolie thought.

CHAPTER TWENTY-FIVE

There was no stronger testimony to the change in Rebecca Grolund's identity than the transformation of her bedroom. Gone was the cheap castle-gray wallpaper, the faux velvet drapes, and the leftover Halloween decorations that had given it its Gothic character. Banished were her posters celebrating My Chemical Romance, Panic, and Linkin Park. Rebecca's room had gone through a full Mary Kaye makeover in her mother's image, complete with lemon chiffon painted walls, ruffled curtains, and Reader's Digest approved inspirational art. In a few years, when they boxed Rebecca's clothes up and sent her off to college, there would be nothing they needed to do except move out the bed. This would be Mrs. Grolund's new sewing room.

The Grolunds had brought in a roll away bed from the garage for Jolie to sleep on, and they'd found an almost matching bedspread so that the two-bed arrangement looked almost planned.

"We'll share my room," Becca announced, happily.

"Did the paint come with sunglasses?" Jolie quipped, squinting against the bright, sunny yellow.

Rebecca laughed. She knew the room wasn't her. She just didn't know who she was right now. Her room and wardrobe had gotten a thorough scrubbing after her Solstice adventure, but it was harder to change people on the inside.

The new Rebecca no longer sought her place in the universe through a fascination with magic, but she was still the same self-conscious kid she'd been when Jolie

Chapter Twenty Five

met her last September. If geek boys got the short end of the stick in high school, geek girls didn't even get to draw straws. They were the outcasts of the outcasts, not accepted into the boys' tech club, not cool enough for the preppy girls' academic click. They were the unclaimed, left to the discard pile.

Becca's interest in the morose and twisted might have been born from a knee-jerk reaction to her parent's Lemon Pledge existence, but it was also an exercise in adventure by a rabidly curious mind starved for meaningful exploration. Rebecca Grolund was a lonely kid--a socially inept kid, but not a stupid kid.

"This is going to be so much fun. It'll be like we're real sisters. What shall we do first?"

Jolie winced. Everything about the Grolund's Brady Bunch re-visited house made Jolie want to tear her hair out.

"Homework?" she suggested. "There's a math quiz on Wednesday." Their focus on academics had been their earliest common denominator. They dug out their math books and laid them out on their beds.

"Thanks for doing this for me, Becca. I really appreciate it," Jolie said, flattening out onto her stomach on the baby blue cotton bedspread.

"What are friends for?"

"Everything all right in here, girls?" Mrs. Grolund appeared at the door. "Do you need anything, Jolie?"

"We're fine, Mom. Don't fuss."

"Everything's good, Mrs. Grolund. Thank you for letting me stay with you."

"It seemed like the Christian thing to do. Having to leave mid-semester is never a good academic choice, and we believe education is important. Don't forget, on weeknights curfew is eight o'clock, but if you're going to be away from the house after six, we need to know where you are. Weekends you can stay out until ten but the same rule applies."

"I understand," Jolie agreed.

Rebecca rolled her eyes. "Do we have to do this now, Mom?"

"Yes, we do." Mrs. Grolund resumed her lecture. "If you skip class or miss a day at school and you weren't actually home sick, you'll be on your way to your mom's in Tecopa, just like that." She snapped her fingers. "No discussion. We don't tolerate drugs, alcohol, tobacco, or profanity; especially taking the lord's name in vain."

"That won't be a problem," Jolie assured Mrs. Grolund.

"I understand that your mother has rather liberal ideas about relationships, and has already allowed you to date, but if you want to go out while you're here, we need to meet the boy, and talk to his parents first."

"I've really only been out on one date and it wasn't really a 'date' date," Jolie explained.

"But you have a boyfriend?"

Jolie cleared her throat. "Not really. I just have friends who are boys."

"I'm not interested in splitting hairs with you. *Little brat. You're the child and I'm the adult and don't forget it,*" Jolie heard her add, silently. "You need to understand the rules you're expected to live by while you're living here, under our roof. *How did Rebecca ever talk me into this?*"

"Thank you," Jolie repeated. The undercurrent of antagonism was not lost on her, but if Mrs. Grolund was so unhappy about Jolie coming to stay, then why had she agreed to it?

"Rebecca has already explained to us how important graduating is to you, so we expect your focus to be on your academics, not partying or getting into trouble."

Chapter Twenty Five

Ah. There it is. Rebecca had moaned, and groaned, and thrown a fit until her mother had given in against her own judgment.

"No, ma'am." Jolie nodded.

"When she messes up, Rebecca will see the little tramp for who she is, and we'll be done with her," Mrs. Grolund thought, satisfied that she would be proven right about the faults in Jolie's character.

"Are you finished, Mom?" Becca asked impatiently. "We've got a lot of homework." Rebecca might be "born again," but she was still a kid who knew how to work the system. No parent who had just announced they were supportive of education was going to stand in the way of homework.

"Welcome to my world," Rebecca moaned as her mother went back downstairs.

*****

"Do I have something in my teeth? Everyone's looking at us." Rebecca and Jolie walked down the hall Monday morning.

Jolie's trouble siren was going off. It wasn't Rebecca; it was her. Kids were looking at her, then turning away and laughing.

"Yo, go, Jolie!" a boy from the stoner crowd, shouted, giving Jolie a big thumbs up as if she had just joined their secret club.

"Burn Webber knows your name?" Rebecca shook her head. "That's not a good sign. What did you do, Jo?"

"Nothing. Honest. I didn't do anything."

Jolie and Rebecca walked toward the sophomore lockers, getting crowd reactions that ranged from the cold shoulder to exuberant cheers, most of them from kids Jolie didn't know.

"You must have some idea," Rebecca groused, annoyed by her friend's meteoric rise in popularity.

"Honestly, I don't, Becca." Jolie checked the hallway for any of the Fus, thinking they might be able to shed some light on the mystery.

The closer they got to the main hallway, the worse it got. The student body's energy was pumped up like it was homecoming or something.

"Awesome," a skater kid shouted when he saw her.

"She's my hero," another boy wrapped his arms around Jolie from behind, hugging her. Before she had time to push him off, he released her, and continued on his way down the hall, repeating: "Jolie Figg is my hero!" Kids in the hallway laughed.

"If they try to expel you, Jo, you just let us know. We've got free speech in this country!" another kid shouted at her.

"Yeah, we'll do a sit-in," a girl from the forensics team chimed in. Several students hooted their agreement.

"Why would you get expelled?" Becca demanded, alarmed. "You can't get expelled, Jolie. My parents will go bonkers."

Jolie stopped in the middle of the hallway. One of Megan Washburn's student council posters was just ahead--at least it looked like her poster, but the slogan had been changed.

"A vote for Megan is a vote for Megan," it read now.

Jolie walked slowly down the hallway, reading the walls. "Megan wants your body," was followed by; "Megan will put your ------ in her mouth" with a crude picture in the blank. Jolie groaned.

"Oh my God." Rebecca stared at the posters, then began to laugh.

Megan Washburn was not laughing.

Chapter Twenty Five

"You! You did this!" Megan shrieked, the moment she saw Jolie.

Rebecca looked askance at Jolie. "Why does everyone think this was you?"

"Because it 'is' her." Megan was shaking with anger. "Because she's a conniving little witch and a terrible person who ruins everything for everyone else. She broke my leg last semester, or did you forget that, Rebecca? You were the one who told me it was her."

Becca glanced at Jolie sheepishly, but as far as Jolie was concerned, that episode was in the past.

"Oh, boo hoo hoo," someone in the crowd mocked Megan.

"Not feeling special, Megan?" another voice added to the humiliation. "What's the matter? Daddy's money can't fix your little boo-boo?"

Megan's knuckles were white. "Losers!" She shouted. "You're all a bunch of losers!" She ran down the hall.

More than a smattering of kids broke into spontaneous applause. Jolie looked around, astounded. The people had spoken. Megan Washburn, golden girl of teachers and administrators, was not as popular as she pretended she was. She was the center of a small visible club of her own friends who had money and powerful parents, and that gave them special privileges, like pushing other kids around. But the rest of the kids didn't support her bullshit.

"It's all in her head," Jolie said, surprised at the realization. "And they think 'I'm' crazy."

The teacher was still taking role when Jolie was called to the office. The student office helper was so nervous, that she could barely look at Jolie.

"Don't worry. Whatever I have, it's not contagious," Jolie assured the girl.

Ms. Warren's office door was open. She came around the desk as Jolie approached.

"Let's go into Principal Maxwell's office, shall we?

"Can we do this here? I need to get back to class. I have a report to work on."

"You may not be going back to class," Ms. Warren threatened. "I've been trying to call your mother. I keep getting voicemail."

Jolie pulled out her cell and pressed her mom's number. Ms. Warren was right, it went to voicemail.

"There's another number I might be able to reach her at." She called Brett's cell. He had given it to her in case of emergencies, but she'd never tried it. It suddenly occurred to her it might be a fake.

"Ms. Warren?" Principal Maxwell called from his office.

"Put the phone away now," Ms. Warren told Jolie. "We can talk about your parent problems later." They went into the Principal's office.

"Please close the door, Ms. Warren." Jolie had never been this close to Mr. Maxwell. He was a ruddy bulwark of a man, the kind who had played football in college and still had his hair in a crew cut. "So, Miss Figg, talk to me about the student council posters."

"The ones that are in the hall now, or the ones before?" Jolie asked.

"Ms. Warren seems to think you had something to do with the current version."

"I didn't. I have witnesses who can vouch for my whereabouts all weekend. Besides that, the school was locked up. How would I have gotten inside?"

"Teachers have keys. Sometimes they give them to students and maybe a student forgot to give them back right away," the principal suggested.

Jolie shook her head. "I'm not part of any clubs. No one gave me a key. Ask your faculty."

"A vote for Megan is a vote for Megan." Principal Maxwell smirked. "It's clever."

"Well, you know what they say, we laugh at what's true," Jolie replied.

"Did you think of that?"

Jolie pressed her lips tight together, then nodded. "Yes, actually. I was walking down the hall a few weeks back and I re-worded some of the slogans, just joking around, you know, but I didn't change those posters. I didn't even write my joke versions down. I was at a wedding with three hundred other people on Saturday, and I went to Rebecca Grolund's on Sunday. I have alibis."

"You admit to authoring the new slogans, but you claim you didn't change them?" Maxwell looked for confirmation.

"Yes, sir. That's right."

"And you don't know who might have?"

"It was between classes. The halls were empty. There wasn't even anybody else around who could have overheard me, except..." She hesitated.

"Except? Who else was there, Ms. Figg?" Principal Maxwell asked.

Jolie didn't want to get Hugo in trouble, but it was starting to look like he had gotten her into some.

"I don't know the kid's name," she lied. "I was just kind of muttering to myself. I don't know if he even heard me."

"Then how did the posters get changed?"

"Your guess is as good as mine, Principal Maxwell, but I'd start with people who had keys."

"Well, it seems we have a little detective work ahead of us. Thank you, Miss Figg. We'll be talking again, soon."

"Her mother--" Ms. Warren started.

"Just got out of the hospital," Jolie explained quickly, going for the sympathy angle. "She was shot at work. That's why I was gone a few days last week, and why I'm staying with the Grolunds now."

"Oh, yes. I remember," Principal Maxwell made the connection. "Some of our students helped stop the attack." He smiled as proudly as if he'd taught the boys their first kick. "I used to be a karate kid myself." He punched the air in a poor imitation of a martial artist. "Are things okay with your mom now?"

Jolie knew she needed this man on her side.

"She's getting better. She can't go back to work yet, though, so we had to give up our apartment. She's staying at a friend's." Her disclosure had the desired effect. Maxwell's instincts to protect one of his students kicked in.

"And you said you're staying where?"

"With the Grolunds," Jolie repeated, grateful that she had not tried to stick out living in the apartment alone for the last few days of the month.

"I tried to notify Jolie's mother about what's happened," Ms. Warren explained. "But she's not answering."

"It could be that cell reception is not good where she's staying," Jolie offered an excuse.

Maxwell chewed on that a moment. "Do you have another number for her, Jolie?"

"Her boyfriend's."

"Then, let's try the boyfriend and see what he knows," Maxwell suggested, lightheartedly.

Chapter Twenty Five

Jolie pulled out her phone, not looking at Ms. Warren. "And while I'm calling him, Ms. Warren, maybe you could call Officer Wrangler and let him know what's going on?" Jolie knew that Ms. Warren would call Wrangler anyway, but by suggesting it, she got the jump on her, and let the counselor know that she was confident the probation officer was in her corner.

"And maybe, call Mrs. Grolund, too, Ms. Warren," Maxwell suggested, "I'd like to talk to her."

By the time Jolie had gotten hold of Brett and he'd confirmed that she was telling the truth about her situation, Pamela Grolund was on her way to the school.

"I'm sorry to bring you down here like this Mrs. Grolund," Mr. Maxwell held out a hand and gave her a hearty handshake. "But I understand that Jolie is staying with you?"

"Her mother is supposed to have signed the temporary custody papers and mailed them to us," Mrs. Grolund explained. "But you know how it is when you're moving. You put something down and it gets packed and no one knows where it got to."

"Of course," Maxwell smiled, understandingly. "I'm sure that can be easily ironed out."

"Is there a problem, Mr. Maxwell? Is Jolie in trouble? She's only been with us one night and since we don't have legal papers, I don't know.... Maybe you should just call her mother and have her come pick Jolie up."

"I don't think that's necessary. Jolie came to your house yesterday, right?" Mrs. Grolund nodded. "And she and Rebecca were there all night?"

"Yes. I went upstairs and checked on them a few times." She glanced nervously at Jolie. "I didn't go in, but I could hear their voices. Rebecca's not in trouble, is she?"

"No one is in trouble, Mrs. Grolund," Mr. Maxwell reminded her. "Jolie is just trying to help us figure out a little school mystery, that's all. She's got quite the brain for it. Don't you, Jolie?"

"I don't like to brag," Jolie played along, triggering a little smile from the brawny principal. He was having way too much fun.

"I'm sorry to have brought you all the way down here on a misunderstanding, Mrs. Grolund, but I am glad I finally met you." He took her hand again. "I hate it when I only meet our finest student's parents on graduation night. We expect to see Rebecca at the Valedictorian's podium in a few years, right, Jolie?"

"I wouldn't be surprised," Jolie agreed.

"Thanks again for coming, Mrs. Grolund." Mr. Maxwell led her out of the office before she figured out what was happening to her. When he returned, he asked Ms. Warren and Jolie to sit. "You have two weeks of school left," he addressed Jolie. "Is this thing at the Grolund's going to work out?"

"I'll make it work," Jolie promised. "I just want to get through to the end of the year, Mister Maxwell."

"And then what, kiddo?"

Jolie shook her head. "I don't know."

"And where is it you said you're mom went?"

"Tecopa."

"For real?"

"That's where her boyfriend said they were going when they drove off with our stuff in the truck on Saturday," Jolie said, flatly. Mr. Maxwell could read between the lines.

"Do you know where in Tecopa?"

"Some place owned by a friend of Brett's."

"Have you seen this place?"

"No."

Chapter Twenty Five

"So you don't actually know where it is?"

Jolie shook her head. "No." *And now Jessie Lynn's not answering her phone.* Silence had never felt so suffocating. "Look, Mister Maxwell, I realize this doesn't look good, but the phone thing is probably just a glitch. Like I said, bad reception or something. My mom didn't run off on me. She wouldn't leave me behind." Jolie bit her lip, her eyes daring him to challenge her.

"The thought never crossed my mind, Miss Figg," Mr. Maxwell lied kindly. "I just want to say that I hope you and your mom can work out some way for you to come back to Chaparral next year. You're a good student. It's easy to be on the Honor Roll when you have supportive parents and everything's good at home, but the kids I really admire are the ones who, against all odds, make honor roll in the face of adversity. I wish I could get inside your brain and bottle whatever it was that made you like this."

No, you don't, Jolie responded silently.

Mr. Maxwell stood. "Well, you'd better get back to class, Miss Figg. We don't want you falling behind."

Ms. Warren watched Jolie go, her lips pressed into a tight line. Jolie needed to be careful. She was making an enemy of the counselor without even trying.

Jolie didn't know what she was going to say to Hugo. The only answer to the puzzle of how the posters had gotten changed, and how people knew that she was the author, was that he had shared. She just couldn't see quiet Hugo stealing a teacher's keys, or breaking into the school, and changing the posters. But who would he have told?

Jolie was still trying to figure it out when she saw a flier for a fundraiser for the school robotics team. Hugo was away on a trip to a conference. Remy had a state track meet and if she saw him at all this week, he'd be exhausted, or distracted by homework. The only kids at the lunch table would be Bodhi, Brutus, and Rebecca. It was going to be a long week.

CHAPTER TWENTY-SIX

"**B**ring those buns over here to me, will you, Little Jo?" Mr. Grolund's boss, Dick Reardon, called from his post at the barbecue grill.

Jolie gave a quick, nervous smile to the other guests at the table, embarrassed by the double entendre.

"You've got two perfectly good feet and the girl isn't your slave, Dick," his wife bellowed back at him. "Walk over here and get them yourself, you lazy bastard." She winked at Jolie. "Don't worry about him, darlin'. He's harmless," the big-haired woman waved a ring-laden hand toward her husband.

Amanda Reardon was a large woman with a large personality, the kind that shrink-fits a room when she enters it, the kind that takes over any event she attends. It was the Grolund's back yard but once the Reardons arrived, it was their barbecue.

"I'm not doing anything anyway." Jolie picked up the platter of hamburger buns. She was a stranger here with no connection to anyone.

The Grolunds had invited people from work and friends from church. A few of them had kids that Rebecca knew, or at least met, and her parents made it clear that, as the host's child, she was expected to entertain the young folk, and not hide out in her bedroom with Jolie. Rebecca's mother called her daughter into the house to welcome some of these young folk twenty minutes ago and Jolie had not seen her friend since.

She walked the plate of hamburger buns over to where Dick Reardon was holding court at the grill.

"The key to perfect barbecue is in the heat," he explained to the dutifully submissive work colleagues clustered around with a beer in their hands. "You've got to know how hot to get your meat, and when to add some sauce. Oh my god, look at those buns." Reardon leaned back from the grill to get a good view of Jolie's derrière as he reached for the platter. "Thank you, darlin'."

"It's nothing." Jolie blushed.

"Oh, it's not nothing. I guarantee you it's not," Reardon smiled lewdly, waving his apron as if fanning his body parts beneath it.

Jolie gritted her teeth. She wanted to punch him. She wanted to shout at him and call him out, but there was a yard full of people acting as if there was nothing wrong, and his jokes and comments were perfectly acceptable. If she'd been with Jessie Lynn's crowd, she wouldn't have hesitated to beat this sucker down, but she knew that she was on thin ice at the Grolund's. Mrs. G was just waiting for a chance to throw her out and get Becca a quality friend.

Jolie couldn't make her exit into the house fast enough.

"Mmm mmm. It's a treat just watching that little delicacy walk across the yard," Reardon said to Mr. Grolund as Jolie reached the stairs up to the back deck. "Who did you say her daddy is?" Reardon took a swig of beer.

"Oh, he doesn't work for us," Mr. Grolund answered, cautiously. "She's a friend of Becca's."

Good, Jolie thought. *At least he has the sense to realize his boss is out of line, even if he doesn't have the balls to do anything about it.*

"Not one of your church going friends either, right?" Reardon's big voice had no volume control. "I can see

Chapter Twenty Six

that. She's not the type. That little peach is ripe for the picking, though if you know what I mean? It's coming off her in waves."

Mr. Grolund frowned. "Jolie is one of Rebecca's friends from high school, Dick," he pointed out delicately, thinking that maybe Reardon didn't understand how young his daughter's guest was.

Jolie could feel Reardon's eyes on her, watching her walk up the stairs, and she was fuming.

"Mmm." Reardon took another swig as Jolie escaped into the house.

Jolie followed the chatter of excited girls' voices and found Rebecca playing a board game with some of the other kids, teenage girls with One Direction tee shirts and expensive salon hairstyles, girls whose home lives were so unlike Jolie's that they might have been from another planet. Boys, clothes, and the color of their nail polish were the big topics of conversation, along with who secretly liked who in their church youth group.

"Here are some snacks for you, girls." Mrs. Grolund set a bowl of chips and dip down beside the group. "*I wish that man's wife would keep him under control*," she thought, annoyed. Jolie didn't need to read the woman's mind to know that Pamela Grolund knew exactly what was going on outside. She was deliberately keeping the church girls away from him. Her protective instincts, however, did not extend to Jolie. "Everything alright outside?" She asked Jolie, pulling her lips into a fake smile.

"Oh, Jolie. I wondered where you'd gotten to. You can play the next game," Rebecca offered.

Jolie wanted to point out that Rebecca knew exactly where she'd gotten to. She had been exactly where her friend left her, but being polite had high value among these people, and causing a scene was taboo, even if the scene was set off just by telling the truth. Jolie had never understood the story about the emperor and his invisible new clothes better.

"Jolie," Mrs. Grolund called as she ducked back into the kitchen. "Can you take this out to Mr. Grolund for me, please?"

Jolie looked the woman straight in the eye and answered silently, *No.* Pamela Grolund just stood there, holding out the relish tray for delivery.

"I'm sorry. It's really unpleasant and hot in the backyard right now. I think I need to drink some water and cool down," Jolie excused herself.

"I'll take it, Mrs. Grolund," one of the church girls offered. The girl was about Jolie and Becca's age, with fully matured curves that her juvenile tee shirt could not hide. Panic crossed Mrs. Grolund's face.

"Oh, no. You're playing, Athena. I'll do it myself." She glanced angrily at Jolie. "It will give me a chance to check and see if anything needs refilling."

Jolie sat down behind the row of players with her glass of water and tried to settle her fluttering stomach. She was already on probation here. She could not afford to lose her temper, seem ungrateful, or unhelpful.

The list of things she could not afford to do in order to stay here was growing.

Jolie expected to run the misogynist gauntlet with Jessie Lynn's bar crowd friends. Somebody inevitably brought along some jerk who decided after a few drinks that Jessie Lynn's daughter was panting to lose her virginity to him. She knew how to handle it. A quick public deflating punch to his ego usually did the trick. But she had not been prepared to face such openly inappropriate talk at a middle-class barbecue at the home of a good family in the suburbs. Church going

Chapter Twenty Six

conservatives were all about family values and protecting their children, weren't they?

Jolie moved into a player's position, rolled the dice and moved her piece around the board, then went into the kitchen.

"Is there anything you need me to do?" she asked Rebecca's mother. "I'd be happy to help out here in the kitchen, where it's not so hot," she hoped she was making her boundary clear.

Mrs. Grolund considered the offer with a tight smile. *"The ungrateful thing had better apologize,"* Jolie heard the woman think.

"I don't want you to think that I'm not willing to help out, Mrs. Grolund, but your husband's boss makes me nervous," Jolie said, just putting it out there bluntly. "The things he says are embarrassing." The look of panic returned to Pamela Grolund's face. She had not expected to be challenged openly by a sixteen-year-old.

"You mean Dick?" she pretended to laugh it off. "Oh, he doesn't mean anything by it. He was a big football player back in his day, and he's still got a locker room sense of humor. I guess you have to get to know him."

"No, thanks," Jolie replied.

Mrs. Grolund's fake smile faded.

"Dick Reardon is the head of Kenneth's division. He's a smart and very successful man," she defended her husband's boss.

"Yeah, I noticed Mrs. Dick's rings." Jolie forgot to edit herself. "What's the deal, do you think? She gets a new ring every time he cheats on her?" Jolie took a cherry off a cupcake and popped it into her mouth. "She must get something out of ignoring his bad behavior. She's too smart not to exploit it."

"You have a filthy mind," Mrs. Grolund accused Jolie. "I know that you don't come from a Christian family, Jolie, but that kind of an accusation will not be tolerated in this house. Do you understand? You can't just take a good man's reputation and ruin it because you're a little oversensitive and don't like his jokes. I think you are right, it would probably be best if you don't go back out to the barbecue."

"That's fine by me. Excuse me." Jolie ran upstairs and locked herself in the upstairs bathroom. Sitting on the closed lid of the toilet, she tried to breathe away her anger.

"Jolie, it's your turn," Rebecca called from the bottom of the stairway.

"Let her be, Becca. She's probably sleeping. She had a headache," Mrs. Grolund lied.

Jolie curled up on the fuzzy throw rug in front of the sink. She could hear the forced laughter in the backyard, Mrs. Reardon shouting ball-breaking snide remarks at her husband, everyone pretending that their dysfunctional repartee' was entertaining. There were other sounds too, little kids playing, too young to understand the awkward nuance of the adult issues. They were probably the only ones actually having a good time. Jolie brought up Remy's number on her phone.

"Hey."

"Hey, yourself, Jo. I wondered when I'd hear from you."

"I told you I wasn't mad."

"I know, but you were hurt."

"I'm fine, Remy. It was my own fault for thinking like a teenage girl."

"You're entitled. You are a teenage girl."

"Not on my best days. All you did was tell me the truth."

"Yeah, but it wasn't a truth you wanted to hear."

"Still, even a truth we don't want to hear is better than a lie, especially from a friend."

"Philosopher Figg, eh? So how's it going at Rebecca's?" Remy changed the subject.

"Fine. They're having a barbecue and there's a bunch of people here."

"Oh. Nice."

Jolie couldn't bear to tell him that it wasn't nice at all, and she hated whining. Her crazy life had caused Remy enough trouble. "Anyway, I'd better get back. They're playing games and I'm up next," she lied. "I just wanted to call and see how you were." *And hear your voice,* she thought privately.

"I'm fine. I placed in the high jump and the relay, yesterday. But we didn't take state."

"Sorry. You still have your track scholarship, though. So you're set, right?" Remy had decided that he would be going to the University in Reno in the fall.

"Yeah. It's a disappointment, is all," Remy acknowledged. "I'm trying to get all my assignments done so I'm back on track for Monday."

"I'll let you go then." Jolie sniffled.

"'You sure you're okay?"

"Yeah. I was just cutting some onions and everything is running, you know?"

"Okay. See you Monday then."

"Yeah. See you Monday."

Jolie lay on the bathroom rug, drifting off to the purr of the window fan. When she woke, it was twilight outside and Becca was knocking on the door.

"Jolie? Are you in there? Are you okay?"

"Yeah, I'm fine, Becca," Jolie replied, sleepily. "I'll be out in a sec." She got up and checked herself in the mirror, straightening out her mussed hair, and rinsing her face and hands. "What's up?" she asked Rebecca at the door.

"Feeling better?"

"Yeah. I think I just got dehydrated. A little nap and a few glasses of water and I'm good."

"Everybody's leaving. Mom wanted me to check and see if you would help clean up."

"Sure." Jolie followed Rebecca downstairs to the kitchen where Mrs. Grolund was putting away leftovers and rinsing dishes to go in the dishwasher.

"There she is." Mrs. Grolund gave Jolie one of her best insincere smiles.

"What can I do?" Jolie asked.

"You can take the garbage out to the cans in the side yard." Mrs. Grolund indicated several bags someone had set by the door. Jolie grabbed one in each hand, letting the lightweight sacks bump against her legs as she walked. The backyard was empty now, the grass pressed down flat by all the careless feet, the tables deserted and bereft of their bright tablecloths. The smell of stale beer, burnt meat, and propane still crowded the air. It was almost dark, one of the best times of the day in Las Vegas, where the skies were super sized like everything else. Released from the weekend's expectations, the neighborhood lingered over the last precious hours before the grind of the work week began. Jolie went through the gate into the long narrow side yard, weaving past the neat stacks of extra project lumber, coiled hoses, and garden tools around the shed.

Her phone rang. She stopped and shuffled the garbage bags so that she could answer it. It was Remy.

"What's up, Rem?"

"Rebecca's house is just North of Twain, right?" he said in a choked voice.

Chapter Twenty Six

"Yeah. The big two story just past the corner of Valencia and La Paloma. Why? What's wrong?" Jolie felt Remy's fear.

"I'm on my way there now. Meet me out front. I just got a call from Bodhi's brother, Jie. Bodhi's in the hospital. Jie thinks that he overdosed."

"Oh my god, Rem. Is he going to be all right?"

"Nobody knows anything yet. We need to get to the hospital. I'll be there in a few minutes."

"Okay." Jolie hung up, rounded the corner and found the garbage cans. Stuffing her bags into them, she turned to head back to Rebecca's room to get her bag and explain to the Grolund's what was going on.

Dick Reardon stood between her and the house.

"Well, there you are, you pretty thing. I wondered where you'd disappeared to."

"I was helping out in the house." Jolie tried to walk past him, but he moved into her path. "The party's over, Mr. Reardon," she said firmly, anger building inside her. "Everyone's taken their wives and kids and gone home."

"Not quite everyone." Reardon smirked.

"Where's your wife?" Jolie demanded.

"On her way home."

"Smart woman. You should follow her example."

"I've never been a follower." He reached out a hand and ran it over Jolie's hair. "I'm more of a take charge kind of guy--top dog and all that." Jolie stepped back. Reardon stepped forward.

"You need to back off, right now," Jolie growled, wondering how well she'd fair in a fight without demons or the benefit of paranormal energy. "Just turn around and go home to your wife."

Reardon shook his head slowly, a sly grin molded onto his greasy lips. "Oh come on, be nice. I just want a little sugar."

"You're drunk," Jolie said, flatly. "And I'm not giving you anything."

He made a feint for her. She dodged the other way and he threw his weight at her, smacking both of their bodies into the block wall behind Jolie. Pushing his overweight body against her, he pressed Jolie hard up against the rough cement. Using his greater weight to keep her in place, his mouth covered hers, chewing disgustingly at her lips. His breath smelled of beer, his sweat like a butcher shop. Revulsion filled Jolie, body, and mind. She bit down on his lip as she jerked her knee up hard into his groin, then stomped down hard onto the closest foot. "Get off me, you pervert." Reardon buckled.

"You little bitch," he gasped breathlessly, tasting the blood on his lip. Jolie slid out of his trap and was backing up along the walkway toward the front of the house when Remy's scooter beeped from the road.

"You're lucky I don't have time to whoop your ass." She flipped him off before running down the side of the house to the street.

"We're out of here." She vaulted onto the back of Remy's scooter.

*****

Remy held Jolie's hand, his eyes red-rimmed, his emotions like an open wound. He wasn't allowed to see Bodhi. He wasn't family, but word had gotten around, and people from the Kung Fu school had packed the hospital waiting room. Many of them had been at the school when they heard the news. With all the black tee shirts and black Kung Fu pants, they looked suspiciously like a ninja conference, but they came together like the brotherhood they were.

Chapter Twenty Six

Every head turned towards the doorway, even before anyone came into the room before most people would have known that someone was approaching.

Jolie watched the Fu family mill around the room. When a new Fu entered, each of their brothers and sisters, locked eyes, taking count of who was there. They marked exit and entrance points in the room, obstacles and potential defensive or offensive objects that might be picked up and thrown. It was what they were trained to do. Confident in their abilities, their movements and stances were precise and wary, but always grounded and no one stood in the corner. They always left themselves someplace to go. No one but a few hangers on and girlfriends sat, casually reading magazines, or watching the TV. The Kung Fu crowd all stood, prepared to fight, their eyes in constant motion, taking in what was going on around them.

Hugo and Brutus entered, like the others, making their way to Jie, to see how he was doing before drifting over to Remy and Jolie. After a few minutes, they moved over to a group of boys standing with a tall thin good looking twenty something young man by the door.

Remy might be the senior Fu at Chaparral but he was not senior in this group. Jolie studied the student's interactions, trying to figure out who was. Was it the tall skinny guy, the sinewy older student, or the other young man who looked like an Asian movie star? Each had followers loyal to them.

When Sifu arrived, the game ended. Whoever led in their teacher's absence, he was unconditionally in charge, not because he strutted, or was loud, or ordered anyone around--he did none of those things. Sifu was soft-spoken, humble, and unassuming, but the moment his students sensed his arrival, they became one group, moving toward the door, waiting for him.

With Bodhi's and Jie's mother out of the country and their father working himself to death in grief over his wife's abandonment, the boys had been living on their own, spending most of their time at the school or hanging out with people they'd met on the strip, people like them, who had no structure and a lot of spare time on their hands. Though Sifu was not Bodhi's biological parent, even the hospital staff accepted his authority and treated him as the patriarch.

Jolie's phone buzzed. She checked it.

"Where are you? My parents are livid," the message from Rebecca read. Jolie texted a short version of the situation, then returned her phone to her pocket.

Jie, a younger version of his Puck-faced older brother, listened to the update the hospital staff gave Sifu, then drifted back to sit by Remy.

"He can't leave me, Rem," the younger boy said. "All we have now is each other."

"We're your family too, Jie." Remy put an arm around the younger boy's shoulders.

Jolie's phone buzzed. Dissatisfied with Jolie's text, Rebecca was calling her. Jolie pressed ignore.

"You don't have just one brother. You have a whole school of us. We'd do anything for you." Remy told his friend's little brother. "You know that, right?"

"Yeah, I know." Jie almost smiled.

It was true. Jolie could see the bond between the students, some of them in their thirties, or older, most in their mid-twenties and younger. They were interlocking pieces of a whole, built around the base of their teacher, each one knowing where they fit.

"He won't die, though," Remy added. "You got him here in time. We just have to make sure that this never happens again, Jie." Jolie could hear him grinding resolve into the marrow of his bones.

Chapter Twenty Six

Jie shook his head. "I don't know, Rem, Bodhi's stubborn. He doesn't listen to anybody anymore, except his own impulses. It's like he can't find any happiness in the world anymore."

"Then we'll just have to find something that will make him happy. I'm working on it, little brother," Remy assured Jie.

Anyone who knows you is going to love you, Remy Bishop. Jolie leaned her head on his shoulder, biting back tears of mourning for what might have been between them. Her phone buzzed like an angry wasp.

"It's Rebecca, again. I'm going to have to answer this." She stood and walked to the hallway where everyone couldn't hear her conversation. "Yes, Becca. What is it?"

"You have to come home, now, Jo. Tell me where you are and Dad and I will come get you."

"I told you where I am. I'm at the hospital."

"With Remy."

"That's right."

"Which hospital?"

"It doesn't matter because I'm not leaving," Jolie told her friend. Jolie could hear Mrs. Grolund in the background.

"Give the phone to me," she ordered her daughter.

"Tell your parents that they have nothing to worry about. I'm perfectly safe here and I'll be back as soon as Bodhi's out of danger." Jolie ended the call and turned off her phone.

The temple kids' heads all turned as she came in, then turned the opposite way as footsteps approached from the ER doors. A doctor came out and Sifu walked forward, motioning Jie to join him. Listening to the doctor, Jie's face brightened. He turned and motioned to Remy to come with them.

"We can see him now. I told him you were our cousin." Jie smiled at his little contrivance. A large group of the students began to crowd in behind them as if to go into the room.

"And how many cousins did you say you had?" Remy laughed as he, Jie, and Sifu went through the double doors into the ER, leaving Jolie and the other Fus in the lobby.

*****

"You knew our rules, and you blatantly threw them in our faces," Mrs. Grolund said, her anger playing second to her unspoken "*I knew this would happen.*"

"My friend was taken to the emergency room at the hospital," Jolie repeated.

"Then you should have come inside the house and told us that so that we could drive you there or--"

"Tell me I couldn't go. Look, I wasn't trying to be a problem. I was just trying to--"

"You went from taking out the garbage to disappearing. No one knew what happened to you."

Someone did, Jolie corrected her interrogator silently.

"Dick Reardon did," she said out loud. Mrs. Grolund looked surprised. "He found me out by the garbage cans. Why don't you ask him why I didn't come back into the house? Or better yet, ask him what he was doing out there? But then, that would be awkward wouldn't it? Because even as I'm saying this, you know, don't you?"

"Jolie, don't make things worse," Rebecca warned her friend. But it was too late. Jolie had her back up and all her Southern Boulette was coming out. "You know that man is trouble. He's a bully and a womanizer, and maybe you even know more than that. That's why you

Chapter Twenty Six

tried to keep Rebecca and the other girls away from him because you just can't afford to find fault with him, can you? After all, he signs your husband's paychecks. But we aren't supposed to talk about that, are we?"

"Jolie, what are you saying?" Rebecca looked from her friend to her mother.

"Rebecca, go to your room. Jolie and I need to talk."

"Dick Reardon was waiting for me outside when I took the garbage out," Jolie said in a quiet, furious voice. "And he trapped me there and tried to force himself on me."

"How dare you?" Mrs. Grolund gasped.

"Oh my God, Jolie. Why would you say such a thing," Rebecca wrung her hands. "You said you wouldn't make any trouble."

"You're just making that up, trying to point the blame at someone else for your misbehavior," Mrs. Grolund argued.

"No, I'm telling a truth that you don't want to hear. Your husband's boss came onto an underage girl while she was living under your roof, and you did nothing to stop it, and now you want to blame 'me'? I thought you were Christians?"

"Get out of my house--now," Mrs. Grolund shouted.

"Mom, you can't!" Rebecca wailed. "She didn't mean it. Tell her you didn't mean it, Jo."

"I won't," Jolie refused. "Because it's the goddamn truth and someone needs to say it."

"Call someone now--anyone." Mrs. Grolund ground her teeth. "Have them come and get you."

"Mom, she's my friend," Becca cried.

"Not anymore, Becca." Mrs. Grolund turned back to Jolie. "I don't want you in my home another minute."

"No problem. We're done here. Sorry, Becca." In minutes, Jolie had gathered her few belongings from upstairs, stuffed them into her backpack and was out the front door.

"Jolie." Jolie jumped as Mr. Grolund appeared from behind the car parked in the driveway.

"It's all right. I'm going," she told him.

"I feel really bad about how this has gone for you," he apologized, lamely.

"Which part, throwing me out of your house, or letting your boss molest me?" Jolie challenged him.

Mr. Grolund looked like a mouse trying to figure out which way to go to get out of the maze.

"Look, I know that you were staying here because you were afraid you'd lose your credits," he recovered himself finally. "I'll pay for a semester of classes for you online so you can finish. I hope this will help smooth things over for you."

"For me, or for your boss?"

"I don't condone what Dick may have done, or who he is, but I still have to work for the man, Jolie." Grolund's eyes begged her to understand the problems of his adult world.

"You must realize, that if you don't confront him and you let this go, it is condoning his behavior? If no one holds him accountable, he will try this with some other girl--maybe even your own daughter?"

Mr. Grolund looked up, a fierceness changing his bland features. "He wouldn't."

"Why? Because he's such a moral, upright member of the community? Because he'd be afraid that you might speak up and expose him? I don't think he's worried about that, Mr. Grolund. I don't think he's worried about that for one minute. He's a predator. He doesn't hunt because he's hungry, he hunts for the twisted pleasure of it. It's not about sex with people like him, it's about power, and if your daughter is there when he feels the

Chapter Twenty Six

need to prove he has a pair, then nothing is going to stop him. Certainly not any fears about you standing up to him, or speaking out against him."

Mr. Grolund's face was like a sheet stretched tight across the bones of his face. "You should leave. I'll pay for the classes if you let this go and don't say anything. That's my offer; take it or leave it." He pulled his self-righteousness on like Mr. Roger's old sweater and walked back into the house.

Iris was there in twenty minutes.

"Tecopa?" she made a face when Jolie told her where she needed to go. "You don't have to do that, Jolie. You could stay here. You could stay with me."

Jolie knew that Iris would make the offer and she thought about what she might say.

"It would be great to live with you, Iris, but I feel like right now, I need to be with my mom. We're a family--a weird one, but still a family. She's trying to get her life together again, and I need to be there to support her."

"I knew you'd say that." Iris smiled as she pulled away from the curb. "Do you know how to get to where we're going?"

"Yeah." Brett had texted Jolie directions before he'd flown out, in case Jolie needed them.

"Okay. We'll pick up some coffee on the way. This could be a long night."

Settled in for the long drive, Iris gave Jolie space.

"So, since I have you here, can we talk about Faith's will?" she opened the subject she was waiting for Jolie to be ready to discuss.

Jolie sighed. "I guess, if we have to, but I don't see what it's got to do with me."

"You know that Faith was very fond of you. She thought of you like her own granddaughter, and she was a big believer in education."

"Yeah." Jolie smiled. "She gave me the college speech a few times."

"Well, she did more than talk. She left a college fund in trust for you." The emotions generated by the memory of their friend and her generous gesture put an uncharacteristic quaver in Iris' voice.

Jolie stared at her. "Why did she do that?"

"Because she could and she believed in you, Jolie."

Jolie turned her face to the window and wept quietly.

When they finally found the overgrown driveway to the new house, Iris repeated her question. "Are you sure about this, Jo?" Jolie assured her that she was. They drove slowly down the long dirt drive, barely able to see what was road and what was not for all the clumps of grass growing up through the thin gravel.

Jessie Lynn came out onto the front porch.

"Are you going to tell your mom about the trust fund?" Iris asked.

Jolie shook her head. "Not now." She got out of the car.

"Do you at least want me to come in before I leave?" Iris asked, leaning across the seat.

"No. This is good. I really do appreciate you going to all this trouble, Iris. I'll keep in touch." Jolie stood on the porch and waved goodbye as Iris drove out.

CHAPTER TWENTY-SEVEN

"**I** didn't know that you drew, Mom," Jolie muttered, looking at each sketch pinned to the stained wall. Jessie Lynn had only been in Tecopa a week, but dozens of pictures were grouped in drunken lines, covering the living room walls of the little house. Bold, emotional charcoals drawn in sweeping scratches, with angry blots of red; abstract images of nightmare dreamscapes, and terrifying creatures, the same ones over and over again, in different places, or positions. The word that came to Jolie's mind was: *disturbing*.

"When I was young. So, what do you think of the house?" Jessie Lynn hugged an old sweater around her emaciated body.

She must have lost twenty pounds. Jolie eyed her mother. Was that even possible in a week?

Calling the shack a house was like calling an outhouse a restroom. Brett's friend hadn't rented the place because it had not been rentable. It had probably not been livable until Brett threw some money and elbow grease at it. New, unpainted wood had been nailed to the old wood with layers of chipped paint, drawing attention to the newly installed window that faced the front of the house and the long dirt driveway. Brett had added boards to make up the difference between the old window's frame and the new smaller standard sized replacement.

There were a zillion bright white spackle spots on every wall that Jessie hadn't covered with her "art". Someone had popped for a used fridge and stove; Jolie suspected Brett. The front door was new; it both closed and locked; a thoughtful touch that Jolie was grateful for. Unopened cans of paint and roller brushes were stacked in the corner, waiting for someone to finish the job. Jessie Lynn had made other choices.

Brett really didn't know her mom very well.

The original interior doors had so many coats of paint that the hardware on the door and that on the frame didn't fit together.

"It was nice of Brett to do all these repairs," Jolie dodged a direct reply to her mom's query. She looked out the curtain-less window at the lonely moonlit landscape. "You could build five houses on this lot," she muttered. They would have in Vegas. The driveway was nearly half a block long, the highway end barely visible behind a strip of salt cedars someone had planted beside the road before people knew that the invasive plants sucked two hundred gallons of water a day. Iris and she had only found the place because Brett had put a shiny new black mailbox on the old weathered post beside the driveway.

The house sat on two acres, but there was no yard-- at least none that was improved. Rotted fence posts lay on the hard dirt. Half standing outbuildings and the rusted metal exoskeletons of dead machinery were all that remained of the dreams that previous tenants had abandoned when they left. Jolie felt the echo of their sadness and wondered what she and Jessie Lynn's future would be living here?

She turned back to the room, examining the leftover bits of hideout style furniture, the mental hospital green paint, scarred windows, the pitted linoleum floors.

"Your art fits perfectly here, Mom," Jolie commented wryly. Her eyes flitted across the collection of pictures. As dark and unsettling as they were, what

Chapter Twenty Seven

bothered her most, was that the artist was the woman who had given her birth, and she was going to sleep in the same house with her tonight. Jolie examined a series of drawings.

I know this place. I've seen it. Her heart began to race. She had walked these dreamscapes in her own dreams. She had seen these images when the demon was inside her mind.

"Brett's taken to calling me his Dark Queen." Jessie Lynn smiled, wistful and self-conscious. "But it's really good therapy." Jolie liked the idea that her mom was thinking about therapy. "I'm finding it very freeing getting the images out of my head and onto the paper."

"Is it working?" Jolie asked, cautiously.

"What?"

"Getting them on the paper, is it getting them out of your head, or are they still there?" Jolie faced her mom.

"Well, of course, they're still there, Jolie. I'm the artists. They come from me."

Jolie wasn't so sure. What had happened to the demon when Hoke banished it from her? Where had it gone? What about Axel? Was the demon's connection to him so strong, that wherever they went now, they would go together? When Axel was chased out of Jolie's mind, where would he have gone? Would he have been drawn back to his old apartment? Would the demon have gone along for the ride because he didn't have anything better to do? Jessie Lynn's artwork had given Jolie a lot of questions.

"Are you sleeping okay, Mom?"

Jessie shrugged. "It's been weird being here alone."

"Brett didn't stay to try out the little love nest once he had it all fixed up?" Jolie teased.

Jessie frowned. "Don't be mean, Jolie. I can't handle it. You know he had to go back to Montana to do business stuff."

Jolie did. She also knew that Brett had not left until Thursday when he texted her. That was four days after he had deposited Jessie Lynn here in Tecopa. He could have visited if he'd chosen to.

"Anyway, it'll be better now that you're here," Jessie Lynn declared, hopefully. "I won't be alone anymore." The echo of the demon's promise was creepy.

Jolie didn't think her mom had been alone for awhile now. She also knew how hard it could be to deal with these particular visitors. They just wouldn't leave, even when they were invited to.

"You've lost a lot of weight. Have you been eating?" Jolie asked her mom.

Jessie sighed, looking at her wall. "I forget. I get to working and...." Her voice faded off. "There's food in the fridge, though. Brett bought groceries before he left, and he asked the neighbors, the Coltons, to check in and see if I needed anything."

"I'll get my license right away," Jolie said.

"Don't bother. The truck isn't working," Jessie dropped another bomb.

"What? When did that happen?" Jolie demanded, imagining living out here in the sticks with no way to get around.

"It blew a...I don't know, it broke down when Brett brought it up the hill."

"We're living out here in the sticks with no wheels?"

"I couldn't drive anyway, and you were going to stay in town. It wasn't at the top of my list of things to deal with. Brett found an old bicycle in one of the sheds. The tires are flat but maybe the Colton's have a pump." Jessie picked up a piece of charcoal and began to scribble around the edges of one of her drawings. Not having a way to get around out here in the middle of nowhere was definitely going to be a problem. "They're nice people, the Coltons--quiet. They keep to themselves," Jessie mused, almost as if she were talking to herself. "Their place is like a horse ranch or something." She stepped back and examined what she'd done. "You know, this is what I was doing when I met your father."

"Drawing?"

"And painting too, back then."

Jolie chewed on her upper lip. "I guess having a baby wasn't part of your big plan."

"No, but I don't regret having you, Jo. The circumstances sucked, though. I begged Lucien not to go to Nicaragua. I just had this feeling that it was dangerous, but he thought I was being paranoid. He probably figured that if there was any danger, one of the Boulettes would have picked up on it--like they're the only ones who ever have visions."

Jolie had heard the story before. Her father, Lucien Boulette, had been working for the Peace Corps when the Casita Volcano mudslide in Nicaragua buried four villages, killing almost two thousand people, including him.

Jessie and Lucien had only met a few months before, while Lucien was home on a visit between assignments. It had been an intense, steamy affair. Jessie had gotten pregnant, and then Lucien's leave was over, and he'd had to leave. He'd been in Nicaragua a week when Hurricane Mitch hit, followed by the devastating mudslide that killed him.

Jessie Lynn was left pregnant, unmarried, and on her own. When word came of his death, Mem had offered Jessie and her child a place in the Boulette family home for as long as they wanted to stay.

If Jessie hadn't gotten pregnant, and Jolie's dad had not died, would her parents have stayed together? Jolie wondered. Lucien Boulette was an educated man from a well-established family; a man with prospects. Jessie Lynn Figg was a nobody from nowhere with no education or upbringing. In time, would Lucien have recognized Jessie Lynn's issues and opted out, or had he been the one person who could have saved her from herself?

"So, do you want to talk about what happened between you and Rebecca's folks?" Jessie interrupted Jolie's thoughts.

"Not really. Let's just call it a difference in parenting styles."

Jessie Lynn chuckled. "You mean they wanted you to be a kid, and leave the parenting to them?"

"Something like that," Jolie agreed. It was easier than explaining the truth, and Jessie would have been on the phone to Pamela Grolund in a hot second if she'd known what really happened. It was easy to label Jessie Lynn a poor parent because of her absence and permissiveness, but there were lines, and someone attempting to abuse her daughter was one of them. Jolie hadn't decided what to do about Mr. Grolund's offer yet, but she wanted the decision to be hers, not someone else's.

There were only certain places on the Tecopa property where you could get cell service. The next day, Jolie walked around until she found one. The tin-man silver fifty-six Ford pickup that sat out in the yard to the east of the house, was in no way original anymore. Someone had jacked up the rear end, put oversized wheels on the back and changed out the guts. The truck's windows had fallen down inside the doors and never gotten back up, leaving them permanently open to the weather, but the deteriorating bench seat was still original. A butt sized hole was worn into the driver's seat where you could see down through the layers to the original straw and horsehair padding.

Previous owners of the unfinished hot rod conversion had used minimum money to start their restoration, adding a hot rod barefoot gas pedal and a fancy leather wrapped mini steering wheel inside the cab. A pair of faded dice attached to the rearview mirror shed sponge rubber fuzz onto the spray-painted dashboard below it. A spider had set up a post-apocalyptic Mad Max web beneath it in the empty hole where a radio had once been.

Jolie flipped down the visor. A set of keys clattered onto the floor.

"Yeah, right. Like this old thing would run," she muttered cynically. Still, she put the key in the ignition, pumped the barefoot pedal a few times and turned. The gas gauge rose above a quarter of a tank and after a little more pumping, the old pickup sparked to life, its glass pack mufflers rumbling like a gangster's boom box. "Amazing." Jolie chuckled. Sitting back with her hands at ten and two o'clock on the little steering wheel, she imagined that she could drive into the sunset, leaving her problems behind her.

For the rest of the world, it was Monday; Remy would be in school, and though Jolie knew she should call Cliff Wrangler to tell him that they had moved out of his jurisdiction, she wasn't ready to break in a new juvy officer today. If the county sent someone out for a site check right now, things could go badly, and not just because of her mom's disturbing self-expressive art. This place was not going to score well on first impressions, and if a social services type looked into Jolie's situation, the worse it would be. They had no income, a finite amount of food, Jolie wasn't in school, and Jessie Lynn had a history of domesticate violence and alcoholism. The likelihood of Jolie being whisked out of her mother's custody and thrown into foster care was pretty high. She needed time to straighten things out before anyone official showed up. She looked around the property and sighed. There was a lot do. But first, there were a few loose ends she wanted to tie up.

Jolie looked up Yanna Maria's shop listing and called.

"Good Morning, Madam Farqueza's psychic readings. This is Madam Farqueza," Yanna Maria answered.

"Hi. It's Jolie." Jolie waited, unsure what the fortune teller's reaction to her call would be.

"Ah. So, you are coming by after school today?" Jolie could just imagine the tight-lipped expression on the woman's face. Yanna Maria was not happy, but she had not completely closed the door between them.

"No, actually, I won't be able to do that anymore, Yanna Maria," Jolie explained.

"I see." An arctic freeze came through the phone.

"It's not because I don't want to, it's that we moved...to California. My mom was in the hospital and couldn't work, so we lost our apartment."

"That is unfortunate," the fortune teller replied after a long hesitation.

"I do have a question that I thought you might be able to answer for me, though?" Jolie went on, hoping that Yanna Maria would be willing to give her this little bit of advice without getting her floor swept, or whatever else it was she was really after. "After Hoke did the wipe down, where would the thing he chased out of me have gone?"

"It is a good question. A question I have asked myself," Yanna Maria replied, more readily than Jolie had hoped.

"Do you know the answer?" she prompted the fortuneteller.

"You knew this entity, Jolie. Where do you think it would go?" Yanna Maria reversed the question.

"Are we talking about a physical place or a dream space?" Jolie asked, trying to gain clarity before she answered.

"What is it exactly that concerns you, Jolie? Has this creature been visiting you again?" the woman's voice had thawed. She seemed almost eager as if she were excited by Jolie's question.

"Yes, but not visiting me, exactly," Jolie hedged.

"Who has it been visiting?"

"My mother," Jolie admitted. "I think it may have gone to my mother."

"Ah." This did not please the santara. "And is your mother a strong woman?"

"No."

"But she is gifted, like you?" Yanna Maria seemed genuinely interested in the subject of the demon, where it had gone, and under what circumstances it now resided. Much more interested than Jolie had realized.

"No. Mom would like to think she is, but.... No."

"Lots of people think they have abilities, but only a very select few truly 'see' and 'hear' things from the other world," Yanna Maria insisted. "It takes years of training and discipline to acquire the skill of being clear and open enough to 'hear' truly," the woman declared.

"My mom has no special skills or training. She's struggled with her own inner demons so long, that she probably doesn't recognize this one as something come from outside of herself. But how could it have found and moved to her?"

"Was there proximity?" Yanna Maria asked.

"What do you mean proximity?"

"Would the demon have gone somewhere that would bring it close to your mother? Was she vulnerable? Could she have drawn it to her?"

"There was a man who lived upstairs from our apartment, who died a few weeks back."

"And that is where you met the creature?" Yanna Maria grasped at every small straw of information with a voracious appetite.

"Yes." It was a partial truth, but though Jolie wanted to understand what might be going on with the demon and her mom, she was becoming reluctant to share more details about what she knew with the fortune teller. There was avarice in Yanna Maria's interest that seemed unhealthy.

"Proximity. You see?" Yanna Maria stated.

"But we were nowhere close to my apartment when Hoke sent it away."

"The spirit would have felt lost, frightened. In that case, it very well could have returned to the last place it had lived."

"And found my mom," Jolie confirmed.

"Yes. But if, as you say, she is not gifted, I don't know why he would have chosen her as a vessel."

"You asked about her being vulnerable. She'd been shot. She couldn't leave the apartment. She was just stuck there, alone," Jolie explained, thinking out loud. "Vulnerable."

"And angry?" Yanna prompted.

"What's her being angry got to do with it?"

Chapter Twenty Seven

"Affinity," Yanna Maria explained. "Like attracts like."

"Well, her ex-boyfriend stalked and shot her, so they fired her from her job, and because she can't work, we lost our apartment. So yeah, I guess she was probably pretty angry. We didn't talk much about it."

"Anger would have created a common bond between them," Yanna Maria explained. "They thought and felt alike; affinity."

"That's how it works; affinity, proximity? That sucks," Jolie complained.

Yanna Maria sniffed. "You asked. I told you."

"So what do I do now, Madrina Yanna? How do I get rid of this thing again; completely this time?"

"Maybe you should ask Hoke." Yanna Maria said, haughtily. "You do not seem to question what he tells you."

"Look, Yanna Maria, Remy brought me to Hoke. I was unconscious at the time and not in any shape to choose who was going to un-possess me. You said you were going to help me, but time ran out, and something had to be done. No one was trying to slight your abilities, Madrina."

"Hoke has no understanding of power or my abilities." Yanna Maria did not disguise her bitterness. "He and his little group mimic ceremonies from a dead culture, trying to gain favor with gods who left this world long ago. He doesn't have a clue what to do with such an ally."

Jolie let the statement stand. "I can't think why anyone would want that thing hanging around," she said.

"Because you are as foolish about the path of power as Hoke is. If you want me to help you, Jolie, you will have to ask."

Jolie sighed. "I can't sweep your floors, Yanna Maria. I'm living in Tecopa. We don't have any money and we don't have a car. We don't have anything anymore."

"You have a demon," Jolie thought she heard the fortune teller think. She wasn't sure; she had never picked anything up over a phone before, but if Yanna Maria thought the demon itself was worth something to her, Jolie was more than ready to let her have the damn thing. "I just want my family to be safe," Jolie said. "I don't care what happens to it. I don't want anything more to do with it."

"I said I would help you and I will," Yanna Maria agreed. "But you must also keep your promise. You remember the rules?"

"Don't talk to anyone about what we are doing and do whatever you tell me to. Yeah, I remember." Jolie sighed.

"You must not speak to outsiders about this; that means Hoke, Rose, your mother--not even your friends at school."

"That won't be hard. I don't have any friends at school," Jolie pointed out. "I don't even go to school anymore."

"I will light a candle and say a prayer for you." Jolie couldn't tell if the fortune teller was serious or sarcastic. "So we are agreed then?"

"Yes," Jolie answered.

"I can remove this demon from your mother," Yanna Maria declared. "But it will not be easy. It may even require battling the creature. It has already been involuntarily removed from one host. It has tasted physical life, and like an addicted person with a drug, it wants more. I think that it will fight unless it sees a better option."

Chapter Twenty Seven

"How long will it take to get it out of her?" Jolie asked.

"How long has it been attached?"

"A couple of weeks maybe."

"How long was it attached to you?"

Jolie did the math. "A little longer than that."

"But you fought against it?"

"Yes."

"And your mother..."

"Probably did not," Jolie admitted.

"It could be quite firmly established by now. There will be no half measures this time, Jolie. I will finish the job," Yanna Maria declared.

"Let me know what I need to do. Whatever it takes to get our lives back."

"I must gain control of the demon," Yanna Maria announced.

Control it? Jolie wondered if the fortune teller knew the meaning of the word hubris.

"What do I do?"

"For now, just keep your mother quiet and stay away from her. Under no circumstances are you to engage this demon yourself. Do you understand?"

"I'm not interested in talking to the demon, but I still have to talk to my mother. There's no one else living here and there's nowhere to go."

"The demon knows the pathway to your mind, Jolie," Yanna Maria warned her. "You cannot risk having it decide that it would prefer to return to you."

"It could do that?" Jolie's mouth went dry.

"I will not let that happen," the older woman assured her. "Keep your mother calm. Do you have alcohol or narcotics if you need them?"

"I'm not going to drug my mom, Yanna Maria. She's trying to get clean and stop doing that shit," Jolie protested. Jessie Lynn, the eternal party girl, usually had alcohol and an assortment of recreational drugs close at hand, but they'd gone into the garbage when she came home from the hospital. Jolie hadn't seen Jessie take so much as a toke or drink anything stronger than water since she'd come to Tecopa. She'd even stopped drinking soda. It probably didn't hurt that Brett had not bought any alcohol when he bought groceries before he left. Still, if Jessie Lynn wanted it, she'd never had any problem finding a party.

"You must understand, that it is possible we will need to sedate your mother in order to separate her from the demon," Yanna Maria explained. "Someone has just come into the shop. We will talk again soon." The fortune teller hung up.

CHAPTER TWENTY-EIGHT

Jolie dug through the stack of unpacked boxes on the porch, searching for anything she could use that would make the little wreck of a house homier.

She found the Betty Boop clock. She had wrapped it in a towel and packed it herself, trying to protect it. She took it inside, found a nail and hung it up in the kitchen. Working inside was definitely going to put Jessie and the demon and her in close proximity, so painting the pigeon poop spotted green walls inside the house would have to wait. Everything outside, however, was fair game.

Without resources, Jolie focused on tasks that required labor rather than materials.

Using a pair of rusty shrub clippers she found in a shed, she cut the salt cedars back so that you could see the driveway. She made a single pile of the trimmings, adding the trash she gathered that had blown into the yard over the years, then covered the pile with old boards so that the trash wouldn't blow away in the next wind.

While trying to pull the grass clumps grown up around the porch, she found an old sunflower thermometer and hung it up on a pre-existing nail on one of the porch posts.

When Jessie Lynn took her afternoon nap, Jolie scrubbed and painted inside. When Jessie was awake, she hauled and clipped outside. By mid-week, the old place was looking like someone with some self-respect, who was not afraid of hard work, lived there.

Jolie set down a bowl of soup and a peanut butter sandwich for her mom.

"What's got into you?" Jessie Lynn asked, an accusation half-hidden in the tone. "You're so domestic."

Jolie thought she saw a glint of her familiar nemesis there, keeping a wary eye on her.

"When was the last time you unloaded a box when we moved, Mom?" she countered.

Jessie Lynn thought about it. "I'm sure I must have done it sometime."

"Eat," Jolie urged. "I'm worried about you. You're too skinny."

"There's no such thing--not at my age," Jessie muttered absently, biting into the sandwich while she examined her drawing, deciding where to make the next line.

"I mean it." Jolie took the charcoal pencil out of Jessie Lynn's hand. "Eat your lunch, all of it, even the crust, and don't forget the soup. It won't be good cold."

"Yes, Mom," Jessie Lynn said, sarcastically. "Jo, what do you feel when you look at this picture?" She held up her latest creation.

What Jolie felt was sick to her stomach with a side of scared shitless; the memories were too vivid. But she couldn't say that. Her mom was a toddler artist struggling to walk, an alcoholic trying to stay sober, a serial domestic violence victim trying to re-create herself. She needed encouraging half truths, not honest criticism.

"It makes me feel uneasy," Jolie found an honest answer. "It's a really dark place."

"And how about this one?" Jessie Lynn turned her sketch book back a page, revealing a picture that Jolie had not seen before. The materials she had used were the same, it was still formed by dark charcoal lines and smudges, but there was a quality of light, created by the empty space on the page, that none of the other pictures had. A girl sat hunched in a tight ball, looking up at a dark Brillo pad creature. She had the saddest look on her face.

"Is that me? Wow." Jolie stared at the picture. "That's different. When did you make that?"

"Last night while you were asleep on the couch. I was looking around at everything you've done around here, how you were making this awful place into a home for us, and it just came to me. What does it make you think of?"

"Hope, Mom. It gives me hope." Jolie kissed the top of her mom's head.

After lunch, she went out to the old Ford pickup and made a call to Mr. Grolund.

"I'll take the classes. I need the credits. I need to graduate on time. They have internet at the library, so I can do it there."

"Okay then. I'll register you at Utah University Online and e-mail you the setup information," Mr. Grolund agreed. "You know, a smart girl like you could probably get a GED tomorrow without any trouble?" he added.

"A smart girl like me expects more for herself," Jolie informed him.

"Just trying to help."

"I'm having to leave school, because you don't have the balls to stand up to your asshole boss, Mr. Grolund," Jolie pointed out the inequity of his help.

"And I'm fixing that," he said, defensively.

"That's not a favor to me. It was your problem."

There was an awkward silence.

"I'll have the account set up within the hour," he promised.

"How's Rebecca?" Jolie asked.

"Angry."

"At you, or at me?"

"I'm not sure she can separate the two, right now."

"She's a smart girl. She'll figure it out." Jolie did not add that she expected Mr. Grolund would not like the outcome when that happened. Not many conservative fundamentalist beliefs made it through the examination process of science focused college geeks. Jolie expected that Rebecca would be born again in quite a different mindset before she graduated college.

"For the record, Jolie, this has got us talking about making some changes," Mr. Grolund said. "Dick Reardon's actions aren't something Pamela and I want our daughter exposed to. Whatever you think, we are good people."

"All we can do is try. Say goodbye to Becca for me," Jolie hung up.

"Who was that?" Jessie Lynn asked when Jolie came back inside the house.

"Mister Grolund. He offered to pay for a semester of classes for me online, and I wanted to thank him." It was close to the truth.

"You're lying," Jessie growled, threateningly. Jolie turned and focused on her mother, warily. The demon was lurking there in Jessie Lynn's eyes.

"I lie to you all the time," Jolie countered, flippantly. "And you lie to me." She picked up the lunch dishes and began to clear them away. "It's how we communicate, that, and a lot of wishful thinking."

"People are always 'doing things' for you, aren't they?" Jessie accused her daughter. "Poor little Jolie, she's practically an orphan. With that loser mom, she'd be better off if she were."

Jolie blanched. "That's not true."

Chapter Twenty Eight

"I know what they say about me behind my back, these friends of yours," Jessie went on. "I'm a slut, and a fool, and an unfit mother."

"No one's saying that, Mom. You're a single parent, people understand that," Jolie tried to side step the tirade she sensed was coming.

"You think Rebecca's father is doing this for you because he cares about you? No one cares about you, Jolie. No one cares about either of us, except us."

Jolie snapped. "That's not true, Mom. Dad's family cared. I had people in Las Vegas that cared, but here we are, on the run again. How come every time I start to build a life and get happy, you mess it up so that we have to move?"

"Oh sure, blame it on me. Go ahead," Jessie fought back.

"I'm sick of starting over, again and again," Jolie gave voice to her frustration. "I'm sick of always being the new kid and having to figure out what my story is. Who am I supposed to like? Who am I supposed to hate? And who does everyone avoid because they're social suicide? Those are the kids I go looking for; the oddballs, the losers--because they're so lonely they'll accept anybody, even me."

"Well, you know how it is, Jo: like attracts like." Jessie smiled, cruelly.

The familiar words, so recently spoken by Yanna Maria made Jolie uneasy. Was there any way the demon could still listen in on her mind? Did it know what she and Yanna were planning?

"God, I hate this," Jolie shouted. "I can hardly wait until I turn eighteen, because then when you say we're leaving, I can say: fuck no, goodbye." Jolie flung herself out of the door, slamming it behind her.

As she was striding down the driveway, she decided she was going to the library. It couldn't be more than five miles away. She needed to start her online classes and there was no time like the present.

There wasn't much traffic on the Tecopa road. The first truck that came along slowed down and stopped alongside her.

"Are you Jessie Lynn's girl?" the man behind the wheel asked. "I'm Ward Colton, your neighbor. Me and my wife, Gemma live on the ranch next door."

"Oh, hi," Jolie tried not to sound angry. "Thanks for looking after my mom."

"It was no trouble. Brett just asked us to check on her in case she needed anything. We'd do that for any neighbor and Brett's more than that."

"I didn't realize that you knew Brett from before?" Jolie couldn't help being curious.

"Oh sure. We go way back. He and Chase Owens used to babysit my boys when they were young." Jolie had no idea who Chase Owens was, and it must have shown on her face because Ward Colton added, "Chase Owens is Brett's friend. He owns the place you're living in. He grew up there. But that was some time ago." Ward squinted at Jolie.

"Brett didn't share the particulars with me," she explained.

"Everything going okay over there?" Ward asked. "I've been hearing a lot of activity."

"I'm trying to fix things up a little," Jolie admitted.

"It could use some of that. It's been vacant more than not since Chase moved to L.A. Look, if you need anything, come over and look around the ranch. Me and the Mrs. have lots of leftover stuff sitting around in sheds and barns just waiting in case somebody needs it. We probably got stuff we don't even know we've got."

Chapter Twenty Eight

"I could use a hammer. I've been using a rock, but you can only do so much with prehistoric tools."

Ward Colton grinned. "Kind of hard on the walls. Are you headed into town? I'm going that way if you want a ride?"

Jolie studied Ward's open sun-browned face and easy manner and decided he was okay. Anyway, he was their neighbor, so it wasn't really like hitchhiking. She climbed in.

"I'm Jolie," she introduced herself.

"You're kind of plucky aren't you, fixing the place up by yourself, and set to walk all the way into town on your own when you could have asked for a ride?"

"I'm used to doing things on my own," Jolie answered in her brief, curt manner. Ward Colton didn't seem to mind.

"Then you ought to get along fine around here. Folks out here are a self-sufficient bunch--not much for asking, but real good at offering. Do you ride?"

"A bicycle if I can get the tires pumped up, but I'm guessing that what you mean is do I ride horses?"

"Yeah."

"When she's working, my mom's a cocktail waitress. We've moved around a lot. So, we kind of skipped the pony thing."

Colton chuckled. "Well come on over. We'll get you up in a saddle. Nothing like riding out here in the open desert to clear your mind."

Jolie wondered what it was about her that made him think her mind was cluttered. Maybe Brett had filled Colton in on the dysfunctional lives of his new neighbors since it appeared he was more an old friend to the Montana rancher than a neighborly stranger.

"If you have any spare time, maybe we could talk about you helping out a bit on the ranch? We can always use an extra pair of willing hands. When my kids were your age, they were always wanting to earn pocket money."

Jolie wondered where they spent it, but thought it would be rude to ask.

"Have you got a kid named Hoss over there, too, Mister Colton? I feel like I've been dropped into an episode of Bonanza."

Colton scratched his head. "Nope, but we did have a Henry and a Maverick, so we didn't completely blow a hole in your theory. What do you know about those old shows? You're too young to remember that stuff."

"I was raised by an old TV," Jolie admitted. "You'd be surprised what you can learn."

Ward eyed her, speculatively. "Less and less surprised, the more I talk to you."

"My first priority right now is finishing my school year online at the library, but I might have some extra time once I get the house and yard fixed up a bit. Let me see how hard the classes are. Okay?"

"Okay, and please call me Ward."

"I'll keep the mister part silent, Ward." Jolie smiled. It was nice to think that there might still be a few places in the world where people were nice just because that's how they were.

Jolie got herself squared away at the library. The sun was beginning to set when she headed home. This time there was no friendly neighbor to help out, but it was a pleasant evening, and the sun on her back had a nice baking quality to it as she walked along the empty road. She was halfway home before the clouds rolled in and the wind started up. There was nothing she could do but press on, squinting against the tooth-rattling wind and gritty dust. When she finally turned into the driveway, only a faint light shone through the sheet she'd hung over the living room window.

Jessie Lynn was sitting on the porch in the dark, a beer bottle in her hand, empty bottles crowded between hers and the open chair beside her.

"What's going on. Mom?" Jolie asked, eyeing the extra chair, suspiciously.

"Nothing. Just enjoying the evening, Jo," Jessie replied, slurring her words.

"I thought you decided not to drink anymore."

"I did. And then I decided not to not drink anymore."

"Where'd you get the beer?" Jolie asked.

"A friend of Chase Owens stopped by. We had a few drinks and got to know each other. We're doing better now." She took another swig. "A real nice guy."

"They always are in the beginning." Jolie began to gather up the empty bottles.

"Don't start with me, Jolie," Jessie warned. "I'm not a sanctimonious little tease like you. I never was." She pointed a drunken finger at her daughter. "If I had been, you wouldn't have been born." It was a common thread in Jessie's defense of her promiscuity: Jolie's existence.

As sudden as a rain squall, Jessie Lynn teared up and began to cry. "I'm sorry, I'm such a mess."

Jolie scooted the extra chair over, sat, and put an arm around her mom's sagging shoulders.

"Oh man, Mom. Don't cry. What am I going to do with you?"

"You should leave me," Jessie sobbed. "You don't have to wait. It would be better for you, alone."

"I'm not going to leave you now," Jolie protested. "You need me. I'm going to leave someday, yeah, but later--like in a few years, when you're on your feet and I'm grown up and graduated."

"I'll never be on my feet." Jessie pouted. "No matter what I do, something always pushes me back down."

"Come on, Mom. You'll make it, someday," Jolie reassured her mom. "You'll get yourself straightened out and off the booze and the drugs. I'm sorry. I know that having a kid hanging around your neck has made it harder on you."

"You didn't make it harder on me, Jo. You were what kept me going. You never needed a mom." Jessie sniffled. "You were always four going on forty. I needed you more than you needed me."

"The eternal teenager," Jolie laughed. "And you still don't look a day over twenty-five."

"Really?" It wasn't true. Jessie Lynn Figg could fit into her daughter's blue jeans, but if you looked close, you could see in her face that she'd been ridden hard and put away wet more than once. Life had taken its toll. But Jolie knew her mom liked to hear that she still had her good looks. It was the only asset she believed she had, and the only one she knew how to use. The trouble was, she'd used it over and over again on the wrong kind of guy, and now, when a decent man came along, all she got was his pity.

"Come on, Mom. Let's get you to bed." Jolie helped Jessie get up. When she touched her mom's skin, she could feel that Jessie Lynn was burning up. She didn't know what it meant. Was it something strictly physical, like an infection from her injuries, or was it a side effect of the demon's possession?

She got Jessie into bed, closed down the house, and went back outside, following the little path that she'd made out to the old pickup.

The wind had swept the sky clean, then moved on, like maids dusting the big house until it sparkled--and it did; it sparkled. Jolie turned her face to the sky, turning

Chapter Twenty Eight

around and around, caught up in the drama of so many stars.

"It's not a just a blanket," she muttered. "It's a field as deep as the universe." Calmed by her communion with the universe, she climbed into the pickup. Sitting sideways in the open door, Jolie put her feet on the truck's running board and called Remy.

"Hey, you," she greeted him when he answered.

"Hey." And suddenly no time had passed between them, and no space separated them.

CHAPTER TWENTY-NINE

In the morning, Jessie Lynn slept in with a hangover. Jolie set out a bowl and a box of cereal for her mother, hoping it would remind her to eat, then headed for the Colton's.

Since the curriculum for the Utah Universities online high school program was based on the Clark County School's and she'd done most of the year's work already, the work had been redundant and easy. Jolie figured she had a little time to spare, and a hammer really was a better tool than a rock.

It was a short walk next door, by rural standards, but a long one compared to Las Vegas, where you could borrow a cup of sugar by opening your window and knocking on the neighbor's window. Jolie climbed through the fence that separated the properties and headed across the pasture toward the buildings. House and barn were set far back from the road, accessed by a gravel driveway with pastures for the livestock running on either side. Horses grazing in the near pasture raised their heads to look at Jolie as she walked through the tall grass, returning to grazing once they decided that she wasn't bringing them treats.

One brown gelding rambled towards her, his head bobbing casually between his shoulders. Jolie tried to out walk him, but it only goaded him into a trot. He circled around in front of her, cutting her off.

"What are you doing?" She froze as the horse nuzzled her hand, then her pants pocket. "Hey, don't get fresh."

Chapter Twenty Nine

"Hello there, neighbor." Ward Colton called out as he approached the inner fence. "He thinks you have something for him to eat."

"I don't. What do I do?"

"Just give him a pet and walk on over here. He's not going to hurt you."

"Okay. I'm going over here to see Ward now," she told the gelding as she moved forward. The horse genially trailed behind her.

"See? He's just a big old pocket pony." The rancher's calloused hands stroked the horse's neck with affection.

"I came to borrow that hammer you said I could use." Jolie cautiously patted the horse's big head.

"Good. I'm glad you did. Have you got a few minutes? Climb through and let me show you around."

There was an old weathered barn that looked like it was about to fall down, full of shadows and broken bits of sunshine that made romance and magic from the dust in the air. There was also a newer pole barn with a painted metal roof, and walls of corrugated steel that was much more solid and far less interesting.

"I like the old barn," Jolie announced. "It looks like it has stories to tell, and if you just sat there on a hay bale it would share them."

"You sound like you have the soul of a writer." Ward Colton grinned. "Yeah. There's character in those old barns, for sure. Even if they aren't the most practical choice out here in the desert."

The house, with its full, wrap-around veranda, was a double wide manufactured home, like most of the houses in the rural desert. This far out of the city, a stick built home was an anomaly unless it was a really old place, like the Owens' shack.

There was a well-tended vegetable garden partially shaded by some large cottonwoods, and a mini orchard surrounding the house in an oasis of greenery. A 60s vintage swing set, recently painted, and a newer playhouse declared that the Colton's were probably grandparents, anyway, that youngsters still visited them.

Farm vehicles and implements were parked near the barns with no order imposed on their placement. It was a working ranch, not a showplace, and therefore, it was exempt from the meticulous manicuring expected of its upscale cousins down in the Vegas valley.

Ward led Jolie into a dusty tool shed attached to the old barn.

"Poke around over there," he pointed. "I think you'll find a hammer. Do you need nails?" He picked up a jar and rattled it before handing it to her. "A shovel?"

"I've got one of those."

"A saw?"

"Nope."

He handed her one. "I'm just trying to think through the basics."

"I've got a broom, a leaky hose, some paint and a bunch of rocks, and I've gotten a lot of use out of all of them," Jolie joked.

"I bet." Ward grinned. On the other side of the wall, they could hear a horse running. "Our trainer's here today, working with one of the youngsters--horses, I mean. Our kids are all long gone. Come on, let's take a look." Jolie followed the rancher out of the tool shed and around the corner to the back. A man in a blue denim work shirt and jeans, with a single long braid hanging down his back, stood in the middle of a circular pen. A black mustang was running around the perimeter of the circle, changing his speed and direction at some invisible command. The trainer put the horse through the

Chapter Twenty Nine

transitions over and over again, until it made them seamlessly as if man and horse shared one mind.

"How's he do that?" Jolie asked, fascinated.

"Magic." Ward chuckled. The trainer turned his body toward them.

It was Hoke. He saw Jolie and Ward and lowered his arms. The horse stopped, taking the opportunity to catch its breath.

"He's looking good, Hoke," Ward complimented the trainer, walking forward to shake the trainer's hand.

"He's coming along," Hoke agreed. "Good morning, Jolie." He did not seem surprised to see her.

"Good morning." Jolie nodded.

"You know each other?" Ward was surprised.

"I was going to school with his nephew, Remy, at Chaparral, until this week," Jolie gave a simple explanation before Hoke could get caught up trying to give a more complicated one.

"Well, isn't that a coincidence?" Ward shook his head. "But then knowing you, Hoke, it's probably not."

Hoke turned back to the horse and resumed his work, without comment.

Jolie and Ward rested their elbows on the fence's third rail, watching the young horse showing off his mastery, going smoothly from one gait to another at Hoke's prompt. "He does good work; one of the best around," Ward commented. "He used to work down in New Mexico on the big ranches there, but when his sister died, he moved up here to be close to her boy. It was a big cut in pay, I tell you, but then most people who live this life don't do it for the money."

Jolie couldn't think why anyone would work without expecting to get paid. Hoke was clearly not a rich man-- not even a middle-class man. He had given up whatever security a career and reputation might have offered him to stay near Remy. On a personal level, she understood that. She would have done anything for Remy, but she didn't think very many adults would have made such a risky financial decision for a kid that wasn't theirs.

"So what do they do it for, if not the money?" she asked.

Ward looked at the sky, the trees, the young horse who was trying so hard to please the man.

"The life," he answered. "When I get up in the morning, I don't need to put on anything to try to please someone else or be someone I'm not. I'm just me. People around here either like me or they don't, but they know what to expect: no games, no pushing to prove something, no scrabbling for position. It's simple here. No one cares about that stuff."

"So you're a bunch of adult dropouts?" Jolie teased.

Ward nodded. "You got a way of looking at things, Jolie Figg, that just makes me smile. Yep, that's it, we're a bunch of adult dropouts. You'd be surprised how many ex-CEOs and PhDs we have out here in Tecopa, mixed in with all the artsy folk, of course."

Jolie thought about that as she watched Hoke work the horse. Watching closely, she was beginning to see the small changes in Hoke's body language that cued the horse. It wasn't magic. It was knowledge. You just had to know how to speak the language.

"Come on, let's see what else we can send home with you today." Ward led her back toward the barn.

With some leftover paint, the hammer, a saw, nails, a length of rope, some agave plants, and a baby trumpet vine snatched from Mrs. Colton's flower beds, all loaded into an old wheelbarrow, Jolie contemplated her foraged loot and the need to get it back home before Ward Colton made the pile any bigger.

Chapter Twenty Nine

"Just load it into the back of my pickup and I'll run you home," Ward said, examining the pile.

"I'm on my way out. I'll take her," Hoke walked up wiping his face with a handkerchief. Ward looked at Jolie to make sure she was okay with that. She shrugged.

"Okay. Thanks, Hoke." They transferred everything into the back of Hoke's truck.

"I'll be back tomorrow. I'll work him every day this week, except Friday," Hoke reminded Ward.

"Got it. See you tomorrow."

Jolie and Hoke got into his truck.

"Remy says that you're doing better. No more bad dreams?" Hoke asked her as they drove slowly along the Colton's driveway.

"No." This was it: her chance to ask Hoke about the demon, Jolie thought. She considered her promise to Yanna Maria and decided that, if she was careful, she could both keep her promise and get information from Hoke. "I still feel like it's around, though," she said. "Is that possible?"

Hoke nodded. "People make rules. Spirits don't--at least none that I know."

"Then how did you know what to do to send it away?"

"I know what I was taught to do for a wipe down. That is all," Hoke answered in his simple way.

"You act so humble, Hoke, like you don't know anything and you're no one special, but I know that you know things." Hoke did not deny it. He also did not own it. "You're not much of a talker, are you?" Jolie added.

"Mostly, people talk to convince someone else to think like they do, but nothing changes." Hoke shrugged. "Why waste the words?"

"What you have to say could mean a lot to me," Jolie claimed. "I have questions and I think that you have answers."

The old trainer shook his head. "Not for you. Your mind is already full. So many problems and plans. So many secrets. You use a lot of words trying to avoid the truth, Girl who Knows Nothing."

Jolie felt his rebuke like a slap in the face. Did he know about the secret pact she and Yanna Maria had made? It sounded like it, but how could he?

"The problems are related," Hoke said, mysteriously.

"What problems?" Jolie bit her lip, afraid he understood too much; half hoping that he did.

"The ones swimming around in your head. You think they are separate, but they are the same. Solve one and you will solve the other."

"Just stop the cowboy Yoda act for a minute and talk to me like a person, okay?" Jolie demanded.

"Truth?"

"Yes, truth," Jolie agreed. "I need to understand what happened to the demon."

"You don't," Hoke disagreed.

"I do."

"You don't. Because you already know," Hoke pinned her.

"So what do I do about it?" Jolie asked.

"I think now it is my turn," Hoke dodged, answering. "Tell me about Remy."

Jolie bit her lip. "Okay. When I first met Remy, I had a vision. I think he's in danger. I think he's going to die--soon and I don't know what to do to stop it."

Hoke's face tightened. "I have seen this possibility as well."

"But you know how to stop it, right?"

Chapter Twenty Nine

"If I did, we would not be talking," Hoke replied.

"But how can that be? You know all kinds of things about the spirit world. How can you not know how to fix this?" Jolie demanded.

"Sometimes we are given sight and sometimes we are left blind."

"Spirits come when you call them. You removed a demon from me. Saving Remy from an accident has to be more simple than that. Isn't there like a protection you can give him, a charm or something?"

"If you believe that the spirit world is confined by man's rules, then you should go back to Sunday school, Wicincala Witko. "

"My name is Jolie."

"To other people maybe, but I will call you Wicincala Witko; Girl Who Knows Nothing, because you know so much, but you pretend to know so little."

"I really do know nothing," Jolie informed him.

"There are several women I know who would argue with you about that," Hoke argued. "Rose and Yanna Maria both think very highly of you and your abilities." Jolie bit her lip. "That makes you uncomfortable."

"I'm not good with compliments," she lied.

"Or with lying, either," he added. The truck stopped. "I hear people say that when the student is ready the teacher will come, but what they do not tell you, is that it is as much a warning as a promise. Yanna Maria is a very complicated woman. She has her own agenda and I do not think any of us understands it yet."

Jolie's mouth went dry. He knew. She climbed out of the truck quickly, to avoid giving a response.

"I can get the stuff in the back myself." She slid the tools and supplies out of the truck bed and set them on the side of the dusty driveway. "Thanks for the ride, Hoke." She waved, keeping her distance.

"Jolie?" He called her closer. There was no way to avoid moving toward him except outright rudeness. She stepped up to the passenger side window. "Do you remember seeing the other spirit lights out in the desert on Solstice?" Hoke surprised her by asking.

"Yeah." Jolie nodded.

"Would you like to meet some of them?"

Jolie's lips bloomed into a smile. "Very much."

"We are going Ridge Walking on Friday night up in the Spring Mountains. You should join us. It is a ceremony to help spirits who are lost to find their way and cross over. Bring along your demon friend. Maybe you can help him find his way home."

Jolie broke out into a huge grin. "I'll try."

"You know the road to Mount Potosi just over the top of the pass on Highway 160?"

Jolie nodded. "Where the sign to the Boy Scout camp is? I've seen it."

"We'll meet there just off the highway at nine o'clock. Tell Remy to pick you up."

"Remy is going?"

Hoke smiled, tipped his hat and put his pickup in drive. He didn't need to answer her. He wouldn't have said it if it weren't true.

"We'll see you Friday. Wear comfortable shoes."

When Jolie went into the house, the demon and her mother were waiting for her.

"Where have you been?" the question sounded like the beginning to an inquisition. Jolie was headed into a mine field.

"I went next door to the Colton's. Ward said I could borrow a hammer, and he gave us some other stuff to help fix things up."

"You brought that man here?"

"No. Ward didn't come--" Jolie saw something in her mom's face. "What man are you talking about, Mom?"

"The one who hurt us. We don't like him," a voice that was not quite Jessie Lynn's hissed.

"Oh my God." Jolie took a few steps back, certain now that the demon was running the Jessie Lynn reality show. "You mean Hoke, don't you?"

"We don't like him." Jessie Lynn looked out the front window at the driveway where Hoke's pickup had been idling just a few minutes ago. "Don't bring him here again. Don't talk to him. He hurt us."

"Well, you shouldn't have tried to take me over, like that," Jolie defended herself. "You weren't invited. You had no right."

"We needed a place to be," the demon whined like a puppy.

"Well, you won't find it here." Jolie remained unsympathetic.

"Oh, but we have." Jessie picked up a new piece of charcoal and a fresh piece of paper and began drawing. "And we were invited," it put special emphasis on the last word.

"You can't live in my mother," Jolie informed it.

"We can. We make her strong and she has always wished to be strong. It is a good bargain," the creature's voice was an eerie, guttural version of Jessie Lynn's.

"It's a terrible bargain." Jolie refused to accept that. "You can't just take over someone's life."

"I can. I have."

"Well, he isn't going to let you," Jolie persisted. "The man, Hoke."

That made the demon nervous. "He is gone," it said, Jessie's eyes flickering to the driveway.

"For now, but I can bring him back," Jolie boasted.

Jessie Lynn's eyes narrowed. "What about the other one?"

Jolie hesitated. "What other one?"

"The woman with the necklaces and the black..."

"Hair?" Jolie finished, sure that he meant Yanna Maria.

"No, the black heart."

That set Jolie back. The fortune teller was crabby and demanding, but did she have a black heart?

"You see her heart?" she questioned. The demon did not answer. "You know this person, from the dream world?"

"Becoming the nurse in your dream was not important. It was just how she slipped in. It was an unimportant role that your mind did not bother to guard. But when you saw her there, you thought it was significant."

Jolie frowned. "What are you saying?"

Jessie Lynn quit drawing and looked at her, the demon's intelligence glowing. "You are mistaken about a good many things, Girl Who Knows Nothing."

Jolie felt her whole world go cold. "You should leave. Leave, or I'll call Hoke," she threatened.

The demon guffawed "You are lying. You lie all the time. You told us so."

"That was sarcasm. This is not a lie. Hoke is looking out for me. So if you try anything, like trying to come back inside my head, he'll know. He'll see it, and he'll chase you out, and send you far away."

"We do not need you," the demon bragged. "This woman will let us stay."

Jolie's fists clenched. "She won't. You leave my mother alone."

Chapter Twenty Nine

"She does not want to be left alone. She is afraid of being alone. You will leave her. It is part of your big plan. I will not."

"I won't let you do this," Jolie argued, unconvincingly.

"You cannot stop me. We are one."

"You're not one. You are two, or three, or however many spirits you've pasted together to create this thing you've become," Jolie declared.

The demon laughed. "This is none of your business. It is not your choice. This is not your body."

"What if I let you back into me? Would you leave my mom and let her go?" Jolie offered.

"So that you can have that man send me away again? No," the demon refused. "This one does not control me. I control her. Go to bed little girl. Sweet dreams."

Jolie grabbed a blanket off the back of the couch and stomped out to the truck. Slamming the pickup's door, Jolie wrapped the blanket around her and curled up in the front seat.

The brilliant pinpoints of the deep starfield twinkled at her through the windshield. Slowly the knot in Jolie's belly began to relax. In spite of everything that was wrong in her life, there were still moments when it felt like the wonder of a single human being suspended time.

Jolie fell asleep on the front seat of the old truck, thinking about how problems came and went like clouds, and whether you chose to curse the gray gloom or see elephants romping across the sky, was more about you and the way you looked at the world than it was about the weather report.

CHAPTER THIRTY

Jolie was awakened by her cell phone buzzing. She blinked the sleep from her eyes, searching for the phone among the folds of the blanket that had become twisted around her while she tossed and turned on the bench seat of the truck, trying to hide from the occasional lights that swept across the yard as cars made the curve to the east along the highway.

Her phone fell onto the truck's floorboards.

"Crap." Jolie retrieved it, sat back up and pressed answer.

"You foolish girl. I said, say nothing!" Yanna Maria shouted. "What do you think nothing means?"

"Good Morning, Yanna Maria. How are you?" Jolie said with sarcastic politeness. "I'm sorry. I'm still a little groggy. I'm just waking up." The fortune teller's blurted accusation gave Jolie no time to wonder how Yanna Maria had found out about yesterday's conversation with Hoke.

"I don't care," Yanna Maria retorted.

"Great, because I don't either." Maybe it was being woken up so suddenly and rudely, or maybe after what the demon had said, Jolie found herself less concerned with staying in the woman's good graces. Either way, she was in no mood to stroke the fortune teller's ego this morning. "So, since you've got your knickers in a twist, let's go for it. I ran into Hoke yesterday and yes, I spoke to him. He offered me a ride. It would have been weird if I'd accepted the ride and refused to talk to him. I didn't say anything about what you were planning to do--

Chapter Thirty

mostly because I don't know. You never tell me anything. So, I don't know what you are so pissed about."

"You made a promise to me, Jolie Figg. You took a vow--"

"And I kept it." Jolie felt more secure in her insistence the further Yanna Maria edged toward insanity.

"We are done," Yanna Maria declared. "Do you hear me? I will not help you anymore."

"Well, since you haven't actually done any helping so far, I don't think I'll miss it." Jolie countered. "But you'll have to find someone else to sweep the dirty little secrets off your floor." The connection went dead. "There's nothing like a clean start to a new day," Jolie said, tucking her phone into her jeans.

*****

It was Friday. The night of the Ridge Walking ceremony. She needed to find a way to get Jessie Lynn and her demon company to go to the mountains with her. Or did she? Jolie examined that assumption. Spirits were not people, they didn't need rides. Yanna Maria's credibility was pretty thin right now, but that didn't mean everything she'd said about the demon was untrue.

Proximity, affinity. When Hoke or Rose sang the Calling Song, the spirits came. Was it only those within hearing range? Jolie threw the assumption out; no. Hoke had cautioned her about trying to apply people rules to the spirit world. Spirits moved within and without space and time. They went where and when they pleased, and they sure as hell didn't have ears with a hearing range.

"They're still praying to gods of a dying culture," Yanna Maria had claimed of Rose and Hoke.

Jolie imagined a bunch of shriveled deaf spirits with horn fashioned hearing aids straining to hear the fading prayers of ancient cultures. It was a very "Hitchhiker's Guide" sort of picture.

If Hoke called the demon to the mountain, would it be compelled to come to him? Did the Native man need to know the demon's true name, like in the fairy tale Rumplestiltskin? Could they use Axel's name?

Jolie ran her hands through her hair, mussing up what was already messy. She shook her head to clear it, then checked her phone to see what time it was. Nine-thirty: still several hours before the school lunch break. Jolie called Remy, knowing the call would go to voice mail.

"Remy, call me when you get this. I'm going with you and Hoke tonight to the Ridge Walking thing. Can you pick me up? Call on a break, or at lunch, or text. I'll keep checking messages in case I miss you." She hung up, climbed out of the truck and headed into the house.

"Mom?"

There was no answer.

Jolie checked Jessie Lynn's bedroom, then the bathroom. There was no one in the house, except her. Jolie went back out onto the porch.

"Mom?" she yelled out over the property; still, no answer. Jolie went back inside, looking for clues to Jessie Lynn's whereabouts. The purse that her mom had stopped using when she got her crutches, was on the floor of the closet. Her wallet was not in it.

Jolie checked the bureau drawers, rifled through the boxes of extra clothes against the wall, and the stash of dirty ones under the bed. Jessie's favorite jeans and her cowboy boots were gone, along with her black leather jacket. It had been cold when she'd left, and she'd wanted to look good. Jolie vaguely remembered waking up in

Chapter Thirty

the middle of the night and seeing headlights flash across the truck's windshield. She'd thought it was a car on the highway or someone coming out of the Colton's.

Someone came and picked Mom up, Jolie decided. *Probably that friend of Chase Owens.*

"Damn." There was no telling where her mother was by now, drunk or sober, drugged or straight, by the side of the road or sleeping it off on a flea-infested mattress in a desert flop house.

Jolie called her mom's cell. It rang from the floor under the bureau. She picked it up, sat down on the edge of the bed, and stared at the phone as her call went to voice mail.

"Where the fuck are you, Mom? Where are you? Don't do this to me, please. Don't do this to us." She pushed the phone screen, ending the call. All she could do now was wait for Jessie to come home or call.

Wanting to stay close to the house in case her mom returned, and hoping Jessie or Remy would call, Jolie set her phone's ringer on high and put it on the seat of the truck. With nothing else to do, she went back to the distraction of cleaning up the property.

Lunch time came and went and still no one called. Trying not to worry, Jolie fixed herself a sandwich, then hurried back outside and ate it, sitting on the pickup's open tailgate.

As the day warmed, the desert grew still, birds and small creatures were seeking safe shady places for their afternoon siestas. Next door at the Colton's, screen doors slammed, truck doors clicked, horses nickered; it was a surreal link to the everyday world that was slipping away.

In what reality did waiting for a ride to a ceremony to help lost spirits cross over to the other world qualify as non-fiction? And yet this was becoming her life.

E.F. Winters

"Mem would be proud," Jolie thought.

The demon doesn't want anything bad to happen to mom any more than I do, she reassured herself. *It's in its interest to keep her alive. It's not going to let her do anything really destructive.* She wanted to believe that, but she kept remembering how eager it had been to kill someone after the fight with Rick. The demon needed to keep a grip on Axel if it wanted to survive. Had the demon's connection to Axel given it the penchant for aggression, or had it come with its own dose?

When Jolie first met the creature, it had been connected to Rory. Its focus had clearly been on power, control, and using others, very much like Rory's own focus. What had happened to the dark minions the demon had commanded that night? Jolie had seen them in her dreams, but there had been no indication of their presence in the physical world. Had the demon's connection to them been severed with Rory's death? Did the demon's focus change with the person it was connected to or was she just trying to make human logic apply where it had no place?

Jolie hammered nails into the loose siding of the house, then began planting the agave starts and trumpet vine Ward had given her, using them to decorate the porch across the front of the house.

When the phone rang, she ran to the truck. She picked it up, muddy fingers making it impossible to use the swipe action to answer. Mud streaked the glass face but the call didn't connect.

"Damn it!" Jolie wiped her hands on her pants and the ringer stopped.

Jolie's consciousness shifted from the desert in Tecopa to a busy street in Las Vegas.

Someone shouted out a warning. Brakes screeched, people screamed, gasping in horror. Like everyone else,

Chapter Thirty

Jolie looked out at the street. Remy was lying on the pavement, his beautiful face swelling with bruises. She looked up at the crowd. Yanna Maria stood across the street looking back at her. Jolie saw the truth in the fortune teller's triumphant eyes; she had caused Remy's accident.

Why? Jolie wailed. He's never done anything to you. He's never hurt anyone. Why would you do this? Jolie let loose her anger like an attacking raptor. The fortune teller looked shocked, then steadied herself, her eyes glittering malevolence.

"This boy's fate has been written since he was born." She thrust her chin into the air.

"No one's fate is written. There is always a choice," Jolie quoted Faith. *"Don't try to hide behind that shit, you coward. You made this happen. It did not have to go like this."*

"Oh, but it did." Yanna Maria faded back into the crowd.

Jolie blinked in the bright sun, back beside the truck in Tecopa, far from Vegas, far from Remy. She pressed Remy's number on speed dial.

It went to voice mail. "You got my voice mail. Leave a message...."

She left no message. She called again, waiting for the system to take her to voice mail.

"You got my voice mail..."

"Remy, it's Jo. Pick up. Please pick up." He didn't. "Okay, listen. Don't go anywhere. Wherever you are, just stay put and don't leave. I mean it. Call me back the minute you get this."

The phone buzzed as a call came in. It was Remy.

"Oh thank you, thank you," Jolie muttered, pressing answer.

"Jo? Oh, Jo, he's dying." Remy's voice was thick, marinated in grief.

"Wait, stop, Remy. Who's dying?"

"Bodhi." Remy sobbed. "They just took him to the hospital. How could he do this? He knows we love him--that I love him. Why would he throw that away?"

Jolie felt a wave of guilty relief. It wasn't Remy. It was Bodhi. The vision had been wrong. It had been Bodhi all along. It was Bodhi's skateboard, Bodhi's destiny, not Remy's.

"I need to go. Will you meet me at the hospital?" Remy's voice cracked. "I need to be there, you know in case...." He stopped himself, unable to say the words. "Just get here as soon as you can, Jo."

And then Jolie realized that the vision had not been wrong. All the elements had slipped into place. Remy would be driving fast to get to the hospital, distracted by emotion, his eyes blurred with tears, his mind somewhere else.

"Remy, don't go," Jolie pleaded. "Wait and have someone drive you, please. You shouldn't be driving in this state."

"I have to go," Remy said as if he hadn't heard her. The phone went dead.

Jolie stuffed it back in her pocket and ran for the Colton's.

Racing through the pasture, she ran through the deserted barnyard and up to the house.

"Ward! Mrs. Colton!" she shouted, banging on the door. "It's Jolie. I need your help. Please." No one answered the door, and no one came ambling around the side of the barn assuring her that whatever she needed, he'd help her.

Jolie scanned the barnyard. Ward's big pickup wasn't there. There was no one on the ranch, except the livestock.

The friendly gelding whinnied at her from the pasture, tossing his mane and pawing the ground.

"This is not a western, and I am not the Lone Ranger, so hi ho some other cowgirl because this one needs another kind of horsepower under her butt."

Jolie jumped off the porch, ducked through the fence, and jogged back to the Owens' place.

Slamming the front door open, she grabbed her backpack and emptied the contents onto the bed. It had been packed for school and then for the move up here. She wouldn't need any of it. She tossed a water bottle back in, a hoody, and a couple of snack bars. Raiding the emergency get away fund in the tin, now stashed under the kitchen sink, she took everything they had left. It wasn't much. There hadn't been much time between emergencies lately. Jolie looked down at her muddy jeans, shirt, and shoes, and dismissed clothes as unimportant. In minutes, she was out the door and in the front seat of the old Ford.

"Please, please, please." She turned the key. The engine started. Pressing her muddy sneaker down on the barefoot pedal, she slowly guided the pick up over the bumpy loose dirt to the driveway, then out onto the highway.

"Just keep going, baby," she patted the truck's dashboard, sitting up as tall as she could so that she could see over the truck's blunt nose. "Just keep going." The truck's glass pack muffler sounded like a thunderstorm gargling. "Too bad I didn't finish Driver's Ed," Jolie muttered. Still, the road from Tecopa to Highway 160 was long and straight. By the time she got to Las Vegas, she'd be a pro.

CHAPTER THIRTY-ONE

Jolie scanned the parking lot for Remy's scooter, parked, then ran into the hospital. The Kung Fu crowd had begun to arrive, but Remy was not among them. Bodhi's little brother sat against a wall beside a forlorn looking older man in construction work clothes.

"Jie," Jolie approached them. "Have you seen Remy? Is he here?" Jie shook his head, his eyes full of tears. Panic rose like bile inside Jolie. She raised her voice "Has anyone seen Remy Bishop?" No one answered. "Oh, shit." Jolie went back outside, punching in the number for the Bishops' house phone.

"Bishop residence," Madison answered.

"Madison, it's Jolie. Is Remy there?"

"No. I thought he was meeting you at the hospital."

"He's not here." Jolie choked back a whimper that threatened to turn into a wail. "How long ago did he leave?"

"I don't know, maybe an hour? He should have been there by now," Madison said.

"He didn't make it," Jolie announced. "I'm at the hospital. He's not here."

"Is something wrong? Jolie, you sound funny. What's happened?"

"Remy's been in an accident," Jolie explained. "I can't tell you how I know, I just do, and I know how crazy that sounds, but these things I see? They come true."

"Just a minute, Jo," Madison interrupted her. "There's another call coming in. I'll be right back."

Chapter Thirty One

Someone screamed a warning. Car brakes screeched, metal crunching against metal. The car struck Remy's scooter, sending him through the air. He hit the windshield of the car that hit the scooter and rolled off the hood onto the street. His backpack split open and Bodhi's yellow skateboard corkscrewed into the sky. Jolie looked up from Remy's swelling face to see Yanna Maria turn and disappear into the crowd. The skateboard fell back down and smashed against the pavement, splintering the vision.

Madison's voice brought Jolie back out. "That was the police, Jo. I have to hang up now. They're taking Remy to Summerlin Hospital. How did you know?" There was a quaver in Madison's voice. "How could you have known?"

"We'll talk about it later," Jolie tried to soothe the girl. "Just get to the hospital. I'll see you when you get here."

"Okay." Madison hung up.

As Jolie walked over to the emergency room ambulance entrance, she punched in the number for Yanna Maria's shop. The fortune teller didn't pick up. Jolie waited for the beep to begin recording her message.

"I saw you," she accused the fortune teller. "I know you did this. How can you live with yourself? You pretend to help people, but the only person you're interested in helping is yourself. If Remy dies, I will make sure you pay--not just in this life. I'll make it my life's work to find a way to wipe out your very soul, you bitch." Jolie ended the call.

She was lingering by the driveway to the ER when the ambulance brought Remy in, lights flashing and sirens screaming.

Jolie was witness to the events in the vision again but this time she watched Yanna Maria put into place each of the seemingly innocent pieces in the chain of events that caused the car in front of Remy to suddenly stop, Remy's scooter to slam into it, and the car behind to hit the scooter, ending with the yellow skateboard spiraling into the air.

The ambulance doors opened and the EMTs pulled Remy out on a gurney. Jolie pushed forward, keeping pace as they wheeled him down the walk.

"I'm here, Rem. I'm right here," she told him. "Don't let go. Do you hear me? This is not the end. You have a life, damn it. You fight for it and don't give up."

"Step away, kid. You can't go any further," the EMT warned her as they rolled the gurney through the ER doors.

Jolie's lips trembled as the gurney pulled away from her.

"Help him," she whispered to the sky. "He's one of your own. Help him, please."

She was pacing in the waiting room when the Bishops arrived, hurrying past her.

Jolie didn't need to hear the scene being played out behind the glass doors. She had seen it before; the broken father, the cold stepmother, the stalwart and loyal younger sister, the three of them trying to come to terms with the reality that Remy was going to die.

Think, Jolie, think. There had to be a point in time when something could be changed; when choice could alter the outcome.

Madison looked out at her through the glass, her pretty face wracked with grief.

Madison, Jolie thought. *Mr. Bishop had been willing to wait for his daughter's consent before taking Remy off life support. She had argued that they needed to wait for Hoke. Madison was the answer. Madison would not let Remy die.*

Chapter Thirty One

Jolie walked up to the glass doors and motioned for Madison to meet her there. "I need to talk to you," she mouthed.

Madison glanced at her parents, her father distraught at Remy's bedside, her mother tense beside him.

"Please," Jolie pleaded, pressing her hands flat against the glass.

Madison stumbled forward, pushing out of the swinging doors.

"Oh, Jolie, what am I going to do?" she wrapped her arms around her brother's friend, sobbing. "I think he's going to die."

"Madison, listen to me." Jolie untangled Madison's arms and held her back at arm's length so that she could look her in the face. "They're going to give you some time with him before they make the decision to take him off life support. I want you to call Hoke, okay? Insist that Hoke has to be here before they let Remy go. Do you understand?" Madison nodded. "Hoke isn't going to be able to answer right now, so just leave him a message, explaining everything, but he will come. You got that?" Madison nodded again. "This is important, Madison. Don't let them take Remy off life support until Hoke comes. No matter what. Your parents will have all kinds of reasonable excuses to let Remy go. Don't let them do it. I'm going to go find Hoke and bring him back. He won't let Remy die."

"Okay. You're going to go find Hoke," Madison repeated. "I won't let them give up on Rem. Hoke won't let him die. I have to go back now." She started through the doors, then stopped. "Wait, Jo, do you know where Hoke is?" she asked.

"I know where he'll be at nine o'clock." Jolie grimaced as she looked at the waiting room clock. "I have to go."

"Yes, go. I'll take care of things here," Madison closed the ER doors.

Jolie turned back to the waiting room, scanning the Kung Fu crowd. There were less of them this time: no Hugo or Brutus or any of the senior students. Jolie walked up to a middle-aged Latino man. "Where's Sifu?"

"He's got some spiritual thing. He doesn't know what's happened."

"I wouldn't bet on it," Jolie muttered.

"How's Remy?" one of the Fu kids asked her.

"Not good." Just saying it made her want to cry. "And Bodhi?"

The student shook his head. "Jie says it's touch and go."

"The school will take this hard," the Latino man said.

"They're not gone yet and I'm not done fighting," Jolie defied the notion that the outcome of the events was already decided. She marched out of the hospital and through the parking lot, praying that the old truck was good for one more adventure.

Every dollar she had left went into the old pickup's gas tank, but when she was done pumping, the gas gauge still registered less than half a tank. She'd driven all the way down from Tecopa on a quarter of a tank, but going back up the steep grade was going to be the greater challenge.

The east end of Highway 160, a steep curvy two lane road before it reached the Spring Mountain Pass, was known as The Widowmaker. While older and larger vehicles struggled to climb up from Vegas on the east side grade, hot shots stuck behind them always tried to pass, often paying for their impatience with their lives or someone else's.

Chapter Thirty One

On a Friday night, the fast traffic was headed downhill toward the big city's nightlife, while the heavily loaded RVs and off-road crowd blocked the slower uphill lane, heading west to play in the wilderness.

Joining the caravan of oversized trucks, trailers, and motor homes winding up the hill, Jolie searched for a way to turn on the headlights, murmuring gratefully when she found a knob and they came on. As the highway gained elevation, she glanced north to where Red Rock Valley and Spring Mountain Ranch Park huddled in the shadows of the grand escarpment that divided the Spring Mountains, from Red Rock. She couldn't see the big pink mountain by Rose's from here, Calico Basin was too far north on the crescent of the valley, but she knew it was there, a quiet reservoir of strength, radiating energy toward her, calming her churning insides.

There was a time for every movie heroine when she faced the necessity of doing something bigger than herself, something she feared was beyond her abilities, and even though she knew she was more likely to fail than succeed, she chose to try anyway, because that was who she was. Jolie Figg knew this was that moment for her.

"Battle stations," she muttered, gathering her resolve.

The old truck slowed, struggling as it chugged and spluttered up the hill, its engine heating slowly. It caught up to the RV, and Jolie stayed there in the larger vehicle's lee.

"Come on, baby. Don't give up on me now," she urged the combustion dinosaur as the temperature gauge hit the red zone. Jolie pulled a few knobs. One released the engine's heat allowing it to flood into the cab. Jolie's hair whipped around in the wind from the open windows and the truck kept going. The temperature gauge slowly edged down.

"Good truck," Jolie patted the spray painted dashboard.

Halfway up the mountain, the single westbound lane of Highway 160 split, giving the impatient a chance to safely pass. Jolie waited until she knew she was close to the summit, moved into the left lane, then turned off toward Mount Potosi at the sign for the Boy Scout camp. Her phone read nine-thirty.

There was no one waiting on the road, but dust still hung in the air above it. Vehicles had been here recently. Jolie drove on, hoping she could catch up. As the road snaked up the hill, she caught a glimpse of headlights ahead.

"That's got to be them." She clenched the steering wheel so tightly that her knuckles locked.

She passed the turn off to the scout camp, then the county recreation area, before coming to a split in the road. With nothing but logic to go by, she followed the branch that went up, watching for any sign of other cars.

There were a few houses; lonely things, out in the middle of nowhere. Once they were behind her, the road became rougher until it was impassable. Jolie stopped, wondering if all the other vehicles the group had taken had four wheel drive, or if she had made a wrong turn, and was in the wrong place entirely. Pulling the Ford over to the side of the road as far as she dared, she turned off the engine and the lights.

It was impossibly dark and silent, the city and the highway now far away. Potosi's summit rose like a dinosaur's backbone to the east.

Jolie got out, pulled her backpack on, and got out her phone. Putting it on flashlight mode, she started to hike up the hill through the desert brush and juniper trees. Above her, real flashlights flared, their beams crisscrossing.

I found them, Jolie thought, pleased with herself. Hoke would be there with them. All she had to do was catch up, but it wasn't an easy climb. The fastest route between two points in this rugged terrain was not a straight line. Jolie missed where the other cars had parked, and she had not found the trail the others were on, even with the help of their flashlights. The ground rose and fell without warning. Boulders, rocks, and prickly bushes were everywhere. The high top tennis shoes which had seemed to fit the bill of comfortable shoes were fine on a city street, but ill-suited to the rougher terrain where some grip was needed.

Jolie stopped and dug a water bottle out of her backpack. She was taking a good long drink when her cell phone flashlight dimmed. If she kept using it, the battery would be dead long before she got off the mountain. She tucked her water bottle back into her pack, powered down the phone, and stashed it in a pocket of her backpack. Starlight would have to do. She waited for her eyes to adjust, then continued up the hill.

A skeleton stepped out from behind a twisted juniper, planting itself in her path, and blocking her way.

"Oh my God, you scared me." Jolie's hand went to her heart. Her new companion offered no reassurance. Jolie examined it.

The white skeleton design had been silk screened onto a black long sleeved turtle neck, a full face mask, and a pair of black pants.

"It's a little early for Halloween, isn't it?" she asked, sardonically. The skeleton continued its silence.

"I'm trying to get up to where Hoke is," Jolie explained. It didn't offer to help. "Fuck you, douche bag." She turned and walked to her left for a bit, staying at the same level on the mountain, then turned right and headed again for the ridge.

Another skeleton rose from behind a rock and put itself in her path.

"Oh, come on," Jolie groaned, turning back. After walking north a ways, she again turned and tried to climb up.

Another skeleton appeared.

"This is ridiculous. Either help me or get out of my way," Jolie warned it as she tried to circle around.

A fourth skeleton barred her progress, a fifth rising out of the darkness behind it. Right and left, more than a dozen skeletons stood like the night watch of the dead.

"Let. Me. Pass," Jolie commanded, separating each word. They did not move unless she moved, always stopping her from going up the hill. "Okay, I get it. You don't want anyone going up. It's a ceremony, and you don't want people just hanging around, but I was invited... by Hoke." No one spoke. No one moved. "I need to talk to Hoke. He's up there. Old Indian, long braid, cowboy hat?"

There was no reaction.

"You stupid jerks. Let me through!" Jolie rushed the closest guard, trying to force her way past him. Arms like iron bars reached out and caught her. The skeleton was rooted like the mountain itself. As determined that she would not go up as she was that she would, it pushed her back down.

"I don't have time for this. Remy is in trouble," she grumbled. Cupping her hands to her mouth, she shouted. "Hoke!" Her voice echoed off the rocks. "Hoke, it's me, Jolie. I have to talk to you. Hoke." The skeleton moved as if to stop her from shouting. Jolie mentally gathered a ball of energy and threw it at him. "Get out of my way!"

Chapter Thirty One

She raced forward past her opponent only to bump into a tall, thin skeleton.

"Jolie Figg?" it asked in a voice that was definitely human and definitely male.

"Yes," Jolie breathed a sigh of relief. "Thank God one of you cretins has evolved enough to talk. Can you please take me to Hoke? I have to talk to him."

"You can talk to me," the skeleton said. She did not doubt his authority; it was in his voice, his body language, the way he carried himself.

"Okay," she gave in. "Hoke's nephew, Remy was in an accident. He's in the hospital," she worked to keep her voice steady.

A man in long black robes, like a priest, appeared.

"Let her go up." His black pants were drawn in at the ankles. Soft soled black leather boots wrapped muscular calves, and long dark hair hung loose around his shoulders. The only thing he wore that was not black, was a string of Buddhist prayer beads strung across his chest.

"Sifu?" Jolie wanted to throw herself into the man's arms in relief, but one look at the dark Taoist stopped her. His energy was like a walking thunderstorm, sparking the air around him. Jolie swallowed hard.

"You can talk to Hoke as soon as he's done," Sifu told her. "Take her up, Rance," he commanded the tall skinny skeleton. With a motion of his hand, two of the other skeletons stepped forward and flanked Jolie while the tall one began to lead her up the hill. The other skeletons faded back into the landscape.

"Just follow Rance," the voice beside Jolie was familiar. "Walk where he walks. He knows the way."

"Hugo?" Jolie stopped to examine the skeleton.

"Sssh. No talking," the skinny one in the lead continued climbing. Jolie reached her hand out for

Hugo's hand and gave it a squeeze. He squeezed hers back, dropping the link between them when Rance looked back at them. They stepped out onto the top of the ridge.

A vast, open sky riffled above them, stars spilling across the deep black. To the northeast, the golden lights of Las Vegas glittered like some mythic god's treasure tumbled over the valley floor.

"Look, the Emerald City is closer and prettier than ever," she whispered to Hugo in quiet delight, surprised at the affection she felt.

Mountain ranges in every direction were visible from the ridge. To the west, jagged ridges were stacked one behind another in fading layers, barely discernible in the fading spring twilight. North, cloaked by a deeper night, the peak of Mount Charleston took focus.

Northwest of where they stood, drawn hard against the indigo sky, a tiny pocket of lights nested on the valley floor between the Spring Mountains to the east and the Nopah Range in the west.

"That's Pahrump," Hugo told Jolie. "It's Paiute for water from the rock because there were springs there back in the day. The Old Spanish Trail came through about where that road is, there." He pointed at the base of the mountain, tracing a line out toward the west.

"How do you know that?" Jolie asked.

"My abuela told me stories. There are a lot of things we don't know about each other," Hugo pointed out.

"Yes. I suppose that's true." Jolie remembered how clean and steady Hugo's spirit flame had burned. People might dismiss the quiet boy, he wasn't flashy like Bodhi, bombastic like Brutus, or handsome like Remy, but he was strong, good, kind, and steady.

"They're starting," Rance informed Jolie.

Chapter Thirty One

She turned around as the dark figure of a woman in a long dress stepped up onto a rocky point a few feet away, outlined against the sky. Another of the Ridge Walkers moved from the dark outline of the trees into range of the starlit backdrop, his silhouette becoming a cut out against it. Jolie continued to make a slow circle, watching the Walkers take their places along the ridge's spine.

Hoke walked out onto a broad flat-topped boulder to her left, his soft voice beginning to call the spirits of the Six Directions. To Jolie's right, Sifu did the same in his own Native language. Each of the participants followed suit, in their own traditions; all different, all connected.

A drum heartbeat joined them as the voices of half a dozen men and women of different spiritual callings reached out, drawing the attention of the universe.

"Do you know what they're doing?" Hugo asked, fascinated and a little fearful.

Jolie closed her eyes, knowing that she would see the spirit world more clearly that way.

The song changed, but not the heartbeat. It remained, anchoring the singers to the physical world as their spirits lifted from their bodies, spreading out and melding their edges until they made one huge multi-colored spirit sail that shimmered against the dark sky.

"They're inviting the lost spirits to join them here," Jolie whispered, afraid to speak too loudly. "They're making a net of their spirits to catch them so that they feel safe."

"How do you know that?" Hugo asked.

"I just do." Jolie opened her eyes. "It's one of those things we don't know about each other, but that we should."

The pull of the Walker's spirit invitation was so compelling that Jolie wanted to fall to her knees on the earth and weep, and sing, to be complete by answering their call and immersing herself in their beautiful light.

A touch on her arm jolted her back.

"Hoke is asking for you."

Jolie followed Rance, to a path that wound up the back side of the rock where Hoke had taken his post.

"Don't talk to him unless he asks you a question," the senior Fu warned her.

She nodded. Cautious of her footing, she climbed up the path and walked out onto the boulder beside Hoke.

A loud crack shattered the Ridge Walker's songs and a spinning vortex slowly opened in the air above them. Swirls of blue and green, light and dark danced, creating a tunnel. At the far end, bright white energy pulsated in rhythm with the earth's heartbeat being beaten out on the drum.

Awestricken, Jolie began to walk forward, toward the swirling vortex. Hoke put an arm out to stop her.

"That is a path for the dead," he cautioned. "Call your demon, Girl Who Knows Nothing. Guide him to the light."

"I don't know how," Jolie faltered.

"Stop lying to yourself," Hoke said, sternly. "It serves no one. Listen with your heart. You already know exactly what this demon needs. Leave behind your anger and fear, and seek this creature in the strength of your compassion."

"Hoke, I have to tell you, Remy--"

"I know." Tears marked the Native man's face. He had made a commitment. He could not go to his nephew until it was finished. His brave anguish made Jolie ashamed of her own selfishness. "You have done your part, Wicincala Witko," Hoke reassured her. "Madison is doing hers. Finish what you came here to do. Call your demon."

Chapter Thirty One

Jolie took a deep, slow breath, settling herself into the peace she had learned to find, even when the demon was hounding her.

"Hear us. Come to us," the ridge walkers called. Jolie gathered a ball of energy, bringing in some of the nurturing invitation the walkers had made, hoping it would lure the demon to return with her to the ridge, then sending her own spirit north and west to Tecopa, she sought Jessie Lynn and the demon.

Her eyes popped back open. "Mom!" she gasped.

CHAPTER THIRTY-TWO

"**H**oke, something's wrong with my mother," Jolie said. Her frantic urgency felt like a rip in the peace around them.

"You can only do one thing at a time," Hoke tried to steady her. "Decide what it's going to be."

"She's in trouble. I have to call nine-one-one!"

Hoke's lip curled "There is no cell service here. You'll never accomplish anything if you lose the threads between what you set out to do and the doing of it, Wicincala Witko."

"But my mom.... She's not moving."

"Everything is connected. Finish the task," Hoke commanded, gently.

Jolie closed her eyes and re-focused, bringing her awareness back to the figure of Jessie Lynn lying by the side of a road. The demon was with her.

"You beast. What have you done to her?" Jolie accused him.

The demon cringed. *"It wasn't me. I couldn't stop her. What you should ask is: what she has done to herself? She took something. It scrambled her mind and now her body is--it's just shutting down. Everything inside her is going too fast, and too slow, and is functioning all wrong. Oh, what will become of me? If she dies, where will I go?"*

"Don't expect me to feel sorry for you," Jolie retorted.

"The form of my life may not be like yours, Jolie Figg, but it is a life." The distraught demon seemed less

terrifying and more like an unwanted puppy, dumped on the side of a high-speed freeway.

"You're a parasite living off others'," she insisted. "The only life you have is what you steal."

"You are young and do not understand as much as you think you do. I am not the evil you make me out to be," it protested.

"You were trying to control me," Jolie countered.

"You needed to be controlled. You had no direction. I provided what you needed."

It was a frightening hypothesis with at least a twist of truth to it. Jolie set aside her anger, centering herself again.

"I'm not here to argue with you. I have brought you something." She moved closer to the demon, opening her hands to reveal the incandescent ball of energy cupped there.

The demon blinked and shrunk away. Jolie just stood, waiting for the invitation to draw it. Cautiously, the creature inched forward.

"Go on, take it," Jolie encouraged. "It's for you."

"What will you demand in return?" it asked, ever suspicious.

"Nothing. It's a gift." Jolie placed the ball before the demon and stepped back, forcing herself not to look at Jessie Lynn lying unconscious a few feet away.

The demon poked at the ball then rolled it around, examining it from every angle before he picked it up.

"It really is quite wonderful, isn't it?" Love and peace folded around him and his face morphed into Axel's wrinkled visage.

"Helen?" Axel looked around disoriented as if all the events between the moment of his death and now had not happened. "Where is Helen?" He asked.

"Helen has gone home to her family," Jolie explained.

"I need to see her." he began to fidget, agitated. *"I need to tell her that I'm sorry."*

"It is okay. She knows," Jolie comforted the grief-twisted man. *"Come with me. I will take you to her."*

"And my boy," Axel pleaded. *"I want to see my boy. He died, you know, years ago, too young...too young."*

"Come with me. I will show you where he's gone." Jolie offered him her hand.

It was much easier to travel towards the ridge walker's invitation than to go away from it. Jolie let go of the will she used to get to her mother, relaxed and allowed her spirit to be drawn back to the swirling multicolored sail, bringing the demon and Axel along with her.

From far across the skies, spirits were converging on the ridge. Some entered the vortex quietly, as if in a peaceful trance. Others remained in their fear and needed encouragement. The Ridge Walkers helped the reluctant, guiding them forward to where the spirits of departed friends and family waited, watching hopefully for their lost loved ones to finally join them.

"Robbie! It's my boy, Robbie." Axel's spirit cried out, recognizing those from his own life.

"It's a trick," the demon growled, pulling him back. *"Don't fall for it. She wants to separate us--to weaken us."*

Axel hesitated, uncertain what to do.

"Don't listen to him," Jolie encouraged. *"He is right there, waiting for you. You do not belong in this world anymore. There is nothing left for you here but bitterness and hate. Go to your boy. The path is open to you."*

Axel stepped out of the demon and walked toward the whirling vortex. Immediately, the demon shrank to the size of a dog, becoming a pale amorphous blob with no resemblance to anything human.

"Don't go. Don't go." It waddled across the ground, its face hidden in the folds of its wrinkled skin like a Basset Hound, as Axel disappeared into the vortex.

"You could go, too," Jolie told the demon, finding that seeing it in its distress, she did not loath it, or wish it ill as she once had.

"No, I cannot. This call is not for my kind," the demon told her, sadly.

"That's your fear talking," Jolie insisted. *"You've been living this borrowed life so long that you don't remember anything else, but there must have been something else once. You don't have to stay like this forever. Go forward and be free."*

"You don't understand," the little demon's ugly, round body trembled. *"In my world, you are the controller or the controlled. She isn't going to let me go."*

"Who?" Jolie demanded.

"The black heart." The gray blob began to twist and roll, this way and that, moaning as if in pain.

Jolie looked around at the walkers gathered on the ridge top.

Yanna Maria stood on the ridge line to the south; her eyes closed, her lips moving. Did they utter quick prayers or curses?

Anger rose inside Jolie. "What is she doing here?"

Hoke's mouth was a grim line. "Trying to subjugate him."

The demon began to sway back and forth as if being tugged between two points.

"It was her, Hoke. She did this to Remy. She caused the accident. I saw it."

"Your mother still anchors the demon," Hoke said. "Yanna cannot take control."

Jolie felt a surge of relief. Jessie Lynn was alive. She turned to face the vortex. Bodhi's spirit was walking toward it.

"No. Oh no," she muttered as Hugo came up beside her.

"What is it, Jo?"

"Bodhi is dead," she told him numbly, happiness leaving her as quickly as it had come. "He didn't make it. He's crossing over."

"How do you--?"

"I can see him," Jolie admitted. "That's what I do, Hugo. I 'see' and 'hear' things in the spirit world." Their hands once again found each other, for the small comfort a friend's support offered. "I'm sorry, Remy," Jolie whispered.

And then another spirit appeared from the darkness. Jolie's face blanched.

"No, Remy. Not you."

"Jo?" Hugo looked confused, unable to see what she saw.

Hoke's hands dropped to his sides, his face sagging with the weight of his grief.

"Remy," he repeated his nephew's name as if it were a prayer. "It's over."

Bodhi turned at the edge of the vortex's funnel and saw his friend. Remy ran to embrace him.

"The hell it is." Jolie jumped down off the boulder, rising from the twelve-foot drop with superhuman speed. "Don't do this, Bodhi." She ran toward the spirits of the two boys, shouting against the storm of energy churning in the vortex. "For once in your life, think about someone besides yourself."

Chapter Thirty Two

Bodhi looked at her, his dark elf features transformed by an inner glow. *"He loves me,"* the tortured boy said, astounded. *"I'm the one he chooses."*

"Yes," Jolie agreed. "Congratulations. You win. But now, does he have to die to prove it?"

"Die?" Bodhi looked at Remy, the two of them lit by their two spirits.

"I want to be with you, Bodhi. I want to share your life," Remy vowed.

Bodhi hesitated. *"I have no life,"* he remembered.

"You could have," Remy insisted. *"You could have a life with me."*

Bodhi shook his head. *"I can't go back, Rem. It's too late for me."*

"Then I'll go with you. I want to go where you go," Remy's spirit persisted.

Bodhi looked at Jolie, then Hugo. One by one he took in the skeleton Fus, his brothers, gathered on the ridge to help do this work.

He turned to Remy. *"You should not die. It's not your time. You have things that you need to do for the people. You have a family that loves you."* He put a hand to Remy's cheek. *"Don't die for me, Rem; live for me."* Bodhi stepped back into the vortex and evaporated into the swirls of energy.

Remy's spirit fluctuated and wavered, becoming less substantial.

"Madison is waiting for you, Remy," Jolie told him. "She's at the hospital, trying to hold onto you. She needs you. Go back to her. Go back to your family."

Remy looked up at Hoke standing on the boulder above them.

Hoke nodded subtly. "I will be there soon."

Remy's spirit rotated, floating east toward the valley and the glittering gold city below.

Jolie looked around, sucking air as if she had been underwater.

It was all right. It was over. Remy was safe. He had decided.

We did it. Remy will live, she thought, relief warming the cold that fear had breathed into her.

The ridge walkers were ushering the last stragglers toward the opening of the vortex.

Jolie stumbled back toward Hoke. Hugo met her at the foot of the boulder.

"We did it. We saved him." She blinked the tears from her eyes. She was moving to hug Hugo when she saw Jessie Lynn.

"Mom?"

Jessie Lynn's spirit floated toward the opening of the vortex.

Jolie's heart sank like heavy metal.

"Mom, no!" She ran forward, reaching out for her mother's spirit. Her hands passed through the image; there was nothing solid to hang onto. "Hoke, do something!" Jolie begged.

A thread of Jessie Lynn's spirit was still attached to the blob of a demon, rolling back and forth at Yanna Maria's feet.

"Stop it, Yanna Maria. Stop it, now," Jolie commanded her.

"I'm trying to separate them." Yanna Maria pushed the girl aside. "If you love your mother, shut up and let me focus."

Inside the vortex, the faces of people from Jessie's life who had crossed over were appearing: Mem, Lucien, others Jolie did not recognize.

The demon twisted and rolled on the ground, tugging Jessie Lynn's spirit this way and that, but always it inched forward.

Chapter Thirty Two

"Leave her alone," Jolie shouted, not sure who she was screaming at. "Let her go!"

With a snap, Jessie Lynn's spirit broke free of the demon and surged forward.

The vortex whirred and hissed and the opening closed.

Jessie Lynn Figg was gone.

"No!" Jolie turned and ran blindly down the hill.

CHAPTER THIRTY-THREE

Jolie abandoned the old pickup when it ran out of gas, leaving time behind without noticing.

She took up her backpack, wrapped the blanket from the front seat around her shoulders, and walked on through the desert night; without direction, destination, or goal, entombed in the numbness of grief.

Jolie walked as the sun came over the mountains and rose high into the sky, kissing her face with fire. Her steps wove and danced with the heat waves, blisters licking her feet.

She walked until she could not walk, slept, beset by dreams of loss, then woke and walked on. Walking required no decisions.

Her mind shunned the thoughts and concerns that could have grounded her to physical reality. Nothing, not her future, not her mother's death, not her friend's precarious hold on life, could entice her mind to stay with her body and remember. Without a shovel, she had buried it all.

As the sun set behind the western mountain range, she walked into the shade.

"What will become of me?" she asked the liquid blue sky, lying down beneath the trees of the pine forest. Diamond tears trickled from the edges of her eyes.

If there had still been magic in the world, a magic plant might have grown where her tears touched the ground, or a small but perfect hero might have leaped up, vowing to help her find her way. But there were no more heroes in the land. She was alone.

Chapter Thirty Three

Jolie closed her eyes, listening to the tiny seeds lying dormant in the dirt, take in the moisture of her tears, and use it to bloom into flowers. Sturdy grasses grew up around her until she was completely hidden.

A pair of bare feet shushed through the grass, walking past her.

Jolie opened her eyes and rolled listlessly onto her side to see who had come.

Mem, sat on a nearby stump, dressed in a long white shift, her long white hair unbound.

"Well, don't just lie there, Cherie. You've come all this way; come over here and talk to me," Mem's voice teased her senses, like the trickle of a hidden spring.

Jolie crawled through the grass, her limbs too heavy to stand, and she lay her head in her grandmother's lap. Long fingers began to gently untangle the strands of Jolie's hair, just as they had when she was a little girl princess, heir to the Boulette kingdom, back in the days before she was changed into the guise of a common girl.

"Mom's dead, isn't she, Mem?" Jolie said quietly after a while.

"Yes," her grandmother replied.

"I tried to make her life better, but I wasn't enough." Her tears stained her grandmother's gown where it stretched over the old woman's knees.

"It wasn't your fault. That wasn't your job," Mem assured her, gently. "Jessie just couldn't make life work this time around. There was too much pain in her. She couldn't let go of it or get past it."

"She tried to run away from it." Jolie sniffled.

"I've never seen that work. Eventually, you have to face what you're running from, especially if it's yourself," Mem mused.

"I never understood what she was running from. Mom never talked about her past or her family," Jolie

thought back. "It was like her life started when she met Dad."

Mem nodded. "We were as close to a family as she ever had."

"But that wasn't enough either," Jolie surmised.

"No."

"Am I going to be like that, Mem?" Jolie sat up and searched her grandmother's face.

"You?" The old woman chuckled. "No, not you. You're a Boulette. Our ancestors have been set upon by outsiders generation after generation. They have tried to persecute us, take our land, our lives, our very souls, but we survived and held, and here we are, still going. You've got the best parts of sturdy old world stock in you, all mixed up together like a grand experiment in what human beings could become, and when things get hard, that gumption packs a wallop of get up and go.

"I am so proud of you, Jolie. You never let yourself get dragged down believing that someone else's approval could make you whole. It takes a lot of courage to honor ourselves like that when all we want is for someone to love us."

"Remy doesn't love me," Jolie confessed, feeling broken inside. "It was Bodhi he loved."

"That's not true," Mem scolded her. "Why that boy loves you like crazy. There are all kinds of love worth having that has nothing to do with sex, Jolie, no matter what you see in the picture shows."

Jolie giggled. "Nobody calls them picture shows anymore, Grandma. They call them movies now."

"I can call them what I like. I'm dead," Mem said, firmly.

"Everyone is, it seems, except me." A silent river of sadness rolled over the top of the dam that Jolie had

built to hold back her despair. "What am I going to do now, Mem? I'm all alone." She wept.

"You're going to figure it out like you always do." Mem stroked Jolie's hair. "You'll think on it awhile, and then pretty soon, you'll come up with a plan. You're smart that way. You'll get back up on your feet, Cherie, and you'll move on."

With their hearts wrapped around each other, the two Boulette women coiled themselves into the forest's silence, breathing with the trees, their eyelids fluttering in rhythm with the butterflies' wings, their heartbeats matching the thump in the chest of the black-tailed deer and the wild mountain mustangs.

When Jolie woke, her arms were wrapped around a tree stump, her face resting on the scar of its cut, her cheek imprinted with the texture of its life's circles. Night was coming again, and the wind was calling her name.

"Jolie.... Jolie...." The voices floated from across the valley, coming to her from where she had been.

Jolie pushed herself to her feet and climbed to the next ridge.

At the peak of the ridge, she looked back at the forested mountainside. Lights flashed among the trees, moving methodically down the hill toward the little field where she had rested on the stump.

Uwipi, she thought, smiling as she turned and continued to climb.

At the top of the mountain, Jolie once again scanned the landscape ahead. The night was advanced now, the sliver of a new moon preparing to set behind the mountains that defined the western horizon. The wind slowed, hushing the forest for the overture that would begin with a new day.

Jolie pulled the blanket more tightly around her shoulders.

"Where are you going?" a passing breeze asked.

"Nowhere," her heart answered.

In the distance, to the northeast, a burro brayed, *"Come home, come home, come home."*

"Red Rock." Jolie's chin trembled and tears rolled down her face. Not everything was gone. Some things remained, eternal. She had a direction. She turned her feet to the northeast and began to walk.

Jolie's mind blended memories of the past with visions of the future, weaving dream into life and life into dream, without a seam between. She saw people she knew and some she had yet to know. Understandings she could never fit into words poured into her; prophecies of the future, terrible and marvelous. But these were the realities of spirit, visions that became clearer the closer the balance tipped toward that world. Physically, everything hurt.

One foot in front of the other; one step, then another.

When she came to the red dirt road that ran east to west across her path, a grateful smile cracked her blistered lips. Stumbling unsteadily, she turned downhill.

She had a destination now. She had a purpose: she would go to Red Rock and sit once more beneath the pink mountain.

Jolie opened her eyes. She could not remember lying down or closing them. The blue had been drained from the sky, replaced by a drape of darkness, sprinkled over with the light of a million suns.

Her swollen tongue felt strange and alien, filling your mouth like a big hot dog in a small bun, and sharp stabs jabbed at her lower back; her kidneys were beginning to shut down.

Chapter Thirty Three

She closed her hand, taking up a fistful of the red dirt beneath her, and smeared it over her cheeks, across her forehead, and down the front of her shirt.

I am done, she announced. Rolling over onto her side, Jolie rested her head on her arm, gazing down the deserted dirt road. It no longer mattered if her eyes were open or closed; she saw the spirit world either way. Her eyelids closed.

When they flickered opened again the old black jack was ambling up the red dirt road toward her.

"Hello, old man," her heart greeted him. "What are you doing here?" The burro's shaggy body stepped from shadow into starlight, the tips of his velvety ears glowing.

"The Mountain sent me. Get up. She is waiting for you."

"I am done with all that now," Jolie told him.

"She says you are not done," he told her, firmly. "She says that you are just beginning." His dark liquid eyes were bright with life but heavy with the understanding of it. "Stand up, Girl Who Knows Nothing. That is the first step."

Holding onto the old jack, Jolie dragged herself to her feet, wound her arms around the burro's thick neck, and pulled herself up onto his back. With her fingers woven through his mane, she lay her head against his dusty shoulder. The old burro turned around and started down the road, back the way he had come.

CHAPTER THIRTY-FOUR

"**H**ere, drink this." Rose handed Jolie a cup of hot tea. "Can you hold it?" It was a solid clay mug, the kind that felt satisfying to wrap your hands around. Jolie nodded. "I'm going to leave you here by the fire while they get the stones ready," Rose went on. "You can sit up, or lie down, or whatever you need to do. If you need to eat something now, I'll get you something easy to digest, but if you can make it, I'd rather you broke your fast in the lodge when we bring you back."

"I don't think I could eat," Jolie rasped. "Bring me back from where, Rose?"

"You've been missing for four days and nights, Jolie. I guess Spirit had a plan. It seems to have sent you on a bit of a walkabout. We're going to bring you back into the world in a lodge."

"There seems to be a lodge for everything." Jolie tried to joke.

"All the important things anyway," Rose agreed. "Just sit here and drink your tea. It's medicine, so drink it all, even if it tastes funny." Tears brightened the kind woman's dark eyes. "We're so very relieved that you're safe." She gave Jolie a quick hug and hurried into the house.

Jolie watched the fire dance, hearing it talk in crackles and hisses. She heard other people talking somewhere nearby too, though they were trying to keep their voices low.

"But how did she get here?" someone that sounded like Yanna Maria asked. Jolie began to shake. She did

Chapter Thirty Four

not want to see the fortuneteller, not yet. She wasn't ready.

"Apparently, she walked," Rose answered the woman.

"From Mount Potosi?"

"Almost. They found the truck she was driving on the highway about fifteen miles west of the pass."

"All those people looking for her and she just walks into Calico Basin?"

"She's a strong girl," Rose said, her admiration clear.

"Does she know about her mother?"

"I haven't asked," Rose's voice suddenly became tight. "And don't you go saying anything about it either, Yanna. Jolie's got more than enough to deal with already without that."

Someone stepped into Jolie's line of sight, adding a log to the fire.

"Nothing can hurt you here. This is a safe space," he said, not looking at her.

Of course, there was a fireman, Jolie realized. She was not really alone. She peered out from inside the blanket that was pulled up like a hood over her head.

"Don't talk, Jolie," Sifu commanded her. "You are still in the spirit world. Just rest."

"I don't want her here," she told him. "Yanna Maria; can you send you away?"

"Of course." He lay a second blanket on the ground, using a third to make a pillow for her head then gently guided her to where she could lie down by the fire.

"How's Remy?"

"Alive."

But Mom isn't. Jolie retreated into the cocoon of the wool blanket, hiding her face.

Spider-Jolie confidently stepped onto the shimmering web stretched out before her in patterns of lines and circles. She did not look down, her spider eyes focused forward as she gracefully navigated the sticky threads that glowed brightly against the dark dreamscape, climbing the universe from the gloom of despair into the winking light above.

Whatever demons lurked below would remain there. She was beyond their ken, a brave blinding spirit from which their greed must shrink. Not hounded, not chased, or ridden by fear, Jolie set aside confusion.

Sloughing off the spider form, she once again became a girl, climbing from the darkness of her fears into the light of her future.

Sensing movement near her, Jolie opened her eyes. Iris sat next to her.

"Rose said to make sure you drank this--all of it." Iris held the cup to Jolie's lips. Tru and Marty slipped quietly in through the gate, their hands linked. They sat down on the plank bench, trying not to look at Jolie, challenged by the idea that they must treat her as if she weren't there. Jolie reached over and grasped their hands in hers, exchanging quick tearful smiles.

Rose came out, carrying four wooden bowls: one with the corn dish, wasna, one with berries, one with buffalo, and one with water.

"We're ready." She set them gently on the little mound outside the lodge door. Hoke crawled out of the lodge.

"Okay, let's bring her in. When she comes back out you can talk to her," he explained to Jolie's friends. "But she will still be very weak and in transition, so choose what you need to say, speak slowly, and don't expect too much." Jolie's friends nodded, their faces shifting between worry and relief.

"Come with me, Jolie." Hoke helped Jolie to her feet, then led her into the lodge. The others followed, with coaching from Rose.

Inside, Hoke told Jolie that she could share what she wished about her experience and keep secret what she did not. He passed the bowls of food and water to her, instructing her to break her fast and begin the process of returning to the physical world.

"The things we have here: corn, buffalo, berries and water, fire and shelter, are all we need to live," Hoke spoke humbly. "Everything else are only things we want." He poured a gourd ladle of spring water over the glowing hot stones. The steam rolled out in a cloud and Jolie raised her face to embrace the wet cleansing heat. "Our relative has returned to us. Welcome back, Winyan Sapa Sunsunla: Black Burro Woman." Jolie could hear him smile.

When the lodge door opened and they came out, the sun was rising over the eastern edge of the Basin, painting it in glorious color.

Jolie's friends clustered around, hugging her, declaring how happy they were that she was safe, and how much they'd been worried. Rose stepped forward.

"I have a surprise for you, Winyan Sapa Sunsunla." A pathway opened and Remy was there. Jolie stumbled into his arms.

"We had to sneak him out of the hospital, but he refused to stay away," Hugo said, coming out from behind his friend.

"Pilamaya. Thank the spirits, you're safe." Remy held Jolie close.

"I was so afraid that we'd lost you," she mumbled.

"That couldn't happen, not with you and Madison working together."

"Welcome back, Jo," Madison was standing awkwardly to one side.

Jolie let go of Remy and hugged his sister.

"Thank you for saving my brother," the blond girl whispered.

"I couldn't have done it without you," Jolie replied.

"I'm not sure that's true." Madison stood back, wiping her eyes. "But two stubborn girls are pretty hard to stop, I guess."

Hoke was next for hugs, followed by Iris, Tru, Marty, Hugo, and an extra long hug for Rose.

"There's a feast inside," Rose announced as she finally let go, wiping tears from her cheeks. "I'm sure you're all hungry. I know some of you've been out with the search parties and probably haven't had a decent meal in days."

"I haven't had one. I've been being tortured with hospital food," Remy joked.

"There's special food for you to break your fast, Jolie," Rose instructed her as everyone began to trickle into the house, talking about Jolie's extraordinary journey, and congratulating Remy on being alive.

Sifu, stayed by the fire, cleaning things up. Jolie went back.

"Thank you, Sifu," she said, handing him back the blanket.

"The hardest part may not be over, yet," he warned her with surprising tenderness.

"I'm a Boulette. Every time they push me down, I get back up and I'm stronger."

Sifu leaned on his pitchfork. "I hear you're a pretty good fighter. Maybe you know this, but I have a school."

Chapter Thirty Four

He smiled, something Jolie had never seen the stern Taoist do before. It didn't suit him. It was like someone took a picture of Batman and re-drew his mouth with a big cheesy smile stolen from the Tick.

"I did hear something about that."

"I could teach you if you wanted."

Jolie nodded. "I'll think about it."

A car pulled up in the driveway, and Cliff Wrangler sidled up to the gate.

"Welcome back," he greeted Jolie as Sifu went into the house. "Everyone's talking about your amazing journey. How are you feeling?"

"I'm alive," Jolie replied. "So, pretty good, considering."

"Look, Jo, I don't know what you've been told but--"

"It's okay. I know about Mom."

"I'm sorry, kid. You said that you didn't have any family here?"

"Sure, I do. I have lots of it." She indicated the crowd inside.

"But legally, there's no one I can send you home with tonight, right?"

"You can send me home with Iris. She'd be happy to have me."

Wrangler took a deep breath, then let it out. "The thing is, Jolie, Iris is not legally your family and she's not an approved foster parent either, so she can apply to become a foster parent, and request that you're placed with her, but there are no guarantees. I can't let you go with her right now."

"But she'll want me," Jolie protested. "She's just inside. Go ask her."

"I know what you're saying, but there's a procedure we have to go through with these things. It's the way the

E.F. Winters

courts are set up. You're an orphan now, Jo. That makes you a ward of the court. You're going to have to go to Child Haven until we can get you into a foster home."

Jolie felt the strength that had returned to her drain away. "You're not serious?"

Wrangler shook his head. "I wish I weren't."

"I shouldn't have come back," she muttered.

"Don't say that. We can work this out. It may take a little time, but it will be okay." Wrangler put a hand on her shoulder. She shrugged it off.

"I hate it when people tell me that." Jolie shut the valve on her escaping courage and lifted her chin. "Keep your sunshine and rainbow bullshit for the little kiddies, I know what's what, Wrangler."

Wrangler looked embarrassed. "Look, there's no hurry. You can eat dinner, say your thank yous, and all that."

Jolie gazed through the window at the happy people inside.

"No. Let them have their celebration. They'll figure it out soon enough. Let's just go." When she got into the probation van, she rolled down the window and leaned her arms on the door, letting the wind feather over her face.

The old black jack stood across the road, watching her. Their eyes met and Jolie remembered how she had really gotten down the mountain and across the valley to Rose's.

"Thank you, my friend," she whispered.

"We will be waiting for you to come home, home, home." The black jack let out a mournful bray as he watched the car drive Jolie away.

THE END

Watch for Book Three: "Catch the Dragon's Tail"